SUDDEN

Vanessa's heart thudded violently. She had only been kissed a few times by young soldiers she had known, and those had been sweet chaste kisses, not a sensual torment that whisked all thoughts from her mind, a kiss that left her feeling hot and weak and made her want more.

He leaned back, and her eyes slowly opened to find him watching her with an unfathomable look. "You are as warm as summer," he said, "a woman meant for loving. Your red hair is like sunshine." He leaned forward to brush her lips again. "Summer," he whispered.

She moaned softly with pleasure, unable to resist, yielding to him and wanting him to kiss her again. When he stopped, she looked up at him.

"You are a beautiful woman."

She felt beautiful with his words even though she knew it was impossible after traveling across country. Her hair was a tangle and her riding habit wrinkled, but his words flowed over her like a golden cape. His hand slid from her head to her shoulder.

"You are ready for a man's loving, Vanessa."

* * *

PRAISE FOR SARA ORWIG

"WARRIOR MOON is a fast-paced, action-packed western romance filled with two great lead characters. Sara Orwig does her customary tremendous story, allowing the audience to enjoy every minute of a mesmerizing read."

—*Affaire de Coeur*

PUT SOME PASSION INTO YOUR
LIFE . . . WITH THIS STEAMY SELECTION OF
ZEBRA *LOVEGRAMS!*

SEA FIRES   (3899, $4.50/$5.50)
by Christine Dorsey

Spirited, impetuous Miranda Chadwick arrives in the untamed New World prepared for any peril. But when the notorious pirate Gentleman Jack Blackstone kidnaps her in order to fulfill his secret plans, she can't help but surrender—to the shameless desires and raging hunger that his bronzed, lean body and demanding caresses ignite within her!

TEXAS MAGIC   (3898, $4.50/$5.50)
by Wanda Owen

After being ambushed by bandits and saved by a ranchhand, headstrong Texas belle Bianca Moreno hires her gorgeous rescuer as a protective escort. But Rick Larkin does more than guard her body—he kisses away her maidenly inhibitions, and teaches her the secrets of wild, reckless love!

SEDUCTIVE CARESS   (3767, $4.50/$5.50)
by Carla Simpson

Determined to find her missing sister, brave beauty Jessamyn Forsythe disguises herself as a simple working girl and follows her only clues to Whitechapel's darkest alleys . . . and the disturbingly handsome Inspector Devlin Burke. Burke, on the trail of a killer, becomes intrigued with the ebon-haired lass and discovers the secrets of her silken lips and the hidden promise of her sweet flesh.

SILVER SURRENDER   (3769, $4.50/$5.50)
by Vivian Vaughan

When Mexican beauty Aurelia Mazón saves a handsome stranger from death, she finds herself on the run from the Federales with the most dangerous man she's ever met. And when Texas Ranger Carson Jarrett steals her heart with his intimate kisses and seductive caresses, she yields to an all-consuming passion from which she hopes to never escape!

ENDLESS SEDUCTION   (3793, $4.50/$5.50)
by Rosalyn Alsobrook

Caught in the middle of a dangerous shoot-out, lovely Leona Stegall falls unconscious and awakens to the gentle touch of a handsome doctor. When her rescuer's caresses turn passionate, Leona surrenders to his fiery embrace and savors a night of soaring ecstasy!

Available wherever paperbacks are sold, or order direct from the Publisher. Send cover price plus 50¢ per copy for mailing and handling to Penguin USA, P.O. Box 999, c/o Dept. 17109, Bergenfield, NJ 07621. Residents of New York and Tennessee must include sales tax. DO NOT SEND CASH.

WARRIOR
MOON

SARA ORWIG

ZEBRA BOOKS
KENSINGTON PUBLISHING CORP.

ZEBRA BOOKS are published by

Kensington Publishing Corp.
850 Third Avenue
New York, NY 10022

First Printing: August, 1995

Printed in the United States of America

To the Rhoades for some answers and insights and to my editor, Beth Lieberman

One

"Haon'yo!" The cry rang in the air as a warrior fell from his pony.

Guipago, Lone Wolf, turned his bay, a Henry rifle in the crook of his arm. His wild whoops added to the din while he fired the rifle as he galloped through the soldiers. Smoke billowed up, the blast of a howitzer drowning out screams and whoops and gunfire.

Out of the thick smoke a soldier loomed before him. Lone Wolf swung the rifle, knocking the bluecoat from his horse. Flames shot skyward as the Kiowa village burned, the acrid smell of flaming hides stinging his nostrils, the stench of gunpowder heavy in the air.

The army attack on the winter camp had come at dawn and the Kiowa and the Comanche had fought all day, only now beginning to drive back the bluecoats, but not before the tipis had been set ablaze. A thick pall of smoke hung over the rolling countryside.

He heard a scream and wheeled his horse. Tainso, his brother's wife, ran with their young daughter in her arms. Tainso's long black hair streamed out behind her as a cavalry officer charged toward her.

Yelling with rage, Lone Wolf kicked his horse. He raced after them as the captain leaned down to yank mother and child up on his horse.

Firing his rifle, Lone Wolf bellowed again while he pounded to catch the officer and his sister-in-law. He had seen his brother, Inhapo, blasted from his horse by one of the two powerful howitzers firing on the village. Inhapo had died instantly, and Tainso had run screaming to his body, throwing herself on him and ignoring the battle raging around her.

Lone Wolf had lost sight of her in the fighting until now. As the soldier galloped away with her, Lone Wolf knew he could not risk a shot because the officer held Tainso close in front of him. Lone Wolf yanked up his bow and pulled arrows from the quiver. He aimed and released an arrow, firing another swiftly. As the arrows struck him in the back, the officer stiffened and fell.

Tainso clung to the horse as the officer fell, then leaned over the animal and galloped away. Following her, Lone Wolf reloaded his rifle. A blond cavalry officer pounded after Tainso even as he turned to fire at Lone Wolf.

Lone Wolf urged his bay faster. But to Lone Wolf's horror, the officer swung his gun around and fired at Tainso. She screamed and fell from the horse while three-year-old Tainguato, whose tiny fists were wound in the paint's mane, remained on the pony as it galloped away. The soldier fired at Lone Wolf.

With a lurch Lone Wolf's horse went down beneath him. When Lone Wolf rolled and raised up to fire, another shot blasted the rifle from his arms and he felt a sting in his shoulder.

In a rage he yanked up his bow and pulled an arrow from the quiver, firing in a fluid motion. The arrow went into the officer's chest, piercing him high on the right.

In spite of the arrow, as he galloped close, the officer raised his rifle. For a moment Lone Wolf looked into the pale man's blue eyes; the officer's face, his thin nose and pointed jaw, became etched in Lone Wolf's memory. His hatred burned hotly as he reached into an empty quiver.

"You die, redskin!" the officer yelled. The blast knocked Lone Wolf to the ground, a hot pain searing his ribs. When he pushed himself up again, the officer had disappeared into the smoke.

Lone Wolf staggered to Tainso, rolling her over. Blood gushed from a large wound in her chest. Her eyes fluttered, and he leaned down to hold her close.

With surprising strength she gripped his arm. "Find Tainguato, my White Bird," she whispered. "Protect her. Promise me."

"I promise."

"Go now," she urged, her hand loosening. Then she shuddered and turned her head.

Agonized, Lone Wolf placed his hand against her throat and knew before he felt there would be no pulse. He let out a searing cry and placed her back on the ground while he looked in the direction in which the pony had raced away with White Bird. He stood, shaking his fist at the wind, crying again, a keening agonized call that was drowned out by the sound of battle.

Lone Wolf glanced at himself. He felt nothing yet, but he was bleeding from wounds in his side and shoulder and thigh. Looking over the battleground, he knelt beside a dead soldier. He took the man's coat and went back to fold Tainso's hands over her breast and cover her with the coat.

He returned to take the soldier's rifle and pistol. He yanked off the man's shirt, ripping it to bind his wounds.

In minutes Lone Wolf caught a riderless horse and leapt into the saddle, pain in his side and leg doubling him over. Regaining his seat, he turned in the direction in which he had seen White Bird's horse race away. The blast of the howitzers had stopped, and Lone Wolf knew the warriors had finally routed the soldiers. He glanced over his shoulder at flames dancing high, a cloud of smoke streaming skyward over the village. Long shadows stretched across the land as the sun flamed in the west. His people had withstood the soldiers and finally driven them away, and he felt a surge of satisfaction along with sadness for the losses. As his gaze swept the ground that was littered with the bodies of his slain kinsmen, hatred rose in him again toward the whites who had killed his loved ones.

He felt a desperate need to find White Bird. In minutes he picked up the trail where it wound west along the river. Pain now throbbed with waves of blackness which threatened to overwhelm him.

He didn't know how many times he stirred and sat up, drifting in and out of consciousness. He was losing blood and needed his wounds tended, but he had to get White Bird before he headed back for help.

Following the river, he rode over rolling grassland. Near the bottomland along the water, cottonwoods and junipers grew. Ahead a movement caught his eye, and he spotted White Bird. He tried to yell, but only a croak came out. His sight blurred, and his head started to loll over. Lone Wolf jerked upright, trying again to call to White Bird.

His heart seemed to miss a beat as the land jutted out in a bluff, and at the crest she disappeared from sight. He was afraid to urge his horse to go faster because any moment he might lose consciousness and fall.

He closed his eyes, his head swimming. A lilting feminine voice rose in song. He jerked upright. He had been on the verge of losing consciousness again, his mind drifting. The voice carried on the wind, and he frowned. Was his mind deluded by shock and pain or did he actually hear someone singing? Where was White Bird?

Fearing for her, Lone Wolf tugged on the reins and dismounted. He staggered and fell, blackness enveloping him. When he opened his eyes, he didn't know how long he had been unconscious, but he still heard singing. He turned to crawl on his hands and knees to the edge of the rise and peer below.

The land gave way, the hillside cut by rainwater. The

sloping bank leveled out in flat land along the river. Cottonwoods grew on the banks, their limbs still bearing yellowed leaves, a bright contrast to the dark junipers. In spite of the cool weather, a woman stood bathing with her back to him, her hands holding up her mass of red ringlets. She sang as she let her hair fall and splashed water on herself.

In the dusky light of early evening, her body was pale. The cascade of thick red hair momentarily caught his attention, and his gaze slid over the enticing curve of her buttocks, down over her long, shapely legs. She stood in shallow water that came below the calves of her legs and left her bare to his gaze.

For an instant he felt the consuming rage he had experienced in battle and the searing loss over a year earlier when he'd found his wife's body after she had been killed by whites. For a moment he wanted to charge down the bluff, grab the woman, and take revenge upon the whites, but then he saw White Bird.

The child was off the paint now, the animal picking its way down the slope behind her, the woman seemingly unaware of the noise. Lone Wolf supposed the splashing of water and her singing had drowned out the sound of hooves.

She stopped singing as a hoof scraped on a stone and the pony moved behind junipers. The woman spun around. Lone Wolf began to cry out to White Bird, and his hand brought up his pistol.

Pain shot through him, and his arm wavered wildly. And then he forgot his anger as he stared at the woman's lush body.

His attention was riveted, her beauty registering through a blur of pain. Her pale, curvaceous body had full rosy-tipped breasts that thrust toward him. Her waist looked tiny enough for his hands to circle. Thick red curls formed a triangle at the juncture of her long legs.

Tearing his gaze from her, he looked at White Bird as he struggled to move the pistol to his left hand. The woman was staring at White Bird, and Lone Wolf's heart thudded because he had never known a white person to like an Indian child.

He wanted to call a warning to White Bird, to protect her from the woman. As he watched, White Bird held out her hands and toddled toward the woman.

"Hah-nay!" His cry of no was a mere croak. The woman looked around, and he ducked down. In seconds he raised his head. She splashed out of the creek, ran a cloth swiftly over her body, and yanked her green gingham dress up to drop it over her head. As the woman fastened buttons, White Bird ran to her.

To his amazement the woman held out her arms and lifted up the child against her body. White Bird wound her thin arms around the woman's neck and hugged her.

"Hah-nay!" he whispered again. The woman had to be traveling with a group; and even if the woman liked White Bird, when the men found the Indian child, Lone Wolf feared what they would do. "Tainguato." He whispered her name as he crawled forward, the pistol clutched in his hand.

Vanessa Sutherland caught up the little girl. The child wrapped her arms around Vanessa's neck and whimpered.

"Shh, love, you're safe. You're safe with me," Vanessa crooned to her, swaying slightly as she stroked the child's tangled black hair.

"Kka-kkoy'," the child murmured. *"Kka-kkoy'."*

"Sweetie, I don't understand." Vanessa looked around again, an eerie feeling making hair rise on the nape of her neck. It was almost dark now, and Vanessa realized she shouldn't have stayed away from camp so long. There was an ominous silence; every bush could be hiding a threatening menace. The child couldn't be out here alone, and Vanessa's gaze swept the area again. And then she forgot her fears as she held the small body close, love pouring out to the little girl.

Vanessa leaned back to look at her, and large, thickly lashed dark eyes gazed up solemnly in return. Red smudges were on the child's buckskin dress and arms and cheek. It was blood. She must have been in a battle or an ambush.

"I'm Vanessa Sutherland," Vanessa said quietly. "Vanessa." She smiled and the child smiled back. Another surge of love rushed through Vanessa. She smoothed long black hair away from the child's face. "You're very beautiful. Where is your mama? Mama?"

The child continued to smile, her tiny fingers touching Vanessa's curls, tugging lightly at one.

"I'll take you to camp," Vanessa continued in a soft voice. She set the little girl on her feet and took her hand. Vanessa glanced down at her and remembered Sergeant Hollings, the officer in charge of the detail to accompany the wagon train to Denver. He despised Indians, and his cruel treatment of one at Fort McKavett had left bitter memories with her. She looked down at the large, trusting eyes gazing up at her and thought about Sergeant Hollings.

The paint whinnied and moved out of the brush into view. Vanessa's heart lurched at the first sound; and then, when she saw it was a riderless horse, probably what the child had ridden, she stared at the animal. And as she looked at it, she remembered overhearing her father's instructions to Sergeant Hollings before they had left Fort McKavett.

"Hollings," he had said in his deep voice, "see to it that my daughter doesn't get her hands on a horse. She is not the obedient child that my other daughters are. I don't want to hear that Vanessa ran away before she reached Denver."

"Yes, sir. I'll personally check on the horses each day. I'll give instructions that she isn't to ride one at any time."

"I'm holding you responsible for her getting to Denver where I can get her locked into the convent."

Now, staring at the paint, Vanessa saw the chance she

had been watching for since leaving Fort McKavett. She didn't want to enter a convent and she had a desperate need to get back to Fort McKavett to try to save her fifteen-year-old sister Phoebe from a loveless marriage arranged by their father.

Before they reached Denver, Vanessa had planned to get a horse in one of the towns they passed through, but here was a horse for the taking and a small child who needed protection.

Vanessa stared at the child, her mind running over possibilities. With a determined lift of her chin, her spirits leaping with excitement, Vanessa knelt beside the child. She touched the little girl's chest with her forefinger.

"You stay." Vanessa took the child's hand and led her to a large rock, seating her there and patting its surface. "You stay." She pointed to herself and tried to convey with her hands what she intended. "I go and come back. You stay."

Dark eyes stared up at her, and Vanessa stood up, moving to take the horse's reins and fasten them to a tree. She started toward camp, glanced back, and smiled. The child smiled in return. Vanessa hurried through the trees, rushing to camp, her pulse jumping at the thought of running away.

Mrs. Parsons, hired by her father to accompany Vanessa to Denver, traveled with her. Vanessa's father, Abbot Sutherland, with his high military connections, had seen to the army escort for the wagon train in order to get his daughter to Denver safely where Mrs. Parsons would place her in the convent.

Vanessa had heard of savage Indians, and the wagon train was traveling beyond the line of frontier forts, the last line of defense with men away fighting in the War Between The States.

If she ran off, she would be alone with the child in a vast desert inhabited by nomadic savages. Vanessa was willing to take her chances because once she reached Denver, her future and Phoebe's would be ruined. Vanessa's thoughts shifted back to the little girl who seemed abandoned or orphaned. Vanessa would take the child with her and go back to Fort McKavett to get Phoebe and their youngest sister Belva. Her father seemed to have love only for his son, so they wouldn't leave Belva behind unless she wanted them to.

She thought of the box of gold and greenbacks her father was sending to the convent. There was enough money in the box to last a long time if she were careful with it. She glanced behind her and saw only the river and trees, no sign of the child. Hurrying, Vanessa reached camp and went straight to her wagon.

People clustered together in the center around a bonfire, and tempting smells of charred meat filled the air. Vanessa climbed into the wagon she shared with Mrs. Parsons. Pausing to look at the crowd gathered in the center of the circle around the fire, Vanessa spotted Ardith Parsons' brown hair and ever-present black hat. Beside her was Ulrich Canton, a man traveling to Denver. With his butter-bean teeth and narrow, dark eyes, he seemed taken with Mrs. Parsons, and the two spent most evenings together over supper and talking afterward.

Thankful the two were together now, Vanessa picked up a portmanteau and emptied its contents.

Her hands shook as she rushed, changing into a blue poplin riding habit with a calico sunbonnet, leaving behind the fancy blue silk hat that would give little protection from the sun. She packed clothing, jars of jam, and cold biscuits, trying to think of everything she might need. She took quilts and finally dropped a portmanteau and a satchel to the ground along with the quilts. With the box of money under her arm, she climbed down and hurried across the campsite to the cluster of people and tables spread with food. Picking up a tin plate, she served herself, smiling at Mrs. Whitaker.

"This smells delicious, doesn't it, Vanessa?" Mrs. Whitaker asked in her raspy voice.

"Yes, ma'am, and I'm hungry," Vanessa replied, taking long strips of beef. She moved around the table, heaping up beans, cornbread, potatoes, and steamed apples. She moved to the edge of the crowd, drifting away from them. No one seemed to pay attention to her, and she turned to hurry to the wagon.

Making two trips until she had her things out of sight of camp, she began to move the first load toward the place where she had left the child and the horse,

Feeling cold with the fear of discovery, she looked over her shoulder because the moment Mrs. Parsons discovered she was gone, she would alert the others and the hunt would begin.

It was dark now, moonlight shedding enough brightness to help her move through the night easily. Her heart raced as she rushed through the woods. Ahead past the trees she spotted the rock where she had left the child, and her heart missed a beat because the girl was gone.

When Vanessa moved closer, her gaze swept the area and she drew in a swift breath. The paint grazed nearby and a bay grazed only yards beyond it. *Two horses?*

The child sat on the ground. A man sprawled beside her, the child's hand on his chest.

Two

Shocked, Vanessa approached them cautiously. Moonlight splashed over a broad-shouldered, black-haired man. Blood-soaked bandages were tied across his shoulder and around his thigh. In spite of his wounds and even though he was unconscious, he seemed formidable.

Looking wild with his long black hair across his cheek, he was clad in torn buckskins. Terrified that he might stir, Vanessa knelt beside him and she saw he also had a wound in his side. The buckskin shirt was ripped and she glimpsed a bandage around his middle. She lifted the bottom of the shirt slightly and drew in her breath because the bandage was crimson with his blood. Placing her hand against his throat, she felt a steady pulse.

"Guipago," the child said, stroking his chest and putting her head against him in a gesture of trust and love. Vanessa hurt for the child.

"Your papa?" Vanessa bit her lip and studied him. Blood oozed from the wounds, and she didn't see how he could survive the next few hours. If she abandoned her plans to save Phoebe and took him to camp, she felt certain Sergeant Hollings would not do anything to help him. He might not allow anyone else to give aid to an Indian.

She bit her lip in indecision. In minutes Hollings and the others might be searching for her. Should she go back and trust some of the people to help the man? She remembered

Hollings' brutality when he had had an Indian beaten so badly at the fort that the man later died.

Studying the unconscious man, she didn't think he would live through the night whatever she did, but she suspected his chances were better if he weren't under Sergeant Hollings' control. She decided to go ahead with her plans and try to take the man along.

The Indian wore a pistol on his belt as well as a scabbard with a knife. She removed the pistol and his knife, placing them in her portmanteau. Then she secured her meager provisions on the two horses after hurrying back to pick up the second armload of belongings. The bay was saddled with a rifle in a scabbard. In minutes she had her things secured on the two horses.

Returning to the man, she leaned forward and placed her hand against his good shoulder to shake him. The moment she touched him, she drew her breath. He was imposing; the solid bulk of his shoulder was hard beneath her hand, the buckskin shirt warm with his body heat. Wounded and unconscious, the man still looked fierce with a hawk-like nose and wide-set prominent cheekbones. She felt reluctant to touch him, yet they had to go.

Knowing any minute they could be discovered, she was panicky. "You have to get up. Soldiers are coming!"

She shook him again, patting his cheek, feeling a tremor run through her when she placed her palm against his warm flesh. It was as if she had reached out to touch a wild animal.

"Please—"

His lashes raised, and dark eyes focused on her with a piercing intensity that was so startling it made her heart leap in fright. She gasped and drew back, staring into his eyes, feeling as if a hot invisible current coursed between them. Along with a twinge of fear, there was a stronger pull on her emotions; she became aware of herself as a woman, intensely conscious of him as a man.

In spite of his overpowering presence, she leaned closer to him. "Soldiers come. You have to get on a horse!"

While he stared at her, she took his hand and slipped an arm beneath his good shoulder. Every touch was like taking hold of a burning branch. What was it about him that conveyed a searing awareness even when he was wounded and next to lifeless?

She glanced at him again to find him studying her with a steady dark gaze that made her feel as if a predatory lion watched her. Judging from appearances, the man was too weak to do anything, yet Vanessa felt at any moment he might overpower her.

"Please get up," she said, trying to lift him, terrified Hollings might come riding out of the woods after her. As she tugged at the warrior, she felt as if she were struggling to pull a tree from the ground. Then suddenly he shifted and sat up, his side pressing against her breast, a solid, hard pressure that was disturbing. She put his arm across her shoulders and tried to stand.

With a grunt of effort he came up beside her. He was taller than she had guessed; her head only came to his shoulder. He stared ahead, his jaw set. Was she making the worst mistake of her life by running away from the wagon train and the safety of the people she knew? Her gaze drifted to the child, and Vanessa knew she wouldn't leave the little girl for the man might not live through the next hour.

"I'll help you get on your horse," she said, waving her free hand. "Only a few more steps." She felt compelled to talk to him, even though both he and the child could not understand her. "That's it," she encouraged his faltering steps. "I know you hurt. I'll try to take care of your wounds when we get away from here. Soldiers are with my wagon train and they'll come looking for me. I'll take care of your little girl."

His horse was only a few feet away; and as they progressed slowly to the animal, she was aware of the warmth of the man's body against her, of the tight muscles in the arm that circled her shoulders. Along with the sour smell of blood, the scents of gunpowder and leather were on him. The bay loomed like a mountain, and she didn't know how she could get the man into the saddle.

"Here we are. This will hurt you, but we have to go. There is a soldier who hates Indians with the wagon train," she said, peering at him, wondering if he understood that word or had heard a white use it. Without a change of expression he stared down at her, and she motioned toward the saddle. For the first time she noticed the U.S. Cavalry insignia on the saddle, and she glanced at him. He was riding an army horse—he had to have taken it in a battle of some kind.

He wrapped his hand around the horn and cantle, then placed his foot in the stirrup. His moccasins were high and made from hides with fur lining the inside. Feeling inadequate and knowing he must be in terrible pain, she placed her hands on his good side and tried to lift him. He pulled up toward the saddle, half up in the air, and she saw him start to sag. She placed one hand on his hip and the other on his buttocks, pushing him. Heat flooded her as she felt his hard buttock beneath her palm, but he didn't look back as he swung his leg across the horse. He swayed and straightened in the saddle, looking down into her eyes.

She held up her palm, hoping he understood she wanted him to wait. She gathered the reins to the paint. Picking up the child and placing her on the paint, Vanessa mounted behind the little girl and put her arm around her.

She looked at the man, who watched her with that same steadfastness that made her pulse flutter every time she encountered it. His steady, direct stare was like a clash with something fiery, causing her nerves to prickle. Did he hate whites and was merely tolerating her because he knew he needed help? He looked as if he could easily wrap his fingers around her throat and choke her. His gaze raked boldly over her and she flushed, knowing that if he weren't wounded, she would be a captive by now. His bandaged shoulder and side were blood soaked. How he was still conscious, she couldn't imagine.

When he motioned and urged his horse forward, she felt a surge of relief because he must have understood that she was trying to help. Then it occurred to her that he could be leading her to his people. She had heard tales of savages and their treatment of women, and she stared at him. She remembered the sun setting to her left when she had been standing in the river. Glancing back at the river, she calculated directions and figured the man was heading north. She caught his reins and pointed the opposite way, tugging on her reins and his to turn them.

"We have to go south. South," she repeated, as if it might help him comprehend. "We have to get away from my camp."

She kept pointing and he only stared at her, so she didn't know whether or not he understood what she was saying. There was a ruthless expression in the set of his jaw and his dark eyes that gave her a chill. Would he try to kill her if he got the chance?

He must be the child's father, but where was the mother? They had to have come from a battle, although no one in the wagon train had heard anything about a battle in the area. Motioning his horse to follow hers, Vanessa turned and rode south through the trees, then climbed a rise.

Leather creaked and the horses' hooves were noisy. She glanced over her shoulder, wondering if she had been missed yet, knowing the soldiers would search all night. Her father's wrath would come down hard on any man who let her escape, for while her father was no longer in the army, but a railroader now, he had powerful connections in the military who would see to it that his wishes were carried out. Hollings and his men wouldn't give up searching for her until they were told to stop.

The land sloped upward and finally leveled, and she glanced behind again. Now the river was lost from sight as they rode over ground sparsely covered with cacti and junipers and grass.

Looking as if he would topple from the horse, the warrior swayed and slumped, but in minutes he straightened again. During the early years of the war she had assisted at the hospital in Shreveport where her father was working and she had tended wounded soldiers. With the terrible wounds this man had, he would likely lose consciousness soon and not revive. They had to get away from the wagon train before she could try to change the bandages on his wounds. But by then, it would probably be too late.

She looked down at the small child nestled against her and stroked the girl's head, lifting long strands of raven hair. The child looked up and smiled, twisting around to hug Vanessa, who squeezed her in return, her love pouring out to the child. Vanessa closed her eyes, imagining for a moment that the little girl belonged to her. To get Phoebe to safety and someday to have her own family, her own children to love and care for, was all Vanessa wanted. And when she went back to Fort McKavett to get Phoebe, they would take their youngest sister, ten-year-old Belva with them because their father had never cared for any of his daughters. They wouldn't leave Belva behind to be sent to a boarding school and then later be given in a loveless marriage.

Would their lives have been different if her mother had lived? The only person her father had ever seemed to truly love was her older brother, his firstborn, Ethan.

Rustling noises around them set her nerves on edge. The moon rose, a big white ball sliding above the horizon, looking as if it hovered close to earth. As it climbed in the sky, its size diminished, seeming to withdraw in distance to a full white brilliance high overhead. The earth was bathed in its light and she felt exposed on the open stretches of land.

They rode down into a wash, following the dry bed with arroyos carved in either side. Prickly pear and mesquite abounded. The man lay on the horse now, his long arms clinging to his mount, and she took the lead. Trying to use the stars as a guide because she knew the north star, she hoped they were continuing south, but she was uncertain. The child was quiet, riding easily, and Vanessa wondered if she were accustomed to traveling like this.

Suddenly the man toppled to the ground. Moonlight spilled over his still form, his outflung arms.

Vanessa's heart missed a beat as she tugged on the reins. Feeling a sense of reluctance, she dismounted. She was certain he was dead. She left the child on the horse as she knelt beside the warrior and placed her hand over his heart.

His chest rose and fell in quick short breaths, and she felt a surge of relief. She went back to the child.

"We'll camp here tonight," she said, wondering if talking helped calm the child's fears, curious if the girl felt any fright. She seemed to accept with stoicism everything that had happened except for the moment she had placed her head on the man's chest. "I'll tend your father's wounds, and we'll sleep and ride again in the morning."

"*Kkaw-Kkoy*'," the child said, looking at Vanessa. "*Kkaw-Kkoy*'?"

"Love, I don't know what you want," Vanessa said, hoping her tone of voice was soothing. She stroked the child's head and in minutes the little girl became interested in the buttons on Vanessa's riding habit.

Setting down the child, Vanessa spread out the quilts, trying to get her bedded down because if she worked on the man's injuries, she was going to cause him more pain and she didn't want the little girl to witness his suffering. Vanessa took down the canteen of water and held it out to the child.

Brushing the girl's head with her hand, she spoke quietly. "I'll call you Hope. You're hope for me, hope for a new life, hope that I escape the convent. Hope that I get Phoebe safely away from Fort McKavett. Hope," she said. "Vanessa," she said and touched her own chest. Vanessa touched the child. "Hope." She took the child's hand and placed it against her cheek. "Vanessa. Van—ess—a."

" 'Nessa," the child repeated solemnly.

"That's it! Very good. Hope."

"Hope," the little girl repeated, handing back the water. As soon as Vanessa had unsaddled and tended the horses, she unpacked the food she had brought from dinner, holding out the cold beef to share with the child.

Finally she had Hope bedded down, pulling a quilt over her and crooning softly until she knew the child was asleep.

With a feeling of dread she stood up and glanced at the unconscious man who hadn't moved since he'd fallen from the horse. She didn't know how much she could help him, but she knew something about tending wounded men. She tore a clean chemise into strips.

Next she spread a quilt on the ground and knelt beside him, staring at his powerful body and feeling hot with embarrassment and a deep reluctance to touch him. However, she placed her hands on his uninjured shoulder to ease him up and slid the quilt beneath him.

Thankful the nights were only mildly cool for the time of year, she began to cut away his shirt. He groaned, and she felt a stab of regret because she knew he was hurting dreadfully.

"I'm sorry. I'm trying to help," she whispered, leaning back to look at him. Her breath caught as moonlight spilled over his broad, muscled chest. In spite of his wounds, he still looked powerful.

She frowned as her gaze roamed down the length of him. His waist narrowed and the buckskin pants were tight across his slender hips. She looked at the bloody wound on his thigh and clamped her jaw closed, taking the knife and cutting away the pant leg, trying not to think about the muscled flesh beneath her fingers. He groaned once, and her gaze flew to his face; but he lay with his dark lashes against his cheeks, his eyes closed.

"Sorry. I don't want to hurt you. I'm trying to take care of you," she whispered and bent to her task.

Finally she had his leg bare to his groin. Her gaze drifted over the front of the buckskin pants and she felt her cheeks flame even though he was unconscious. She let her hand drift across his chest. "You frighten me," she whispered. "I want you to live; but if you do, I hope you won't hurt me."

Steeling herself for the task ahead, Vanessa turned to unpack one of the portmanteaus. She had brought a small bottle of smelling salts, a bottle of alcohol that Mrs. Parsons had packed away, and a bottle of laudanum. With water from the canteen, Vanessa washed his wounds. He gasped and stiffened.

"I'm sorry. I'm trying to help you," she whispered, leaning close to his ear. She continued, finally pouring alcohol on the wound. All three wounds had torn through his body from front to back. She wasn't certain if that meant the shots had passed through him and nothing was lodged in him. If he had a shot still remaining in his body, she did not have the experience to try to cut him open and remove it.

As she poured alcohol on his side, he groaned. "I know this hurts," she whispered. "I'll be through soon. You must be terribly strong to have survived this far." She leaned closer to him. "If anything happens, I will take care of your little girl. I will love her as if she were my own," she said, feeling a tightness in her throat because she already loved the child. "I call her Hope and I think she's precious."

Vanessa sat up and cleaned the wound in his thigh. Finally she bandaged him, winding the strips of her white chemise over his shoulder. She bandaged his thigh next, blushing again as her hands moved on his leg. She had never touched a man intimately. Even when she had tended the wounded soldiers, she never had taken care of them in the manner she was helping this man.

She stared at his side and knew she had to get him up to bandage it. She leaned down to tug on him, placing her face beside his, her mouth at his ear. "You have to sit up for me to bandage you."

She pulled on him and felt his muscles tense as he sat up. Surprised, she leaned back and gazed into black eyes that made her want to jump away from him. Dark as a moonless sky, his eyes seemed to pull and tug on her senses and hold her captive. Again, she had that intense awareness of herself as a woman as he studied her.

"You don't understand me, but I'm trying to help," she said, making an effort to look away. She pressed a folded pad of clean cotton against his side and placed his large hand over the bandage to hold it in place.

"I'm sorry if this hurts you. I've run away from my camp and I have to take you and your little girl with me. The soldiers traveling with my wagon train don't like—" She paused, glancing at him, looking into his unfathomable gaze. "Sergeant Hollings hates Indians, and you wouldn't want to be in his care."

She worked fast, talking rapidly, feeling nervous again. What was it about the warrior that was so disturbing when he regained consciousness? She wrapped strips of the chemise around him, her breasts brushing against his chest as she tried to get the strips in place. Finally she had the bandages secured and she pulled out the bottle of laudanum.

"This will help you."

He pushed it away and stared at her, his dark eyes locking with hers, the air becoming charged again as she gazed at him. Was it anger in him that made every moment volatile? Or was it his virile, powerful male body, his awareness of her as a woman?

"It's for pain." She felt helpless, trying to convey to him

what the laudanum would do. She held it to her lips. "You drink. You won't hurt."

When she held it to his mouth again, he pushed it away. His lashes fluttered, and she wondered if he were about to lose consciousness. Holding his broad shoulders, her breasts brushing his chest in a contact she could feel through her shirt and chemise, she eased him down on the quilt. Leaning back, she looked at him. Only inches separated them, and she was caught in another compelling stare.

"You frighten me," she said softly. "I want you to live for your child's sake, but you frighten me." Even as she said the words, she knew fright wasn't what she was experiencing. He disturbed her in a way no man had before. He wasn't touching her, yet her nerves felt as tingly as if he were.

In spite of his injuries, he was strong and wild and like no man she had known. Savage was the way she had heard Indians described. This one hadn't acted savagely toward her, but he awed her. His eyes fluttered and closed.

She stared at him, touching his cheek. He felt hot, and she wondered if he were running a fever. As if she had no control of her hand, her fingers drifted down lightly over the full underlip that was cracked from wind and sun, yet soft to touch. She ran her fingers over his nose, the arrogant arch in the bone. Her hand moved along the plane of his cheek, over his jawbone, and along the strong column of his throat. His pulse was steady and strong, and she felt a flicker of amazement. How could he survive such terrible wounds, the hours of riding, and his loss of blood?

The white bandages across his shoulder and around his middle were a stark contrast to his dark skin. Blushing, yet yielding to curiosity, she slid her fingers over his chest. She had never touched a man this way and her hand tingled, her nerves quivering as she felt his muscles and ribs. His skin was warm and smooth, his body hard everywhere she touched.

"You're a powerful man," she whispered. "I don't know

how to care for gunshots. I don't know much about men. And I know nothing about a man like you." She let her hand slide to his flat stomach, and the touch seemed to sizzle from her fingers up through her arm and down into the center of her body, stirring a heat that suffused her.

Lone Wolf lay without moving. A steady pain coursed through him while he listened to the woman. Having been an army scout for two years for white soldiers, he spoke English and understood every word, but he didn't want to let her know yet. Why was she running from her people? She wasn't running from a husband, because she wasn't accustomed to a man. Lone Wolf opened his eyes a fraction, gazing at her through his lashes as she slid her hand across his stomach. In spite of his pain, her hand moving low on his bare stomach was stirring his desire.

The cascade of red hair he had seen at the river was looped and pinned up on her head now. He felt darkness overtaking him and knotted his fists, trying to cling to consciousness. Her voice was soft, and she smelled like spring flowers.

The darkness passed, and he became aware of her again, her hand moving on his thigh. Suddenly she stilled, and he opened his eyes a fraction. She was staring at him, and then she jerked her hand away. He closed his eyes, knowing she had seen his arousal.

She was too beautiful to be without a man—had the war or a protective father or brother interfered with her life? Why would she leave the people she knew and go with an Indian child and man who didn't speak the same language? She had to be desperate. What was the woman running away from?

When she had offered laudanum, he had been tempted because the pain was bad. His side burned and throbbed; his shoulder and leg hurt as well, but he wanted to stay conscious. He needed more help than the woman could give. He glanced at her and saw her remove his pistol from a saddlebag. She stretched out on a quilt only a few feet from him with the pistol close at hand.

In minutes she was quiet, and he turned his head to look at her. She lay on her side, White Bird pulled close against her. He felt a peculiar rush of sympathy for the woman because she must love children greatly. Her care for White Bird was constant, and he was still amazed that a white woman would be so loving with an Indian child. Vanessa. The name played in his mind. Locks of her hair had come undone and fallen over her shoulder. His pistol was near her head. He reached up to move it where he could get it if necessary, yet he wondered how much longer he could stay conscious.

If he didn't survive, she had promised to care for White Bird, but how could a woman alone take care of an Indian child? And the woman knew nothing about traveling across country this way. As soon as they had left the river and she had taken the lead, she had said she wanted to go south, but she was angling to the west. She seemed determined to get to a certain destination—was she riding back to a lover?

His people were to the north and if he could get to them, he would get the help he needed for his wounds. But right now he was too weak to protest and could only ride in silence. He needed the woman. When he regained his strength, he would go north and take her with him to his people. His love was still with Eyes That Smile, his wife killed savagely by whites after they had used her for their pleasure. Thus he could take the white woman and use her in turn, taking a measure of revenge.

A wave of pain came, and darkness enveloped him.

The soft cry of a dove woke Vanessa. The cool morning air was fresh; and when she stretched, she was startled by a warm body moving against her. She looked down at the small child. Hope. She remembered and glanced only a few feet away at the man. His chest rose and fell steadily, and Vanessa let out her breath in relief. He was still alive.

All her life her father had talked about savages. Abbot Sutherland hated Indians and had battled them viciously when he started to build his railroad in Kansas. Too well she remembered his offer to the men who worked for him of ten dollars bonus for any dead Indian they brought in. When she had asked him about it, reminding him the Indians were humans, he had flown into one of his rages, shouting about savages and telling her she knew nothing about Indians or about building a railroad.

The wounded warrior did not seem savage, yet she knew he was too weak from his injuries to cause harm.

Vanessa extricated herself from Hope and sat up, stretching and looking around. The sky was lightest behind her, a star still twinkling in the dark sky ahead, and she realized she was facing west. She stood up to get her bearings and then looked down at the unconscious Indian. Her gaze ran over the man's long length, and a shiver coursed through her as she looked at his bronzed skin and powerful muscles.

When the wagon train had left Fort McKavett, they had taken a trail north into isolated land beyond the frontier. Sergeant Hollings had protested because, he'd said, they were riding into a vast desert where only tribes of savages roamed; but the wagon master had been adamant about avoiding Comancheros. Now how far would she have to ride to find a settlement? The man had made it through the night, but could he last another day—or days—until they reached a town and a doctor? Her gaze returned to the man, who stared back with an enigmatic gaze.

"You're awake!" she exclaimed, startled to find him watching her. In the light of day he looked younger than she had guessed last night.

"I'll get water." She stood and went to get a canteen, returning to kneel beside him. Acutely conscious of touching him, she raised his head onto her lap and held the canteen to his mouth. His hand curled over hers as he held the canteen while he drank, his blunt, well-shaped, brown fingers covered her pale hand.

"You're as tough as this land," she said quietly. "I didn't think you'd make it through the night. For the child's sake, I'm glad you did."

She took the canteen away and glanced at the girl, who was still asleep. As the man watched her, she stared back at him, her gaze drifting over him. "We'll have to travel soon because the soldiers will be searching for me. If my father learns I'm with you—" She paused, looking into his dark eyes. "He would kill you, and I don't know what he would do to me. If I'm caught traveling with you, my reputation will be ruined even though there is no real reason for it to be."

When she started to move away, the warrior caught her wrist. Surprised, she looked at him as he struggled to sit up. She leaned against him, taking his weight; his shoulder pressed against her soft breast as Vanessa helped him.

Amazed that he was able to sit up, she stared at him. The bandages held dark stains of blood, and his shoulder and side had the bright red of fresh blood seeping from the wound.

"You should be careful," she said, knowing it was useless to warn him. He ignored her, putting weight on her as he rose to his feet and swayed.

"You can't—" He turned his head to look at her, and she bit back her protest. As wild and fierce as he looked, he was also ruggedly handsome with an air of determination that was impossible to ignore.

"You don't understand what I say, and even if you did, I know you wouldn't obey me," she added swiftly, "but you should get off your feet." She pushed against him gently and motioned toward the ground. Her fingers were on his right arm and his good side, and she yanked her hand away as soon as she touched him.

"I'm glad you don't know that you frighten me," she said, trying to get some force into her voice. "You should sit down."

He placed his hand on her shoulder. "I won't get my strength back." His voice was deep and strong and clear.

Three

Shocked, she stared at him while her mouth dropped open. He stared back, and her cheeks flushed with heat. "You speak English!"

"Not as well as you do," he said.

"You made me think you didn't know what I was saying—" She bit off her words, angry that he hadn't told her sooner.

"You said nothing that should worry you," he stated. "Now I will tend to myself for a few moments. I'll need your help later because my injuries pain me."

As he struggled to remain standing, she reached out to steady him; and the moment her fingers touched his warm skin and her arm went around his waist, she drew her breath. He looked at her, his dark brows arching.

"It was easier to care for you when I thought you didn't comprehend what I said to you!" she snapped, flustered.

"My understanding should make it easier, not more difficult," he remarked dryly.

He moved away in an unsteady limp, disappearing behind a bushy mesquite. She turned her back, looking through her portmanteau for food. She was stunned that he had understood everything she had said to him, and she remembered babbling when she had tended his wounds.

In minutes he returned. In spite of walking slowly with a limp, he was formidable, and her heart beat faster. When he approached, she stood up to help him. Her hair spilled over her shoulders, and she was aware of her disheveled appearance as he watched her walk to him.

"Why did you leave your people?" he asked. Before she could answer, he stumbled and she caught him, feeling his weight come down on her, his arm circling her shoulders and his body pressing against hers, sending shocks of awareness through her everywhere she touched him. She helped him ease down onto the quilt.

"I have some food," she said, ignoring his question and getting out beef, apples, and cold cornbread from the night before. She handed him the canteen, and he tilted it up to drink. Her gaze ran over his chest; she was mesmerized by the play of muscles as he lowered the canteen. She looked up and found him watching her while he handed her the water.

"You didn't answer my question. Why did you leave your people?"

"My father intends to place me in a convent. He wants me to become a nun. Do you know what a nun is?"

"Yes. Why would he do that?"

"He didn't know what else to do with me," she answered bluntly, looking beyond him and thinking about her father. "He travels a great deal, and my mother is dead. My brother is in Virginia; Papa thought I should go into a convent in Denver."

"Why didn't you marry someone instead?"

She blushed, looking into the warrior's dark eyes. "My father wanted me to marry one of his friends, but none of them would have me."

The dark eyes raked over her, settling on her burning face. "I find that difficult to believe."

"They said I was too strong-willed."

He studied her. "That wouldn't stop many men."

"It stopped the ones my father would have approved of, and the others he kept from courting me. What is your name?"

"I am Lone Wolf, Vanessa," he said, her name rolling across his tongue with the accent on the first syllable, sounding different from the way anyone else said it and sending a rush of warmth through her.

She glanced at the child. "What's her name?"

"White Bird."

"Where is her mother?"

"She's dead," he answered flatly. "She was killed by white soldiers in a battle yesterday," he said, the anger unmistakable in his voice.

"That's where you were injured." Vanessa looked at White Bird and felt saddened by the little girl's loss. "What tribe are you?"

"Kiowa," he answered. "We were camped for winter with the Comanche. In the winter we don't move around as in warm weather when we follow the buffalo."

"I suppose you want me to take you back to your people."

When he didn't answer, she looked around. He was sprawled on the quilt and she moved beside him quickly, seeing he had lost consciousness again. She knelt over him, knowing he must have been incredibly strong and fit before he was wounded.

His anger toward the white soldiers had been obvious. How would he feel toward her when he learned she was the sister of an officer in the Union Army? She prayed he would never learn how her father hated Indians and had offered money to have them killed. Vanessa heard White Bird stirring and turned to find the child rubbing her eyes.

Within the hour she had fed White Bird apple, cornbread, and damson jam. Fascinated by the little girl, Vanessa brushed White Bird's hair, plaiting it into one long braid.

The moment Lone Wolf regained consciousness, the child ran to him. She knelt beside him, and he hugged her with his good arm while the two of them talked in harsh sounding words that Vanessa couldn't understand.

His eyes fluttered and closed; White Bird sat quietly by

him, stroking his chest, and Vanessa felt another wrench to
her heart. The child had already lost her mother; now she
was likely to lose her father, and Vanessa hurt for her.

A bird flapped noisily skyward and Vanessa came to her
feet, chilled with fear as she looked back the way they had
come. Since soldiers might not be far off, she hurried to
pack. In another ten minutes they were ready to mount up.
Lone Wolf was conscious again, and she knelt down beside
him. "We have to keep moving because we're still close
enough to my wagon train that the soldiers might find us."

"We go north. We can get to my people, who will tend
my wounds," he answered.

Intimidated by him, but knowing he was too weak to
cause her trouble, Vanessa shook her head. "I have to go
south to Fort McKavett."

"I can't get any help if we go south. You'll be riding
through Comanche territory, so you can't go without me."

"I'm not going north with you," she said, feeling the
clash of wills, seeing the anger coming to his eyes, and
feeling another chill because if he were well, she couldn't
oppose him.

"You can't go alone; and if I lose consciousness, White
Bird needs you," he said.

"If I have to leave you behind, I will," she replied forcefully. "You can't travel without me, and White Bird won't
be safe going with you because you're too weak to protect
her. I have to go south to get back home to get my sister."

"I won't survive if we ride south."

"You'll be as likely to survive as you will if we ride
north," she persisted, feeling desperate to get back to
Phoebe.

"Why do you have to get to your sister?"

"My father has promised her to Major Thompkins, a man
she doesn't love. I told her I would come back and get her
and we would go west where Papa can't find us. The major
is cruel and selfish, and Phoebe is terrified of him."

"Why would your father promise his daughter to a man like that?"

Hurting, Vanessa looked away, knowing that their father did not care for any of his girls. All his love had always gone to his golden-haired son, never to his daughters. "My father doesn't want us around now, and the major is wealthy and powerful. As far as my father is concerned, this is a good match. I have to rescue Phoebe!" Lone Wolf stared at her, and she felt his anger and frustration. "You don't have a choice," she added quietly. "This is one time you're going to have to do what someone else tells you."

Fury blazed in his dark eyes, but she stared back steadily in spite of her pounding heart. Suddenly his hand shot out and closed around her wrist, pulling her close to him. He caught her off balance, and she threw her other hand up against his chest to brace herself. She yanked her hand away as if she had touched burning coals instead of his warm, bare skin.

He drew her close to him, leaning his face near hers. "You will kill me if we ride south."

Her heart thudded in fear, but she felt a flash of anger for his arrogant treatment of her when she had saved his life by her attention. "You're too tough to kill!" she snapped, angry with him, jerking her wrist to try to break free. His fingers tightened around her slender wrist and he caught her other hand, holding them both easily with one hand while she struggled against him.

"If you tie me up and go north, I can't help you when you lose consciousness!" she snapped, glaring at him. She felt his anger as she looked into his brown eyes. He leaned closer to her and her heart pounded in fright, yet she wasn't going to give up on going south to rescue Phoebe.

"I don't know that I can stay conscious, so you'll get your way; but beware the day I'm well," he said in a quiet voice that frightened her.

"When we get to a town, I'll get help for you."

"A white doctor won't tend me," he said, closing his eyes as if he were in pain.

"I'll tell him you're my husband, and then he will."

Lone Wolf focused on her again. "Don't tell anyone that. You'll be persecuted or they'll think you're a captive and take you to the nearest fort. Or worse."

She frowned, staring at him, wondering what experiences he'd had to make him have such an opinion of whites. She thought about her father and his hatred of Indians, of Hollings and his mistreatment of them, and she realized that Lone Wolf was probably correct.

"I'll get help for you some way. I have to go south and get my sister. My father intends her to marry next month on her sixteenth birthday. I don't have time to ride north with you. And if you were going to die, you already would have!" She knew better than that because she had seen soldiers look on the mend and then suddenly they were gone, but she had to get Phoebe.

Vanessa pulled her wrist from his grasp, and his eyes narrowed. "We're in danger of being found, so we should go," she added.

"How many soldiers are with your wagon train?"

"Fifteen."

He frowned and placed his hand on her shoulder, sitting up straighter. She knelt to let him place his arm across her shoulders. Avoiding his wounds and keenly aware of his body, she put her arm around his back above his narrow waist.

"Ready?" she asked, his face only inches from hers.

He nodded and they stood. She felt his weight sag against her, and then he was on his feet and they moved toward his saddled horse. He mounted slowly, inching his leg across the horse and settling in the saddle. "Give me my knife and pistol."

She hesitated, looking into his dark eyes and feeling un-

certain what he might do once he was armed. She shook
her head. "How do I know you won't use them on me?"

He stared at her and his anger was unmistakable. "I won't
harm you because I need you. If I don't live, White Bird
can't survive out here alone," he answered solemnly.

Vanessa retrieved his gun and knife and handed them to
him, watching him place the knife in a scabbard at his belt,
the gun in the waist of the buckskin pants.

She placed White Bird on her saddle and mounted to
turn toward the south. She looked over her shoulder at him
and saw him following her, his dark eyes filled with anger.

After a time she dropped back to ride beside him.

"Why doesn't your sister run away as you did?" he asked,
studying her.

"She's younger and much more obedient so she needs
my help. Phoebe does what Papa tells her to do."

"And you don't?" he asked, still gazing at her with curiosity in his eyes.

She raised her chin. "Sometimes I've opposed him; that's
why I'm being sent to a convent. I'm eighteen; and Papa
thinks after a year at a convent, I will be submissive enough
that one of his friends will marry me."

"You'll never reach that convent," Lone Wolf said matter-
of-factly. She looked at him sharply, wondering if his prediction were a threat against her life.

"I have another sister, Belva, who is ten years old.
Phoebe and I won't run away and leave her with Papa, so
I'll get both Phoebe and Belva and then we'll all go out
West."

"Two sisters? How can you get two sisters away from
your father if he doesn't want you to?"

"I will," she said, determined to succeed.

"If your father doesn't want any of you, why doesn't he
just let you go?"

"Because he expects to make a marriage for Phoebe and

later for Belva that will give him good connections in high places and make his daughters wealthy women."

"There is an advantage to our way of life," Lone Wolf remarked, and she glanced at him, surprised at his intelligence and subtlety.

They became quiet, and she glanced back over her shoulders, looking at the vast expanse of land. She experienced a momentary fright because she couldn't tell the direction unless she could see the sun or the north star.

Lone Wolf gritted his teeth against the pain, wondering if he would survive to get White Bird back to their people. His anger smoldered because for the first time in his adult life he was helpless and had to do what someone else ordered. He looked at the woman, knowing the moment he got his strength back he would take her and go north. He could satisfy his body with her because he would not bed a Kiowa maiden without marriage and he was not ready to wed again, but the white woman was different. He felt a grudging respect for her, though, because she had stood up to him today even when he knew she was frightened by him.

He worried about White Bird; he had to live for her sake. He didn't want her raised by whites—the woman might be kind, but others would persecute the child.

They were riding to an army fort. His anger increased, burning as steadily as the pain in his wounds. The woman could not possibly ride into a fort, take her two younger sisters, and ride out without her father stopping her.

Lone Wolf knew it would be his death if they reached that fort or anywhere close to it.

If he survived, he should regain some of his strength and, before they reached the vicinity of the fort, he would take charge and turn north. And when he did, he would take the woman with him. When he remembered the pale-skinned lieutenant deliberately shooting Tainso, Lone Wolf drew a deep breath, his hatred fanning bright like flames in a prairie wind.

Lone Wolf glanced at Vanessa, his gaze drifting over her. She was innocent—and the thought of taking revenge on an innocent left him with a bitter taste.

Toward noon the sun rose high overhead. A hawk circled above them on rising air currents while they rode toward a line of junipers and cottonwoods; and Vanessa hoped to find a creek, praying there would be water. Her stomach churned with hunger, and Lone Wolf was beginning to sway in the saddle.

They rode into the trees, moving beneath branches in the cool shade. After a time they approached a meandering muddy creek that looked welcome to her. They rode alongside it for a quarter of an hour with Lone Wolf in the lead. She kept expecting him to stop to allow the horses to drink; but when he didn't, she moved beside him to tell him to halt. Before she could speak, he reached across and placed his hand on her arm.

She glanced at him and watched him withdraw his knife. Her pulse drummed as he reined his horse close to her, his leg touching hers. Leaning over, he clasped her shoulder. His warm breath fanned on her, and once again that blazing awareness of him shot through her.

"If there's trouble, take White Bird and go," he whispered. "Someone's behind us."

Startled, Vanessa gazed up at him. "If you'll give me the pistol, I'll help you."

"No," he said. "Now get down off your horse." He held White Bird's arm and whispered in her ear, and she nodded.

Glancing behind them, Vanessa dismounted. She didn't see anyone approaching or hear anything out of the ordinary. Nearby a bird whistled and a breeze rustled cottonwood leaves, but there was no other sound.

Lone Wolf dismounted as well, then he led the horses between junipers, motioning to Vanessa to follow. With White Bird still on the back of the paint, Lone Wolf held the reins to both horses, standing between the two.

Branches scraped Vanessa and she paused, facing him. He reached out, his dark eyes as unreadable as ever, and pulled her to him, turning her so her back was against him. Her heart thudded, and she was aware of his strong arm banding her waist, of standing against his long length.

For the next few minutes, she forgot danger. Instead, she was intensely aware of her body against his, startled by the reaction she had to him every time she was close to him. And then she decided he had been imagining noises because nothing was happening. There was only silence and the warble of a bird. She shifted impatiently, trying to turn to look at him.

"I don't—"

He placed his hand over her mouth. It was a light pressure, his dark eyes boring into her, and she blinked in surprise. He moved his fingers, tracing them across her lips slowly and shaking his head. She knew he was signaling her to stop talking, yet her awareness was of the light drag of his fingertips over her lips, a sensual touch that made her breath catch. As her lips parted, his eyes narrowed. She realized her reaction to him and his perception of it, and she blushed hotly.

A harness jingled and she turned, feeling cold because someone approached. The sounds of hoofbeats and the deep voices of men mingled with the creak of saddle leather and her heart quickened with fear. Lone Wolf's arm tightened around her waist and he pulled her tightly against him, his hand holding his knife.

Four

"Who the hell could she have met? Who could she be riding with?" The snarling voice carried loudly, and Vanessa felt a chill run down her spine as she recognized Sergeant Hollings' voice.

Vanessa glanced up at Lone Wolf, who stared ahead. Afraid White Bird would be terrified, Vanessa twisted around to look at her. White Bird stared at Vanessa and sat still, and Vanessa realized the child must have been accustomed to situations like this because of the clashes between the Indians and the soldiers.

The noise of the soldiers and their mounts grew louder, bridles jingling and horses snorting. The riders sounded as if they were headed straight toward them, and Vanessa felt a momentary panic.

With impassive features, Lone Wolf gazed over her head, and then his eyes shifted to meet hers. Forgetting her fright, she stared back at him, wondering about him and his feelings toward her because he must be accustomed to considering all whites his enemy.

His dark eyes were impassive, devoid of emotion. Did he ever show fear or joy? Was he capable of laughter? When her gaze lowered to his mouth, her breath caught.

Behind her, bushes rustled and her attention was drawn back to Hollings, her fear returning with a rush. The voices were louder now. Hollings sounded angry. If he found them, he would kill Lone Wolf, and she suspected he would kill White Bird as well.

Growing more alarmed, Vanessa glanced around again to see if White Bird were afraid. The child lay on the horse's neck, and she watched the white woman with the same unfathomable expression that Lone Wolf exhibited. With their dark skin and buckskin clothing, Lone Wolf and White Bird blended into the surroundings, but Vanessa's blue dress and pale skin might be discernible.

As the men rode closer, Lone Wolf drew her against him, shielding her body with his. She was pressed against his chest, his arm around her, and Vanessa's heart thudded wildly. She felt his smooth, warm flesh beneath her cheek, the heat from his body, his strong arm encircling her.

Voices and horses were loud, yet Vanessa was more aware of the man holding her. Without thought, she reached up and placed her hand on his right side. She inhaled his male scent, the faint traces of the smell of leather. His muscles were as solid as the rocks that dotted the land.

Twisting to look over her shoulder, she saw Hollings ride into view only yards away. His wrinkled blue uniform was stretched tight over his squat, thick body. Long tufts of pale yellow hair stuck out from beneath his hat brim. Private Jergen rode beside him, and the other soldiers followed. She counted swiftly, determining that there were eight men in all, only one rider not in uniform. She didn't recognize him, but she remembered seeing him in the wagon train.

The soldiers splashed across the creek. To Vanessa's horror, Sergeant Hollings and Private Jergen stopped to water their horses while the others rode on.

"How the hell could she find someone to travel with out in this godforsaken desert?"

"I dunno, sergeant. No one else is missing from the wagon train."

"If someone had followed us from Fort McKavett, we would have seen them. Out here you can see five hundred miles in any direction until you're near a river and trees. She didn't take any horses, yet we're following two horses; so she's traveling with someone. Who the hell is it?"

"Maybe a renegade took her. That Parsons woman said the colonel's daughter went down to the river alone to bathe."

Sergeant Hollings spat a long stream of brown tobacco juice at the ground and wiped his mouth with the back of his hand. "I wish I'd known that. I'd like to have that wench under me. Damn waste to put her in a convent without a few good rides first."

"Lordy, the colonel would kill you!"

"Her pa would never know. She'd be 'shamed to tell and she's headed for a convent anyway. If we find her, we'll pleasure ourselves before we take her back. Get her off alone."

"That woman's body makes a man nearly burst just looking at her. You don't think she'd tell?"

"Hell, no. I know these prissy women. They get 'shamed and they don't want any of their menfolks to know what happened."

Vanessa's face flamed, and she couldn't look at Lone Wolf.

With a jangle of spurs, both men dismounted and knelt to splash water on their faces from the stream. As they stood up, the private pushed back his hat. "Maybe she had a lover and he trailed after her and met up with her."

"No." Hollings shook his head. "I've been stationed at McKavett and I've been in a detail assigned to her pa. He's working on the railroads for the army. He watches his older girls like a hawk. No one can even steal a kiss unless he has the old man's approval and no one has that except some old buzzards those girls wouldn't want to kiss. He's marrying the middle one off to Major Thompkins."

The soldier sneered. "Damn. Feel sorry for her. All kinds of rumors about how his last two wives died."

"Last three. There were three wives, and they all died violently. And each time he gets a new one, she's younger. The middle sis is the prettiest one."

"I've seen her," the private said. "She'll be wasted on old Thompkins. He must be forty years older than she is."

"We ought to catch up with them today. Judging from the tracks, we're not far behind at all. We've got to get his daughter back; our careers will end if she gets away from us. The colonel has powerful friends in the army. And when we get her, we'll make this trip worthwhile. Let's go."

They mounted and she watched them, her cheek still pressed against Lone Wolf's bare chest. It seemed impossible that they would lose the trail, but she hoped it happened. She could hear Lone Wolf's heart beat in a steady thump that wasn't accelerated with fear the way hers was.

When Lone Wolf released his grip, she looked up into his eyes. They were so dark brown they appeared black, the difference between the irises and pupils barely discernible. He gazed down at her with a steadfastness that caused her pulse to drum. He touched her cheek lightly. The touch was gentle, so at variance with the wild, rugged man he appeared to be. Her gaze lowered to his sensual mouth, the full, prominent lower lip, and she wondered what it would be like to kiss him.

Blushing because she knew little about kisses, she shifted, turning to look at White Bird.

"They're gone, but we'll wait," Lone Wolf whispered, his warm breath fanning on her temple, and she was acutely aware of even that faint contact. "They could double back. They have a scout who is leading them."

His words chilled her. How could anyone find tracks on this dry, pebbly, grass-covered ground? "Hollings doesn't like Indians," she whispered. "I don't think he would be kind."

"No, he would not be kind," Lone Wolf whispered in return, a sardonic glint in his eyes. "No soldier would be."

She wondered about his experiences with white soldiers. Was that who had caused his terrible wounds? She still felt embarrassed by Hollings' crude talk. And now she knew she wouldn't be safe with him either.

"White Bird hasn't made a sound," she said.

"Early in life, Kiowa children learn to keep quiet. Babies are allowed to grow as they please, except they all must learn to avoid crying, because it could jeopardize everyone else in moments like this." He looked down at her solemnly. "If the soldiers catch us, I'm not strong enough to defend us. If we turn north now, we can get to my people."

And she wondered how safe she would be with them. She shook her head. "I have to get to my sister. The wedding is set for next month." She looked at White Bird. "Someday I want my own children, and I'll never have any if I'm in a convent."

He tilted up her chin and looked into her eyes. "You will have your own, Vanessa."

Her breath caught in her throat as she gazed at him. She felt uncertain with him because she had never known a man like him. He was as wild as this land they crossed. He ran his finger across her mouth again, and her heart thudded against her rib cage. It was another slight touch, the faintest friction, yet it became intimate as he stood watching her. Her lips parted, and she felt overwhelmed by him, knowing she was having an intense reaction to a man she could trust only because he was so weak he needed her.

She felt unable to get her breath or move, and then he stroked her forehead and looked beyond her and the spell ended. "We go quickly now," he whispered. "We can't head south for a time because that's the way they're going. If you won't go north, we'll go west."

She mounted, holding White Bird whose eyes were large and solemn. Vanessa kissed the girl's forehead and squeezed her; and when the child looked up at her, Vanessa smiled.

As White Bird smiled in return, Vanessa hoped she wasn't afraid.

Lone Wolf led the way, and she wondered what it was costing him to sit up and take the lead. They rode down the center of the muddy creek. It seemed a risky thing to make so much noise, yet she was certain Lone Wolf knew more about survival than she did. He swayed, and she felt a stab of fear for him. They needed to keep traveling to get away from Hollings. In seconds Lone Wolf squared his shoulders and sat up straight again.

The soldiers had tracked them easily and quickly. With Lone Wolf's wounds, the three of them couldn't travel fast. Would Hollings catch them? She shivered, thinking about Hollings' words.

For the next hour, they followed the creek, riding through water that would leave no trail. When they finally emerged from the water, they followed the line of trees. To her right, she could see the sun slanting in the sky and was satisfied they were headed southwest. Lone Wolf reined in to look at her.

"We stop here and eat and rest. We'll travel at night because when we leave this creek, we'll be in the open."

As he faced her, she saw the grim lines of pain around his mouth. The bandages were soaked again with bright red blood. "Your wounds are bleeding," she said, fearful for him, wanting him to survive even though she barely knew him.

He nodded, and she suspected he had pushed himself to his limit. He swayed in the saddle and then gripped it, dismounting awkwardly. As his feet touched the ground, he kept going, slumping and collapsing to sprawl unconscious.

Vanessa dismounted quickly, lifting White Bird down and moving the horses away. Vanessa rushed back to feel Lone Wolf's pulse. It was fluttery. He had to stop traveling and get medical attention. Should she have ridden north with him? She felt torn between her need to get to Phoebe and the need to get help for him. Vanessa unpacked quickly, handing a plum to White Bird and spreading a quilt for her.

Unpacking a quilt and getting a canteen of water and the bottle of alcohol, she worked swiftly. Wondering if she would have anything left to wear if she had to keep tearing her clothing into strips for bandages, she took out her night-gown.

She knelt beside him again, trying to get a quilt beneath him, so he would be off the ground where she could wash his wounds and avoid getting dirt in them.

His eyes fluttered and opened and he shifted, moving onto the quilt and sitting up.

"You're bleeding badly. I have to change your bandages," she said, suddenly disconcerted because it was easier to touch his bare skin when he was unconscious. "I've seen doctors take care of the wounded at the hospital in Shreve-port," she said. She was rambling, her words tumbling out too fast. "My first home was in Shreveport and then I went to Kansas. Now we're living in Texas. My father takes his family with him when he moves around." She sat back to look at Lone Wolf. "I'll try to tend your wounds."

He nodded, staring at her with a distracting directness that addled her thoughts. She glanced at White Bird, who was seated on the ground, her small dark fingers busy stack-ing a pile of pebbles.

"I'll get her something to eat first," Vanessa added. Aware of his constant watchfulness, Vanessa handed White Bird an apple. When Vanessa gazed at their meager food supply, she had a new worry because they had eaten nearly everything. Shoving that concern aside, she picked up her nightgown and moved back to him.

"May I have your knife?"

He handed it to her, and she sat on the quilt beside him and shook out the gown. He caught her wrist, and his touch sent currents of heat across her nerves.

"You tear your good clothing." His dark hand slid to the

white gown. As he held it, she drew her breath, gazing at his blunt fingers. He stared at the gown, and she realized he was imagining her in it. Her cheeks flushed hotly as she stared back at him. He reached out to take a lock of her hair in his hand. "Your hair is red like a sunset in the time of snows."

His voice was deep, playing over her senses like his touch. She drew in her breath and with an effort looked down, taking the knife to cut the gown. He placed his hand on her wrist again.

"I can't replace it for you," he said quietly.

"I don't mind. I can get another gown." She ripped it, and he reached over to help. In minutes they had the gown in long strips. She dreaded the next part, wishing he would close his eyes. "I have to cut away the bandages."

He nodded and sat up straight, his legs in front of him. She scooted close, intensely aware of his constant observation. His face was only inches away; her hands brushed his chest. She slipped the knife beneath the strip of cloth on his shoulder and she cut the binding. When it came away, she rose to her knees to unwrap it, trying to reach around him, feeling self-conscious as her breasts brushed against his shoulder. Finally the bandages came away, and he drew in his breath.

"I'm sorry I hurt you."

Dark eyes stared at her in another impassive look. She shifted her attention to the wound.

It was still draining, but it held no offensive odor and she hoped no infection had set in. "I want to take away all the bandages at once and then redo them," she explained, sliding the knife under the bindings across his rib cage. As she unwound them, he held up his arms. Her fingers fluttered over his skin, and she was acutely conscious of each slight contact.

She met his dark eyes and wondered what he was thinking. He seemed stoic and solemn, keeping his thoughts to himself. Lone Wolf was a good name because even in the brief time she had known him, he seemed a solitary man, fierce, arrogant, and a leader.

When the bandages on his side came free, he inhaled as she pulled away the pad of cloth.

"I know I hurt you."

"I'm aware you try to avoid hurting me. This is nothing."

She glanced at him, suspecting he meant what he said because he seemed as tough as an old steer. "I think many men would not be alive now with wounds like this." She tried to work as gently as possible. "I put alcohol on your wounds before because one of the soldiers at the hospital in Shreveport said that's what someone did to clean his wound when he was in the field. You weren't conscious the last time I put alcohol on you. It'll hurt dreadfully, but it might keep infection from setting in."

He merely nodded and waited in silence while she looked down at his leg. His large fingers brushed her slender ones as he took the knife from her, cutting away the bandage around his thigh. When he handed the knife back to her, amusement seemed to dance in his dark eyes. It was the first time she had caught such an expression in them.

She blushed, knowing she was shy around him. She knew little about men, and even though she had worked in the hospital, the staff had shielded her as much as possible. Most of her work had involved taking mail to patients and reading letters to them, writing letters for them, or helping feed them. Never had she cared for a man's body as she was having to now.

He unwrapped the bandage, and she tossed it with the other blood-soaked pads to wash because she would have to use them again. She poured water on his wounds and then she got the bottle of alcohol, looking at the small amount of liquid she had left. She bit her lip, dreading putting alcohol on him while he was conscious.

He took the bottle from her and poured the liquid on his

wounded leg without a change in his expression, and she was amazed at his toleration of what must have been terrible pain.

She picked up a bandage, and he took it from her as she placed a clean pad of folded cloth against his dark leg. His leg was sinew and muscle and bone, as fit and strong as the rest of his body. Vanessa tried to keep her gaze from drifting to the front of his tight buckskins, remembering his arousal when she had tended him before.

He wrapped a strip of cloth around his leg, and she reached out to secure it. "I think the more you move your arm, the more your shoulder bleeds," she said in a low voice, conscious of touching his inner thigh.

She looked at his side, aware this was the worst wound with a jagged tear in his flesh. "Ready?" she asked, and he nodded.

As she poured the amber liquid on his wound, he drew in his breath. Pouring it on the back side, she felt a tight knot of sympathy, glad it was over and done. She folded a cloth and placed it against his side in front, another in back.

"Hold these in place." She began to wrap a long strip around his middle, brushing against him even more than when she had removed the bandage. She was inches from his face again, trying to avoid looking at him, but her gaze seemed drawn with a compelling force.

Suddenly, she became aware that the top buttons of her riding habit and shirt were unbuttoned, that she was leaning over him, and the only place he could look was down her dress. She tried to shift away, but as she looked into his dark eyes, her hands became still, her heart missing a beat. When his gaze lowered to her mouth, she felt on fire. He leaned closer and her lips parted, her breath catching in her throat.

He was so close; the expression on his face showed clearly his intention, and she shut her eyes. His lips touched hers, a faint contact that seemed to shift the ground beneath her with its impact. His lips brushed hers, warm and firm, a touch that kindled heat low inside her. He slid his hand behind her head, his lips settling on hers firmly, parting hers.

Lone Wolf's mouth moved on hers, and then his tongue touched her lower lip and her eyes flew open in shock. Heavy-lidded, with lowered lashes, he watched her, his dark eyes stirring a tremor inside of her. As his hand behind her head pulled her closer, his tongue slipped over her lower lip, touching her tongue.

Her heart raced, and the heat building in her made her shift her hips. A soft moan caught in her throat while his tongue played over hers and went deep into her mouth in a possessive thrust. She felt faint with the sensations which streaked through her. Without thinking, she reached out and placed her hand on his arm and was dimly aware of the firm muscle. He continued to kiss her until she trembled from the fires he had kindled. Unaware of what she was doing, she placed her right hand on his thigh.

Vanessa's heart thudded violently. She had only been kissed a few times by young soldiers she had known, and those had been sweet chaste kisses, not a sensual torment that whisked all thoughts from her mind, a kiss that left her feeling hot and weak and made her want more.

He leaned back, and her eyes slowly opened to find him watching her with an unfathomable look. "You are as warm as summer," he said, "a woman meant for loving. Your red hair is like sunshine." He leaned forward to brush her lips again. "Summer," he whispered.

She moaned softly with pleasure, unable to resist, yielding to him and wanting him to kiss her again. When he stopped, she looked up at him.

"You are a beautiful woman."

She felt beautiful with his words even though she knew it was impossible after traveling across country. Her hair was a tangle and her riding habit wrinkled, but his words flowed over her like a golden cape. His hand slid from her head to her shoulder.

"You are ready for a man's loving, Vanessa." His words stirred another rush of warmth. He closed his eyes, and a frown crossed his brow. "I lie down now. The blackness is coming."

Startled, she placed her arm around him, more aware than ever of his body against hers as she eased him to the quilt. Her gaze traveled the length of him, and she stared at the thick bulge against the front of his buckskins and realized how aroused he was from their kisses.

He caught her hand, and she looked at him, blushing because she had been staring. "Go back and look for the soldiers. White Bird will stay with me."

Vanessa nodded and stood up, moving away from him, but unable to avoid taking one more glance that raked down his long body.

Turning away, she walked without seeing where she was going, her thoughts a jumble over his kisses, her mouth still tingling, and her body aching strangely.

She heard him say something in a low tone to White Bird. Vanessa walked back the way they had come, climbing up the slope. She moved cautiously, keeping close to the ground and peering over the top of the rise across the open land they had covered.

No one was in sight, and she felt a rush of relief. If the soldiers trailed them now, there was nowhere to hide or run and Lone Wolf was in no shape to flee.

She slid down the embankment and went back, looking at him sprawled on the ground, thinking about his kisses and feeling hot all over again. She had never been kissed in such a bold manner. Her heart drummed, knowing she had yielded with shameful eagerness. She had resisted boys at home who had wanted to kiss her; why was she so susceptible to Lone Wolf? And she knew he was no boy. He was a man in every sense. He was self-assured, arrogant, brave. And so far there had been nothing savage about him toward her, yet he had no strength to do anything harmful.

She thought of her father's tirades when Indians had attacked his railroad crews. How he hated Indians! And if he knew she was traveling with one—

Vanessa's mind slid away from that image, and she shivered and rubbed her arms. He would have Lone Wolf beaten and killed and he might banish her from home forever, yet he had all but done that when he had decided to place her in the convent.

Kneeling beside White Bird, she pointed to the rocks. "You're building something grand. A house?"

"House?" the child repeated, smiling at Vanessa. " 'Nessa." She climbed into Vanessa's lap, hugging her and turning a lock of hair in her fingers.

Vanessa held her close, feeling the tiny body in her arms, thinking White Bird was sweet. At the thought that White Bird's mother had been killed in a battle, Vanessa tightened her arms around the child and crooned softly to her.

She couldn't bear to think about the little girl's loss. White Bird was still too young to understand what had happened, but the bond between a mother and child was so close that White Bird had to feel the void.

Vanessa reached for the portmanteau and pulled out one of the hard, dried biscuits and a jar of damson jam. In minutes, she had the biscuit broken apart, covered with jam. She fed bites to White Bird, singing to her all the while.

Lone Wolf heard the singing and turned his head slightly to watch Vanessa feed White Bird. She seemed to love the little girl as if she were her own child, and the love between them grew with each hour even though they didn't speak the same language.

His gaze slid to Vanessa's mouth; it was hot and ripe for a man's love. She was innocent, unawakened by any man. He felt his body heat as he remembered her soft moan of pleasure when he had kissed her, her surprise when he had invaded her mouth with his tongue. What should he do with her?

Had he been well when he'd first found her alone at the river, he would have taken revenge. The whites had violated Eyes That Smile, and then they had stabbed her and left her to die slowly and painfully. It had been a crew of men working on a railroad. Lone Wolf and six other warriors had hunted them down and taken revenge, but it hadn't been enough to stop the hurt that he felt every time he remembered finding his wife's body. He felt the familiar hurt that still tore his insides, particularly when he learned the men had been paid a bounty for killing her.

He heard Hollings say Vanessa's father was a railroad man. Lone Wolf hated them more than the soldiers.

He could take Vanessa captive, take her back to his tribe. She would fight him, but he knew from the few stolen kisses that she would not fight long. Anger surged in him. The whites hadn't cared how much pain they had inflicted on Eyes That Smile. Nor on the people who loved her. And the same with Tainso and his brother, his mother, all his loved ones who had died at the hands of whites. As he watched Vanessa rock White Bird, emotions warred in him. She was brave and intelligent and loving, and he admired her even as he still wanted to take her for revenge against the hated whites.

He was weak in body and spirit, Lone Wolf chided himself angrily. When he was stronger, he would take revenge; and then he and White Bird would ride north. As swiftly as he made the decision for revenge, logic argued that Vanessa was innocent where Eyes That Smile's death was concerned. Almost twelve moons ago she had died, and he had not been with a woman since. His body was clamoring for satisfaction.

He looked at Vanessa again. He ached from the few sweet, hot kisses he had taken. Lone Wolf studied the spill of red-gold hair over her back and shoulders. When she had leaned over him, her clothing had gaped open and he had seen the full, lush curves of her pale breasts.

He remembered that moment when he had seen her in the river. She was hardy, bathing in the river in November, riding with him and running away from her people. And she was brave and loving, so loving to White Bird, who responded fully. The child had lost both parents. At the thought, he felt another tight knot of pain constrict his heart.

He needed to be with his people. His gaze drifted over Vanessa again. He must take her captive. She would fight at first like a she-lion, but he knew the way to win the battle. Once again, Eyes That Smile's vision floated in mind. He hated whites. Even as good as Vanessa had been to them, there were moments when he felt his anger burn fiercely.

He stared at the sky, calculating the hour and how many days' ride before they would near Fort McKavett. Now they were headed southwest and if they didn't change course soon, they would cross into New Mexico Territory. Another wave of faintness came. He ached and hurt all over, but there was no putrid odor so the wounds were clean. The shots had gone through him without striking anything vital. He felt as if ribs were cracked because of the pain he felt when he moved and took a deep breath. His head swam and he closed his eyes, listening to Vanessa's lilting song, which soothed him to sleep.

After a few hours of rest they ate the last of the cornbread that night. Afterward White Bird climbed onto Vanessa's lap. Vanessa held and rocked her, humming softly until White Bird's eyes closed and she snuggled against Vanessa and went to sleep.

"Do you think it's safe to stay here tonight?" Vanessa asked him later as they both sat on quilts while he ate the last of the beef.

"No. We need to keep moving. We'll wait a little longer and them mount up and ride." He sat near her, and he reached out to touch her knee with his forefinger. She drew a deep breath, feeling the contact through the thick poplin.

"You were going to a convent. Was there a man left behind?"

"No," she replied, gazing into the darkness beyond him. "I'm eighteen now; and after the war came, the boys I knew went to fight. Papa wouldn't allow me to have callers often, and most of the time I've traveled with him, so there is no one."

Lone Wolf placed his hand beneath her chin. "I can understand your father's protecting you, but only the war could have kept the men away. Even then, I find that amazing."

"The war took the boys my age from home."

"How do you think you can ride into a fort and take your sisters out without your father's discovery and without his stopping you?"

"Phoebe and I discussed it before I left. There's a church in a small town near the fort, and Phoebe and Belva often go there with the Carters, a family we know. We agreed that Sunday mornings will be my best chance to get them away without our papa's knowing it."

"How can two young women and a child expect to get away from the soldiers who will be sent to hunt you?"

She raised her chin, and he saw the glint of defiance in her eyes. "I don't know, but I have to try to save Phoebe."

"The soldiers called your father colonel. Is he stationed at Fort McKavett?"

"No. He's there only temporarily, traveling across the United States. Men call Papa colonel from years ago when he fought in the Mexican War, but he hasn't been a soldier since. He builds railroads."

Lone Wolf's eyes narrowed only a fraction, the slightest change, yet she felt as if her answer had stirred his wrath. "Do you know men with the railroads?" she asked.

"They killed my wife."

"I'm sorry," she said, remembering the struggles her father had had against Indians, wondering if he had clashed with Lone Wolf's people.

"He's a railroad advisor to President Lincoln, and he's in Fort McKavett to see about a railroad across Texas."

"What's your full name, Vanessa?"

As his dark eyes bore into her, she felt a tremor of caution. Her father had paid to have Indians killed, and Lone Wolf had had a bad experience with railroaders.

"Vanessa Sutton," she answered with a twinge of guilt, yet uncertain about him and afraid to tell him her last name.

"Your people will build a railroad across Texas and across our lands." Lone Wolf lay back on the quilt and studied her. The railroad men wanted the land, and they were ruthless in taking it. The war had stopped them and concentrated their attention in the east; but once the war was over, he expected them to try to build more railroads across the land. Had her father been any part of the crews who had taken his wife's life? From what she had said to him, Lone Wolf suspected her father shared little of his life with his daughters.

Thinking about revenge, feeling an unaccustomed conflict, Lone Wolf stared at her. In spite of his hatred of railroad men and white soldiers, Vanessa was a warm, giving woman and his respect for her was growing.

Vanessa finished feeding White Bird the last of the jam. "I'm worried about food. We're running low. I just brought what I could find the other night along with a few provisions Mrs. Parsons and I had packed in the wagon."

"Who is Mrs. Parsons?"

"My father hired her to travel from Fort McKavett to Denver with me to see that I behaved properly before she placed me in the convent in Denver. Someday Papa expects to buy a house and settle in Denver, so he selected a convent there." Vanessa looked down at White Bird, curling a long strand of black hair over her hand.

"You were talking about food."

"I have only a few plums and apples, some strips of dried beef, one more jar of damson jam. We ate the last biscuits tonight. I brought three large canteens of water, and we've used one and part of another."

"Use what you have. We'll find food and water."

He answered with such certainty, she stopped worrying about it. "I have laudanum if you want some for the pain."

"No. I don't want to sleep because we'll ride soon. We need the cover of darkness to travel."

They fell silent for a time, and then she asked, "Why did you learn English?"

"I was a scout for the army. My father was a chief and he urged our people to peaceful dealings with the white man. Chief Dohasan follows this road now. My father wanted his sons to learn the white man's language and ways, so I was a scout."

"You sound bitter about it," she said, hearing the harsh note in his voice.

"White soldiers killed my wife and my mother. They just killed my brother and his wife—White Bird's parents."

Startled, Vanessa looked at him sharply. "You're not her father? I thought—"

"No. I'm her uncle. I saw no reason to correct you."

Vanessa looked down at White Bird and stroked her head, tears suddenly coming and her throat constricting. "She lost both parents yesterday?" she whispered.

There was a pause, and she heard a rustle. With a grunt of effort, Lone Wolf scooted closer and ran his finger over her cheek to wipe away tears. "You cry for her. Your heart is tender, Vanessa."

"I lost my mother when I was eleven. She died in childbirth. I have a brother, Ethan, who is twenty-three, five years older than I am. My father has always favored my brother—my father wanted only boys. I know what it is to be without parents and without love," she said to him.

She could see Lone Wolf's expression was solemn, but

beyond that she couldn't tell what he was thinking. "She's a precious child," she added, looking down again at White Bird, nestled in her arms. Lone Wolf eased down next to her, closed his eyes, and drifted to sleep.

Later, as the moon rose in the sky, Lone Wolf stirred and sat up. Vanessa faced him. Feeling disheveled and dusty, she raked her fingers through her tangled hair.

"We go now."

"Sit still," she said, standing up. "I'll saddle the horses."

She glanced at White Bird, who was curled into a ball, her hair over her shoulder. Moving away from them, Vanessa gathered the saddle blankets and began to get the horses ready. All the time she worked, she was aware of Lone Wolf's watchful gaze on her. Soon they were mounted with the sleeping child in front of Vanessa.

They rode through mesquite and cedars, finally turning to emerge from the trees. Ahead, open ground sparsely covered by mesquite stretched for miles, broken by washes and gullies. Lone Wolf rode beside her, his gaze sweeping the horizon.

"Where do you think the soldiers are?" she asked, feeling exposed.

"They were headed south, but by this time they could have doubled back."

His answer didn't reassure her. "If we ride across that open land, anyone can see us."

"We can't stay here. They'll eventually pick up the trail if they have a good tracker. If they come after us, do what I told you before—take White Bird and get away."

"I will never let anyone hurt her," Vanessa said so fiercely he turned to her.

"She's not your blood, yet you treat her as if she were."

"I told you, I love children. And when she came to me, you weren't with her," Vanessa said, stroking White Bird's black hair and remembering that moment. "It was as if she had been given to me."

"The child isn't yours," he said flatly. "When I get my strength back, I'll take her and go."

Vanessa looked away quickly, but not before he saw her flinch as if from a blow. He stared at her head bent over White Bird as she stroked the child's hair.

"You'll have your own children some day. And I find it impossible to imagine a white woman who would want an Indian child."

"She's a beautiful child," Vanessa whispered, and he realized she was crying.

"You surely didn't think I'd leave her with you," he said, feeling annoyed with her.

"No. But when I first found her, she was alone. No, I've known all along that you'll take her and go when you're well. But I love her and I hurt for her losing her parents."

"You will have been with her only a few days and you'll forget her. If you feel that strongly, I'm surprised you've cared for me."

She glanced at him. "I couldn't let another person die."

He looked at her, feeling the irony of her statement, knowing her white colonel father not only would have been glad to have let him die, but would have killed him.

"You're too gentle for this land, Vanessa," he said quietly, yet he wondered if he were wrong because she was courageous enough to run away and take them along with her and determined enough to battle him about which direction they would ride. "We'll go now," he ordered bluntly. He led the way again, urging his horse faster, and she knew it must be causing him dreadful pain.

She clung to White Bird and flicked her reins, looking at Lone Wolf, who rode tall in the saddle in spite of his injuries, his black hair flowing behind him. His back was bare, his skin taut over the powerful muscles.

Expecting at any moment to see the soldiers galloping after them, she glanced behind her, but no one was in sight.

Her heart raced because they were in full view of anyone who rode out of the trees bordering the creek's banks.

Finally, Lone Wolf dipped down out of sight into a gully. She followed as he slowed.

By dawn, he knew he couldn't ride much longer. He was in terrible pain and he felt light-headed from the loss of blood. They were leaving an easy-to-follow trail. And he knew he should watch for game, try to kill something, so they could have fresh meat. White Bird wiggled and wanted down from the horse, suddenly crying out, *"Kkaw-Kkoy', Kkaw-Kkoy'!"*

"What's she saying?" Vanessa asked, dismounting and hugging White Bird when the child began to cry.

"That's our word for mother," Lone Wolf replied solemnly, and Vanessa felt as if someone had plunged a knife into her heart.

She hugged White Bird more tightly. "Oh, love, you want your mother. Sweet child," she said, burying her face against White Bird's neck and rocking her back and forth. She began to sing softly as she stroked White Bird.

Lone Wolf saw the tears spill from Vanessa's eyes, and he was astounded at her kind heart. The women he had known were more accustomed to death and accepted the violence they met. Their lives had never been as sheltered as Vanessa's, he was certain. As he watched her comfort White Bird, the child quieted.

Trying to get her emotions under control, Vanessa stroked White Bird's head. She hurt for White Bird's loss and wanted to reassure the little girl. Finally, setting her on her feet, Vanessa held out her hand to take White Bird's small one and they walked back to the horses.

"She has to be hungry," she said, rummaging in the bag. The few strips of dried beef were gone, the apples gone; the only things left were the jar of damson preserves and the last canteen of water.

"May I teach her our word for mother?" Vanessa asked him.

"Yes, but it won't change things. When I am well, I take her and ride north," he said harshly, angry with himself for feeling kindness toward her when he intended to take her captive. He wondered if perhaps she would prefer life as a prisoner to having to return to her father; Lone Wolf was certain she would never escape her father.

"Thank you. I'd rather she say mama than Vanessa. Besides, someday you'll marry again and you and your wife will be mother and father to her."

He nodded, frowning as he studied her.

"That displeases you even when you say I may teach her the word."

"Since it's not our word for mother, it will hold no meaning for her. I frown because of your words. I don't intend to marry again for several years, yet you're right. I should take a wife to give White Bird a mother."

Vanessa nodded and moved away to get a canteen of water. Lone Wolf touched White Bird's head lightly. She seemed content enough now, so Vanessa must have calmed her.

After a short rest, they mounted to continue traveling. They rode that day until dark and he felt he could go no farther. He stretched out on a quilt as soon as Vanessa placed one on the ground. Later, she changed the bandages, her fingers light and gentle as they moved over him. Her voice was low and quiet and soothing, and she smelled of flowers. As she helped ease him down, he held her, feeling her slender waist and delicate bones, wanting to pull her beside him and hold her close because it was long since a woman had been in his arms.

With dawn, he mounted, feeling weak and in pain and wondering if he would survive. As they rode, he studied the landscape, trying to spot a line of trees that would indicate water.

Hours later, when he saw a snaking line of dark cedars, he motioned to Vanessa and they headed toward the meandering stream, finally riding into a draw. The cottonwood were interspersed with dark green bushy cedars that gave good cover if the men were still following them.

Refreshed, their canteens replenished, and the horses watered, Vanessa helped Lone Wolf mount. To her relief, on the countless times she looked back during the day, she did not see anyone following.

By noon the next day, Lone Wolf rode ahead of them, winding slowly through the trees toward a meandering stream. Vanessa marveled at him, sitting straight in spite of his injuries. She was exhausted, hungry, and thirsty, and she knew his bandages should be changed. How could he keep riding? She stared at his shoulders, thinking about the demands he made on himself as well as on them. She glanced down at White Bird and refused to think about parting with her.

He dropped back beside them, swaying slightly as he rode close. "We'll stop soon when we find a good place. It's time to get water for us and the horses and to find food."

"I don't know how you'll find anything to eat, but I pray you do."

As they rode, they topped a rise. Her heart seemed to leap in her chest as she stared at rooftops in the distance. "Look!"

She touched his arm and then instantly forgot the town as she realized what she had done. His warm flesh beneath her fingers stirred a flash of awareness, and she glanced up at him.

"There's a town," she said, more subdued.

He shook his head. "You won't be safe there, and soldiers can pick up our trail easily."

Feeling he was wrong, she looked at the town. If there were a doctor, they could get medical attention and they could buy supplies. She glanced back and gasped.

Lone Wolf lay slumped over his horse. She studied him and looked at the town again. With a lift of her chin, she rode close to him to take the fallen reins.

Lone Wolf's fists were wound in the horse's mane, and Vanessa prayed he wouldn't fall off the horse or rally and realize what she was doing as she headed south toward the town.

Five

As they approached the town, a crooked wooden sign shot full of holes proclaimed Martin Gulch. There were few houses, and most of the ramshackle wooden buildings were saloons.

A prickle ran across Vanessa's nape when she remembered Lone Wolf saying they would be in danger, yet she had to try to get medical attention for him. Along the wide dusty street that ran down the center of town, she saw another battered sign that stated there were rooms for rent.

While they rode toward the one-story rambling frame structure, men in open doors of saloons turned to stare, and Vanessa's nervousness grew. When she gazed the length of the street, her apprehension deepened because there were no women in sight.

In front of the house with rooms for rent, she stopped at the hitching rail and dismounted, setting White Bird on her feet and taking her hand. At any moment she expected Lone Wolf to fall, so she picked up White Bird and hurried inside, the bell over the door ringing when she entered.

The small room with a dusty bare floor held a desk and chairs. One windowpane was cracked, and an iron pot-bellied stove glowed warmly. From a doorway, a short, bearded man appeared, his brown eyes sweeping over her in a glance that added to her discomfort. "Help you, miss?" When his gaze went from her to White Bird, he frowned.

"Yes. I'm Hepzibah Grant. I need to rent a room for my husband and child and me."

"That child looks like an Indian," the man said coldly, continuing to look at White Bird. His gaze lifted to Vanessa, and she received another bold appraisal that made her flesh crawl.

Vanessa set White Bird on her feet and pulled up the dainty silk reticule her father had purchased long ago in Shreveport. She placed a gold piece on the desk and drew herself up. "Sir, my father is a colonel in the army and my brother is an officer. My husband has some Indian blood, but he is a scout for the army."

The man stared at the gold. "We don't allow breeds," he said without taking his eyes from the gold.

"But this one pays in gold, which is getting more scarce as the war drags on," she reminded him firmly. "My father will be most unhappy to hear I've been turned away from here."

"He's a colonel?"

"Yes, and he's stationed in Texas. He can be here in a day."

The man licked his lips and pocketed the gold piece. "You can stay in a back room."

"My husband was shot by renegades. I need someone to help carry him inside. Is there a doctor in this town?"

"We have a horse doctor. But Doc Wilkens won't treat your husband. If you're staying here, let's get your husband off the street. Lead him around behind the building, Mrs. Grant. I'll get him inside. What's the child's name?"

"Hope. My husband is Robert Grant."

"I'm Elwood Parsons," he said. "Take him around back. I don't want trouble," he said with a shake of his head. Long oily strands of his brown hair touched his shoulders. "Folks won't want a redskin in town."

Trying to control her anger, she raised her chin and went outside. Across the street, outside the saloon, men stood in a cluster and watched her. Vanessa set White Bird on the horse and picked up the reins to lead the animals around the house.

At the back was an unused wagon, one wheel gone, with weeds growing high around it. A rusty pump stood close to the door of the building, and two windows were broken. An alley ran behind the place, with a fenced pasture across from the yard and two small structures fronting the alley. Glancing at the sagging board fence along one side of the yard, she disliked both house and grounds, but she had paid and she would try to find the doctor as soon as she got Lone Wolf into bed.

Elwood Parsons stepped into the sunshine, his fists on his hips and a scowl on his face. "Ma'am, that don't look like a scout to me. He's in buckskins and he looks full blood."

"You said we could stay."

"One night. You get out of here before noon tomorrow. This ain't a town for an Injun and his squaw." He waved his hand. "That's my lot behind the alley. You can put the horses in the shed and there's feed."

"Thank you," she replied stiffly.

Parsons moved forward and pulled on Lone Wolf's arm. Lone Wolf toppled to the ground, and Elwood Parsons let him fall.

"Sure he ain't dead?"

"He will be if you keep that up!" she snapped, kneeling to try to get her arm around Lone Wolf to pull him up.

"Just a minute." Elwood Parsons disappeared and in seconds returned with a tall, rangy man with a thatch of blond hair. The two men picked up Lone Wolf, who groaned.

"Careful!" she exclaimed, hating the way they handled him and wondering if Elwood Parsons hoped he could kill Lone Wolf.

Entering a narrow hallway, they carried him a short distance into a room that held an iron bed, a washstand, a rocking chair, a tin tub, and nothing else. Holding White Bird's hand, Vanessa followed them into the room.

"I'd like water fetched for the bath," she said.

"That'll cost you five dollars."

"Five dollars should buy the rooming house!" she replied, glaring at him.

Elwood Parsons shrugged. "That's it, Mrs. Grant," he said rolling the name in an insolent manner, eyeing her again.

She pulled out five dollars in greenbacks, and he reached out to take the money. "I'd stay off the streets with them two if'n I were you," he said to her, jerking his hand toward White Bird and Lone Wolf.

Vanessa nodded, her anger growing.

"Here's a key. We'll fetch the water. Be out of here by mid-morning tomorrow."

As soon as she closed the door behind him, she rushed to the bed to feel Lone Wolf's pulse. It was erratic, but she suspected hers might be, too, after the encounter with Parsons. White Bird had climbed into the rocker and was rocking back and forth, a smile on her face.

"I wish we had a calico dress for you instead of buckskin. It would make our lives easier," Vanessa said. She combed and refastened her hair, parting it in the middle. She smoothed her riding habit and finally felt she was as neat as possible under the circumstances. There was a knock at the door, and the blond man entered with buckets of water.

His gaze raked over her with a bold insolence, and she felt a prickle of fear because she had little protection.

"You lonesome, missy?" he asked.

"Put the water in the tub."

He set a bucket on the floor and poured water from the other one slowly into the tin tub, looking at her as he filled the tub. "Going to bathe now?"

"Just pour the water and go."

His gaze slid to the bed. "Looks like your husband is at

death's door. Course an Injun ain't much loss." The blond set down the empty bucket and picked up the other to pour slowly. "I'm Jethro Hankins. I live just two doors down the alley, so if you get lonesome, just let me know." She stood in stony silence while his gaze went over her again. "You're wasting yourself on that sorry excuse for a human," he remarked.

"Will you get out now!"

"You're mighty uppity for a squaw," he said, crossing the room to her. She drew a deep breath as he reached out to touch her. Vanessa stepped back quickly, yanking Lone Wolf's knife from its scabbard.

"Get out of here."

The man stared at her, and his lip curled in a contemptuous smile. "I'll go. But I'll be around tonight. You might change your mind. We can dance at the saloon."

He picked up the empty buckets and left the room, leaving the door open behind him.

She took White Bird's hand and glanced again at Lone Wolf, who looked ashen. Deciding to tend to errands first and bathe later, she stepped into the hall, looking around for any sign of Jethro Hankins. Hurrying down the corridor, she entered the front room where Elwood Parsons was behind the desk.

"Where can I find the doctor?"

"Two blocks down, across the street, and in a back room at the barber shop. Won't do you any good. Doc hates redskins."

Without replying, she left, praying she could convince the doctor to come take care of Lone Wolf. Angry and astounded at the hate they had already encountered, she moved along, becoming more curious as to why she hadn't seen any women. All she saw were men and hastily built structures. Her gaze ran the few blocks of the main street and took in five saloons, a barber shop, a blacksmith, and a general store.

Her nervousness was increasing because this wasn't a town filled with families. She saw two signs—one stating *Hair Cuts, Two Bits* and below it, dangling by one nail, hung a board reading, *Horace Wilkens, Veterinarian.*

She opened the door to a barber shop where one man was getting a hair cut and another was waiting. Embarrassed and frightened, she stood in the doorway and held White Bird's hand tightly. All three men turned to stare at her, and the one in the barber chair looked at her as insolently as Jethro Hankins and Elwood Parsons had. A chill ran down her spine, but she faced them squarely. "I'm looking for Dr. Wilkens."

"He's in the back room," the barber said, jerking his head toward the door.

"What's a purty woman like you doing with a little redskin?" one of the men asked.

"This is my child," she answered stiffly, wanting to pull White Bird up into her arms and protect her from their remarks, thankful that White Bird couldn't understand the hatred directed toward her. "My husband and I are passing through town on our way to meet my father, who is a colonel in the army."

She crossed the room aware of the scrutiny of the three men. Relieved to leave them, she stepped through a door.

A lanky man in rumpled denim pants was in a chair, his feet crossed at the ankles on a billiard table while he snored.

"Doctor!"

He jumped and sat up, turning to look at her with bloodshot blue eyes, his gaze roaming down to her toes, and her annoyance grew. "What can I do for you, ma'am?" he asked, coming to his feet with the first note of respect she had heard in Martin Gulch. His gaze shifted to White Bird, and he frowned. "That yourn?"

"She's my daughter," Vanessa said, staring him directly in the eye. "My husband was attacked by renegades. He's been shot, and his wounds need tending. We're renting a room from Elwood Parsons."

He looked again at White Bird. "Your husband must be a full-blood Injun."

"He's a wounded man who needs medical attention," she answered tersely.

The veterinarian sank down on the chair and studied her. "I work on animals and people, but not on redskins."

Her anger soared, but she quietly opened her reticule and took out a twenty dollar gold piece.

"Maybe this will change your mind," she said, holding out the gold.

His fuzzy brown eyebrows raised, and his eyes widened. "Gold?" He stood up and crossed the room to get a black bag. "For gold, I'll work on ole Abe Lincoln hisself. Next to hating redskins, I hate Yankees; but for gold, I'll do most anything," he replied cheerfully.

Vanessa closed her eyes in relief, praying he could help Lone Wolf and thankful he would try.

He nodded to her. "Let's go out the back. There will be fewer questions that way. I want the gold now."

She handed the coin to him, and it disappeared into his pocket. He motioned with his head, and she followed him outside.

"How did this town come to be?" she asked, looking at a building on the other side of the alley. Its boards were weathered, and the roof was full of holes. Vines grew through cracks between the warped planks in the walls. Torn, yellowed curtains hung limply in the open windows. The first woman Vanessa had seen sat on the step of the open doorway. Shocked, Vanessa stared at her, aware that the woman was in a chemise and drawers. Her brown hair was unkempt, and she was smoking a cheroot.

"Hey, doc." She stared at Vanessa, and Vanessa nodded, realizing the woman was a soiled dove, the first Vanessa had ever encountered.

"Afternoon, Dusty." They walked on past, and he glanced at Vanessa.

"This was on a trail west to the territory, but it never was used enough. The Comanche, the snakes, no water—no sane person would stay here."

She wondered why he did, but decided she didn't want his answer.

When she opened the door to the room, Doc Wilkens crossed to the bedside. Rolling back his sleeves, he leaned over Lone Wolf. "I'll do what I can, but he's shot the hell up." He turned to study her and White Bird. "Looks like to me the U.S. Army wanted him gone."

"It was renegades. He's been an army scout."

He studied her. "People out here don't ask too many questions and a man's business is his own, but you look like you come from decent folks. Let me give you some advice. Get out of here as fast as you can get him on a horse and go. Word gets around that you're married to an Injun or word gets around that you've got gold, you're not going to be safe. As pretty as you are, ma'am, you're not safe now."

"Thank you," she said quietly. "Can you do something for my husband?"

He studied her a moment longer and shook his head. "I'll bet that gold piece your folks don't know where you are." He turned back to the bed.

"Doc," she said quietly, and he glanced at her. "Just because you don't like Indians, don't let him die on you. I would be most unhappy, and my husband's people would be unhappy."

He nodded. "You paid me. I'll do my job right. First, I want to get this gunbelt and knife off."

He bent over Lone Wolf, who groaned, and she moved restlessly around the room, going to the window to look at the alley. Jethro Hankins was chopping wood. He had taken off his shirt, and she could see he was as muscled as Lone

Wolf. She shivered, feeling alone and afraid. She glanced over her shoulder at White Bird, who was in the rocker again, happily wiggling to get the chair moving.

Vanessa crossed the room to take the child in her lap and rock her, and in minutes White Bird was asleep. The doctor had placed Lone Wolf's gunbelt over the chipped and scarred headboard so the revolver hung close to his pillow. The knife was on the table beside the bed.

Finally Wilkens straightened up, rolled down his sleeves, and put his things away in the black bag. He turned to face Vanessa. "Ma'am, I don't know if he can make it. His pulse is weak, and I imagine he's lost lots of blood. He ought to stay in bed until he begins to heal. I've given him something for pain, so he'll sleep tonight. He looks as if he needs it badly."

"Thank you," she said, relieved that someone who knew what he was doing had finally tended Lone Wolf's wounds.

"If you do stay here, keep off the streets. There aren't any decent women in town. There are only two women here at all. Don't let any of these men get you alone."

Frightened, Vanessa felt cold as she listened to him, at last comprehending that all three of them were in danger. He looked at the sleeping child in her arms.

"They won't be any better to her. She's a redskin." He shrugged. "Might be the girls would take her because she could earn her keep by the time she's ten."

Annoyed and even more frightened than before, Vanessa tightened her hold on White Bird. She stood up, gently placing the child back in the chair. "Thank you for coming to help and for the advice."

He grinned. "I got my gold for it. I'm satisfied." He moved to the door. "Ma'am. When you leave here, head south. About a mile south, you'll hit a dry creek bed. Most likely you won't find water for the next twenty miles or more, but there are creek beds with cedars along the banks where you can ride without anyone seeing you easily. You go any other direction, and people can see you for miles."

"Thank you. I'll remember that."

He hesitated, studying her. "We don't get many pretty women through here. I'd say it's been two years since I last saw a real pretty woman—until now."

"Thank you," Vanessa answered quietly. "And thank you for your help."

When he turned and left, she closed the door behind him, moving to the window. Jethro Hankins stopped chopping wood, and she stepped back so he wouldn't see her watching through the tattered, faded curtain. He talked to Doc Wilkens and looked toward her room. She took another step back.

She wished she had learned how to fire a pistol. She didn't know how, and she was sure if Lone Wolf's revolver were loaded and ready to fire, she still wouldn't be able to hit anything. And she had to go out to get supplies. They needed food desperately.

She moved to the bed and wiped Lone Wolf's heated brow. He was damp with perspiration. She took a pillow from the bed and placed it beneath White Bird's head.

Both of them slept; and after a moment's indecision, Vanessa took some money from the portmanteau and stuffed greenbacks into her reticule. She hurried into the hall and down the street to the next block where the general store was located.

The floor was dirty, goods piled in a haphazard fashion, the pans and lanterns and other goods covered with a thick layer of dust. At a table by a pot-bellied stove, men gambled, paying little heed to their game as they watched her and talked in low tones. Aware of the men's interest, she hurriedly selected what she needed. Occasionally, she heard one of the men laugh. Nervous and feeling vulnerable, she wanted only to get out of the place and hurried to the counter to pay for the goods.

"If I go to the livery stable, can I buy a mule or horse to carry all this?" she asked the man behind the counter.

"I'll carry all of it," a brawny man said, standing up with a scrape of his chair. He wore a faded chambray shirt with sleeves turned back, his blond hair sticking out in long strands beneath a gray, battered hat. As he sauntered toward her, her heartbeat quickened. "I'll help," he repeated.

"Thank you, no. I need a pack animal. I'll be traveling out of here soon."

"I'd be obliged to accompany you," he said, his blue eyes studying her. "First pretty woman in this town in a bear's winter. What's your name, miss?"

"Mrs. Robert Grant. Thank you, but no; I'll get a horse to carry these things. I already have a husband, and we join up with my father and three of his officers. My father is a colonel in the army."

The moment she said her father was a colonel, the man straightened up and nodded, exchanging a long look with the clerk. "Nice to meet you, Mrs. Grant," he said politely and sauntered back to the others. He leaned across the table to talk to them in a low voice, and two of the men glanced at her. She turned away to look at the clerk.

"You might get a mule or horse if you can pay enough," the stocky man behind the counter said. The light reflected off his balding head, and he tugged at his thick black beard. "You pay Abner enough, and he'll sell you his own horse."

"I'd like to take care of that and come back to get these things."

"Yes, ma'am," he said, looking at her as boldly as the others had. Her flesh prickled and she longed to get Lone Wolf and White Bird and ride out of town, but she had to get supplies before they could go.

She hurried out of the store, dreading walking through the entire town to the livery stable, but she had no choice. When she passed the open saloons, she clamped her jaw tightly closed, conscious of men coming out to watch her.

Within twenty minutes she had purchased a sorrel gelding, a worn saddle, and a bridle, and was headed back up the street. The wind had sprung up, stirring the dust with a cold bite. A gust whipped tiny grains of sand against her skin, and she squinted her eyes.

Doc Wilkens leaned against a post. He straightened and strolled to the middle of the street to fall into step beside her and take the rope to the sorrel. "Everyone in town knows you're here."

"Does everyone know about my husband or his condition?" she asked, trying to keep her anger from showing.

"Nope, not yet, but they will by tonight because Jethro Hankins will talk. I guess I don't need to tell you to stay away from Jethro. I heard you'd gone to buy a horse."

"Word gets around."

"There's nothing else to do here, and a pretty woman is a fascination for every man in town. I'll pack your horse. If you can get your husband mounted up in the next day or two, you go."

"How far is the next town?" She glanced up at him, wind whipping locks of her hair across her cheek.

"There's not a town in any direction for fifty miles or more."

Disturbed and wondering if they should try to ride out of town under the cover of darkness, she halted in front of the general store. As frightening as the town was, she hated even more to think about moving Lone Wolf when he was finally getting the rest he needed.

"You stay right here, and I'll get your things," Wilkens said. He disappeared inside and promptly reappeared, carrying flour, sugar, jars of pickles, a skillet, dried beef, and new canteens that she intended to fill at the pump. With the rope she had just purchased, he lashed the goods onto the sorrel, finally stepping back to survey his work.

"If you take all that off when you get to your room, can you load it up again?"

"Yes, I can."

"Better keep the goods where you can pack and go in a hurry. Tonight Jethro will spread the word that you're married to a redskin—an *ailing* redskin."

Knowing Lone Wolf should not travel yet, she thought about the danger. "Will I be safe here tomorrow if I stay in the room?"

Wilkens rubbed his thin jaw and pursed his lips. "I'd say you'd better be gone after two days. If you need help getting your husband on a horse, send for me."

"Thank you for what you've done," she said, smiling up at him.

He looked at her solemnly. "I keep thinking I'll get out of this miserable place and back to civilization. It's been too long since I've been around a decent, pretty woman."

"You can ride with us."

Amusement flared in his blue eyes. "Thank you, ma'am, but I don't want to take on that kind of trouble. One thing about this town—there's no law here."

She wondered if he were hiding from the law. "Thank you."

He nodded and stepped aside. She led the horse to the back of the rooming house and tethered it to a rail. Was she making a mistake in planning to stay several days? Could she talk Elwood Parsons into letting them stay beyond tomorrow?

"Nice evening," said a deep voice, and she spun around as Jethro Hankins walked up. Dried grass swished against his boots, and he smelled of alcohol and tobacco. "Looks like you bought up the general store."

"We needed some things."

"Want me to help you unload it?"

"No, thank you. I'll take care of it shortly."

He shrugged. "That's a lot of work. Sack of flour, sack of sugar." His gaze shifted from the supplies to her. "We could go out tonight," he said, his voice dropping slyly.

"Leave the kid asleep here with your husband. There's a place to dance."

"Sorry, but no."

"You don't like me, do you?"

She glanced at him. "I'm a married woman and I don't socialize with men other than my husband." She turned to go, her back prickling. She would have to come back out and unload all the things she had bought, but she wanted to get away from Hankins. As she held her skirt and walked away from him, she half-expected him to try to stop her, but she entered the boarding house without interference.

She waited in the room for a quarter of an hour and then stepped into the hall and looked outside. She didn't see Jethro and quickly slipped out to unload her belongings, her nerves raw. She had the uneasy sensation that he was watching her.

Making several trips, she carried her purchases into the room. The sun was setting, and the night was cold. The wind hadn't died down and came in gusts, whistling around the corner of the house and adding to her nervousness.

With darkness, her fear for their safety grew. She felt unprotected because she couldn't stop a group of men from trying to harm Lone Wolf or from taking her.

Moving to the bed, she gazed down. Lone Wolf was ashen, his breathing shallow and fast, and she knew they had to stay.

Six

Within the hour she went down the hall to talk to Elwood Parsons. "Where can I get something to eat?"

"For ten dollars each, I can cook you up something."

"For thirty dollars, I can buy all the food in the general store!" She started to walk away in disgust, deciding they would eat some of the dried food she had bought at the store.

"Wait a minute. All right. Five dollars for each of you. Fried chicken, potatoes, corn bread, corn, and coffee."

"Ten dollars would be exorbitant. In any city I can get a dinner like that for two dollars or less."

He scowled at her. "All right. Ten dollars."

"Do you have milk for my husband and daughter?"

"Yep."

"Fine. I'll pay when I get the food. For that amount, you can bring it to our room."

"Intended to. Don't want you folks out here where everyone will see you. I run a quiet place."

It *was* quiet, and she wondered if anyone else lived there. She hadn't seen any other people, and doors along the hall were open and the rooms looked unoccupied.

An hour later, she heard a knock on the door, and Elwood Parsons appeared with a tray filled with food. The golden fried chicken made her mouth water, and she ushered him into the room. He placed the tray on a chest and she paid him.

"Thank you."

"It's nothing. Just bring the tray down to the desk when you're finished." He left and closed the door, and she patted the rocker for White Bird, who climbed up quickly. Vanessa placed a plate in front of the little girl, and the two of them ate quietly.

The tender, hot chicken tasted delicious; and as Vanessa bit off a piece of chicken, she glanced at the bed, wondering if Lone Wolf would stir and be able to eat anything.

Finally, she and White Bird finished. Vanessa undressed the child and placed her in the tub of tepid water to bathe her, then dried her and dressed her in the blood-soaked buckskin because that was all she had to wear for the moment. At the general store, Vanessa had bought material, needles, thread, and hooks to make White Bird a red gingham dress. However, that would take some time.

Vanessa glanced at the bed. They would all sleep in it tonight. She hadn't been in a bed since she had left Fort McKavett; and even though it meant sharing the mattress with Lone Wolf, she was going to sleep in it.

When she lifted White Bird up onto the bed, the child shook her head and pointed at the floor, saying a word that Vanessa didn't recognize. Vanessa tried again; but White Bird became stiff and motioned to the floor, so Vanessa folded a blanket and made a nest beside the bed, putting a pillow on the blanket. White Bird stretched out and was asleep in minutes.

Moving the rocker close to the table with the lamp, Vanessa began to work on the dress for White Bird. Wind whistled around the corner and rattled the windowpanes, coming in through the cracks, and the room grew cold. Vanessa knelt to tuck the quilt around White Bird, who felt warm and was sleeping soundly.

With a swell of love, she vowed to keep the child safe. She brushed the girl's dark hair off her cheek and gave her a light kiss. Vanessa returned to her sewing for an hour and then she folded the material. She moved to the door to jiggle the knob. The door was locked, but she did not feel particularly secure.

Vanessa removed her clothes, then eased into the cool water in the tub, shivering, but relishing a bath. She took her time washing her hair, finally stepping out to dry and put on one of the two dresses she had packed. The red and blue gingham was wrinkled, but it was clean and she had clean underclothing. Without putting on her stockings, she brushed her hair dry.

Finally, she put out the lamp and moved to the window to look outside. The backyard was quiet; the horses grazed in the lot across the alley. Moonlight shone on the yard, but the shadows seemed threatening because she could imagine Jethro Hankins out there in the dark. Wind stirred dust in the alley, sweeping it up to spin in a dust devil that gradually dissipated.

She walked to the bed to look down at Lone Wolf. Beams of moonlight spilled across the counterpane, and she could see the rise and fall of his chest. She placed her hand against his throat and was shocked by the flutter of his pulse.

Feeling her cheeks flush with embarrassment even though he was sound asleep, she climbed onto the bed as far from him as she could manage. Easing down quietly, she sighed with pleasure. She slid beneath the thin blanket, glancing at him.

Her pulse jumped as she looked at his profile in the darkness. Her gaze ran across his bare chest, and she sat up slightly to pull the blanket up to cover him. He shifted and turned, causing the blanket to slide back to his waist. His face was toward her, and his black hair spilled on the pillow. Vanessa's gaze took in his long frame and the drape of the blanket over him. She felt hot, ill-at-ease, yet she was curious and couldn't resist studying him. Even wounded, he looked strong and virile.

When he began to get his strength back, how safe would

she be? She knew he had an abiding hatred of whites because of the loss of his wife and family.

All tiredness gone, she rolled on her side to study him fully, flushing again with embarrassment, yet openly curious about him because she had never been in an intimate situation with a man. She didn't want to go to a convent. She wanted marriage and love and her own babies. She knew from the brief time with White Bird that she wanted children badly. And she wanted a man's love and companionship. She thought of Lone Wolf's kisses and grew warm, recalling the thrust of his tongue over hers and the sensations that had assailed her.

She reached out tentatively to touch his chest, placing her hand lightly against him, feeling his heartbeat, his warm flesh beneath her hand. Unable to resist, she let her fingers drift over his chest, feeling his flat nipples, the smooth skin, and taut muscles. Her hand slid to his throat; his pulse seemed steady and stronger now.

Uncomfortable, yet still overcome with curiosity, her hand slid down to his flat stomach and then up over the blanket that covered his hip and thigh, a current of heat seeming to run from him through her fingertips into her body.

She looked at his face and touched his mouth lightly, tracing her finger along his lower lip and remembering when he had done that to her and how sensual the slight contact had been.

As if memorizing him feature by feature, she trailed her index finger along the bony ridge of his nose and across his thick brow. His lashes were thick, dark against his prominent cheekbones. She touched his ear, looking at his mouth, recalling too clearly the devastating kisses that she wanted to experience again.

Hot and suffering clamorings of her body that she had never known before meeting Lone Wolf, she rolled onto her back and stared into the darkness, her thoughts shifting to the problems that lay ahead. Could she actually get Phoebe and Belva away from their father's control? Phoebe could never survive marriage to a cruel man like Reginald Thompkins, and Vanessa had no intention of entering a convent.

As she grew still, she became cold. Glancing at Lone Wolf, she edged closer to him, absorbing the heat from his body as she would heat from a stove and drifting off to sleep.

In the night Vanessa stirred, her eyes flying wide. She felt his warm body pressed against her. Lone Wolf moved closer to her and slid his arm around her waist. Vanessa held her breath, afraid to move, wondering if he would kiss her. Then she realized he was still asleep. She closed her eyes, fighting the urge to scoot closer to him.

The next morning when she opened her eyes, she stared at the cracked ceiling. When she remembered where she was, she turned to look at Lone Wolf. His chest rose and fell evenly, his breathing deeper than the night before. Vanessa slid off the bed and studied White Bird. The child still slept, curled on the blanket on the floor.

Listening to a rooster crowing in the yard, Vanessa combed her hair and moved restlessly around the room. Finally, as the sun streamed through the windows, she went down the hall to talk to Elwood Parsons.

"Mr. Parsons, we need to stay two more days."

"Not in my place," he said curtly without looking up.

She put a twenty dollar gold piece on the counter. "Two days, plus meals," she said, adding a stack of greenbacks.

He stared at the money and looked at her. "If I say you can stay, you have to keep off the street."

"I'll be glad to do that. I bought everything I need yesterday. I won't go outside except to care for my horses."

He looked at the money and reached out to take it, dropping it into a vest pocket. "Very well. But if there's trouble, I won't stop anyone."

"Fair enough. I never thought you would. Now about breakfast—"

She returned to the room and only had to wait an hour before Parsons knocked on the door with a tray ladened with eggs, ham, grits, and biscuits with gravy. She took the tray and fed White Bird, talking to her as she fed her. White Bird touched Vanessa's hand. "Vanessa," she said, smiling. "Hand."

"Hah!" Vanessa exclaimed, surprised and pleased and using the Kiowa word for yes that she had heard Lone Wolf say to White Bird.

"Where are we?" Lone Wolf's voice was deep and strong.

Startled, she whirled around to look at him. "We're in Martin Gulch—the town we saw," she said. When he struggled to get up, she hurried to help, plumping pillows behind him. "Stay where you are," she said. "I have our breakfast."

She placed a plate on his lap and brought him a glass of milk. "Be still and I'll feed you," she said, perching on the side of the bed. "That way you don't have to move your arm. The doctor said you should stay in bed several days." She lifted a forkful of eggs to his mouth. He watched her as he took the bite, his dark eyes enveloping her, and suddenly she wished she had let him feed himself.

"You blush easily, Vanessa," he remarked, his voice deep.

She felt a tremor run through her. "I told you, I'm unaccustomed to men."

"You slept in this bed with me last night."

This time she burned from the blush that flooded her throat and cheeks. "Yes, I did. I haven't slept in a bed since I left Fort McKavett, and I didn't think you would know."

"Of course, I knew," he replied solemnly. She raised the fork, and he took it from her hands. "I'll do this," he said quietly. "Go back to White Bird."

She fled, sitting down on the floor to help the little girl, aware of Lone Wolf's every movement behind her, remembering how she had touched him and looked at him last night, stunned that he had been awake and aware of it.

After they finished eating, she carried the tray and dishes back to the dining room to hand them over to Elwood Parsons. She returned to the room.

"I'm going to feed and water the horses. I'll take White Bird with me."

Lone Wolf nodded, closing his eyes and leaning back against the pillows. She paused to look at him, realizing he already looked stronger. She went outside into the cool morning air. Dew was thick on the grass, sparkling in the early sunshine. There was a chilly nip in the air.

When she returned to the room, Lone Wolf had shifted and was flat on his back, asleep. She stood beside the bed, brushing strands of hair from his face, wondering how much he had been aware of her last night.

She spent the day trying to entertain White Bird, telling her stories that she knew the child couldn't understand, yet she seemed to enjoy hearing. Vanessa made a rag doll out of the gingham for White Bird, sewing button eyes and stitching a red mouth, finally stuffing it with clean rags from a torn chemise.

White Bird sat beside Vanessa on the floor and played with bits of gingham and, as Vanessa sewed on the button eyes, White Bird scooted closer to lean against her.

"Doll," Vanessa said, holding the rag creation in front of White Bird.

Tiny fingers reached out to touch it. "Doll," White Bird repeated. As Vanessa stitched the smiling mouth, White Bird curled a lock of Vanessa's hair in her fingers. Vanessa smiled at her, and White Bird smiled in return.

"I love you," Vanessa said softly.

"Love you," White Bird repeated. Vanessa gave her a quick hug and returned to sewing on the doll. She glanced at the bed to find Lone Wolf's head turned and his dark eyes on her, sending tiny shocks to her system.

"Do you want water?" she asked him, trying to sound undisturbed.

"Not now. When you get up."

She stood and crossed to the pitcher to pour a tin cup full of water. "Here," she said, leaning down to slide her arm beneath him and help him. His hand closed around hers on the cup, and he raised his head to drink. Drops of water sloshed on his jaw, and silver drops ran down across his bare chest. Vanessa brushed them away, exquisitely aware that she touched his chest. His gaze slid up to meet hers and she stared at him, feeling unaccountably drawn to him.

"Guipago," White Bird said, climbing on the bed.

Vanessa started to reach for her, but Lone Wolf shook his head. "She's all right."

"She might hurt your wounds."

"I'll watch her." He drank and then pulled White Bird close against his good side. She sat facing him, touching his black hair while they conversed in words Vanessa couldn't understand.

She returned to the doll, and in a few minutes White Bird slid off the bed and toddled back to sit beside Vanessa. Lone Wolf was propped against pillows, his head turned so he could watch her sew. Bending her head over her task, Vanessa tried to forget his intense scrutiny, but her skin prickled and she could not shake her awareness of him.

When Vanessa finally finished the doll, she handed it to White Bird, who took it and climbed into the rocker, holding the rag doll against her heart while she rocked and sang.

"Now what do you sew?" Lone Wolf asked.

She glanced at the gingham in her lap. "I'm making a dress for her."

"She won't need it. She can wear buckskin."

"It would be easier for us when we're in towns if she wore something besides buckskin."

His gaze bore into her. "You received hatred because she

is Indian. I heard some of the remarks when the doctor was in here."

"How much were you aware of what was happening?" she asked, newly embarrassed at having touched him in the night and having shared the bed with him.

"Just little things, Vanessa," he said, leaving her as uncertain as before. "I grow hungry, and I see chicken on a plate."

"It's from last night." She helped him, watching him eat everything left on the tray. Now that he had been treated and had some rest, he was recovering quickly. After drinking two cups of water, he pushed the tray away.

"You may take that and help me up to tend to myself."

"There's a privy down the hall. I'll help you." She removed the tray and went back to him. He had swung his legs over the bed and was sitting up. She moved close, and his arm went around her as he stood. For an instant she felt his weight sag against her, and then he stood alone.

"Now I'm fine," he said, stepping away from her. Taking down his pistol, she followed him, leaving White Bird playing with the doll.

"Vanessa," he said, sounding amused, "I don't need you."

"I just want to make certain you're all right. I don't think anyone in this town likes Indians, and a man lives on the alley and works for Elwood Parsons—"

"Hankins. I heard him talking to you. Give me the pistol. I'll be all right."

She handed it to him, hoping he could manage to get around in spite of his weak condition. She remembered Jethro chopping wood and the play of his muscles, and she knew Lone Wolf would be no match for him without the pistol.

She stood in the darkened hall and waited, relieved when Lone Wolf returned. He moved slowly, but, although he was still weak, he looked better than yesterday. Another two days and he would be far better. When Lone Wolf climbed back into bed, she pulled the blanket over him. By the time she had tucked it across his chest, he had closed his eyes.

"Guipago?" she asked softly, letting the name roll across her tongue. She received no answer.

To Vanessa's relief, she didn't see Jethro Hankins until late in the day. As soon as she spotted him coming down the alley, she hurried inside to stay behind a locked door until it was time for a dinner tray of steak and potatoes from Elwood Parsons.

She helped Lone Wolf, who ate his dinner and what White Bird and Vanessa left of theirs. Once again, Vanessa helped him outside. She stood at the doorway while a cold wind blew. Worried about Hankins, she waited and was again relieved to see Lone Wolf return to the house without interference.

In the distance thunder rumbled, and she shivered as another blast of cold air struck her. The minute Lone Wolf settled in bed, he fell asleep again.

After trying the basted gingham dress on White Bird, Vanessa bathed the child, preferring yesterday's bath water to having Jethro bring a fresh supply to their room.

While White Bird and Lone Wolf slept, Vanessa hemmed the red dress that needed only hooks and eyes to be finished.

At nearly midnight, Vanessa stripped and stepped into the tub to bathe. She dressed again in the gingham, put out the lamp, and finally climbed up on the bed beside Lone Wolf.

His head turned as he looked at her. She inhaled swiftly and sat up, starting to get out of the bed. His hand caught her wrist. "Lie back down. You slept here last night."

"Tonight, you know I'm here. Last night, you were unconscious."

"I knew you were here," he said. "Lie down," he ordered. She stretched out as if she were reclining on hot coals.

"Vanessa, you'll never escape from Fort McKavett with your sisters," he said, his voice deep and resonant in the quiet. "Even if you did, where would you go?"

"We can head south and catch the stage to El Paso and then go on to California."

"Why California?" he asked, turning on his good side and propping his head on his hand to look at her.

"I don't think my father will follow us that far," she answered, intensely aware of Lone Wolf stretched out so close to her. "Also, my sister Phoebe has a wonderful voice. When we were living in St. Louis, Missouri, Phoebe met a woman, Eleanor Rosati with the San Francisco Opera. When she heard Phoebe sing at a party, she invited Phoebe to stay with her in San Francisco. I want to take Phoebe there and see if she can get into the opera."

Lone Wolf reached out to stroke Vanessa's hair away from her face, and she felt a tingle from his faint touch. Her gaze drifted down to his mouth, and she inhaled deeply. "How can the three of you live?" he asked, his deep voice like a caress.

"I have some of father's money and I can sew, so I can earn wages. Eleanor said she would help Phoebe."

"Why won't your father let Phoebe do something with her singing?"

"He thinks the opera is foolish. He sees a chance for a marriage for Phoebe that will unite him with a wealthy, influential family. My father has political ambitions. He wants to be a United States senator. Frankly, I think he'd like to be the president, but he knows that's out of his reach."

"And will you be content to sew, care for Belva, help Phoebe, and perhaps watch her rise to fame?"

"Yes, of course. I have no inclinations for fame. All I want is—" She broke off, suddenly embarrassed.

"Is what, Vanessa?" he asked insistently, and her pulse jumped. He lay on his good side, facing her, his dark eyes studying her. He was only inches away, both of them stretched out, and she felt a yearning for his kisses that threatened all propriety.

"It isn't important," she answered awkwardly.

He caught her chin. "What is it you want?" he demanded with a quiet persistence, his gaze boring into her, his warm fingers holding her so she had to look into his eyes.

"I want a husband who loves me, and I want children," she confessed, blushing. "I love White Bird," she said firmly, wishing he would turn to another subject.

"Ahh, a husband and children," Lone Wolf said. He traced his finger across her lips, and she felt as if she were melting inside. "You will have that, I promise you."

"It isn't up to you whether or not I marry, so don't promise it," she chided.

"It's a prediction. You're a woman meant for a man." His finger slipped across her lips again, and she gazed at him through the darkness. He leaned closer to her, tilting her face up. His brown eyes were compelling, his rugged features handsome.

As she gazed back at him, her heart pounded. Lone Wolf looked arrogant and virile; his desire for her was evident. With deliberation, he leaned closer. His mouth brushed hers, and the faint contact was magical.

She closed her eyes, wanting his kiss, feeling a heat kindle inside her. Lone Wolf's strong arm banded her, pulling her against him. She put her hand against his chest and ran her fingers across his flesh, hearing him groan, the noise muffled by their kisses.

His tongue played in her mouth, touching her tongue, sending wave after wave of pleasure through her. His hand slid down to her breast, and she felt as if she would faint from his touch, her body swelling toward him as she slid her arm carefully around his neck.

Logic told her to resist, to avoid sharing a bed with him, to stop the kisses. He was a tough, solitary man who was still grieving over his wife. Vanessa knew she was vulnerable, that she lacked experience. It would be disastrous to fall in love with him, she reminded herself. They belonged to different worlds. She suspected he hated most whites, and she knew nothing about his way of life.

Yet moving out of his arms was impossible. He leaned over her; his kisses deepened, becoming more demanding. His hand played across her breast, and his thumb circled her taut nipple as warmth flooded through her. He shifted closer, his hand banding her waist and pulling her against him.

"Don't!" she gasped. "Your wounds will—"

His mouth stopped her words, and she was lost because she was in his arms, stretched against his powerful body, his arm around her, his hard erection pressing against her.

Dazed, on fire with new sensations, she felt her breasts swell against his solid chest. As her hips moved, she ached for more of him.

With a silken touch that made her gasp with pleasure, his hand slid over her hip, down to her thigh in a fiery trail that stormed her senses.

His kisses were passionate, deep and demanding, and she returned them wildly, her fingers winding in his thick black hair, her hand sliding over his smooth back. Logic told her she was running risks; at the same time, to be in his arms felt right and good, as if she belonged there.

She moaned, her hips thrusting against him, feeling his erect manhood pressing against her belly. The ache low in her body between her thighs was unfamiliar, a yearning that was overwhelming.

His leg nudged hers apart, and she moaned at the warm friction as he slid between her thighs. His big fingers slipped beneath the neck of the gingham to cup her bare breast, his thumb playing over her nipple.

Vanessa's soft cries were muffled by his kisses as he caressed her, driving her to a frenzy.

Trying to cling to reason, knowing she had to stop now or be hopelessly lost to passion, she caught his hand, scooting away from him.

"No!" She gasped, not meaning the word to come out so forcefully. As he became still, she looked up at him. "We have to stop," she said, starting to get out of bed. Again he caught her and pulled her down.

"Stay where you are. I'll leave you alone."

Gasping for breath, with her heart racing wildly, she faced him. She ran her fingers lightly along his jaw, and his eyes narrowed.

"I'm so inexperienced," she said, her voice little more than a whisper. "I know we should stop now or I won't stop at all. And if I fall in love with you, I'll be hurt—terribly."

"It is not my intent to hurt you, Vanessa," he said solemnly. "If it were, I could have done so that first day."

"I didn't mean that kind of hurt. I meant if I fall in love with you," she said, her voice tight with the emotion of baring her soul to him. "You never would love me in return, and our lives have to part. Your way is not the same as mine."

Lone Wolf ran his fingers through her hair and caressed her slender throat. He was torn between taking her and wreaking revenge, and respecting her. And the latter was winning in the battle because he admired her. She had been courageous, resourceful, and at the same time she had obeyed him when it seemed necessary. She had saved White Bird that first night and had also saved his life by tending his wounds.

He ached with wanting her, and he tried to push his desire aside as he pondered what to do with her; but it was difficult to ignore the clamorings of his body when Vanessa was stretched out only inches away from him. He let his hand slide down her arm, shifting to her hip, down to her thigh. Her eyelashes fluttered and closed for an instant, and he wanted to lean forward and kiss her again.

Instead, he stroked her thigh and slid his hand back up, brushing one soft breast. She inhaled swiftly, and he was amazed again that her father deemed her unmarriageable because she was a beautiful, warm, responsive woman.

And at the thought of her father, he frowned. Her father was a railroad man; and all the railroaders Lone Wolf had known were ruthless, filled with greed, and Indian-haters.

Lone Wolf wound his fingers in Vanessa's hair and tilted her face up toward his. "You said you lived in Kansas. Has your father been connected with a railroad in Kansas?"

The question hung in the silence between them, and he guessed her answer before she spoke.

Suddenly cautious and uncertain, Vanessa knew she should answer with care. At the same time, she wanted to be truthful. Remembering that she had lied to him about her name, she looked him directly in the eye.

"Papa started to build a line across northern Kansas at Topeka and headed west, but the war interfered."

"A Kansas railroad crew killed my wife. They used her for their pleasure and then stabbed her and left her to die."

Vanessa gasped and touched his cheek with her hand. "How dreadful," she said, hurting for him, suspecting her father might have encouraged the killing by his bounty on dead Indians.

"Would your father fire such men from his crew if he knew what they had done?" Lone Wolf asked, his voice harsh with smoldering anger.

She stared into Lone Wolf's eyes. She wanted to answer *yes,* but the truth was *no.* Her father would condone what they had done because he had no use for Indians. He treated them with far more contempt than he had for stray dogs.

"Answer me, Vanessa," Lone Wolf demanded, pulling her hair so her head was tilted back further.

"No, he wouldn't care," she replied forthrightly. "My father doesn't like Indians."

Fury surged in Lone Wolf and he leaned closer, his mouth coming down hard on hers, his tongue thrusting deep into her mouth. He yanked her against him, his arousal pressing against her. For a moment he wanted revenge, wanted to inflict his will on the white woman and her hated father. He shifted over her, pushing her legs apart. And then her slender arm circled his neck and she pulled him down, moaning softly as she kissed him back.

He felt the softness of the lips beneath his, felt her pliant yielding to him; and he remembered it was Vanessa he held, not a stranger, not a white woman who hated him or his people, but a warmhearted woman who had tended him and cried over White Bird.

As she tightened her arm around his neck and clung to him, he released her abruptly, his emotions seething. He was on the brink of revenge, anger tearing at him; yet too easily he could recall her facing him bravely or holding White Bird and crooning softly to her. He was caught between two warring urges. She was a virgin, and it would be as important to her people as to his that she remain pure for marriage.

His breathing was ragged while he struggled with his emotions and this time she turned on her side and propped her head up to look down at him. "You're angry with me—only it's anger against my father more than me."

"I loved my wife, and she was treated brutally. She was innocent and had done nothing. I have hated all whites for what those men did to her. They were Kansas railroad men—like your father—so I find that difficult, Vanessa. I've dreamed of revenge."

She turned on her back, unable to answer him because she could understand his hurt and hatred. And in spite of the chasm between their worlds, her body raged with fire for him. She was beginning to feel a closeness to him she had known only with her sisters. Suddenly she rolled over to touch his jaw.

"I'm sorry for what happened, for your loss, and your hurt."

He stroked her hair away from her face, gazing at her, and she couldn't tell whether his anger had abated or not. She lay back down and gazed into the darkness, wishing he would turn and pull her into his arms again and kiss her, yet knowing it was better that he had stopped.

Thunder rumbled and lightning flashed, and in seconds rain pattered lightly against the windows.

"I find it difficult to believe that your father couldn't find someone to marry you," Lone Wolf said, the words coming out gruffly.

"He would only approve of someone wealthy, high in the military or political life, and the suitable men we knew were not interested in marrying me." While Lone Wolf turned his head to study her, she rubbed the bridge of her nose. "I'll have to admit, I didn't cooperate when I was introduced to them because I didn't want to marry any of them."

Lone Wolf tugged lightly on one of her curls, and she felt the faint pull against her scalp. Her nerves tingled; her body still felt on fire, and he was only inches away. She fought the urge to reach out and slip her arm around his neck again.

"And there was no young man who wanted to court you?"

"Anyone I might have liked Papa detained from calling or arranged to have transferred. My father has been at military forts most of my life. He was an officer for years. The brief time in between his military service and the War Between the States was the only time we didn't live at forts." She looked into Lone Wolf's dark eyes. "After a while, if Hollings doesn't find me, I imagine my father will offer a reward."

"Why would he offer a reward when he was sending you to a convent to get you out of his life?"

"He doesn't like to have his way thwarted. And he may suspect I'll come back for Phoebe and Belva. I could be wrong—perhaps he will let me go and consider himself well rid of me, but I don't think so. He has always had to have his way."

"Do you think you can do better raising your sister Belva than your father?"

"Phoebe and I discussed that and, yes, I think I can," Vanessa replied firmly, turning to face him and propping her head on her hand, "because I'll love her. Life may not be as easy, but love is more important than comfort."

"Not all women would agree with that," he replied dryly.

"If you're caught with me, it could be very dangerous for you."

"I know it's dangerous for me. I could be killed for traveling with you. But don't forget, if we're discovered like this, your reputation is destroyed."

"I don't see that my reputation matters if Papa is sending me to a convent anyway." She studied Lone Wolf, curious about him. "What is White Bird's Kiowa name?"

"Tainguato."

"Tainguato," she said. "Guipago and Tainguato. How did you get the name Lone Wolf?"

"It was Gray Wolf, but after my wife's death I have wanted to keep to myself and not take another wife. I loved my wife and cannot imagine loving another. Not yet. My name was changed to Lone Wolf because I am alone and I dwell in my tipi without anyone. They have all been killed. My father died in a battle with Apaches; my mother and wife were killed by whites. My brother and his wife were killed by soldiers."

"You have White Bird."

"Yes. And I promised to care for her and I will." He

tugged a lock of Vanessa's hair through his fingers. "Now I also have you with me."

"That's not permanent. Soon you'll be well enough to get along without me, and I'll go." She studied him solemnly. "And if you decide to do so, you can get rid of me easily."

They stared at each other, and her heartbeat quickened. What ran through his mind? Would he take her captive as soon as he could? As she stared at him, she suspected he would. He was accustomed to a fierce life that involved fighting for survival so he would not be bound by the polite constrictions that would hamper many white men. On the other hand, many white men would not be bound at all, but would have tried to possess her by now or take her gold.

Lone Wolf stroked her head, his fingers combing through her hair. "I would never destroy you," he said in a husky voice. "I might keep you and take you back with me, Vanessa, but I will never hurt you."

"I don't want you to take me back," she answered quietly, "because I have to take care of my sisters. And Phoebe should have her chance at the opera. She has a beautiful voice that's wasted out here." She turned to study him. "What is it like for women in your tribe? Do they obey the men?"

He smiled faintly, stroking her cheek. "Yes, they obey. But they also are treated as equals in many ways, and they are consulted about decisions. Some of them ride on raids and some accompany their men on hunts. They work and they do a great deal of the tasks that keep the village running—the cooking and sewing, putting up the tipis and taking them down, caring for the families. They have a voice in what happens."

"I had the impression they didn't."

"Not at all, Vanessa."

Lone Wolf rolled over and was silent. "I took the pill the doctor left, and I think it makes me want to sleep. We need to get out of this town, Vanessa. We're in danger." His voice trailed off, and soon he was asleep. She touched his straight black hair, feeling the thick coarseness of the strands. She traced her finger across his good shoulder and drew a deep breath. Even that slight touch made her ache for his arms and his kisses; and every time he said her name, it still sent a tiny shock of response through her.

She turned over and stared at the ceiling, knowing she should be careful. If she began to love Lone Wolf, the only thing that could come of it was terrible hurt when they parted.

She glanced at him. She had told herself that once he regained his strength, she wouldn't be safe with him. Now she wondered if he would simply tell her goodbye and ride north without her. She had heard of women captives and seen them brought into the forts. The few she had seen were pitiful creatures, frightened, humiliated, treated insolently by her father when he had to cross paths with them.

If Lone Wolf recovered before they reached Fort McKavett, would he force her to return to his people with him? She glanced at the gunbelt that hung over the headboard and wished she knew how to use the revolver.

Thunder boomed again, and Vanessa shivered. She scooted close against Lone Wolf, and his arm went around her. Startled, she turned to look at him, but his breathing stayed the same, deep and regular. She fitted herself against him, flirting with a longing that she knew was dangerous.

As dawn filled the room with light, Vanessa stirred and got out of bed. She checked Lone Wolf; he was breathing evenly. He already looked stronger, and the bandages were clean—not blood-soaked. Turning, she looked at White Bird, who was curled beneath a blanket, her thumb in her mouth.

Vanessa knelt down to brush White Bird's long hair from her face. The doorknob jiggled. At the faint sound, Vanessa's head came up and she stared as the knob turned and a key grated in the lock.

Seven

Vanessa stood up, her heart pounding. The door swung open, and Jethro Hankins stood framed in the doorway. He was shirtless, his eyes bloodshot. As his gaze raked over her, he smiled. "Elwood sent me to see if you want breakfast."

Cold with fear, she inhaled deeply and faced him. "You can tell him yes, and I'll come get it soon. After this, don't unlock my door."

Jethro stepped into the room, glancing at the bed. "Husband still alive?"

"Yes, he is."

"There's something wrong with your horse. I think you'd better come look." He moved back into the hall and waited.

She didn't want to go with him; yet if something were wrong with one of the horses, she had to find out. Wishing Hankins would go on outside, she walked through the doorway and into the hall, trying to sweep past him and ignore him. She caught the odor of his sweat and avoided looking at his bare chest, revulsion rising in her.

As they turned toward the back door, he walked beside her, his shoulder brushing hers. When they passed the open door of the empty room across the hall, Jethro pushed her, spinning her into the room.

Vanessa's heart thudded, and she struggled against him in silence. Grasping her upper arms, he pulled her up close.

He smelled of whiskey and sweat, and his body was damp. Repulsed, she shoved against him angrily.

"Let me go before I scream."

"You scream and get that husband of yours in here, and I'll kill him. He's in no shape for a fight," Jethro said, grinning at her and squeezing her tightly. He shifted, his thick fingers closing on the neck of her red-and-blue gingham dress. He ripped open the front of her dress, the buttons popping, cool air rushing over her skin, his gaze lascivious and revolting.

Biting back a scream because she didn't want Lone Wolf hurt, she twisted and tried to break away, but she was powerless against Hankin's strength. He slid his hand beneath her chemise and squeezed her breast. With a swift yank of his arm at her waist, he spun them both around and jammed her back against the wall, his hands pulling up her skirts.

"Don't cry out or scream if you want him to live," Jethro warned, trying to kiss her as he pulled her skirts high.

She turned her head to avoid his kiss, biting his ear. He growled and shoved her into the wall until she could barely breath.

"Hellcat. You'll pay—"

Struggling with him, she stomped as hard as she could on his foot, but his boot protected him and he laughed. "I'm taking you, squaw—"

Tears of anger and frustration spilled on her cheeks as she fought him, but her blows were useless. His leg slid between hers, forcing her legs apart.

Her heart racing in fear, she bit his shoulder. He growled, squeezing her hard until she cried out.

The click of the hammer of the revolver was a slight sound, but Jethro froze.

"Let her go," Lone Wolf said from the doorway in perfect English that held a quiet, deadly force.

Taking advantage of Jethro's loosened grip, she wriggled

out of his grasp and tried to button her dress, yanking up two buttons from the floor.

"You'll hang if you shoot," Jethro snarled as he turned around.

"No, he won't!" she said, "because I'll say I did it, and no one will hang a woman for defending herself!"

"Move," Lone Wolf said to Jethro, motioning with the revolver and stepping back.

"Where are you taking him?" she asked, suddenly afraid Lone Wolf would take the other man out and shoot him.

"I'll tie him up outside where he won't be found for a while. You pack."

His words were terse, and his dark eyes flashed with anger. She glanced at the clean white bandages and was relieved to see that they weren't bloody in spite of his moving around.

With shaking hands, hurrying as quickly as possible, she changed to the poplin riding habit. White Bird continued to sleep as Vanessa rushed around the room gathering their belongings and carrying them outside to saddle the horses and pack the provisions on the sorrel.

The ground was wet from rain, the water trough filled to the top, and water still dripped from the bare branches of a tall hackberry. Trying to avoid puddles, she rushed back inside.

As time passed, she began to worry about Lone Wolf, but when she dragged out the portmanteau, she saw him crossing the yard.

"We get out of here now," he said harshly. "I heard the doctor talking to you, and I know what kind of town this is."

"If you heard him, you also heard him say to ride south."

Lone Wolf nodded and looked at the sorrel. "How did we acquire the horse?"

"I have money my father was sending to the convent for taking me in. I bought supplies and a horse." She thought she saw a flicker of amusement in his dark eyes, but she could not be certain.

"I hope you got a bargain."

"Nothing in this town is a bargain. They know I have gold. If you're ready, I'll get White Bird."

She ran inside and picked up White Bird, glancing around the room and staring at the bed, remembering sleeping beside Lone Wolf, knowing she never would forget the past night. Even though it had been little more than kisses and a few caresses, they had shared an intimacy that she suspected he rarely allowed and she had never had.

When they mounted, she noticed that Lone Wolf did so with more ease than before. The morning was chilly, and she wondered if he were cool.

"Mama," White Bird whimpered sleepily. Vanessa held her close and gave her a plum and a bandanna to wipe her fingers with. She glanced at Lone Wolf and found him watching her.

"Are you cold without a shirt?"

"No. I'm accustomed to the weather, and the day will be warm. We ride now."

He led the way down the alley, staying off the main street all the way through town. Twice, men stood in open doorways and watched them pass. Finally, they rode through the few blocks that comprised the town and then they had to move into the open. Her neck prickled, and she turned to look back. She saw two men mounting up. "Lone Wolf," she said quietly, and his head swung around. He glanced over his shoulder.

"We need to get away." He reached across to take White Bird, who finished the plum and was wiping her fingers daintily with the bandanna.

"Shouldn't I keep her with me?"

"We're going to have to run. I'll slow down if I feel I'm losing consciousness. I'm better now."

She knew he was better without his having to tell her,

and she wondered again about her safety. One minute, she remembered the quiet moments in the night and she didn't think she could possibly be harmed by him. The next minute, she looked at his arrogant profile, the hawk nose and strong jaw, and she could imagine his taking her captive to return to his people.

She glanced back and saw six men strung out in a line riding out of town behind them.

"What about the packhorse? With all our supplies, the sorrel may not be able to keep up."

"See the line of trees ahead?"

She saw the cedars and guessed it was the creek bed that Wilkens had told her about. "Yes."

"We'll try to keep the sorrel with us that far. I'll turn the horse loose in the trees, and we may have to leave it behind."

"If you do that, we won't have food. I've packed the water on these two horses, but most of the food is on the sorrel."

"You made a wise choice. If we have water, we can get along. You ride ahead of me."

She suspected he was doing that to shield White Bird and her. As soon as Vanessa was a few yards beyond him, she turned to look back at the men who were steadily coming behind them. Her gaze slid to Lone Wolf.

"Go," he ordered, his expression fierce.

At his command, she flicked the reins and the paint surged ahead. It was a short-legged horse, thick through the hindquarters, and she expected it to be slow; but to her surprise, it was fast and the wind whipped against her as they galloped across the flat land.

The long-legged bay pounded directly behind her, and White Bird had her fists knotted in the horse's mane. The little girl's face was raised to the wind, and Vanessa was thankful the child didn't realize the danger, but simply enjoyed the race.

She glanced at the lagging packhorse and saw a pan fly loose from her packing and tumble to the ground. The horses were lathered and hers was slowing as the trees loomed closer. A shot rang out, and Vanessa glanced over her shoulder, terror gripping her. Lone Wolf leaned low over the bay, and Vanessa was amazed that White Bird didn't look terrified.

Another shot was fired, and then Vanessa reined slightly as the land dipped and her pony slowed to go down an embankment to the dry creek bed.

"Keep going!" Lone Wolf yelled, sliding off his horse and tossing the reins to Vanessa.

In a reflex action she caught them while Lone Wolf sprawled against the bank and raised his rifle to fire at the riders.

"Go!" he shouted at her. Hating to leave him to fight half a dozen men but knowing she must, she rode along the creek bank.

Gunfire exploded in rapid succession. At a bend, she looked back to see him firing steadily. She urged her horse forward until they had rounded the bend. She halted there and dismounted, tethering the horses.

Motioning to White Bird to stay where she was, Vanessa walked back as gunshots continued to shatter the quiet.

Lone Wolf lay sprawled on the bank, firing over the rim. As she watched, he lowered his rifle. Silence fell like a heavy cloak, enveloping the land. He turned his head to look at her and he scowled. Then he stood up and, to her horror, the bandage around his side was crimson again.

He walked toward her with the rifle in one hand, his revolver in the other. As he approached, he replaced the revolver in the holster on his hip. He looked fierce and angry, and her pulse drummed as he approached her. Only yards away, he halted. "I told you to ride out of here."

"I couldn't leave you behind. Besides, they're gone now, aren't they?"

"If they had killed me, you could have gotten White Bird to safety if you had continued on. If they'd found you here, they would have taken you for their pleasure and killed her."

She felt his anger like a lash. Raising her chin, she studied him, hoping he didn't know how much he had frightened her. "I didn't think they could kill you."

"You couldn't know any such thing," he said quietly, moving closer to her.

She felt the elemental clash with him, but overriding it came another explosion that was repeating itself with greater frequency. They were at odds because she didn't want to yield to the attraction she felt for him or their growing friendship. And she suspected he despised the moments he felt drawn to her, preferring the familiar ground of his passionate hatred for whites.

As she faced him, her heart pounding, she wondered if he were going to strike her. He stopped only inches from her, his black eyes filled with fire. With a grunt of disgust, he tossed down his rifle and reached for her, his arm sweeping around her waist and drawing her up against him.

"You disobey the most reasonable order." He ground out the words, his fury evident while his dark eyes revealed his desire. Then his mouth covered hers, stopping her reply as his tongue thrust deep, sending heat streaking throughout her body.

Thrown off guard, she was devastated by her reaction to him. He was both friend and foe. Last night she had felt closer to him than to anyone except her sisters; yet for a few moments as he had faced her with obvious fury, she had been frightened and uncertain what he would do. And then as his tongue slid over hers, touching the insides of her mouth, conscious thought receded and she reacted primitively, following her heart. She wound her arms around his neck and returned his wild kisses.

He leaned over her, pulling her to him, his arousal hard

against her. His solid body felt marvelous; his strong arms held her tightly. His hand slid over her buttocks as his tongue thrust in a primeval rhythm. Her eyes closed, Vanessa clung to him, her heart beating wildly because it seemed so right to be in his arms. She kissed him in return, knowing he wanted her, her heart thudding at her response to him.

Finally, she leaned back; both of them were breathing as if they had run the last mile on foot.

"White Bird—" Vanessa waved her hand. "We should go."

"Woman, don't run risks like that again." He ground out the words, his fingers digging into her shoulders.

"You run risks. Look at your side. And I told you, I knew you would hold them off."

Lone Wolf curbed the urge to shake her. Eyes That Smile had been an obedient and loving wife. Vanessa was fiery with the independent mind of a warrior. Lone Wolf stared at her, alternately wanting to shake her and kiss her. And he didn't want the wild attraction that was growing daily between them. Never did he want to lose his heart to a white woman, the daughter of a detested railroader, particularly a woman who would be as obedient as a wild stallion.

Had she really been that confident he could hold off six renegades when he was wounded and had only one rifle and one revolver? He let out a deep breath, trying to bank his anger.

She wriggled out of his grasp, walking away from him, her hips twisting with a saucy wiggle.

Angry at the upheaval she was causing in his life, he strode after her. White Bird sat quietly waiting on the paint, and he was thankful one of the females with him was obedient. He walked to her and swung her off the horse. A pain ripped up his side and he grimaced, but he pulled the child to his chest and hugged her.

"I love you," she said to him and his eyes narrowed. He looked beyond her to Vanessa.

"You've taught her English. How does she know what that means?"

"Because I say it to her when I hug and kiss her," Vanessa replied airily.

"I don't want her to know English."

Vanessa placed her hands on her hips, a smile playing over her features that shot his temper higher. "You don't? When you learned English, it was because your father said you'd have to share your world with whites so you might as well be equipped to deal with them. Yet you would deny White Bird that knowledge?"

"Her men will protect her, that is a trust and security you could afford to learn!"

"Right now I have you to protect me, and I'm very well aware of your abilities. You just performed beautifully."

He saw her smile widen before she turned her back, and his anger churned because he knew she was right about teaching White Bird words of English. He knew Kiowa, Spanish, Comanche, and English; and he had never regretted the knowledge.

He hated to admit what lay at the bottom of all his anger—the fright he had felt that moment he had turned and seen Vanessa standing in the bend of the creek bed where she could have been easily captured if the white men had killed him. Lone Wolf clamped his mouth shut. He did not want his heart to jump with fear for Vanessa Sutton's well-being.

He set White Bird on the ground. "Vanessa, stand watch. Go back around the curve and climb the bank while I repack the sorrel."

To his surprise she went without a word of argument, adding to his anger because she was not only self-reliant, she was unpredictable.

He worked quickly, his side and shoulder throbbing with

pain now. He wanted to get away from the town because he was certain the men would get others and come after them again. They knew Vanessa had gold and traveled with a wounded Indian and an Indian baby. He wanted to put distance between them quickly.

He whistled and Vanessa reappeared, hurrying around the bend, holding her riding skirt up slightly to keep it from getting dusty, her trim ankles showing.

"We go now. I think they'll return." As soon as Vanessa mounted, he handed White Bird to her. He swung up into the saddle and they moved off. Except for occasional puddles, the creek bed was dry; the horses's hooves crunched on the rocks.

Lone Wolf glanced at her. "How much did you spend in town?"

"I spent greenbacks and gold pieces," she replied with a shrug. "I had to give Doc Wilkens a twenty-dollar gold piece to tend you."

"That's a fortune!" Lone Wolf frowned, astounded that she had paid that to have him cared for. "He must not have wanted an Indian patient."

"No, he didn't. But he said for gold he would tend President Lincoln."

"That amount is a fortune to the men in town." Lone Wolf fell silent and then in a moment he turned to study her again. "You don't have any great interest in money, Vanessa," he said dryly.

Vanessa saw the amusement in his eyes. "No, I don't. Papa has always taken care of us, and I don't care about fancy dresses. We've moved so much I've never had many things."

"Then you would be a good Kiowa because we move too often to accumulate many things."

She smiled at him, and he reached out to catch her chin in his hand.

"A smile of summer sunshine," he said quietly, and she felt a rush of pleasure.

Lone Wolf headed up the slight bank. At the top, her gaze swept the land, noting the sparse mesquite bent to the north by the prevailing southern winds and the prickly pear that were dark splotches near the ground. It was quiet except for the horses's hooves. Hawks circled high overhead, gliding and drifting. The day was pleasant, warming as the sun rose in the sky.

She halted and glanced down at White Bird, who slumped against her while she dozed. Glad the little girl felt no fright, Vanessa brushed the child's hair back from her face.

An hour later, she drew in her breath because the bandage on Lone Wolf's shoulder looked bloody. "You should stop. Your shoulder and your side are bleeding again."

"No. If we stop, they can catch up with us. We keep going."

"How do I know you're not leading me back north?"

He gave her a level look. "You have to trust me."

His answer irked her, and she continued to ride in silence. When they didn't stop as the sun moved across the sky, she realized he must be greatly concerned about being followed.

White Bird awoke and wriggled, and Vanessa caught up with him. "We need to stop. White Bird should get down and run, and we haven't eaten all day."

"Drink water. We keep going."

Annoyed, but afraid to argue because they might be in terrible danger, she nodded.

"When we go through another town," Vanessa said, "I want to purchase a pistol and I want you to teach me to shoot."

He glanced at her, his dark eyes twinkling. "And you will turn it on me, Vanessa?"

Shaking her head, she smiled. "You'd take it away from me."

"Why do you want to learn to use a weapon?"

"Because we've been in danger and I felt helpless. You were unconscious, and Jethro Hankins frightened me."

Lone Wolf nodded. "It is good you learn to use a pistol, but I'll probably regret it."

"No, you won't. And I wish you would teach me some words or some signs in your language because I feel helpless when I'm unable to converse with White Bird. I know a few Kiowa words, but not many."

"It is not an easy language, but I shall teach you—and some sign language as well. There's no *r* in the Kiowa vocabulary, and sometimes meaning depends upon pronunciation. Sign language is easier." He clapped his hands in front of his chest. "That means peace. Keep the palm of your left hand up."

She followed his example, reaching around White Bird. He shook his own hand. "Friend."

Gradually, she began to learn the sign language as they rode. He glanced at her. "If I lose consciousness again and you encounter the Comanche, make the sign for peace and make the sign for husband. You'll be safer if they think you're my woman."

He held up his right index finger, the back of his hand away from his face, the finger in front of his face. "That's man. Now add to it the sign for marry." He joined his index fingers side by side, pointing away from himself. "That's the sign for trade or marry. But together with the sign for man, it will indicate that I'm your husband."

The words were ordinary, but their effect on her was not. When he'd said *I'm your husband,* the words had carried an emotional impact. She glanced at him, studying his profile, remembering the moments in the quiet of the night when she had been close beside him, remembering his hard, powerful body.

At last the sun slanted close to the horizon, and she realized they were heading southeast. "You've turned back east."

"Otherwise we'd be in New Mexico Territory."

"Do you think we're still in danger from the men of Martin's Gulch?"

"Yes. That looked like a hideaway of men on the run from the law. If they thought they could get even one hundred dollars in gold, they would ride after us with eagerness. Vanessa, do you know how much you carry?"

His gaze was intent and she dreaded answering him, suspecting her gold had placed them in greater danger.

"No one in town saw or knew how much I had."

"That isn't what I asked."

She drew a deep breath. "I left the wagon train with five hundred dollars in gold and another two hundred in greenbacks."

"Eha'eho'!" he exclaimed, his brow furrowing, his expression fierce. "For that amount the entire town would ride after us! Did the Parsons woman know how much your father was sending?"

"Yes, she did."

"So by now, the soldiers that accompanied the wagon train know. When you made purchases in town, did anyone see how much money you carried?"

"No. I divided it up and left most of the money in the room with you."

He nodded, glancing behind them, speculating.

"How far until you'll feel we're safe from them?"

"Tonight we can change course. If we ride all night, I don't think they can catch up—"

"You can't ride all night!"

His dark eyes bored into her. "I'm stronger than I was. If we stop, they may find us. I had the advantage today because they were on open ground and I had cover so I could pick them off, but next time I probably won't be as lucky. I think they could number as high as twenty men. Maybe more. I can't battle that many."

She nodded, trying to reassure herself that if he had made

it this far, he would survive, but as her gaze drifted over his bandages, she felt a stirring of alarm because they were now thoroughly soaked with blood.

Knowing it was useless to argue, she grew silent. As the moon rose in the sky that night, she kept dozing and jerking awake. She was too weary and groggy to try to figure out in what direction they were headed and hoped he hadn't circled around and turned north. She jerked upright and glanced at him. How he managed staying awake now, she couldn't imagine.

Vanessa battled sleep until they reached some trees and moved down onto a creek bed. A faint trickle of water— only inches wide—ran through it, but it was enough for the horses. Lone Wolf reined in and dismounted. He stepped in front of her to take White Bird.

"Spread a blanket, and I'll put her down while we get some water and food."

Too weary to protest, she spread the blanket and, as he lowered White Bird to it, Vanessa stretched out beside her and closed her eyes.

The next thing she knew, Lone Wolf was gripping her shoulder. "Vanessa," he whispered loudly. "Get up. We have to go." He pulled her to her feet, picked up White Bird, and handed the child to Vanessa, who settled the little girl on the saddle in front of her.

Finally, Lone Wolf mounted up and led the way as they followed the stream.

At the first faint glow of dawn, Lone Wolf turned to ride beside her. He reached over to place his hand on her arm, and his fingers felt warm against her flesh. His brow furrowed in a frown, and she realized there must be trouble. He tugged her reins, and the paint halted. Lone Wolf leaned close. "We're being followed. Stay with me," he ordered.

Tiredness vanished as fear replaced it, and she glanced over her shoulder.

"When I see a place where we can ride out of this low

spot and make a break for it again, I'll motion to you and you ride away with White Bird." He tilted Vanessa's chin up and gazed into her eyes. "This time, don't stop. I think many men follow us."

A chill ran down her spine, and she glanced behind them. She couldn't see or hear anything unusual, but she remembered how long he had known Hollings was following them before Hollings and the soldiers had appeared.

As she nodded, he motioned her to go ahead. Frightened, she rode quietly, her skin prickling because she didn't doubt for a moment that Lone Wolf was correct in his assumption that they were being pursued.

She hadn't heard a sound, but suddenly an arrow struck the tree beside Lone Wolf with a solid *thunk,* the shaft quivering.

She flinched and tightened her arm around White Bird, ready to gallop away, but waiting for a signal from Lone Wolf.

"Bo'dalk'inago!" he called. *"Kai'wa! Aho'."*

As if materializing out of the air, dozens of warriors emerged at the top of the embankment and surrounded them.

Vanessa's heart throbbed violently. All the men looked menacing with black paint on their faces, feathers in their long hair, their expressions solemn and intent. Some of them wore buckskin shirts; others were bare-chested. They looked as strong and formidable as Lone Wolf.

She felt a rising panic that she hoped didn't show. She hadn't feared Lone Wolf because he had been too weak to harm her, but now she was at the mercy of the warriors.

While the warriors spread out, circling them, Vanessa sat still. Were they his people? Now would she be their captive?

Eight

Lone Wolf rode forward. He made a motion with his hands, closing his fists, thumbs down, bringing them in front of his chest. She remembered that this was his sign for soldiers and wondered if he told them they were being pursued by soldiers. Along with the sign language, he spoke in words she couldn't understand. One of the men answered Lone Wolf, and the two conversed. The man talking to Lone Wolf looked at her and said something. Reaching up with his right hand, Lone Wolf combed his fingers through his hair as he answered, and the man nodded. They both glanced at White Bird.

Lone Wolf turned his horse to ride back beside her. "We go with them. They're Comanche. Their medicine man will tend my wounds. The warrior I talked with is Huusibe, Draw Knife. The Kiowa and the Comanche have made peace with each other. These men are a war party, returning to their camp."

"They'll accept me?"

"They think you're my woman," Lone Wolf said quietly. Again, she felt a strange flutter inside at the words.

"I'm afraid of them."

"If you go as my wife, you'll be safe. And do not speak. If you were my wife, you would know Kiowa words." He turned and looked at the man he had talked to. The Comanche nodded to the others, and they turned their ponies to ride south.

Surrounded by the Comanche, she felt a tremor of fear. What would happen to her if Lone Wolf died from his wounds? None of these men spoke English, and she knew little sign language or words to converse with them. Her gaze ran over two of the warriors who rode in front of her. One's barrel-chested body appeared hard with muscle, and his thick shoulders were broad. She shivered at the thought of being at their mercy. She looked at the pistol on Lone Wolf's hip and wished now she had kept it.

He turned to look at her, caught her glancing down at his pistol, and rode closer. "You're with me. Do not act afraid."

"Don't you die and leave me with them!" she snapped.

His gaze shifted ahead as if he hadn't heard her request, but in a moment he leaned close again. "You will be with the women. Do as they say. They'll be doing winter chores, making new tipi coverings, tanning hides, making pemmican. When I recover, I'll join you."

His words didn't reassure her because she didn't know what they would do to treat him. She glanced at him, her gaze going over his wide shoulders and long length and she felt better when she thought how strong he was. As he looked at her, his gaze held hers and she forgot the problems, remembering the night and being in his arms. How much had those moments meant to him?

They rode through the morning, entering a camp at noon. She worried about Lone Wolf because his wounds were bleeding even more profusely. He rode ahead of her, his back straight, and she prayed he was all right.

As they entered the camp, people came out of tipis to look at them. Her fear increased at the thought of being at the mercy of the Comanche.

He dropped back to ride beside her, glancing at her. "Cooperate with them."

She saw the lines of pain around his mouth, the crimson blood-soaked bandage. His eyes fluttered, and her heart thudded because she knew he was on the verge of losing consciousness.

He leaned forward, slumping over the horse, and she reined in. "Please!" she cried, feeling helpless and at a loss, wanting to get Lone Wolf off the horse before he collapsed and fell.

Two of the warriors rode beside him; one tugged on Lone Wolf's reins while the other jumped to the ground to ease Lone Wolf down.

A warrior took the reins from her hands, and she looked into dark brown eyes and an impassive face. She reached for the reins, wanting to dismount to see about Lone Wolf. But the moment she pulled on the reins, the warrior met her gaze and yanked the reins from her hands.

"Yee!" he said fiercely, the word drawn out in a hiss, and she drew in her breath, letting him have his way.

She glanced back over her shoulder. A short, broad-shouldered man strode to Lone Wolf and stood over him, shaking an object above him and then talking to the others. A man took Lone Wolf by the arm to drag him across the ground, and she cried out.

She glanced at the warrior who led her horse. He didn't look around; and when she turned back to look at Lone Wolf, he was no longer in sight. White Bird wriggled and Vanessa smiled at the little girl and brushed a long strand of hair from her face.

White Bird smiled in return and then leaned around her to look back toward Lone Wolf. "Guipago?" the child asked, but Vanessa could only shake her head and motion with her hand toward the direction the men had taken him.

As she looked across a clearing, she saw men clustered around Lone Wolf, who was stretched near a firepit. Smoke rose beside him, curling in the air. The short man stood over Lone Wolf, facing east. He had a gourd rattle decorated with feathers high over his head. He turned to face south, and she heard the faint sounds of his voice chanting in words she didn't understand.

She turned around when they halted. The warrior motioned to her to dismount, and a small boy appeared to take her horse. The warrior unfastened her portmanteau, canteen, and quilt, handing them to her. She felt a sense of loss as she watched the boy lead her horse away. She stood holding the portmanteau with one hand and White Bird's hand with her other.

Three women came toward her. One, who looked about Vanessa's age, was tall with a cascade of thick black hair. Her prominent cheekbones and an arched nose gave her a noble air. The woman next to her was short-legged, stocky, with black hair that had jagged ends just above her shoulders. Her face was broad, her eyes large, and she gave Vanessa a smile that revealed a missing front tooth. The third woman reminded Vanessa of a tiny bird. Looking old enough to be Vanessa's grandmother, the woman was small, slightly hunched. Silver dangled from her ears and glinted around her wrinkled neck; bracelets clinked on her arms. She wore silver in her hair, and silver glittered at the end of her braid. Less than five feet tall, she gazed up at Vanessa with bright eyes and then smiled at White Bird.

The warrior left them alone; and while Vanessa gazed at the women, the youngest one reached down to pat White Bird's head. The woman looked at Vanessa.

"Siiko," she said, thumping her chest, and Vanessa guessed that must be her name.

"Vanessa," she said, touching herself in return.

"Vanessa," two of them said.

"Tsihpoma," another woman said, and Vanessa echoed the sounds. She patted White Bird's head.

"White Bird. Tainguato."

They repeated the names, and she wondered if they knew they were speaking English when they said White Bird. The elderly woman patted herself.

"Muaahap," she said, looking down at White Bird and taking her hand. *"Kaku."*

Siiko motioned to Vanessa to follow, and they walked through the circles of tipis that all faced east. With Muaahap and White Bird trailing behind, Siiko led Vanessa to a large tipi. Outside the door, a warrior's shield hung on a tripod made of lances. The tipi of translucent hides was lined with skins. The lining was tucked beneath the bedding to keep out winter wind. The spacious tipi was far roomier than Vanessa would have guessed, with hides stretched on poles to give privacy and divide sleeping areas.

Through signs and guess, Vanessa learned that they were to share Siiko's family's tent with seven already in the family unit. Muaahap also shared the tent, but Vanessa did not understand the connection between Muaahap and Siiko.

Ten hides and buffalo robes lay on the ground for sleeping. Warming the tipi, a cozy fire smoldered in the firepit in the center of the area. Siiko and Tsihpoma unpacked the portmanteau while Muaahap brushed White Bird's hair. Then Muaahap left and came back with a doeskin dress to put on White Bird.

Siiko and Tsihpoma studied Vanessa's blue and red gingham dress, turning it in their hands and talking to each other. They looked just as long at the pink muslin that she had packed away. One of them crossed to a rawhide bag and returned with folded buckskin, extending it to Vanessa.

She shook out a deerskin dress, and the two women helped her change. Siiko braided her hair. *"Tso yaa,"* she said, holding up locks of hair.

"Tso yaa," Vanessa repeated, causing Siiko to smile.

"Tainguato," Muaahap said, and White Bird smiled at her.

Vanessa hoped they understood her pleasure when they presented her with a pair of moccasins. Different from Lone Wolf's plainer ones, these moccasins were heavily fringed and comfortable to Vanessa's feet.

That night after eating a thick stew with chunks of deer meat, Muaahap caught Vanessa's wrist and motioned her and White Bird to follow. As she crossed the camp area, Vanessa looked for Lone Wolf, but saw no sign of him.

Muaahap turned to face Vanessa, her wrinkled hands moving quickly, making the sign for sleep by holding both palms up, fingertips pointed to the right, fingertips of the left hand almost touching her right wrist, and tilting her head as if to cradle it.

"Sleep. Sleep," Vanessa said, repeating the sign, saying what she thought it was in English.

"Sleep," Muaahap repeated and changed the sign, closing her fists except for the two index fingers she pointed together to form a tent shape. She pointed toward a tipi and made the sign again.

"Tipi," Vanessa guessed, pointing toward the tipi and making the same sign back to Muaahap who grinned and nodded.

"*Kahni,*" Muaahap said. "Tipi."

"*Kahni,*" Vanessa repeated, pleased that she was beginning to learn a few words.

While Muaahap held White Bird's hand, they went back to the tipi where Muaahap sat on one of the hides and pulled White Bird down onto her lap to croon to her and rock her.

Vanessa realized they had settled for the night, wondering if others would join them in the tent. She stretched on a hide and pulled another soft buffalo robe over her. In the chill of the night, the robe and the smoldering fire soon brought warmth and she closed her eyes, listening to the raspy voice of Muaahap as she sang to White Bird.

"*He'e'yo! He'e'yo!*" Muaahap sang, and the words echoed in Vanessa's mind. Where was Lone Wolf? Was he all right?

As she watched Muaahap sing, Vanessa wondered how safe she would be if something happened to Lone Wolf. She suspected she would be kept captive by the tribe. She thought about the last two nights in Martin Gulch, the intimate moments during the night with Lone Wolf, and she missed his presence now.

In early morning she stirred and woke to see Siiko and Muaahap combing White Bird's hair. Vanessa rose, and Siiko moved to her side to hand her a brush for her hair.

After dressing and eating, Siiko led Vanessa to a gathering of women who worked on deerskin, shaping and cutting and sewing the hide into dresses.

Given thread made from sinew and a needle sharpened from bone, she watched as Siiko showed her how to lay out the pale-brown, pliable deerskin. The skirt was made in two pieces sewed together with buckskin thongs. The hem was heavily fringed with shorter fringe up the sides to the waist.

Vanessa learned to bead, sewing the geometric designs that would decorate the top of the dress and the moccasins.

White Bird watched for a time and then returned to Muaahap's side while Muaahap made a tiny buckskin dress for the child's rag doll.

During the day, when they stopped to eat or to sit and chat or to wash, Vanessa watched for a sign of Lone Wolf, but she didn't see him and she was helpless to ask about him.

By the third day in the camp, she had begun to keep track of the days, placing a small red bead beside her portmanteau in the tipi.

Two afternoons later, she paused as she placed the fifth red bead on the ground. She glanced at Muaahap, who was combing White Bird's hair and braiding it, winding a bright red ribbon through the braid. Vanessa picked up the silver-and-sapphire earbobs her father had given her on her seventeenth birthday. She also had a delicate silver bracelet with tiny dark sapphires that matched the earbobs. She carried them to Muaahap and took Muaahap's hand to place them in her hand.

"These are for you. To you from me," she said, motioning from herself to Muaahap.

Muaahap looked down at them and then at Vanessa and a wide grin covered Muaahap's face. "Ahh," she let out a long sigh of pleasure and put on the jewelry. She looked at Vanessa and smiled again, nodding.

"They are pretty on you," Vanessa said, and Muaahap bobbed her head and patted Vanessa's hand.

Muaahap moved behind Vanessa, beginning to comb her hair. Vanessa sat still while Muaahap parted it in the center and braided it, binding the braid and starting on the other half of her hair. When she finished, she painted yellow down the part and then moved in front of Vanessa. Rubbing a thin coating of grease over Vanessa's cheeks, Muaahap placed stripes of yellow paint across Vanessa's cheeks.

She sat back and smiled, pleased with her handiwork, and Vanessa smiled in return. She rummaged in the portmanteau for a mirror and when she looked at herself felt a mild shock. The days in the winter sun had bleached her hair, and her skin had darkened, making her eyes look greener than ever. Now with paint on her face and her hair in braids, she was shocked at the transformation; she looked more like the women in the tribe, her red hair and green eyes were a startling difference. She was comfortable in the soft buckskin, although she was unable to part with the cotton underdrawers that Muaahap found amusing.

When they began their work, she saw they were going to paint a robe and realized this was a special garment. The women took the gelatinous scrapings from the underside of a hide and boiled them in water. This was spread over the surface that was to be painted. She sat back to watch the painting as Siiko and three other women bent over the hide to draw designs. After an hour, Vanessa joined them in the work, deciding it was a robe for a victorious warrior or a chief.

Three days later, a north wind sprang up and Muaahap

gave her a blanket that provided warmth from the cold. During the afternoon the work stopped as men paraded through the village driving a string of horses ahead of them.

They stirred up dust, shouting and singing. Vanessa stood beside Muaahap, who was dancing and laughing, and through a series of signs, Vanessa learned that a victorious war party had returned from a raid, bringing back horses.

That night, the drums began to beat and Muaahap combed Vanessa's hair, chattering to her. Siiko and the members of her family had painted themselves; Siiko's younger sisters and her small daughter were all dressed in beaded dresses and wore black paint. Siiko's husband, Puhihwi Wehki, left the tipi early in the evening; and Vanessa saw him crossing the camp, eagle feathers in his hair, a painted robe thrown around his shoulders, red streaking his face.

Uncertain as to what was happening, yet feeling the current of excitement running through the village, she sat still as Muaahap parted her hair. Soon she had two long braids with black paint down the part and black paint streaked on her face. Her braids were fastened with bits of copper wire, and she wore gold earrings that she had brought from home. Muaahap brought her a beaded deerskin dress, and Vanessa gasped with pleasure as she took it and ran her hands over the geometric patterns of brilliant beads.

She dressed and pulled on her fringed moccasins, finally letting Muaahap take her hand along with White Bird and lead them outside. The drums beat loudly, a steady rhythm that vibrated in the air while men's voices raised in a chant.

Poles had been erected at the midpoint of the dance circle. Beneath the poles a fire roared in the center of camp and caldrons of stew bubbled and gave off tempting smells.

As Vanessa approached the fire, she saw men sitting in a ring around the blaze. She looked across the dancing flames and her breath caught as she gazed into Lone Wolf's dark eyes.

Startled, her heart seeming to miss a beat, she stared at him, for an instant forgetting the raging fire and the people. As drums thumped, she felt as if her heartbeat matched the throbbing sounds. The world narrowed to Lone Wolf, who looked fit and strong, and so handsome! He wore red streaks of paint across his cheeks and along the center part in his hair.

His chest was bare, the bandages on his shoulder were gone. He was painted with stripes across his chest, and he had eagle feathers in his dark hair. A buffalo robe was tossed casually around his waist, and he sat cross-legged near the fire, the flickering orange flames casting light across his striking features.

He gazed back impassively, yet his steady look held her and she could not turn away as she felt a bond burn fiercely between them. She wanted to run across the campsite to him. Instead she waited because she knew she had to follow the rituals but she was uncertain of the proper etiquette. And while she wondered, she continued to meet Lone Wolf's smoldering stare.

Breaking Lone Wolf's spell, Muaahap took her hand and Vanessa turned to go with her to sit in an area with the women as the men stood up to dance. Lone Wolf rose, too, chanting with the other men as they shuffled around the fire.

He had shed the buffalo robe, and she could see the scar on his shoulder. His side was still wrapped with a cloth secured by a narrow strip of leather. He wore only a breechcloth and moccasins; his body was streaked with paint. Her gaze ran the length of his body, as she noticed that the breechcloth covered so little and his muscles rippled as he moved. She looked up to meet his mocking gaze, a hungry expression in his dark eyes that caressed her raw nerves.

When the women formed a second group, Muaahap took her hand, pulling her into the dancers. She tried to follow the shuffling steps and listened to the chanting as they stomped in a circle around the fire, going in the opposite direction of the men. The drums thumped steadily; the chanting was a deep, mesmerizing sound.

Bathing her in its warmth, the fire burned brightly, orange sparks spinning upward into the night sky, filling the air with the smell of woodsmoke. Her awareness centered on Lone Wolf as he approached her on the inner circle. His dark gaze met hers as he danced toward her and she moved toward him, aching to touch him. And then he danced past and they parted, shuffling around the circle to meet again.

Lone Wolf stared at Vanessa, watching her dance. Her slender body moved gracefully in the circle of dancers. She looked like the other women with her braids and painted face and deerskin dress. And yet she was different. Her hair was the color of the fire and her eyes were a vibrant green, a look of passion in their depths that heated him more than the camp flames.

As they danced, he motioned to her to leave. She frowned as if she were uncertain, but then she stepped out of the circle of dancers and turned toward the tipis.

He waited a moment and then drifted out of the dance, moving away from the fire and light and crowd into the quiet night. He saw her waiting, and he lengthened his stride.

Vanessa watched him glide toward her, and her heart thudded violently. With the feathers in his hair and paint on his face and chest, he looked like a fierce warrior. When he walked up to her, her pulse jumped wildly. He reached out to slide his arm around her waist and draw her to him, bending down to kiss her.

Trembling with eagerness, she wound her arms around his neck and strained against him, wanting him, kissing him back fully. Her tongue entered his mouth as she kissed him, her hands running over his smooth back, and then she recalled how little he wore. Always before he had worn the heavy buckskin pants, but the breechcloth was almost nothing. She touched his thigh lightly with her fingertips and heard a groan that was muffled by their kisses.

Finally, he raised his head to look at her, framing her face with his hands. "You belong here, Vanessa. And you look beautiful."

Warmth flooded her, and she touched his jaw. "They've been good to me. And to you. You look well."

"I feel well. My side still heals, but the other injuries have mended and I have my strength again."

And now we will part. She gazed up at him, knowing that everything between them would change when he was no longer dependent on her. How long before they would leave the Comanche camp and part ways? At the thought, she drew a deep breath, her fingers trailing along his jaw.

"White Bird is coddled every minute that she's awake," Vanessa said, not even certain what she was saying to him, wanting his kisses again. "There is a small, older woman, Muaahap, who adores the child, and White Bird loves her in return. They're together constantly."

"That's good. And this is good," he said, his fingers trailing down over the soft deerskin, his fingertips drawing slowly down over her shoulder, sliding to her breast. Vanessa gasped, closing her eyes, her arms sliding around him again as he pulled her to him to kiss her.

He leaned over her and she clung to him. Lone Wolf wanted to carry her to a tipi and possess her, but he knew he held an innocent virgin. He would not take Vanessa's virginity when his heart was still with Eyes That Smile.

Vanessa could feel his thick, erect manhood pressing against her. She had an aching need for him that made her hips thrust against him while she stroked his back, her hand sliding over his firm buttocks. He groaned again, the sound muffled by their kisses as his arms tightened around her.

He released her reluctantly, gazing down at her. He had never known a woman like her and he had spent the last few idle days of his recovery speculating and thinking about Vanessa.

"I must go back and join the others," he said in a husky voice. "I'll come to you later because the medicine man said I may rejoin my family. They think White Bird is our child," he said, his voice deep. He stroked her cheek with his knuckles, the slight touch enough to make her want to step back into his arms.

Instead, Vanessa nodded and watched him stride away. His long legs were powerful, well-shaped. She turned to go to the tipi, knowing that Muaahap would care for White Bird.

Vanessa's body ached for Lone Wolf's loving. He was awakening her to new feelings, a sweet torment that needed assuaging. Restless, wanting him to join her, she moved around the empty tipi and finally stretched out on the hides to sleep. Muaahap and White Bird eventually returned, and Vanessa listened to the drums and chanting that continued while the others went to sleep.

Then Siiko and her family came back as well. Vanessa could hear the quiet whisperings of Siiko and Puhihwi Wehki, and they made her long for Lone Wolf and the moments they had spent quietly talking in the night. Thunder rumbled in the distance, and Vanessa pulled a robe high over her shoulders.

She could not sleep, but kept thinking about Lone Wolf and his handsome face as firelight played over it. Lightning flashed, giving an instant's illumination, and she saw the translucent beauty of the hides. The soft drum of rain beat against the hides.

As lightning flashed again, she glanced at the opening flap. It lifted, and Lone Wolf entered.

Nine

She sat up, her pulse jumping while he moved noiselessly across the tipi to kneel beside her. Without thinking, she placed her palm against his cheek. With the next flash of lightning, for an instant she saw his dark eyes and there was no mistaking the look of desire in them.

His arm slid around her waist, and he pulled her up hard against him. His mouth covered hers, his tongue an insistent raider as he kissed her. With pounding heart, Vanessa wrapped her arms around his neck and kissed him in return, relishing his hard body against her, his strong arms holding her.

Finally, he released her and gazed down at her. His jaw was set, and in the lightning's flash she saw the stormy look in his eyes and wondered what was in his thoughts.

"I'm glad you're well," she whispered.

"Your hands are cold," he said, taking her hand in his large warm palms.

"They're warming," she said, aware her other hand was tangled in his long hair.

"The medicine man has done his work. Now I sleep in here." With a lithe movement, he slid beneath the robe.

"You can't sleep here!" she whispered fervently, shocked as his long body settled against hers and he pulled her beside him. His body was hot, almost naked. Their legs touched, his manhood hard, pressed against her, her breasts against his chest. She felt on fire, unable to breathe, her nerves raw pinpricks of awareness.

"Shh, Vanessa. They think you're my wife. If I don't sleep here, this family will know; and then by tomorrow, the entire camp will know that we are not married. I'll only hold you."

She started to protest while her heart thudded. His fingertips pressed lightly against her lips, and even that casual touch made her tremble with a longing she didn't wish to feel.

Wanting her beside him, Lone Wolf held her close. He could sleep on his own hides away from her, and Muaahap and the others would think it was because of his wounds that he didn't sleep with his wife. But he was getting his strength back and along with it was coming a compelling urge to possess Vanessa. Added to his desire was the knowledge that very soon he would take White Bird and return to his people. If he took Vanessa captive, he would possess her. If he parted with her, she would never get to Fort McKavett on her own, for she would either fall prey to men like those in Martin Gulch or she would become a captive of the Comanche.

He would not marry a white woman because his hatred ran too deep and too strong, yet he wanted this one. He wanted her soft body beneath his. He had been too long without a woman, and this one would not fight him. Or the fight would be only seconds, a struggle he could kiss away easily.

He was still surprised how much she had adapted to the Indian way. He had seen captives fight for months before they accepted their new lives. Maybe, he mused, she didn't have as much to go back to. From what she had told him, there was little affection in her household between parent and daughters, although the sisters seemed to love each other.

He stroked her hair and tried to curb the impulse to kiss her and take her now. His body responded to her softness against him, his erection throbbing as he fought to control his needs. She was soft and warm and he had been too long without a woman.

He remembered Vanessa dancing, firelight making a halo of flames around her head when it threw its orange glow on her red hair. She fit in with his way of life. He frowned, anger stirring because he didn't want to love again. And never a white because whites had caused him so much pain and hurt.

Possess her soon and get her out of your blood. He would possess her and he would take her back to his people.

The rain drummed lightly on the tent, but beneath the buffalo robes and in Lone Wolf's arms, Vanessa felt on fire. Her hips moved against him and she tried to stop her body's intense reaction; but her breasts tingled, her body yearned for fulfillment, and she wanted his kisses.

"I can satisfy your longing if that is what you want," he whispered in her ear, his warm breath tickling her and heightening desire.

"No!" she said, her hips becoming still at once. Fighting the longing that made her as taut as his bowstring, she tried to be still, knowing he shouldn't be here, yet feeling that this seemed more right than being alone and thinking about him constantly.

As she listened to the strong, steady beat of his heart, she clung to him, realizing that he was growing more important to her with each moment they spent together. And that was the greatest danger to her heart. He was a tough warrior who would soon tell her goodbye and ride out of her life forever. She didn't want her heart and love to go with him.

Tonight, when he had entered the tipi and crossed to her, she had almost flung herself into his arms. And it seemed the most natural thing in the world to raise her lips for his kiss.

She stared into the darkness, knowing if she loved him,

gave him her heart, it would be disastrous for her when they parted, which would be soon because he looked strong and fit now. She did not want to fall in love with a fierce warrior, a man who still loved and mourned his dead wife, a man who would be relentless about his way of life.

Vanessa had to find Phoebe and Belva and go west. She had promised them she would get them, and she intended to keep her promise.

She could feel Lone Wolf's chest rise and fall in the deep, steady breathing that indicated he was asleep. Vanessa pressed tightly against him, touching his jaw. Any day now they would part, and she would have to go on alone. The thought frightened her because they had encountered many dangers along the way. How would she fare without him?

She slid her hand across his chest, wanting to hold him forever. Was she already in love with him? she wondered.

He shifted, his leg sliding over her, across her thigh, a warm, sensual weight. Vanessa felt the blush burn in her cheeks as she held him. Eventually, she fell asleep, and when she stirred in the morning and opened her eyes, Lone Wolf had gone.

A light rain came down, and at mid-morning she was alone in the tipi when Lone Wolf entered and closed the flap. While there was the steady patter of rain outside, in the cozy, warm tipi was the crackle of a fire burning low in the firepit.

Today, Lone Wolf was dressed in a Comanche buckskin fringed shirt and pants. The shirt was open at the throat in a deep V, revealing a powerful chest that was beaded with raindrops. He didn't look as if he had ever been injured. With his height, broad shoulders, and commanding presence, he dominated the large tipi.

"I wanted to talk to you," he said, his gaze sliding over her in a manner that made her more conscious of herself. "I am ready to go back to my people. We leave tomorrow."

She drew in her breath as his words cut into her like an

icy wind. From the beginning, she had known they would have to part; but now that the time had come, it hurt. She nodded. "Will you ride out of here with me? If they see you leave me—"

He waved his hand as if to stop her. "We've traveled west into New Mexico Territory. I'll ride east back into Texas before I turn north, so you can have my protection that long."

She gazed up at him. She would have to say goodbye to him and White Bird, but for a few more days, they would be together. The thought of parting stirred a devastating ache, and she was honest enough with herself to admit it wasn't solely because of the loss of White Bird.

She nodded. "Very well. Guipago," she said quietly, using his Kiowa name, which came easily to her now. "I want to discuss something else with you."

"What's that?" he asked. Moving closer, he touched her braid.

"Muaahap has no family here. I thought she belonged with Siiko and her family, but she doesn't. Muaahap lost all her family in battles and illness and accident. She has grown to love White Bird." Vanessa locked her fingers together nervously. "When we go, I have given her permission to come with us."

"Hah-nay!" he snapped, reverting to Kiowa and then shaking his head. "No. I have taken on two females already—"

Vanessa touched his mouth with her fingertips as he had done on occasion to silence her. His lower lip was soft beneath her fingers. Something flickered in the depths of his dark eyes, and he stopped talking.

"Please," Vanessa pleaded quietly, determined to convince him to take Muaahap. "Muaahap is old and may not live much longer and she loves White Bird with a strong love. White Bird has lost her parents and for now you have no woman. White Bird needs a grandmother."

"She will have grandmothers when I get back to my people."

"But what is one more small woman who has great love for your niece?" Vanessa argued, seeing the stubborn lift of his jaw. "She has a great love that White Bird needs because the loss of a mother is disastrous. I know what this loss is. And Muaahap has lost her family; you know her loss. Now she loves this little child. Don't separate them."

He looked over her head. "I do not want three females traveling with me."

"Then I will part from you," she said quietly, "and you take Muaahap."

"You won't survive out here; and if we part now, the Comanche will keep you."

"Take Muaahap with you," she urged, determined Muaahap would not be separated from White Bird.

He gazed over her head again, staring into space as if looking into the future. He inhaled, making his broad chest expand a fraction, and her gaze lowered. She was intensely aware of his closeness, aware he would soon ride out of her life. Her gaze ran across his powerful chest, down to his narrow hips. As she looked at him, warmth kindled in her, a desire that was impossible to ignore.

"Please," she whispered, thinking of Muaahap who had gazed up at her with longing in her dark, bird-like eyes and who cradled White Bird and cared for her constantly.

Lone Wolf wondered if his life would ever return to the quiet he had known before the battle with the white soldiers. Yet did he want the emptiness he had known then? He glanced at Vanessa and saw the tears brimming in her eyes before she hastily wiped them away and looked down. Her fingers were locked together, the knuckles white; and once again, he felt a jolt of shock that she would be so caring about an old Comanche woman and his tiny niece.

Vanessa Sutton was so different from all the whites he had known; the few female captives they had taken had been hysterical with fright and then docile and submissive, attitudes Vanessa seemed to know nothing about. And the other whites, the males, had been savage and brutal, taking the life of Eyes That Smile in a cruel way. He recalled the blond officer who had killed Tainso with deliberation. The captain could see he was shooting a woman who had a child in her arms, killing her during the heat of battle when he should have been fighting the men.

Lone Wolf mulled over Vanessa's request. His people wintered with the Comanche, so if he allowed Muaahap to return with him, she would be near her own people when he joined his. He tilted Vanessa's face up and saw she had fought back the tears. The tip of her nose was red and her lashes were wet, making them look thicker and darker and framing her lustrous, large green eyes.

"You're soft-hearted, Vanessa. And this is not a world for soft-hearted women. The frontier is harsh and demanding and you must change or it will break you."

She raised her chin and gazed at him with a glint of defiance in her lustrous green eyes. "The frontier needs a few soft hearts to take the hardness away. I've already told Muaahap she may travel with us. If you say no now, you'll hurt her."

"It was not your place to give permission, and she knows that."

"She is small and will make little trouble."

"Any female is trouble," he said, studying Vanessa, amused because she was more trouble than half a dozen angry young braves. "She snores at night."

"She has already said she will sleep far from you."

"She can't possibly get far enough that I won't hear her. And she clinks with every move."

"I'll tell her to remove her bracelets."

"If she does, she may come along," he said, unable to resist pleasing Vanessa, amused by her bargaining with him. Surprise widened Vanessa's eyes, and then she smiled at him, the first full joyful smile she had bestowed upon him. Her green eyes sparkled. Her white teeth were small and even except for one eyetooth that was slightly crooked. His breath caught in his chest, and he felt his heart lurch because she was even more beautiful when she smiled. It was as if the light around them had suddenly increased and become brighter.

Lone Wolf touched the corner of her mouth. "If you had smiled at me like that when you first asked, I would have consented sooner," he said in a deep, husky voice.

"Thank you!" she exclaimed, seemingly unaware of the effect her smile was having on him. She threw her arms around him and stood on tiptoe to kiss his cheek. "Oh, thank you!"

His arm banded her waist instantly, his senses bombarded by the sweet scent of rosewater on her skin, by her slender body pressed against him. He turned his head, his mouth covering hers, which was open in surprise. He bent over her, his tongue sliding into the satiny, wet inside of her mouth, for a moment all his control gone as he kissed her hungrily. He wanted her, all of her joy, her sweetness, her fire. And she was fiery and passionate, responding to him instantly, her tongue thrusting deep into his mouth, arousing him swiftly. As his hands roamed over her, he felt a desperate need for her, wanting to feel her softness and warmth envelope him.

He trembled with need, aching to take her, to get peace of mind again so he could view Vanessa in a casual manner. He needed relief so when he looked at her, his pulse would not race or his breath catch. His mouth covered hers in a long, slow kiss that was done with deliberation that made her quiver.

His hand slid down her back over her buttocks, and then he released her, pulling up the top half of the buckskin dress, his hands brushing her skin as he tugged the top over her head and tossed it away.

"Someone may come," she whispered, trembling, wanting him, a tiny voice within her clamoring a warning that she was on the brink of disaster, that she should leave him now while she could.

The air was cool on her skin, and Lone Wolf stood looking at her as if he would devour her. He reached out, filling his large dark hands with the soft weight of her breasts, his thumbs circling her taut nipples, making her moan softly.

She closed her eyes, her hands going to his chest, moving lightly over his shirt. Caution and reason were gone. She wanted to touch him, to let him stroke and kiss her. She inhaled, her gaze going over his broad chest, and she leaned forward to kiss him, pushing open his shirt and flicking her tongue over his flat nipple.

The sound in his throat was like a growl as he caught her up against him to kiss her hungrily, bending over her. He paused and straightened to yank off his buckskin shirt.

Although the air had chilled her, they stood close to the small fire and it warmed her side. Lone Wolf pushed her away, his dark hands resting on her pale hips as he stepped back to look at her, and the expression in his eyes made her want to throw herself in his arms. He made her feel loved, wanted, desired.

"You're a beautiful woman," he whispered as he leaned forward to cup her breast and kiss her, his tongue flicking over her nipple. She gasped with pleasure, her hands playing across his broad, powerful shoulders and then sliding down. With shyness, she paused; her fingers drifted lower to touch his erection beneath the breechcloth.

He gasped; his mouth covered hers as he kissed her long and hard. His hand slid along the inside of her thighs, and Vanessa felt on fire. With tantalizing strokes, his large fingers moved between her legs to the moist warmth and her feminine bud. She gasped, clinging to him. His hand moved on her, a sensuous pressure that rocked her. Her soft cries of passion were muffled by their kisses.

Lone Wolf wanted to push her down and take her, to drive into her soft body, to teach her passion. He slid his finger into her, feeling the tight maidenhead, sobering as she clung to him, her eyes squeezed tightly shut. He moved his hand against her, feeling her response, her hips undulating when who he took her to the brink.

"Vanessa," he whispered and pulled her against him again, bending over her to kiss her until she moaned, her hands winding in his hair, her hips thrusting against him.

With a sudden twist, she pulled away to look at him in a long, searching gaze. "I have to stop," she said, her protest tumbling out breathlessly, her green eyes belying her words. "If we go on, I will love you forever and saying goodbye to you and White Bird will hurt me deeply."

He stared at her, his chest heaving. He would take her captive, make her his woman, so it was merely a postponement if he didn't take her now. And his body clamored to possess her; he ached badly, needed release, and he wanted her in his bed without reservation. He wanted her to be ready, to want him as badly as he wanted her. And she would soon. She was too passionate to continue to say no, and each foray built fires of need within her because her response was greater each time.

She took a step back away from him and inhaled deeply. Her pale body was perfection—full, lush pink-tipped breasts, a tiny waist, and slender thighs. There would be another time; and she would be even more ready and more eager because she trembled now and her body was taut, moist, and as ready for love as his.

Vanessa gasped for breath, looking at his heavy-lidded eyes so filled with flaming desire. She caught up the buckskin to yank it on.

With another long, yearning assessment, he pulled on his shirt and brushed past her, untying the tent flap and leaving, dropping it back in place.

The moment he was gone, she closed her eyes and

swayed, aching for him, yet knowing this was best. She moved around the tipi without thought, her emotions seething because she wanted Lone Wolf's kisses. She wanted his *love.*

Shocked, she stared at the smoldering embers in the firepit. Was she already in love with him?

She thought of the past few minutes, the night, the dance, his smoldering looks at her, their passionate kisses—she was losing her heart to him. She would be hurt badly, yet how could she stop her heart?

She looked at the tent flap, her body aching for his touch and his loving. *Think, Vanessa, before you do something foolish that you might regret all your life!*

She closed her eyes, remembering, his hands and arms holding her. He was a hard man and yet he had relented on Muaahap. At the thought of the small woman, Vanessa let out her breath and smiled again, thankful that he had consented to take Muaahap. Vanessa raked her fingers through her hair. She would have to convince Muaahap to remove her bracelets.

That night all of the women retired to the tipi earlier than the men, who had a council and shared a pipe. The rain had stopped and Vanessa was warm beneath the buffalo robe, but her nerves were raw and sleep was impossible. She waited for Lone Wolf, knowing he would sleep with her in his arms. At the thought, her body tingled. His kisses earlier in the day had set her aflame, kindling a fire that could only be quenched one way.

Puhihwi Wehki returned with Lone Wolf, and she heard the whispers and rustlings as Puhihwi Wehki bedded down with Siiko.

And then Lone Wolf slid beneath the robes and pulled her against his already-aroused body. She turned her head. His mouth slanted over hers, and he kissed her hungrily. She clung to him, returning his kiss, her heart pounding and her pulse roaring in her ears.

Finally, she turned her head. "We must stop."

He placed his mouth close to her ear. "Someday, Vanessa, you will not tell me to stop. You'll want me and you'll tell me you want me to love you."

His warm breath tickled her ear and his words dazzled her. He was right. Against all good judgment, his caresses and kisses were melting the barriers she kept around her heart; and when they were gone, the defenses she raised for her body would end. And then, she would have to tell him her name was Sutherland, not Sutton. Lone Wolf already knew her father hated Indians, but he needed to know her real identity.

Lone Wolf slid away and left the tipi, and she suspected he needed to calm his body because he had been fully aroused, wanting her. A long time later, she stirred and his arms tightened around her. She didn't know when he had returned, but she was sleeping against him. She felt his strong arms wrapped around her and wondered if this were the last time she would sleep with him. Too soon they would say goodbye.

The next morning, as shadows slanted across the campsite and a dewy freshness still filled the air, they were ready to travel. Their friends had gathered and, impulsively, Vanessa reached out to hug Siiko and Tsihpoma.

Dressed in buckskin with pouches of medicine and supplies hanging from her belt, Muaahap mounted the sorrel and reached down when Vanessa lifted White Bird in front of her. Muaahap had removed all her bracelets except one on each arm so they would have nothing to clink against. She wore silver in her hair and ears and around her neck.

Puhihwi Wehki had given Lone Wolf two more horses, a black and a chestnut, so their things were distributed over three horses. A parfleche filled with pemmican was over each saddle, along with the two rawhide carrying cases fastened with rawhide cords that went over the cantle and pommel of each packsaddle.

Muaahap had a long, thin stick tucked beneath her belongings, and Vanessa wondered what it was for. She understood the Comanche did not eat fish, so Muaahap had no need for a fishing pole.

They mounted up and Lone Wolf led the way with Muaahap behind him and Vanessa coming last. As they left the camp, she turned to look back at her Comanche friends, glancing at the tipi where she had spent nights in Lone Wolf's arms.

She felt a twisting loss for the world she was leaving behind. It had been an idyll in her life and the thought surprised her. She had worked harder than ever before, helping prepare the meals and sew the skins into dresses, yet camp life had seemed a very special time and place. Her gaze went beyond Muaahap to Lone Wolf, who sat straight-backed on his horse, and she knew why.

Mid-morning, she saw White Bird wriggling in Muaahap's arms. Vanessa started to flick the reins, to ride alongside Muaahap and take White Bird; but before she could, Muaahap pulled the long pole free. She leaned forward and reached out to jab Lone Wolf in the back.

He swung around and scowled at Muaahap.

"Sua yurahpitu!" Muaahap said and pointed at the ground, reining in her horse and staring at him.

He shook his head and motioned to keep riding, turning his back on her.

Muaahap leaned forward to jab him again, giving him two swift stabs. His head swung around, his expression fierce.

"Sua yurahpitu!" Muaahap repeated, reining her horse and dismounting quickly.

Vanessa halted, too. She lifted down White Bird, who wriggled to get free and run around. Muaahap tucked the pole back in place. She scurried away after the child as Lone Wolf came toward Vanessa, an angry glint in his eye. He reached for the pole.

Instantly, they heard a loud shriek and Muaahap dashed back to fling herself against the side of the horse and grasp the pole.

"Kee!" she snapped, wailing loudly. White Bird began to cry and Vanessa turned away swiftly, leaving Muaahap and Lone Wolf to settle their dispute. She hurried to White Bird as Lone Wolf said something in a quiet, deep voice to Muaahap, whose shrieks became louder.

Quiet suddenly descended, and Vanessa turned around. Looking serene with a faint smile on her face, Muaahap approached. She took White Bird's hand and wiped the child's tears away, talking to her softly in Comanche.

As they walked away through the trees, Vanessa looked at Lone Wolf, who stood with his hands on his hips. His forehead was creased in a frown. His gaze shifted from Muaahap to her. He came toward her and she pursed her lips as she tried to hold back a smile.

"She is nothing but trouble. I don't care to have that old woman stab me in the back every time she wants to stop!"

"I think White Bird was growing tired."

He shook his head. "Muaahap should not cause trouble when danger comes."

"I'll tell her."

"Tell her I don't like her stick." His gaze returned from Muaahap to Vanessa. "Why does she obey you instead of me? That is not the way with Comanche or Kiowa women. She knows you're white and don't speak her language or mine."

Vanessa smiled and shrugged and saw amusement finally flare in his gaze. He tilted up her chin. "She is trouble, but she is with me because of you. You are the wind storm in my life, Vanessa Sutton," he said softly, and her heart drummed. "And when we part, you will leave her with me," he added. "I suspect unless I beat her or abandon her, she won't obey me. It's my misfortune to travel with the two most obstinate women on the earth." Lone Wolf took her arm, his fingers warm and light on her flesh. "We've stopped. We'll walk and let the horses drink."

"I want you to teach me to use a revolver. And I want to learn a few words of Kiowa. I'm becoming familiar with sign language—"

"I've noticed," he said dryly. "I've seen you with Muaahap." He looked down at her. "And so, Vanessa, as I said before, I teach you to use the pistol and the next argument, you will turn one on me," he teased, smiling at her.

The smile was warm enough to kindle a fire within her. His teeth were even and white, a sharp contrast to his dark skin, and she stared at him, enthralled. "I like your smile."

"And I like your smile," he said softly, tracing his finger across her lower lip, a soft touch that ignited a flame of longing. How easily he could make her heart race! "Go tell Muaahap that I will teach you to use my revolver."

As he led the horses to water, Vanessa hurried to tell Muaahap, feeling amused that Lone Wolf asked her to deal with the other woman as if she were the one who spoke Muaahap's language instead of him.

When she rejoined him, he stood in the sunlight, his dark hair framing his face, muscles outlined by light and shadow. He was imposing, handsome, and her heart raced as she approached him. "We'll move away from the horses and Muaahap and Tainguato."

"Will they be safe?"

"The old woman would let out such a screech that no one would want her," he said dryly.

After walking far enough away, he halted and removed his revolver from his holster. It looked big and deadly to Vanessa, yet she knew she must learn to shoot.

"Take it and don't point it at anything you don't want to shoot." He placed her fingers around the grip, and she put her index finger on the trigger as she had seen him do. He moved behind her and raised her arm, his breath fanning on her ear as he talked softly. "Now raise your arm and choose a target."

His body was warm against hers, his breath tickling her slightly, and she was more aware of him than the revolver in her hand.

"What is your target?"

"I don't know," she answered, dazed by his closeness.

"Select something, Vanessa," he said softly. His voice changed, the tone becoming deeper. "The base of the trunk of the mesquite." She held out the heavy revolver with Lone Wolf's arm steadying her. "Now look down the barrel and line it up with your target," he said quietly. "Is it in line?"

"What line?" she asked and looked over her shoulder at him. His eyes narrowed as they stared at each other. Her pulse leaped and all thought of shooting vanished.

"Are your thoughts on your target?"

"It would be better if you didn't stand so close," she answered, knowing her voice was breathless. He towered only inches from her.

"Vanessa," he said, frowning, and then he shifted, taking the pistol from her hand and sliding his arm around her waist to lean forward to kiss her.

She clung to him, returning his kiss, knowing it forged a stronger bond between them, yet wanting his arms around her. Then he released her and looked down at her, desire clear in his expression. He stepped back and handed her the pistol.

"We will concentrate on your shooting. When you look down the barrel and it is lined up with your target, squeeze your finger against the trigger," he said quietly.

Her gaze drifted down to his mouth. With an effort she turned away from him and tried to concentrate and follow his instructions.

She pulled the trigger, and the gun fired. Her hand flew up from the kick, and leaves fluttered off a branch of the mesquite yards to the right and considerably higher than the base of the trunk.

"Look down the barrel," he repeated. "See how it should line up."

"I think I would have less distractions if you would move farther away from me," she stated, blushing and staring ahead.

He stepped away. Concentrating, she aimed again, and this time her shot was into the ground a half-yard away. She turned to find Lone Wolf watching her. He stood with his arms akimbo, his gaze steady. Crossing to her, he took the pistol from her hands and showed her again how to fire and how to reload. He stepped away as she began again.

Lone Wolf watched as a breeze blew the gingham skirt around her long legs and caught strands of her red hair. He thought about her request for him to move away from her. The attraction was strong and he wanted to possess her. He had waited long enough.

His body reacted to his thoughts and he shifted until he could look across the rolling land. Within days, he would have to turn north.

He clamped his jaw closed, torn between warring desires. He wanted to protect her, but he also wanted to take her back to camp with him and keep her.

She had fit into the Comanche way as easily as if she had been born to it. Her interests were in the people around her, not possessions, and he suspected she cared nothing about a fine house or beautiful, expensive furniture. And if he got her with child, he knew she would love the baby. He studied Vanessa's slender body that was ripe for loving.

Disturbed by the feelings she stirred in him, Lone Wolf raked his fingers through his hair. He would never have allowed Muaahap to travel with him if it hadn't been for Vanessa. The old crone was trouble. He thought about the jab in the back this morning and Muaahap's demanding they stop. He looked at Vanessa. She had more control over

Muaahap than he did. Vanessa turned around to face him and smiled. "I hit my target!"

"Fine. Now hit it again."

She shook her head. "My wrist hurts, and my hand is shaking. This weapon is heavy."

He walked over to her to take the revolver and reload it. Then he tossed a rock into the air and fired, striking and shattering it. He lowered the revolver and moved closer to her. "We go back now, and I'll show you how to clean the weapon because you must care for one if you have it."

"Did you learn to shoot when you were young?"

"Not with a revolver. I learned with a bow and arrow and then a rifle. I learned to fire this with accuracy when I was an army scout. I don't want to forget because we must fight whites with guns, not bows and arrows," he said, thinking about the recent battle and the cannon the soldiers had used with such a catastrophic effect on his people.

Once they returned to White Bird and Muaahap they ate, and then Lone Wolf stood up. "Now we go."

In minutes they were on the trail again. As they traveled, they angled to the southeast. Vanessa's pulse leaped and she wondered if Lone Wolf had had a change of heart and would accompany her closer to McKavett. The land began to roll; the mesquite grew thicker, and weeds and cactus covered more ground.

In early afternoon, when White Bird began to wriggle, Muaahap pulled up the long stick and once again jabbed Lone Wolf in the back.

Ten

Lone Wolf jerked his head around, his gaze fierce. Muaahap motioned with her fist to stop as she reined her horse.

She lowered White Bird to the ground then dismounted spryly, rushing to join the child. Then both of them hurried away from Lone Wolf.

He scowled as he watched them go, and then he walked over to Vanessa as she dismounted and took down a canteen from the saddle.

"Will you tell that woman to stop jabbing me with her stick! I'd like to break the damned stick into pieces, but she might set up such a howl we would never get her quiet."

"Why am I the one to tell her? You two speak the same language," Vanessa said with great innocence, and his head swung around.

"You're enjoying yourself, aren't you?"

She placed her finger alongside her nose and tried to gaze at him solemnly. "It's interesting to travel with her."

"Vanessa, she's here solely because of you. Do something about her."

"Yes, sir," she answered, grinning.

He shook his head, looking at Muaahap, who was picking acorns with Tainguato.

Vanessa crossed to the pair, and he watched as she and Muaahap struggled to communicate, both using signs and a few words—Vanessa's in English and halting Comanche, Muaahap in Comanche. He understood them and wished he had never said Muaahap could travel with them. She had no intention of getting rid of her long stick.

Vanessa came striding back. "She says her stick is the safest way to get you to stop traveling because it makes no noise."

"That woman is trouble."

"Has she hurt you with her stick?"

His gaze focused on Vanessa and he moved closer, his long arm stretching out to block her. "No, she has not hurt me! She tries my patience!"

"It's time you had women in your life again."

"That is not the woman I want when I decide to share my life again. You're amused by this. I ought to teach you a lesson, Vanessa, about having someone bully you."

She laughed and tried to duck under his arm, but he caught her and turned her to face him. "You're the trouble here, woman," he said in a husky voice. "You're the one who causes me worries and who robs me of sleep."

"I rob you of sleep?" she asked in surprise.

"Yes," he said, his amusement vanishing as his gaze lowered to her mouth. He bent his head to kiss her, a long, lingering kiss that he didn't want to end. All too soon, he raised his head, wanting her, knowing he should move away from her now.

Her eyes were heavy-lidded, her breathing as ragged as his as she looked up at him and then she pushed away, hurrying around the horse and putting distance between them. He gazed after her, aware that Vanessa was changing his life, making him feel alive again.

He followed her as she knelt to splash water from the creek on her face. He opened a canteen to take a long drink and then offered it to her.

She accepted it, tilting it to drink.

"Who were the men your father wanted you to marry and why weren't they interested?"

"There was Major Dempsey. He was in his fifties and had gout and thought I was insubordinate."

"And how many times were you with this Major Dempsey for him to get to know you, Vanessa?"

"We had two dinners together with friends of his. He was quite happy to send me home."

"Well, I agree with Major Dempsey. You are definitely insubordinate. Who else?"

She smiled at him. "Captain Cantillion. He found me hopelessly shy—"

"Shy?" Lone Wolf asked, arching his brows.

"I was shy with him. The man seemed to have a dozen hands, all trying to grasp me. With Colonel Van Thoff, I was too talkative."

Lone Wolf hung the canteen on his belt and turned to her. He touched her hair, turning a curl in his fingers as he studied her features. "Insubordinate, too shy, too talkative. Those are contrary traits." He tilted up her chin. "I suspect contrary fits, doesn't it? And I'm glad you were contrary or you wouldn't be out here now and I never would have known you."

"And I wouldn't have known you," she replied solemnly. "I know things now that I didn't then."

"What things?"

"That I want my own family. I always thought I did; but now that I've been with White Bird, I'm certain that I want children and a family."

"Even if you have to marry a Colonel Van Thoff or a Captain Cantillion or a Major Dempsey?"

"No, I don't want to marry a man I don't love. But the men whom I found interesting were younger and not as high-ranking and, unfortunately, not as wealthy, so Papa had no interest in them."

"Nor do I, Vanessa," Lone Wolf said dryly. "I don't care to hear about the suitors you liked," he said, pulling off a twig from a cottonwood and dragging the leaves lightly across her throat, tickling her slightly. He trailed them along the neckline of the buckskin dress, and the faint brush tickled as he moved it to her ear. She smiled and shook her head.

"How old were you when you married?" she asked him.

"I was twenty-two and had returned from being an army scout. Eyes That Smile was eighteen when we wed. She lost one child at birth and then we never had another."

"I'm sorry," Vanessa said quietly.

He looked down at her. "You won't be able to get your sisters away from McKavett."

"I have to try. I would never feel right if I didn't go back and try to rescue Phoebe and Belva."

"And when your father takes you captive, will he see that you enter a convent?"

"Yes. Only this time, I'm sure he'll accompany me there himself. Papa always insists that if you want something done right, you have to do it yourself."

"That is not the Kiowa way. We work together on many things— hunting, fighting, daily life." He touched her cheek with the cottonwood. "You won't be happy in a convent. And the convent will never be the same again," he added with amusement.

"I'll get Phoebe and Belva, and we'll run away. We'll go to El Paso and catch the stage for California where I will meet a man and marry. He'll love me and I'll love him and we will have babies—"

Lone Wolf caught her up against him hard, holding her tightly, his dark eyes piercing as he gazed down at her. Her heart lurched, all thought vanishing as he lowered his head and his mouth covered hers. His tongue entered her mouth forcefully, demanding her response. Her heart drummed as he held her and kissed her.

Her hands rested on the smooth, hard muscles of his upper arms and her pulse raced while she returned his kiss. As abruptly as he had taken her into his arms, he released her, looking down at her. "We should go back," he said gruffly and turned to walk away from her.

Puzzled by his mercurial change of mood, she followed, wondering what had brought about the change. Her remarks about loving a man and a man loving her couldn't have triggered such a reaction. Why would he care? Her eyes narrowed and she studied him. They were growing closer with each day; and when it came time to say goodbye, would it hurt him to part? *Was he beginning to care?*

They mounted their horses, moving into a single-file line, and Vanessa's lips tingled as she watched Lone Wolf and knew they both were risking their hearts by the continual kisses and touches and shared moments.

Within an hour she glimpsed a town on the horizon, and her pulse jumped with eagerness. She hurried past Muaahap to catch up to Lone Wolf and ride beside him.

"There's a town. Tonight can we stay in a hotel? I have money and I'd like a bed. It would be good for you until you've completely recovered."

"It's far riskier. Remember the last town."

She looked at the rooftops in the distance, the number of trees. "This is different. It's larger and it looks like a regular town. We can get some supplies."

He stared ahead and finally nodded. "The hotel may not take us because we're Indian."

"They'll take my gold, and then they'll take us in. Gold has become scarce because of the war."

She rode back to try to explain to Muaahap. Finally, Lone Wolf glanced back to say something to Muaahap in Comanche and she nodded.

Vanessa pulled up her reticule and handed it to him. He took it, his fingers brushing hers. The silk purse looked ridiculous in his big hands as he opened it and jiggled it. He reached inside and pulled out gold pieces that glittered in the sunshine. He frowned and looked at her. "You're a wealthy woman with all this."

"The rest of the money is packed in my portmanteau."

"If we take rooms, Muaahap will expect you to stay in a room with me because she thinks you're my wife."

Blushing, Vanessa thought of the nights they had already spent in the same bed. "We've done that before without succumbing to urges, so yes, I'll share the room with you."

"So we'll get a room in the hotel," he said, knowing Muaahap would accept wherever Vanessa chose to sleep. But he wanted her in his bed because each time he kissed her, her response was swifter and more intense than the time before.

It was over an hour later when they passed a neatly painted sign reading Jenksboro. They entered the town, and Vanessa was reassured by the rows of houses down the dusty streets leading off the main artery. The town stretched a distance of almost eight blocks of busy shops, patronized by women in buggies and men on horseback and on foot. A two-story wooden building had a sign in front with bright red letters that proclaimed it the Jenksboro Hotel, and they halted at its hitching rail. They walked inside, and Lone Wolf rang a silver bell. Vanessa glanced around the lobby while they waited. It was plain, but clean, with potted palms, a polished plank floor, and simple wooden furniture.

A door closed and a pale, thin man straightened rimless spectacles and approached them. He smiled at her; but when he looked at Lone Wolf, his smile was replaced by a frown.

"I want two rooms," Lone Wolf said quietly to the clerk, who again adjusted his spectacles as Lone Wolf placed several greenbacks on the counter.

"I'm sorry we don't have any vacancies."

"I want two rooms for my family," Lone Wolf said as if he hadn't heard the man. He produced a twenty-dollar gold piece and placed it beside the greenbacks. "We'll be gone early."

The clerk looked at the gold, glanced at Vanessa, looked at the gold and greenbacks again, and nodded, slipping the gold into his pocket. "Very well. I'll show you to your rooms."

"Thank you," Lone Wolf said politely. "And bring two tubs for baths."

The man nodded without looking around at Lone Wolf. They followed the clerk, who took down two keys from hooks on the wall and came around the counter. "If you'll come with me."

They motioned to Muaahap and White Bird to follow, then waited while the clerk opened the door to a room.

"Here's one room, and the other is next door." The clerk opened the adjoining door and motioned to Muaahap to enter. She seemed dazzled by the room as she walked in and tentatively touched a chair.

Soon the tubs were brought to the rooms and filled with water. Vanessa joined Muaahap and helped her bathe White Bird and wash her hair, and then Vanessa bathed. She changed from the buckskin to the pink muslin, wearing it for the first time in her travels and wondering if Lone Wolf would prefer she continue to wear the buckskins. She parted her hair in the center and combed it, fastening it high on the sides of her head to let it cascade freely in back. She brushed White Bird's hair and fastened it in the same manner, placing tiny red silk bows on both sides of her face. Then she dressed White Bird in the red gingham dress she had made in Martin Gulch.

Muaahap clapped her hands and grinned. *"Nananisuyake!"*

Her pleasure was obvious, and Vanessa motioned toward the door to Lone Wolf's room. "I'll be back," she said, waving her hands. She knocked on his door and when he swung it open, she entered.

He closed the door and turned to look at her, his gaze drifting over her in a manner she had not often seen.

She saw the pleasure light his eyes as his gaze raised to meet hers. He was bare-chested, his hair wet from bathing.

"You look beautiful, Vanessa," he said quietly, moving toward her and touching her hair.

Her heart raced and she could smell his soapy scent. "I didn't know if you would prefer the buckskin; but since we're in town, I thought I should wear this."

"You look beautiful," he repeated. He trailed his fingers along her throat, letting them drift down over the scooped neck of the pink muslin. His fingertips caused a feathery, fiery trail across her skin as he ran his hand lightly across the curves of her breasts. "This dress wouldn't be practical in our lives."

"They may not allow us to eat in the hotel dining room—" she said, conscious of his bare chest, her gaze drifting down and focusing on his muscles.

He shook his head. "They will allow you to do so if you go down there without any of us."

"I'll go get us food, and we can eat here," she said, trying to concentrate as his fingers moved from her throat, to trace the soft rise of her breasts. She inhaled deeply and tried to think what else she had intended to tell him. "You'll have to take my money and purchase a revolver for me. I won't know what I'm buying."

He nodded. "I'll get a pistol."

"I want another horse. Will you get that also? I'll need one for my belongings when I leave you."

He nodded.

"I want to go to the general store and get some supplies and material for another dress. I'll wait until later to get the food because it's early to eat." As she talked and tried to recall her list, he leaned closer.

His hand drifted over her nape, and her pulse drummed from the slight touch. Her nerves were taut, his constant touches building a fire in her that threatened to rage out of control. The slightest contact increased her yearning for him.

He gazed at her with desire in his eyes and a solemn,

intense expression, and she wondered if she should insist on staying the night with Muaahap. As swiftly as the thought came, she knew she wouldn't. She wanted Lone Wolf's kisses and loving, for she knew that within hours, he would tell her goodbye and she would part from him forever.

"I'm leaving for the store," she said in a breathless voice as she moved past him to the other room, excited because she would be with him tonight.

By sign she conveyed to Muaahap that they were going shopping. Muaahap had begun to pick up a few words of English just as Vanessa had learned a smattering of Comanche and Kiowa.

They stepped into sunshine beneath a cloudless blue sky with only a slight breeze. The women on the street stared. A few nodded and smiled; but the others gazed at Muaahap and White Bird and frowned, turning away.

In the general store, they meandered about and Vanessa bought a bracelet and earbobs and a red ribbon for Muaahap. She purchased a small rag doll for White Bird, some ribbons for her hair, and a locket. She also selected material for a dress, and supplies for their journey.

At the hotel, Muaahap helped carry things to their room and then she motioned to Vanessa that she was taking White Bird out to walk.

Vanessa waved them on and waited, guessing from the late afternoon hour that Lone Wolf would return shortly. She went to his room, moving around and wondering about him because none of his possessions were in sight. The room held a four-poster mahogany bed, a washstand, a rocking chair, a high chest of drawers, and an oval rag rug on the clean floor. A scratched mahogany armoire stood along one wall. She thought about her things, packed in the portmanteau and reticule; the satchel with White Bird's clothes, ribbons, and toys, and Muaahap's bundle. Yet Lone Wolf traveled only with what he wore on his person.

She moved to the window to look below, trying to spot his dark hair, knowing if he would cut it or hide it beneath a hat, it might save him some abuse from the whites.

She wondered if her father had given up the search for her now, and she prayed he never learned she had traveled with Lone Wolf.

She felt a burning excitement to be here with him tonight and longed for him to return without encountering any hostile whites or soldiers.

Two blocks away, Lone Wolf leaned against the counter and looked at the revolvers. He pointed to one. The clerk handed it to him. "You're Injun, ain't you?"

"Yes," he said, taking the revolver and holding it in his hand, sighting down the barrel. "I'm an army scout and I've been back to see my people. Now I return to Fort McKavett."

The man nodded. "I thought you'd be in a uniform. Didn't know the U.S. Army would allow buckskins."

"They allow buckskins for scouts because they need the scouts. Let me see the one with the polished grip," he said, replacing the revolver on the counter.

The man got out another revolver and put away the Smith & Wesson.

Lone Wolf held it, clicking the trigger on the empty chambers. "I'll take this one. Do you have a derringer?"

"Yes. Right here."

He needed very little time to purchase a revolver for himself and a derringer for Vanessa. "Thank you," Lone Wolf said as he accepted the guns.

"You're welcome." The man squinted at him. "Mister, some people in town don't like Injuns, army scout or not. I'd stay out of the barber shop, away from the tinsmith, and off the street in general. You'll get along better."

"Thanks," Lone Wolf said, placing the revolver and the derringer in his waistband. He walked to the livery stable and within the hour had purchased a black gelding and made arrangements for the stable to keep it along with their other horses until the next day.

As he headed back down the street, he noticed a flyer nailed to a post. It fluttered in the breeze and at first his gaze slid past it. But he paused to read it and then he frowned. He moved closer to stare at a picture of a smiling Vanessa. It was a good picture and there was no mistaking her face or the bold black letters across the top that sent a chill down his spine as he read: *$1,000 REWARD.*

A thousand-dollar reward. He looked at buildings and posts along the street and spotted three more flyers. She could be under arrest now!

He yanked the flyer off the post, his gaze raking over it as he started toward the hotel, and then he stopped in his tracks, his heart missing a beat. He stood in the dusty street in the warm afternoon sun and stared at the flyer, rage rising within him, his pulse roaring in his ears as he read: *$1,000 REWARD. Vanessa Mae Sutherland, daughter of Colonel Abbot Sutherland . . .*

Lone Wolf stopped reading, his head jerking up as he looked at the hotel. Vanessa Sutton was actually Vanessa Sutherland, and her father was the man who had condoned Eyes That Smile's death, the man who paid ten dollars for each Indian killed, a man Lone Wolf despised and hated.

Enraged, he held the flyer and started toward the hotel.

Eleven

Vanessa spotted Lone Wolf striding toward the hotel. His legs covered the distance swiftly, and her heart raced as she wished he would look up, but he didn't. She turned from the window and crossed the room to wait for him. The key grated and the door swung open, slamming against the wall.

Shocked, she stared at him.

He stepped inside, then closed and locked the door, and her heart lurched because the moment she saw his fierce expression, she knew something was dreadfully wrong.

His dark eyes were filled with rage as he crossed the room. "You lied to me, Vanessa Sutherland," he said in a quiet voice that sent a chill running down her spine. "You're the daughter of Abbot Sutherland, the man who condoned what his men did to my wife, the man who has offered ten dollars to his men for any dead Indian. Ten dollars," he said in an even quieter, more deadly voice.

Terrified, Vanessa raised her chin in spite of her fear and faced him. "I said Vanessa Sutton because I knew how you would feel if you learned I was the daughter of Abbot Sutherland. You knew who he was and what he had done."

"You're his daughter and you're like all whites—deceitful, telling untruths because it will meet your needs. When I think—" He strode forward and looked down at her, and she felt his anger washing over her in waves. Her heart pounded wildly because he looked as if he could close his fingers around her throat and squeeze the breath from her.

"They took my wife and raped her and stabbed her, and your father paid them ten dollars for it!"

"I didn't have anything to do with it."

"How do I know you're not lying again?" Yanking his shirt over his head, he flung it away. Her eyes widened, and he saw the momentary flash of fear.

He stepped toward her, expecting her to try to run. Instead she faced him as he reached out to grab her pink muslin and rip it down the front.

"I will have you, Vanessa Sutherland." He ground out the words as he ripped away her chemise. "I'll take you as they took her!"

She faced him and caught his hands, her fingers closing on his thick, strong wrists. "You'll not do this in anger!" she said, trying to wrench away from him. He held her and wound his fingers in her hair, yanking her face up toward his.

He shook with rage, wanting to throw her down on the floor and possess her and take his revenge. Stunned that she had lied to him, he felt betrayed by her deceit. She jerked her knee up and he twisted to avoid her, taking the blow on his thigh as he pushed her back against the wall. He bent his head to kiss her, his mouth hard on hers, his tongue going deep while he tore away her underdrawers.

Suddenly, she lunged against him, breaking her arms free of his grasp and placing her hands on both sides of his face. She looked at him, and the expression in her green eyes made him pause.

"I swear to you, I have told you the truth in all else."

"You lied to me, Vanessa, as whites have lied again and again." He was breathing hard, his anger blinding him.

"Only in that one thing," she answered. She stood on tiptoe and placed her mouth on his.

He made a sound like a growl in his throat, his arm banding her waist as he bent over her and kissed her hard.

She spun away to look at him. "I did not lie in anything else," she whispered. "And my father does not love me."

Lone Wolf exhaled, shaking from his anger, feeling her hands touching his chest.

He tightened his arm around her, pulling her to him to kiss her, wanting to punish her, wanting to love her. He hurt from the deceit, yet he knew Vanessa well enough to believe her. He could understand why she had told him Sutton.

He groaned, his hands coming up to roam over her body, cupping her pale, soft breasts, and a tremor ran through him. He wanted revenge for her lies; he wanted *her*. He wanted to make her cry out and to feel her warmth envelop him.

"The first time between us will not be out of anger!" she snapped, wresting her face from his and struggling with him. "I will always carry the first time in my heart."

Her words registered through his rage, and he looked at her. Her green eyes gazed back, enflamed with anger and longing, but no fear. Here was a woman who could match his temperament and his needs. He framed her face with one hand under her jaw. He wanted to hear her cries of passion not pain.

"If I ever find again that you have lied to me—"

Her lashes fluttered and she gave him an open, fearless look. And he remembered that once as a boy, when he had been running in the wilds, he had crossed paths with a mountain lion. For one startled moment they had faced each other only a few yards apart and he had pulled his arrow to kill the cat. It had confronted him, tail switching, and then it had turned and walked away and he had lowered his arrow because the animal had been fearless. Vanessa had that same steadfast stare as she met his gaze.

"I haven't lied to you about anything else," she whispered.

His hand slid down her body over her curves as his arm

tightened around her waist and he drew her closer, bending his head to kiss her. Her head tilted back and she clung to him, her body pressing his, her curves tantalizing to his touch.

With a groan he covered her mouth with his, and she yielded to him. He held her tightly. As his hand slid along her smooth back and down over the curve of her bottom, his anger changed to a throbbing need. He had waited long enough, wanted her for so long now.

His hands cupped her breasts and his thumbs drew circles around her taut nipples. Her breasts swelled against his palm, and the stiffness left her body as her tongue thrust against his.

His anger gone, knowing she was blameless, he kissed her. His pulse jumped and he ached for her. Bending his head, he took her breast in his mouth.

Vanessa felt the wet heat of his mouth on her nipple and she gasped as pleasure shot through her. His hand moved over her belly, down between her legs to touch her in an exquisite friction.

Lone Wolf found the bud and stroked her. She gasped with pleasure, thrusting her hips against his hand, her body tightening. He increased the pressure and his strokes until she was moving against him in a wild rhythm.

Vanessa held him as he stroked her, his hand on her feminine warmth, sensations rocking her. She felt a need that tore at her. Her eyes were closed, and he leaned forward to kiss her while she clung to him. His hand drove her to the brink of release until her passion burst inside her, washing over her in waves as she rocked against him.

Trailing kisses from her mouth to her breast, he shed his buckskins, his shaft thick and erect, throbbing with readiness.

He placed his large hands on her hips. Her green eyes were huge, filled with passion and curiosity as she reached out slowly to touch him, her fingers lightly grasping his erection.

Closing his eyes, he drew his breath, feeling as if he would burst in her hand. He looked at the body that he had seen that first evening in the river when her lush beauty had been etched in his memory.

"Vanessa." He pulled her down on the floor, moving between her legs. Vanessa gazed up at him, her heart pounding wildly. He was virile, his broad shoulders tapering to his narrow waist, his manhood so large she felt it would be impossible to mate.

Her breath caught as she looked at him because he was magnificent, his wild mane of black hair touching his shoulders. She stared up at him, knowing every inch of her wanted to belong to him. She loved him and she wanted him to love her, if only this once.

Lone Wolf gazed down into her fiery green eyes and knew she was caught in the throes of passion. His pulse drummed as he lowered himself to enter her, his shaft sliding into her softness. Her maidenhead was tight, and he would hurt her. Dimly he wondered if she would think he was doing it deliberately.

He eased into her and felt her hips rise to take him. She gasped and closed her eyes, her slender arms winding around his neck to pull him closer.

He moved slowly, the effort costing him as sweat beaded his back and shoulders and forehead. He braced himself on her, sliding his shaft out of her. She gasped and her hips arched beneath him and he met her, his member entering into her again to slide slowly against the tightness. And as he moved, she began to thrust more quickly. Then he covered her mouth with his when he thrust deeply, feeling the tight membrane yield and surround him.

He made a sound deep in his throat as he kissed away her cry, feeling her body tighten against the pain and then relax slightly, moving with him.

"Put your legs around me," he whispered, turning his head as he moved. Her long legs wrapped around him and she slid her hands along his back and arched beneath him. He knew when the pain changed and she began to feel the ecstasy.

Vanessa clung to his strong body, waves of pain assaulting her. She felt as if he had torn her open, but then it changed. She moved against him and the pain diminished more, transforming to a need that was greater than she had ever known. She gasped, raising her hips, wanting more of him, feeling an urgency that tore at her.

He thrust slowly again, so carefully, and his deliberation made her wild with need. Her hips moved beneath him and she slid her hands down his smooth back and over his firm buttocks, pulling on him, wanting him inside her.

Lone Wolf tried to hold back, fighting the urgency that was building in him. He wanted her with a hunger that dismayed him. He had to move, to feel the tightness of her around the length of his shaft. He kissed her, muffling her cries, her hips moving with his as she clung to him. Her arms tightened, and she arched against him.

Vanessa felt as if she were drowning in the torrent of sensations that assailed her, yet the need seemed to grow. Pain ripped through her, and her cry was stopped by his mouth and tongue; but then the pain faded, replaced by a driving need.

Her pulse drowned out all else, and ecstasy rippled through her. She moved with him and clung to his hard body and, for this moment in time, reveled that she had all of him.

Lights burst behind her closed eyelids. The roaring in her ears shut out Lone Wolf's cries, and her body responded to him in ways she had never known possible.

"Please—" she gasped, arching against him, her hips moving with his; and then she felt the bursting release that brought rapture.

"Vanessa!" He cried out, and this time she heard his

words. His mouth covered hers, and he kissed her passionately while they slowed and, at last, quieted.

She held him, still joined with him, their hearts beating together. She opened her eyes, reality returning. She had given him her virginity, given him her heart.

And he had not taken her in anger or revenge. She had no regrets, suspecting that whatever lay ahead in her life, she would always love Lone Wolf.

He stroked her hair and raised on his elbows to look down at her, tracing her lips with his finger. And he knew in that moment that he would never tell her goodbye and let her go south alone to Fort McKavett. He would take her with him back to his people. He was not going to give her up. She would fight him, but her sister would survive. Only an unwanted marriage threatened the sister, not death. Lone Wolf would keep Vanessa for himself. Her wide green eyes studied him solemnly, and he wondered what she was thinking. Regrets? Anger? Knowing Vanessa, she had given herself freely and was neither angry nor regretful, but he could only guess.

"Next time you will like it better," he said softly, kissing the corner of her mouth, thinking nothing in the world could be as soft as her lips. He settled her in the crook of his shoulder and toyed with her hair. "Don't leave me yet. Stay here, Vanessa."

"I didn't want you to know that Abbot Sutherland was my father," she said, the words coming out in a rush, her voice low and urgent. "I didn't know what his men had done to your wife, but I knew that my father offered a ten dollar bonus for any dead Indian because the Indians were interfering with his building a railroad. We had a fight about it, and he was so angry. He slapped me—he has only done that twice in my life—and he said I didn't know anything about Indians or railroads and I was not to talk to him about his business. He locked me in my room."

"Your father is cruel. How long were you locked in your room?"

"Only that night. I climbed out a window and stayed with a friend, then went back before Papa was up in the morning."

Lone Wolf rolled on his side and propped his head on his hand and regarded her as she ran her fingers across his chest, touching the red scar on his shoulder. "You've finally healed; I was so frightened those first nights until we found a doctor."

Solemnly he reached for her hand. "Vanessa," he said, "I understand why you told me your name was Sutton. And I've lost my anger toward you, but I haven't lost it toward your father. Some day our paths may cross."

"I realize that. His feelings won't change either," she admitted, growing equally solemn as she faced again the great differences in their worlds.

She ran her fingers down his arm over the bulge of firm muscle. "I should bathe and dress. Muaahap will soon return with White Bird."

He picked her up easily. He was warm, a solid bulk against her, his strong arms holding her. He crossed to the tin tub that still held water to the brim.

"What are you doing—"

Ignoring her question, he sank down in the water. Vanessa yelped, struggling in his arms. Suddenly, they looked at each other and she laughed.

Lone Wolf felt his heart twist. Her laughter was like sunshine, and the last shreds of anger burned away. He grinned at her, shifting and settling her over him, their warm bodies slippery with water.

"This is the way you should be, Vanessa. Laughter lights your eyes."

"This tub is too small," she teased, but her smile was gone and her hands played across his chest, her fingers touching his firm muscles. In minutes he was aroused and he shifted and moved her, pulling her down on him, relishing her gasp of pleasure.

Later, she gathered her torn clothing. He stopped her, his large hand closing on the pink muslin. "I don't carry money to have more made for you."

"I have two other dresses, and this wasn't a good one to travel in. Besides, I can repair it."

"You looked beautiful in it, Vanessa," he said. Then he reached behind him and picked up the flyer he had tossed aside. He held it out to her. Holding the pink muslin in front of her, she took the flyer from his hand and looked at it.

"A thousand dollar reward is enough to make many men search for you and make anyone turn you in the moment he's found you."

"I've been in several stores this afternoon and nothing happened."

"That doesn't mean it won't. We must leave town before daylight. If we can go while it's dark, we'll be safer."

"I have to go downstairs to order our dinner."

"I'll get dinner sent up for us," he said firmly, and she nodded.

"I should go dress."

He caught her wrist and held her, pushing away the pink muslin to caress her. Tilting up her chin, he leaned down and brushed her lips with his. Her heart beat wildly, and she returned his kisses, amazed by the swift rush of desire she felt.

She turned away reluctantly, going to the other room and closing the door. She dressed in the patched gingham and brushed her hair, tying it behind her head with a ribbon, staring at her image and seeing Lone Wolf's dark eyes, his virile naked body poised above her.

"I love him," she whispered, knowing she had given him more than her body. She had given her heart as well. And now when she parted with him, it would hurt more than ever.

She closed her eyes, refusing to think yet about parting, anticipating tonight when she would again be with him.

Hours later, as they ate dinner together in Lone Wolf's room, over plates heaping with golden roasted duck, fluffy potatoes covered with cream gravy, and hot cornbread, Lone Wolf held out the flyer to Muaahap, conveying to her in sign and Comanche that men would be watching for Vanessa and that they should ride out of town before daylight.

Muaahap took the flyer from his hand to study it, and then she reached over to squeeze Vanessa's hand. She gestured, and Vanessa understood that she had Muaahap's sympathy.

"I think you have a grandmother as well as a daughter," Lone Wolf remarked.

"I never really knew either of my grandmothers very well. My mother's mother died young, and my father's mother was back east. When we visited her a few times, she seemed cold and I didn't like her."

"I find it difficult to imagine you disliking anyone, Vanessa," he said, his hand brushing her shoulder. She smiled at him and he smiled in return and suddenly she felt as if they were alone. She remembered their lovemaking and blushed beneath the steady gaze of his dark eyes.

Tearing away from his scrutiny, she glanced at the flyer again. "My hair is up on my head in the picture, so maybe people didn't recognize me today." She studied her image. "Do you think we should go now and not sleep here?"

"No. If someone had recognized you today, we would know it by now unless they have sent for your father. If that's the case, you'll still be safe tonight. And you were with Muaahap and Tainguato. No one is looking for a woman with a family. Still, it's a good likeness." He folded the flyer and tossed it on a chest of drawers.

Soon after they ate, Muaahap took White Bird to their room, closing the door behind them. Suddenly shy, Vanessa watched Lone Wolf as he crossed the room to wrap his arms around her.

"I wanted you here tonight. We won't be alone on the trail, so this may be the last time we'll be together," he said in a husky voice, brushing her lips with his. His mouth settled over hers, and then he lifted her and carried her to bed. He took his time, stroking her, his large hands caressing her slender legs, moving up over her thighs. He took the hem of the dress in his fingers, eased the garment over her head and tossed it to the floor. He sat up beside her to remove his shirt.

Caressing his broad chest, she wanted his love, knowing she had given her heart to him as completely as she had her body. Too aware that they would part soon and she would never see him again, she wound her arms around his neck.

"This time will be better, Vanessa," he said quietly, looking at her as his hands cupped her breasts. He leaned down to kiss one. His tongue was moist and warm on her flesh, and she arched against him. Pleasure radiated from his touch and kisses.

Bending over her, his dark hair falling forward, he trailed kisses across her stomach down to her thighs. His breath was hot and erotic on her flesh.

She stroked his shoulders, moaning with pleasure as he pushed her legs apart, his tongue seeking her soft folds.

Vanessa gasped and arched her back, her body tightening as he took her to a dizzying brink. Release burst in her, her body shuddering while she clung to him.

He stripped away the rest of his clothing and slipped between her thighs. She felt the hot, velvet tip of his shaft press against her then slide into her, and waves of pleasure drove her to move wildly with him. As she moaned softly and cried with pleasure, she wrapped her legs around him, stroking him, feeling his firm buttocks and smooth back.

He covered her mouth with kisses and they rode each

other, the rhythm increasing until she felt the burst of rapture and heard his hoarse cry. His large body was heavy as he thrust swiftly, his hot seed spilling into her; and then his weight came down and she held him tightly, wishing that he would be in her arms every night.

She shut her thoughts to parting and stroked his back.

"And this time was better, wasn't it, Vanessa?"

"Yes. I don't want to tell you goodbye, but I know we have to go our own ways."

He turned his head to kiss her, and she held him closely. Later, she lay in his arms, suspecting it would be the last time they would be together like this. Sleep didn't come easily because she wanted to hold him and touch him, to let her fingers glide over his smooth skin and strong body while he slept.

It was still dark when he woke her with kisses and said they should go. She slid out of bed and dressed, moving around the darkened room with him. As she brushed her hair, he came up behind her, then turned her to face him as he leaned down to kiss her one more time.

His arms banded her waist, pulling her up against him. He smelled of soap and buckskin, his hair still damp from bathing. She wound her arms around his neck to hold him, feeling his long length while he bent over her, his arousal pressing against her.

He held her tightly, his hand winding in her hair, and finally he released her. Both of them were breathing raggedly, and his dark eyes devoured her as he gazed into her eyes her and rubbed his knuckles lightly on her cheek. "We must go," he said.

Reluctantly, she broke away from him. "Shall I wake Muaahap now?"

"Yes. I'll get the horses and bring them behind the hotel. Vanessa," he said quietly, his voice sobering, "if anyone starts after us, ride quickly and I will follow. I don't know if Muaahap can keep up, but she isn't wanted and doesn't have a reward offered for her."

"I won't wait."

He left, closing the door quietly. She moved into the next room to awaken Muaahap. Within the hour, they were saddled and riding through the sleeping town. The air was still and cold; she felt chilled and wished she had one of the buffalo robes they had left behind at the camp.

Lone Wolf rode next to her and she glanced at him, feeling safer with him by her side, not wanting to think about traveling without him. His back was straight, his black hair touching his shoulders, his jaw set. He looked commanding and handsome, and she had to curb the urge to reach over and touch his hand.

Buildings were dark; and even though no one stirred, her back tingled. A flyer fluttering on a post was a reminder her father had men searching for her. His anger would know no bounds and he would kill Lone Wolf if he caught them. She looked at Muaahap and White Bird and wondered if he would pay men to kill them as well.

They left town and rode east all day, camping that night on hides and riding the next day until noon. As the sun moved across the sky in the late afternoon, they stopped to water the animals and Vanessa gazed at the long shadows cast by the slanting sun.

Muaahap and White Bird meandered farther along the creek bank with Lone Wolf standing close to her. Vanessa stood up slowly and studied the sun, looking back in the direction they had come. She looked at it again carefully because the sun was setting to her left.

They were heading north!

Twelve

When she looked at Lone Wolf, who was straightening the load on the sorrel, anger flooded her. She thought how enraged he had been when he had discovered she had lied to him, yet here he was riding north without telling her!

She calculated again, wanting to make certain, shocked by his duplicity and doubly furious when she thought how he had acted about her deceit.

"Damn you," she said quietly, clenching her fists.

His head swung around, and his eyes narrowed. He yanked at the saddle and turned toward her, looking around as if to spot Muaahap and White Bird.

"Keep your voice down," he said quietly, and her rage flamed until she shook.

"You were so angry with me for lying to you! Yet, you have deceived me all day. We're riding north toward your people. You've turned north without telling me."

He looked hard and tough, as he had when she had first met him, and she drew a deep breath, feeling the first flicker of worry and uncertainty about him.

"Yes, we're riding north. Your sister will survive, but there is no way you can rescue her and your youngest sister then escape from a fort filled with soldiers."

"Damn you for not telling me!" She shook her fist at him. "That's worse than what I did!"

"You cannot rescue her and you should face that fact,

Vanessa," he replied firmly. "You'll be caught and placed in a convent. Is that what you want?"

"Of course it isn't what I want, but I don't intend to be caught."

"You can't get her. All the soldiers know you on sight, and your father will be watching her like a hawk. He may suspect what you plan to do."

"How long have we been riding north?" she asked, feeling betrayed, her rage growing.

"Since mid-morning." Lone Wolf's tone was grim.

"I'm going back. I don't care if I have to go alone. I won't abandon Phoebe, and you're not going to stop me," she said, turning to look at the western sun again.

He drew closer until he caught her, encircling her wrists with his hands. She tried to yank away, but he held her firmly and shook his head again. "You're not going. You wouldn't get half-a-day's journey without encountering someone. And the first white men who found you would take you; the first tribe would make you their captive."

"You'll not take me with you!" she snapped, trying to wriggle free, her anger soaring.

He withdrew a strip of rawhide from beneath his shirt. She saw what he intended and kicked, struggling to get away from him. He held her calmly, turning slightly so her kicks had little effect.

"Don't stop me! I'll hate you for it! And I'll run away the first chance I get!"

"Be still, Vanessa. It will do you no good to fight me. I'm taking you back with me to my people."

She stared at him in shocked disbelief. "No! You can't."

"Yes, I can," he said quietly, his dark eyes holding an implacable glint, his voice unyielding. He towered over her, his broad shoulders intimidating, and she knew his strength would be impossible to counter.

"I can take you as you are now or I can throw you over the horse and tie you down so you'll travel on your stomach.

You won't like it. And Muaahap won't help you. She'll
know I'm right, and I imagine she'll agree with me. If she
doesn't, I'll leave her behind. If you cause trouble with
Muaahap and White Bird, it will only go harder for them
because I am taking you with me."

"I will never let you—"

He caught her up against him so swiftly it took away her
breath. His face was only inches from hers. "Don't threaten
me with what you'll never let me do because I can easily
overcome your anger. If we were alone, I would show you
what you want and what you would ask me to do to you,"
he said in a husky voice.

Furious with him, she jerked her knee up. He took the
blow high on his thigh.

He caught her up and strode to her horse, tossing her
across the saddle on her stomach. He stood close to her
face, holding her wrists with one of his hands as she struggled futilely.

"Do you want to travel this way?"

She turned her head away from him, but he wound his
fingers in her hair and jerked her face back toward his.
"Answer me now or this is the way you'll ride!"

"No!" she snapped, her green eyes fiery. Lone Wolf
knew she would fight, but he wasn't going to let her ride
away alone. She would never reach McKavett, but she was
too stubborn to admit it and too inexperienced to know the
dangers she faced. He lifted her off the horse to set her on
her feet.

"I'll water the horses," he said.

"I hate you for this," she stated, her voice low and quak-
ing with anger, spots of color turning her cheeks red. "I'll
never forgive you if Phoebe's marriage ruins her life."

"Your sister should run away as you did. She's almost
sixteen, that's old enough to escape if escape is possible at
all. I'll not let you go back alone for her. You would never
get to McKavett, Vanessa. Never."

"I have to try. I won't cooperate with you. The first chance I have, I'll run away."

His dark eyes gazed at her, and then he walked away with the horses.

Angry, frustrated, and frightened for Phoebe, Vanessa stared helplessly at his broad back. She ran to the horse and yanked the rifle from the scabbard, grasping the bolt. When she yanked up the rifle, he turned. Trying to hold the heavy weapon, she braced the stock against her shoulder.

He ran toward her, his head down, coursing like a snake. She swung the rifle lower, and he leapt at her, tackling her. The shot reverberated in the air, an echoing bang that sent birds flying.

Lone Wolf's weight came down on her, knocking the breath from her lungs and stunning her as she hit the ground hard. He yanked the rifle from her hands and tossed it away, pausing with his face only inches above her, his brown eyes blazing with fury.

"You wanted to kill me!"

"I just want to be free! Let me go! You'll wish you had!"

He stared at her, rage churning in him. He had known she would fight him, but he had misjudged how hard she would fight. And he hadn't guessed that she would try to shoot him, not after having spent days and nights at great risk to nurse him back to health from gunshot wounds.

Trying to control his anger, he stood up, turning in the direction Muaahap and White Bird had gone. In seconds, Muaahap came trotting through the trees. He waved to her and held up the rifle, shrugging his shoulders.

She waved and turned to hurry back to White Bird, disappearing into the trees again.

Lone Wolf looked down at Vanessa and knew he had to make her understand that she was not going to go free. And he was going to give vent to some of his fury.

Vanessa met his dark gaze and saw the rage that blazed

in his eyes. He walked away, placing the rifle in the scabbard, and then he came back to her. "Get up, Vanessa."

She stared at him, suddenly afraid of what he intended. It wouldn't do any good to tell him she hadn't intended to shoot to kill, only to stop him and get away from him. Feeling a stubborn contrariness, she gazed up at him without moving, determined to cooperate as little as possible.

He reached down and picked her up roughly, swinging her over his shoulder on her stomach and striding downstream with her. Angry, embarrassed, and hating hanging over his shoulder and bouncing like a sack of flour, she kicked and wiggled.

"Put me down! I'll walk!"

Ignoring her, he strode away from the horses and Muaahap. He stopped and swung her down, setting her on her feet. "We're going to settle this. You tried to kill me just then. I think you need to understand that you're my captive, Vanessa, and that I'm not letting you ride away alone. By nightfall, someone else would have you."

"I want to take that chance, and you shouldn't stop me! I have to try to get my sister!"

"No, Vanessa. You're foolish and young, and you know nothing about the harshness of this land or the men that roam it. You've seen a little, enough that you should know in your heart that I'm right. You heard what Hollings said he would do if he caught you. You know what Hankins wanted from you. You're going with me, and you're not going to fight me every step of the way," he said, moving closer to her.

She backed up. "I will fight you," she snapped. "I've helped you and cared for you, and now you can repay that by letting me go."

"Did you hear what I just said to you? Someone else would have you by nightfall."

"I want to take that chance," she said, backing into the

trunk of a cottonwood. He reached out and caught her, pulling her to him.

She fought him as Lone Wolf had known she would, her green eyes blazing with anger. "Let me go! I don't want your kisses, and I don't want you to touch me!"

"You're talking in anger and I don't believe you," he said quietly, pulling her into his arms, holding her tightly against him while he ignored her struggles. He bent to kiss her and she twisted away. He lowered his head, kissing her throat, his hand moving to her breast to stroke her.

Vanessa felt bombarded by the sensations that he stirred. As angry as she was with him, she also loved him and his touch was not unwelcome or repugnant. He kissed her throat, unfastening the thongs that held the top of the buckskin to the skirt and pushing up the top to take her breast in his mouth.

With a gasp, her struggles ceased. She gave a cry, her hands becoming still on his shoulders. "Let me go," she whispered, but all force was gone from her voice and her eyes were closed. "You're fighting unfairly," she whimpered as his large hands cupped her breasts and his thumbs played over her taut nipples. She clung to his arms, her eyes squeezed shut as her anger dissipated like fog beneath the onslaught of a hot sun.

"You won't fight me, Vanessa, because you belong with me. You do not give your heart lightly to men and you have never given your body to a man before. When you fight me, I will remind you that the fight is easy to end," he said in a husky voice.

"I want to—" He silenced her words, his mouth coming down over hers, his tongue thrusting into her mouth. She yielded, forgetting the battle and everything else as she wound her arms around his neck.

Lone Wolf knew he had taken advantage of her passionate nature, but he was determined to settle the battle quickly.

She was going back with him. Any other course would be a disaster for her.

He unfastened the skirt and pushed it away, tugging at the cotton underdrawers that she wore. His hands trailed over her, stroking her inner thighs until her legs parted. He touched her moist warmth; his fingers, feeling her readiness for him, stroked her velvety folds.

He shed his clothes swiftly, seeing her change as her thoughts returned. He caught her around the waist and kissed her, stopping her words as she opened her mouth to speak. He turned her, nudging her legs apart, pushing his bare thigh up against her softness, against the bud that he had already stroked.

She gasped, undulating, and he jammed his thigh against her more tightly, holding her hips as she moved and clung to him.

"Guipago," she whispered, reverting to his Kiowa name in her passion. Her eyes were closed, her white teeth biting into her lower lip. He stroked her breasts and leaned forward to kiss her, winding his hands in her hair as her hips moved wildly.

Vanessa felt the tightening in her body, the urgency as his warm, muscled thigh pressed against her, and she couldn't hold back or stop now. Pleasure bathed her in waves; and then, with her release, she cried out and reached for him, wanting him, her fingers stroking his thick shaft.

He lifted her up easily and settled her on him, sliding into her as she wrapped her legs around him. She cried out again as another climax burst within her, and she moved with him, her fingers wound in his thick hair.

"I hate you for this," she whispered, knowing it wasn't so, but still feeling the smoldering anger that had given way to passion.

"No, you don't. I've seen you with the men you hate," he murmured, kissing her throat and her ear, trailing kisses to her mouth and then kissing her hard as he thrust into her and pulled her down tightly on his hot shaft.

She cried out with this new climax, rapture bursting over her, everything gone from existence except his big, hard body, his mouth on hers, his arms holding her tightly.

Lone Wolf held her against him and thrust swiftly in release, hearing her cries and knowing she had found satisfaction, knowing she had yielded completely and for the moment forgotten her anger. He lay down on the grass and pulled her over him.

"You can't go across the country alone," he told her fiercely. "I won't let you. You can't get your sister. It is foolishness, Vanessa. I've seen bloody battles where men were killed because of their foolishness. You're my woman, and I'm taking you with me."

She stared at him, part of her knowing he was right, part of her refusing to accept what he was saying. Even if she lost her life trying to get Phoebe, she firmly believed she had to try.

"I want to go back," she said, turning her head to stare beyond him. "Nothing you can do or say will change how I feel about my promise to my sister."

He picked her up and waded into the cold stream, sinking down with her in his arms. Icy water splashed against her, but his warm body was pressed close and she had one arm wrapped around his neck.

"Look at me, Vanessa," he commanded.

She turned her head, anger still smoldering, knowing she wouldn't stop fighting him. "You won't be able to hold me."

"Yes, I will. And every time we get into a heated battle, I'll remind you that part of you wants what I do. You'll stop fighting me then, but you could save yourself trouble if you stop now. And if you ever take a gun to me again—" he threatened, turning her chin and tilting her face up.

Lone Wolf had intended to tell her he would beat her; but as he looked into her wide, fearless green eyes that sparked with anger, he knew he never would hurt her. He admired her and respected her, and he wasn't going to let her go to her death or to rape or captivity.

He leaned forward to kiss her, feeling her body stiffen and her lips clamp shut in resistance. He held her face, his tongue playing over her lips, and then her mouth parted and he kissed her long and passionately.

He raised his head and looked at her. Her eyes were closed, her head tilted back, her red lips parted, wet from his kisses. Then her eyes opened and he could see the arguments coming. He stood up, with a splash of water and set her on her feet, leaving her as he strode out of the river.

He glanced back at her and drew his breath. Her red hair spilled over her shoulders; her body was white and pink with the thick triangle of red curls at the base of her belly. Her long silky legs were wet with sparkling drops of water. He could stride back and pick her up and take her again. Instead, he turned away, yanking on his buckskins, ignoring her as she passed him and dressed.

As soon as she had her clothing on, he stepped to her and caught her wrists. Her head came up, her nostrils flaring, fire sparking in her eyes.

"Don't bind my wrists."

"You won't cooperate. You've already told me that," he replied calmly. "You tried to kill me, Vanessa. You'll stay tied when we travel."

She glared at him. "I hate what you're doing! I won't cooperate. You know you can——" She bit off the words and looked away, spots of color in her cheeks.

He caught her chin with his fingers and turned her head. "I know I can *what?*

"You can kiss me and make me forget everything," she said swiftly in a low voice, her face flushing. "I can't change or stop that, but the rest of the time I can think and remember and hate you for what you're doing."

He picked her up, wanting her in his arms, wanting her

anger to go and knowing in time it would. He strode back to the horses with her and set her on a log while he changed the saddle from the paint to the sorrel.

"This horse is the slowest. I'm sorry if that reflects on your horse-buying, Vanessa, but I imagine you have little experience in purchasing horses."

"Or stealing them," she said sharply to him, certain that he had stolen horses often as part of his way of life.

He glanced at her and she thought she saw amusement in his dark eyes, which only fueled her anger further. She raised her chin and looked away from him.

"You'll ride the sorrel. That way, if you see a chance to run away, I'll be able to catch you easily because the bay and the paint are both fine and fast horses."

"Muaahap will help me," she said.

"No, she won't because she will understand completely what kind of danger you would place yourself in by riding off alone. You'll see that she will agree with me in this. I won't have to threaten her or argue with her."

"I think you will threaten her," Vanessa replied darkly, furious with him and wanting to argue with anything he said.

He wheeled abruptly and strode to her. This time, there was no mistaking the amusement in his eyes. He tilted her chin and gazed at her, the look causing a rush of warmth in spite of her anger.

"So!" he exclaimed. "No matter how desperate you are—desperate enough to shoot at me!—you do not beg as so many women would. You shed no tears of despair. You do not plead."

"I can cry," she threatened. He ran his thumb along her chin.

"I doubt it," he mused. "How much more like you that you took my rifle and tried to shoot me. I should have guessed."

"And I'll do it again if I get the chance!" she retorted.

He grinned, his white teeth flashing—unbearably handsome at a time when she did not want to find him so, when she preferred not to see him as charming. She jerked away from him.

He knelt in front of her. "Vanessa," he said softly, "there is a wind that roars over this land occasionally during summer storms. It tears up everything in its path and it does the impossible. I find you are this wind in my life."

Startled by his words, she swung around to look at him. His dark eyes studied her, the faint smile still on his face. At another time she would have slipped her arms around his neck and leaned forward to kiss him, but not now. She put her chin down so she could look into his eyes. "I wish I were that wind and could tear you out of my way and go where I want!"

He grinned again as he stood up to move away from her.

She wanted to cry out and beg for freedom, but she knew it was useless. The only way was either help from Muaahap or escaping on her own.

He continued to prepare the horses for travel. He placed her pistol in his saddlebag. Soon, she heard White Bird's happy voice. Muaahap strode up, looking at her, glancing at her wrists, and then turning to frown at Lone Wolf as he walked toward her. White Bird toddled past them, enticed by a rock pile, and her uncle remained with Muaahap.

Lone Wolf spoke in Comanche, most of the words lost on Vanessa, but she knew he was explaining what had happened. Listening quietly, Muaahap glanced at Vanessa and back at him. Finally, Muaahap nodded and Vanessa's hopes sank. Muaahap walked to Vanessa and motioned to her. She passed her right hand downward over her heart, then made a fist and shoved it downward, opening her hand. The signs indicated danger.

Frustrated that Muaahap would agree with him, Vanessa tried to indicate how desperately she needed to get free. Muaahap merely shook her head and patted Vanessa's hand.

She walked away while Lone Wolf talked to White Bird, who turned to stare at Vanessa with wide eyes, her gaze going to Vanessa's bound wrists. She toddled to Vanessa and leaned her head against her, patting her and holding her. Vanessa stroked her head and, when White Bird looked up, kissed her forehead.

"I love you," she said softly.

"I love you," White Bird repeated. Muaahap called to her, and she scampered away as Lone Wolf approached.

"What did you tell Muaahap?" he asked.

"I told her the truth. I told her you want to go to Fort McKavett to rescue your sister from marriage, but your father would catch you and place you in a convent. She likes the idea of your being my wife better, so she has agreed to give me her cooperation. Also, I told her that you want to go away alone and you don't know how dangerous it is so I've done this to protect you. White Bird doesn't understand what's happening, but I told her it would save your life."

"Damn you," Vanessa said again in a low, angry voice.

He hunkered down in front of her, his eyes on a level with hers. "Vanessa, you saved my life and cared for White Bird. I don't want to go to Fort McKavett and get myself killed. And I care too much for you to let you go by yourself."

"You just want me," she snapped, knowing she was being unfair, but still angry with him.

"Yes, I do want you," he replied, and her head swung around. She gazed into his dark eyes. "I want you and I don't want you to be hurt. If you part from us and ride away alone, you'll be hurt badly. Now we go," he said, as if the subject were closed.

She glared at him as he straightened up and stood over her. Then he bent down and picked her up, easing her onto the sorrel. She raised her chin, staring ahead, knowing that she would have to watch for a chance to escape. She decided to forget her anger and try to plan logically.

Muaahap mounted and Lone Wolf lifted White Bird in front of her. He swung into the saddle as if he had never been injured, and they moved off. Vanessa looked at the sun, now on her left, and knew they were going due north. She glanced over her shoulder. Lone Wolf held the reins to the sorrel, and Muaahap and White Bird brought up the rear.

Vanessa's anger smoldered as she rode, and she began to devise ways to escape, determining what she should try to take. Her pistol was in his saddlebag and would be impossible to get. Her portmanteau, however, filled with the gold so essential to her mission, was loaded on a packhorse. She needed the gold for their stagecoach tickets to California.

Phoebe planned to bring some money; but she had saved only a small amount through the years, and it would not be enough to get them to California. Vanessa stared at Lone Wolf's back. It would be difficult to get away from him, but she would bide her time until the moment when he let down his guard.

And now she would have to escape Muaahap's watchful eyes as well. Since the old woman agreed with him, she would let him know if Vanessa tried to get away.

When they stopped for the night, he lifted her down from the horse, his hands lingering on her waist. He took her wrists in his hand. "I'll free you and you may stay free much of the time as long as you don't try to escape. The moment you try to get away, then I'll keep you tied all the time."

"You'll never know how much you're hurting me."

"Then you are too softhearted and too impractical."

Anger filled her again, and she stared down at him coldly. "Untie me. I won't run," she lied. She would have only one good chance at freedom, and she had to be very sure before she took it.

His large fingers loosened the rawhide and pulled it free. He massaged her wrists where the cord had dug into them. "Come here, Vanessa," he said, holding her hand and leading her to his horse. He removed a leather pouch from his saddlebag. She had seen many such pouches in the Comanche camp and suspected it came from there.

"The medicine man gave me this to rub on my wounds as they healed. It might help your wrists." His blunt fingers massaged the thick salve over her slender wrists, and she looked up to find him watching her, desire evident in his gaze. She lifted her chin and looked away from him.

"You can kiss me until I yield to you, but my feelings for you will gradually change and die."

"Perhaps, perhaps not. I can take you back to my people and give you to another man."

She looked up at him and drew a deep breath, wondering if he threatened her. "I don't think I'll care."

He tilted up her chin. "I think you will. You fight for what you want, Vanessa."

He replaced the pouch in the saddlebag and she moved away from him, helping with supper in silence, trying to talk to White Bird, but leaving her to Muaahap's care most of the time.

They ate in silence and soon were all stretched on the ground to rest for the night. Lone Wolf's hides were beside her quilt and he took her wrist.

"You said you wouldn't tie me."

"I said I wouldn't most of the time. You've been untied since we stopped. Now I have to make certain you're still here in the morning," he said, lashing their wrists together.

Surprised, she watched him and yanked against the leather that wasn't knotted yet and slipped free. He pulled her wrist back against his own and tied them together. "Now we sleep."

"Unless I can reach your knife during the night," she snapped.

"Don't try, Vanessa," he cautioned. He stretched out and she glared at him frustrated and betrayed.

"I hate what you're doing. If you knew my sister—"

She bit off the words because he knew a harsher world than she did and he would not change his mind because Phoebe was a gentle person and easily frightened.

Vanessa lay down, staring at the stars overhead, knowing she would have to cooperate with him and try to get away when she wasn't bound. She thought about the reticule with the gold that he now carried with his things, packed on his horse. And she seethed because she had to get away within the next few days. Every hour, they put more miles between her and Fort McKavett; soon she would have an impossible journey back. Time was running out. Phoebe was to marry at the end of December. Vanessa had to get back before then.

Her best chance of escape would have been after dark, but because she would be bound to him while he slept, she would have to try when they were awake.

The next day she rode in silence; and when no one else spoke either, she suspected Lone Wolf welcomed the quiet.

By the fourth day of their northward trek, her calm deliberation had turned to panic. She had had no chance to get her gold. The land was flat, stretching away to the horizon with mesquite and prickly pear, and she felt the distance widening between Phoebe and herself.

That night, as they made camp, Lone Wolf unsaddled the horses and turned his back to her. The portmanteau lay on the ground beside his saddle, a quilt tossed over it.

Lone Wolf led the black horse to a narrow stream of water. Muaahap and White Bird piled up sticks they had gathered along the way for a fire.

Deciding this might be her only opportunity, Vanessa rushed to the portmanteau. She pushed aside the quilt and rummaged through the suitcase. Her fingers closed around the box that was heavy with gold, and her pulse jumped as she lifted it, feeling its reassuring solid weight. A shadow fell across her.

Thirteen

Lone Wolf's hand closed over hers. "What do you want, Vanessa? What's in your hand?"

"Let me go!" She stood up and faced him, secreting the box behind her back. "I'll help Muaahap."

She started to pass him, but he caught her, his hand sliding around her waist to hold her. He took the gold from her, his dark fingers closing around the box.

"You have my money. It's mine and I want it!"

"I'll keep it until you need it," he answered with a maddening calm, his hand still on her waist.

"When next month comes, if I am still with you, part of me will die because my sister will die," she said in a low voice, shaking with anger, her fists clenched at her sides. She wanted to leap at him and try to grab the box, but recognized that the action would have been futile.

"No one dies from marriage," he snapped.

"Phoebe will from marriage to this major. The man is a beast, and my sister is as innocent and childlike as White Bird."

"Your sister is a woman on the verge of wedlock."

"No, she isn't. You don't know Phoebe. I've sheltered her, and our father has sheltered both of us. He has kept us from society and from men. You of all people know I was innocent."

Lone Wolf studied her and she eyed him defiantly, aware of the increase in the tension between them. His dark eyes were implacable and her hopes sank because nothing she had said had affected him.

"When she doesn't have you to rely on, she may become strong. We're far from McKavett now."

Defeated, she turned away, wanting to lash out at him even though she knew it was useless.

He placed the gold in his saddlebag and carried the saddle farther away as she watched. Removing another saddle, he took the paint to water. Still saddled and munching on mesquite beans, the bay stood near her. Lone Wolf was only yards away, but she was within a few feet of the bay, the last horse with a saddle. The bay was the best horse. If she tried to get away now, she would have a few yards head start.

In desperation, she flung herself into the saddle and wheeled the horse around, kicking its sides and leaning low over its neck as the bay sprang forward. She raced away, wind whipping against her, knowing without looking that Lone Wolf would give chase and continue without stopping.

And she intended to ride until he caught her or the horse couldn't go any longer. The bay's long legs stretched out and pounded over the flat ground. She clung to the horse, her gaze scanning the horizon for any break in the land that might give her an advantage.

The animal became covered with lather, its dark mane flowing while wind whipped her hair. Finally, she glanced over her shoulder and felt a stab of fear because Lone Wolf was only yards behind her. He rode easily, his face set grimly, his black hair flowing behind him.

Tears of frustration filled her eyes, but she ignored them as she urged the bay to go faster. Lone Wolf was on the black horse that had been given to him as a gift by Puhihwi Wehki. She didn't know the speed or stamina of the horse, but she knew Lone Wolf's determination.

Within minutes, Lone Wolf pulled alongside her and reached over to yank the reins from her hands. As soon as the horse slowed, Lone Wolf grabbed her, pulling her onto the saddle in front of him, his arm around her so tightly that it cut her breath.

"No!" Vanessa cried, beating against his solid chest, her hopes crumbling. She could not escape from him.

He pulled her more tightly against him, pinning her arms and scowling at her. She felt their clash of wills, their determination. And she felt the wild attraction that blazed steadily whether they were at cross-purposes or in harmony.

"I wish I could beat you into submission, Vanessa."

She stared at him, surprised that he hadn't since he came from a world that would accept such treatment. "I'm surprised you haven't," she admitted, her breathing as ragged as his and her heartbeat fluttering because, in spite of the anger in his expression, her desire ran rampant.

She felt a need for him that was too strong to be destroyed by their arguments. His arms had not been around her since their clash the first day he had turned north. Now he held her pressed against him, his desire obvious in his hungry gaze, and her pulse raced.

With a growl in his throat, he yanked on the reins. The horses stopped and her heart thudded wildly as he swung his leg over and jumped to the ground with her in his arms. He stood her on her feet to face him, holding her upper arms. His dark eyes were filled with a desire that burned through her.

She placed her hands on his forearms, feeling the strong muscles, knowing she was no match for his strength. The wind blew against her, catching long red locks and drawing them across her cheek. She tossed her head, swinging her hair away from her face as he shook her slightly.

"We're not safe out here and we have to get back because Muaahap and White Bird are not safe alone." His voice was low and intense. "I should beat you, but all I want to do is hold you in my arms and kiss you. You're brave, Vanessa, too brave, too obstinate, and as wild as that red hair of

yours!" He ground out the words and pushed up the skirt
of the buckskin and yanked down the drawers she wore.
The thin cotton slid over her hips; falling around her ankles;
the night air cooled her heated skin.

She wanted to fight him, but at the same time she longed
to be in his arms. Her primitive need for him was as strong
as her urge to run from him.

"I want you to let me go!"

"No, I'm not going to let you ride across this land alone."
He pushed away his buckskins, yanking off his shirt and
pulling her down. The tiny rocks and pebbles on the ground
were rough against her skin. The wind tangled his black
hair; his shaft was dark against his powerful body, and her
heart thudded with a searing longing. Suddenly, she wanted
him as desperately as he seemed to want her. He spread
her legs and moved between them. As he leaned down to
kiss her, his dark eyes bored to her soul.

"You are a red-haired wildcat, Vanessa, as brave as any
lioness fighting for her cubs. I want your fire and your
warmth."

Excitement shot through her from his words and the need
in his eyes, a longing that burned away the clash of oppos-
ing wills, leaving only the bond she had felt with him for
so long now.

The moment his mouth came down on hers, desire rocked
her, washing up in hot waves from the depths of her being.
She wound her arms around his neck, sliding her hands
across his wide shoulders and arching her hips to meet him.

He slid his shaft into her softness, and Vanessa's cry was
muffled by his mouth as they both moved frantically with
a need that consumed them like wildfire.

His body was heavy, his thrusts deep and swift as he
drove her to a blinding ecstasy.

"Vanessa, Vanessa!"

Dimly hearing his deep voice cry her name, she climaxed
swiftly, rapture washing over her.

Her heart thudded and she felt torn between wanting him and hating him for keeping her from Phoebe. She held him tightly as their movements gradually slowed.

Her awareness changed as her mind began functioning again. When he moved away, he reached down to pull her up. He tilted her face, his fingers holding her chin tightly. "Don't fight me."

The wind whipped against her with a chilling blast as she pulled on her clothes. Her problems returned swiftly, along with her anger. As soon as she was dressed, she stepped in front of him.

"Let me go back to her," she said, her voice filled with determination. "If you don't, I'll never forgive you."

"You will in time," he said flatly in a tone that indicated the end of the conversation.

She moved away from him, watching him obliquely as he dressed. He had recovered from the gunshots. The scars were still fresh and red, but otherwise, his body was strong and fit. Why did she succumb so easily to him? Was she that deeply in love with him? Was he right that she would forgive him in time? She didn't think so because she loved Phoebe and Belva and she had promised to go back.

She mounted the bay and rode silently beside him back to camp. Muaahap merely stared at her impassively and continued cleaning utensils while White Bird played with her rag dolls. Later, Muaahap patted Vanessa's shoulder. Helpless, Vanessa wiped away her tears and helped with supper.

That night Lone Wolf bound her wrist to his, moving his bedding close to her quilt, covering her with a hide. He lay only inches away, his dark eyes on her. "She will get along better than you think."

"You don't know my sister at all. She isn't able to cope with problems. And I promised her I'd come."

"You did all you could, Vanessa." He turned away and

she stared at his broad back, remembering the moments of wild passion earlier, wishing she could resist him.

The next day they rode northeast, and her hopes dwindled for escape. At night, Lone Wolf slept like a cat, waking at the slightest sound, occasionally opening only one eye as he looked to see what she was doing.

She knew there was no chance to get to Fort McKavett, and something seemed to wither and die inside her. She rode quietly, her thoughts on Phoebe and Belva.

One evening four days later, Lone Wolf studied Vanessa as she shoved away her plate with only a few bites eaten. She had stopped fighting him. He had realized that two days earlier. After her mad dash for freedom, she had seemed to finally accept what lay ahead. Only she had changed, and he didn't think she was sulking.

She seemed to have lost all interest in life. She left White Bird to Muaahap's care. She did the chores to help with meals and with White Bird, but she moved about in silence, totally submissive and docile.

The joy had gone out of her green eyes, and her lifelessness worried him. Each day she grew thinner, the buckskin dress hanging on her slender frame. She was kind to Muaahap and to White Bird, but she was unreceptive to him. He knew he could overcome her lack of physical response because her body would react to his touch, but he felt that Vanessa's heart was locked away and he would never have the warm woman he had known before he had turned north and taken her captive.

He studied Muaahap, who looked up and then quietly turned her back on him. She, too, was worrying about Vanessa, yet she would agree that Vanessa should not go alone across the plains. He knew what Muaahap wanted him to do. Even White Bird seemed unhappy and restless, whining in an uncharacteristic manner.

His gaze roamed over Vanessa as she unfolded her quilt. He repaired the cinch to one of the saddles. As he worked, his thoughts were on Vanessa. If he rode south to McKavett, he would risk all their lives. How could she expect to whisk away her sisters from a fort of soldiers? If he helped, he would bring down the wrath of the U.S. Army on the Kiowa and jeopardize their safety, and he didn't see how he could succeed because he would be alone, pitted against the fort of soldiers. And if by some miracle they escaped from McKavett, three young women would be easy to find.

He eyed her over his shoulder. Vanessa was stretched on the quilt, her hands behind her head as she stared at the sky. She was important to him—how she had become so important, he didn't know. He still loved Eyes That Smile and he did not want to love or wed a white woman, but he felt as if he had plunged a knife into Vanessa and was slowly turning it each day. He swore softly under his breath, wanting to shake her, wanting even more to see the light back in her eyes.

He looked toward the south, wondering if he had become soft in the head and soft in the heart. With a swift motion, he tossed aside the cinch and stood up, striding to Vanessa. Was he sealing his own fate and committing himself to an act he couldn't survive?

He grasped her wrist and pulled her to her feet.

For one startled moment her eyes flew wide, and then she stood, following him, rushing to keep up.

Anger and determination filled him as he strode from camp. He clamped his jaw closed, traveling far enough away that they would have privacy. Vanessa followed docilely. At one time he would have been overjoyed to have had her so obedient to him, but he wasn't now.

When they were alone, he faced her, placing his hands on his hips. She stared at him with little curiosity. Her hair was a tangle, and he knew she had stopped combing it. Her skin was pale in spite of hours in the winter sun.

"I do not want to kill you, Vanessa, and you act as if I am trying to. You don't eat. I know you don't sleep."

She shrugged, watching him quietly.

"I feel I am riding to my death," he said in a grating voice. "You know we can never succeed."

She frowned and stared at him, and he knew his last chance for reason and survival were drowning in her wide, green eyes.

"Succeed at what?"

"What do you think?" he snapped, wondering if he had gone mad. He was not wildly in love with her, yet he couldn't bear her suffering. He still loved Eyes That Smile, but he had to do this for Vanessa. "I will free you and I will accompany you to get your sister," he said, grinding out the words, experiencing a stab of disbelief even as he said them. "And then, Vanessa, if by some miracle I survive, I am taking you north with me. You are mine. You're my woman now," he snapped.

Stunned, Vanessa stared at him, unable to believe what he had said. He looked fierce and angry, yet he had agreed to go after Phoebe! Her mouth fell open, and she blinked in dismay. She felt as if a crushing weight had lifted from her shoulders.

Vanessa closed her eyes and swayed as joy surged in her like a tidal wave. Opening her eyes, overwhelmed by gratitude, she flung herself at him. "Thank you! Oh, thank you! Thank you!"

It was the first time in days he had held her against him, and he was aroused instantly, his arm banding her waist as he pulled her up against him even more tightly. "You have torn my life apart, woman, from the first day!" he grumbled as she showered quick, light kisses over him. Her tears were salty on his lips.

"Dammit, Vanessa," he said, "you know I won't live to go home to my people."

"Of course you will! It'll be easy for you compared to what you went through before. Thank you!"

His emotions tore at him. Every bit of logic in him said he was riding to his death; yet he wanted her and he wanted her like this—joyous, giving, warm, and passionate, the woman he had taken to bed and traveled with for so long.

He kissed her hard, holding her against him, suddenly wanting her with a desperation for he felt as if his days were numbered.

She wound her arms around his neck and kissed him back, her tongue sliding over his. Her hands were all over him, caressing him, setting him aflame.

His erection was swift and hard, and he caught Vanessa's hand to draw her farther away from their camp. "White Bird will be orphaned because of this!"

"Of course, she won't. I know you'll get home again. You'll see. We'll just whisk Phoebe and Belva away, and Papa will never know. We'll have a long head start, and he won't have any idea where to search. Thank you," she said, squeezing his hand. "Oh, thank you!" Tears of joy streamed unheeded down her cheeks, and he wiped them away with his thumb.

"Now you cry! You don't shed tears until I tell you I'll do what you want, and now you can't stop crying!"

"I'm crying because I'm happy," she said, a sob shaking her as she stood on tiptoe to kiss him. He tasted her salty tears, reaching for her, but she pushed against him and caught the ends of his shirt. She tugged his shirt up eagerly, pulling it over his head while he watched her with a feeling of amazement as she seemed to come alive and glow with joy.

"I'm so happy I feel as if I'll burst!" she cried exuberantly, and he clamped his hand over her mouth.

"Shh! Vanessa, we're in the wilds. Be quiet!"

She laughed, her hand drifting down the front of his buckskin pants over the bulge of his arousal. He drew in his breath and watched as she pushed away his pants, stepping closer to kiss him.

He caught her up, his arms banding her waist. "I suppose I'll willingly ride to my death for this!" He kissed her hard and then pulled her down with him to the ground.

She laughed and wriggled against him, pushing at him. "This time you're the one whose backside is on the rocky ground!" She scooted away, turning him, and sliding over him. He pulled up her dress, bunching it above her waist and then tugging it over her head to toss it away.

"Those damned drawers that you don't need—"

She stood and shed them, looking down at him. Moonlight splashed on her alabaster skin, on her breasts that were high and full. She was thin, her ribs showing, her hipbones jutting out, and he reached up to pull her down over him, his shaft touching her softness, sliding into her. She gasped with pleasure as she moved on him, and he cupped her soft breasts, rubbing her taut nipples against his palm.

Vanessa moved wildly, filled with joy and love and exhilaration, knowing he was doing all this for her and feeling as if the bond between them had grown stronger. Sensations rocked her while her heart pounded with joy.

With a cry of ecstasy, she climaxed. Rapture came in waves that rippled through her. She felt his body shudder with his release, and finally she sprawled, exhausted, on him.

His skin was damp with sweat, his body heated against hers, feeling marvelous to her. She stroked his head and shoulders, wanting to give to him, so joyful that he would do this for her.

"Thank you! I'll always be grateful." She showered light kisses on him. "You don't have to go near the fort. I'll get Phoebe and Belva when they go to church with the Carters. Papa always stays at the fort and doesn't attend church. He's not religious."

"Enough, Vanessa. I don't want to contemplate what lies

ahead. I have never known a lone warrior to take on an entire fort of soldiers."

She laughed softly against his throat, and he wondered again if he had lost all his senses because of this slender woman.

"Vanessa," he whispered. "You have ended my solitude and my quiet life. Lone Wolf no longer is a fitting name. Donkey with a She-Pack would be more like it because I think I must have the sense of a jackass to consent to this."

She laughed. "That's absurd! Your name should be Brave Warrior with Kind Heart."

He studied her as she lay in his arms, turning her on her side and shifting to look at her. "We should get back. This ground is less than comfortable."

"You thought it was fine when I was the one on my back," she said, chuckling with amusement. "I'm so happy!" she exclaimed, stroking him, certain they could rescue Phoebe and Belva.

"I'm glad you're happy," he stated, raking her hair away from her face with his fingers. "You can break your news to Muaahap, and she'll be overjoyed for you. But she'd better not kiss me."

Vanessa laughed, and he raised up to prop his head on his hand and stare at her. "Vanessa, for your laughter I would ride into Fort McKavett unarmed and try to bring Phoebe and Belva out," he said quietly, and her wide green eyes studied him. "And that is the remark of a man who has lost all reason." He kissed her gently. "We go back before we are missed."

She kept glancing at him as she dressed. Joy overwhelmed her, and she hummed and felt like jumping in the air with happiness. But along with it was curiosity over his last few statements. *". . . For your laughter I would ride into Fort McKavett unarmed and try to bring Phoebe and Belva out . . ."* How much did he care about her? It had to be a great deal for him to think he was riding to his death to please her.

She caught his hand and kissed his knuckles, brushing them lightly with her lips, feeling his rough skin. "Thank you. You make me very happy."

He placed his hand behind her head, holding her. "Remind me of that every day, Vanessa," he stated solemnly and strode away from her.

They walked back, and she ran to Muaahap, who was snoring softly. "I should wait to tell her in the morning," Vanessa said to him in a loud whisper. She went back to her quilt. Lone Wolf pulled her down into his arms, holding her tightly against him, and sleep came quickly.

The next morning when Vanessa woke, Lone Wolf was packing the horses and Muaahap was folding her bedding. White Bird still slept. Dawn had lightened the sky, and the soft coo of a mourning dove could be heard. Vanessa stared at the sky, the last star still twinkling in the west, and she remembered the night before. Excitement filling her, she rose, slipping on her moccasins, and hurried to tell Muaahap her news.

Lone Wolf eyed them, wondering what Muaahap would think, knowing she would probably be happy if Vanessa were happy.

The old woman peered around Vanessa at Lone Wolf, and he looked away. He placed his folded hides on the horse and then he picked up a coil of rawhide. Sitting on the ground, he began to untangle a rawhide rope he intended to use for packing. As a shadow fell over him, he looked up.

Muaahap squatted in front of him, and for a startled moment he braced himself in case she were going to throw herself at him and kiss him for pleasing Vanessa.

"*Aho,*" she said, signing to indicate her pleasure. She had a sly look on her face, and he wondered what she was leading up to.

He nodded his head and made the sign of danger.

She nodded. "You, brave warrior," she gestured.

"Brave warrior cannot battle fort of soldiers."

"Brave warrior can," she said, touching his chest with her finger. "Brave warrior. Make woman happy." She reached into her buckskin sleeve to withdraw a packet wrapped in deerskin.

"For brave warrior," she said and held it out to him.

Curious, he took the gift and nodded, knowing it wasn't given lightly, half-expecting one of her silver bracelets. The moment his fingers closed on it, he looked at her in surprise. He unfolded the hide, revealing a fine, large bowie knife with a carved ivory handle. When he glanced at her, she smiled at him. "Make woman happy."

He motioned his thanks; with a grin, Muaahap returned to her tasks. He turned the knife in his hands and wondered how she had acquired it. It was sharp and looked as if it had never seen use. He pulled out his old knife, which was worn and scarred and thin from being sharpened often. Pleased, he replaced it with the new one.

"She is very happy with you," Vanessa said in a quiet voice that was filled with the warmth he had missed so badly.

"Where did she get this knife?" he asked.

Vanessa shrugged. "I don't know. She only told me she had a gift for you."

He touched Vanessa's cheek. "You sleep at my side tonight. You are my woman now, Vanessa."

She gazed up at him with a strange mixture of emotions. She was overcome with gratitude toward him, and a thrill went through her at his words. Yet she felt a longing for something more. He had been married before, had loved a woman enough to make her his wife. Vanessa had given herself to him because she thought they would part and never see each other again; but they weren't going to part, and she did not want to be his woman indefinitely without a commitment from him. She drew a deep breath and faced him.

"We aren't man and wife."

"We are the same as man and wife."

"No, we're not. I thought I wouldn't see you again, that we would part ways," she said softly, looking away from him, unable to stop her blush. "Now our feelings for each other are more important. I must give it thought."

Lone Wolf saw the spots of color in her cheeks and guessed she was leading up to marriage. But he still hurt over the loss of Eyes That Smile and he was not ready to take a wife. Vanessa had given herself freely to him, so he was taken aback now by her reply. He nodded, giving her time. She didn't realize she was fully his captive and that he could possess her when he wanted. Yet this was not a woman to be taken by force; she was as strong-willed as a warrior. She walked away from him, and his pulse drummed as he remembered her wild abandon and joyous lovemaking last night.

During the days of riding with her before he had taken her virginity, he had thought that once he possessed her, the urges he felt toward her would lessen. Instead they were stronger, and his body clamored for her slender form beneath him even though he had possessed her only hours earlier. Her eagerness and vitality took his breath and made his pulse pound.

Her red hair swung with each step, swirling across her shoulders, and he wanted to bury his face in its softness. The flaming color fitted her; she was passionate and fiery. She had a proud walk, although in many ways she was unselfish and undemanding. Only when it came to someone she loved was she fiercely demanding and protective.

Vanessa Sutherland. The Sutherland name left a bitter taste in his mouth. How he hated Abbot Sutherland! When he had been with the army, he had encountered the man once at Fort Garland. Sutherland had asked why a redskin was present; and when he had been told Lone Wolf was a scout, he had demanded Lone Wolf not be allowed in the same tent with the officers as they discussed the railroad. Lone Wolf had left, but he remembered Sutherland as a tall, blue-eyed, brown-haired, pompous man.

Vanessa was Sutherland's daughter, the child of a man hated by all Indians. Yet she was treated badly by her father and from what she said, Abbot Sutherland withheld his love from his daughters. Lone Wolf glanced at Vanessa, and his anger left him. She could not be held responsible for her father's actions.

He crossed the camp toward her, looking at the hair that fell over her shoulders, curling around her like flames. He drew in his breath because she was beautiful and desirable. He wanted her in his arms. And he knew she wanted more. She wanted to be loved and to be his wife, but he wasn't ready to give that part of himself yet, to say goodbye to his memories of Eyes That Smile.

"We ride within the hour. White Bird should eat first."

She nodded and he turned away although he wanted to pull her into his arms, knowing he'd better start thinking with a clear mind about Fort McKavett.

Fourteen

They headed south, riding hard across open land. Days later, the land changed to rolling grassland with mesquite, cedars, and cottonwoods. Because of the flyers offering a reward and bearing her picture, Lone Wolf thought Vanessa should avoid all towns; so, as they neared Fort McKavett, he and Muaahap rode into Menard to get supplies and learn what day it was. Lone Wolf took Vanessa's gold and bought two rifles, ammunition, and a long list of supplies. Muaahap purchased a hat for Vanessa and yards of green muslin for a dress. Lone Wolf bought woolen trousers, a shirt and vest, a coat, a hat, and a pair of boots.

When they rejoined Vanessa, he dismounted and began to unpack all they had purchased.

"Now I need to teach you and Muaahap to fire a rifle. Also, I bought the clothing we'll need but I do not like to shed my buckskins."

"You won't stand out as much if you wear the white man's clothing or if you cut your hair."

He nodded solemnly. "I only cut my hair this one time. You cut it, Vanessa. Although even with it cut in the white man's style, anyone who glances at me will know I'm Indian." She had to agree as her gaze ran over his features.

He had honored her wishes and had not kissed her since they had turned to ride south. The occasional brush of his fingers when he handed her something or of his shoulder against hers as he moved past sent tingles through her. With each passing hour, she grew more aware of him and the longing she felt for him increased.

"Today is Thursday. We can be close to McKavett and Glen Hollow tomorrow; then we will camp and wait for Sunday. I want to see this church and plan what we'll have to do."

"I think we should find a safe place for Muaahap and White Bird and leave them, then come back and get them."

He nodded solemnly, and she wondered if he had already decided on a similar plan.

That evening when they camped, he sat on a stump while she combed his thick black hair. The strands were coarse, as black as raven feathers. Her fingers moved over his head, brushing his neck, his ear, while he sat still. She leaned against him, parting his hair in the center and combing it, picking up strands, feeling strange about cutting his hair as if she were violating some primitive law.

Lone Wolf sat still, inhaling the faint scent of rosewater as her fingers brushed his nape and head. She leaned against him and her body was warm. Her fingers offered the faintest contact, yet her light touches stirred his desire for her.

As she tried to part his hair, he spread his knees and she stepped between them. Since her concentration was on his hair, Lone Wolf suspected she was unaware that she was arousing him.

She stood between his thighs, her breasts in front of his eyes. The buckskin was belted, the soft leather clinging to her. His imagination stripped away the clothing, and he thought of her standing between his legs without the dress.

As his body responded swiftly, he tried to shift his thinking to something else, to forget how close Vanessa stood, how sweet she smelled. She stepped behind him and tilted his head back slightly, her soft breast brushing against him.

A lock of dark hair fell on the back of his hand. She was changing him just as she had changed his life. He was going on an impossible journey that might take him to his death, a ridiculous risk to attempt to take two young women from a fort of soldiers.

He had no intention of marrying the daughter of a man he hated and had sworn to kill. And if the father came after them and there were a confrontation, if he killed Abbot Sutherland, what would that do to Vanessa?

Locks of black hair fell on the ground and on his knees. Vanessa worked slowly, not wanting to cut it too short. She brushed his nape, looking at his smooth, brown skin. She trimmed over his ears carefully. If he tired, he gave no indication, but sat as still as a statue.

She stepped in front of him, placing her hands on his cheeks to tilt his face up so she could see if she had cut his hair evenly. She parted it on the right side and then on the left, finally deciding on the right.

She paused in front of him again, her gaze going over his features. She drew in her breath. The look of wildness about him was diminished but not banished. In its place, though, was a strikingly handsome man with distinctive features—the dark brown eyes that now seemed larger than before, the arrogant hawk-like nose, the sensuous, masculine mouth, and the firm jawline that was now even more noticeable.

"You're handsome," she said quietly.

"Don't tell me I look white."

As her gaze shifted from his hair to his eyes, she wondered if he were teasing her, but he gazed back solemnly. "I don't know whether you meant that or not, but you look—" She paused, at a loss to describe him. "You look noticeable. Maybe more than you did before."

"That, Vanessa, is not what we hoped to accomplish with this haircut. How could I look more noticeable?"

Muaahap and White Bird joined them. White Bird picked up the shorn locks of black hair, gathering them carefully while Muaahap stared at Lone Wolf.

"Taiboo," Muaahap said cheerfully.

"Hah-nay'! he snapped.

Muaahap chuckled and nodded her head, and Vanessa suspected she was annoying him. Vanessa caught Muaahap's wrist and pointed toward the hides, motioning toward White Bird and indicating it was her bedtime.

Muaahap took White Bird's hand and left, chuckling as she went.

"Vanessa, she tries my patience."

"What did she say?"

"She called me a white man."

Vanessa smiled. "That's not such an insult!"

"She did it to aggravate me."

"Well, perhaps she teased a little. By no stretch of the imagination could anyone who looks at you closely take you for a white."

"My hair will grow out again, but I don't think my life will ever return to the peace I once knew."

"Perhaps it was time for you to lose that peace and come back into the world," she said lightly, walking away from him while he stared at her.

Two days later on a cool December day, he stood beneath the bare branches of a tall hackberry on the edge of Glen Hollow and looked at a small frame church that was quiet and empty. It was painted white with plain glass windows, a tall steeple over the door, and an iron bell at the top of the steeple. Lone Wolf scrutinized the area.

The church was on the edge of Glen Hollow, a small town that had built up because of the fort. There were nine blocks of houses, a small store, a smithy, a livery stable, a saddlery, a wheelwright, one saloon, and little else. If they took Phoebe and the soldiers or Sutherland gave chase, there was nowhere in town to hide.

Lone Wolf mounted his horse, hating the woolen pants and boots that pinched his feet. He turned and rode north through the rolling land that was thick with cedars and mesquite and high grass. There were creeks and gullies and places to hide, and he felt slightly better as he began to get a feel for the land.

In an hour he came back through the town and turned south. He rode in a wide circle, trying to decide which direction to take to lose anyone who might give chase, where they could hide, where they could get water and supplies. He needed to know the area as well as he did his own campsite, to know which direction would give him the most water, the most cover.

That night at camp, he sat close to Vanessa in front of a dying fire. He had killed rabbits and roasted them on a spit for their supper and now he was relaxed, drawing with a stick in the ashes. "Here's the church, Vanessa. We will leave our extra horses here in a shallow ravine while we take a buggy and ride to the church."

Looking up from her sewing, she nodded. She and Muaahap had spent each evening sewing to make a new green muslin dress for Vanessa, one that her father would not recognize. "I can buy a buggy in town."

"I'll buy the buggy, and you stay out of sight." He thought about her plans. "You said you wanted to get to the stage at El Paso to get tickets to California. Tucumcari is about one hundred miles closer, and it will be on the way back to my people."

"As long as a stage goes through heading to California, it's fine if we go to Tucumcari."

"So we ride for Tucumcari. Now when we leave the church, we'll go straight north and then turn west." He looked at her. "I would feel better if we went this Sunday and you pointed Phoebe and Belva out to me. Then I could go back next Sunday and try to get them."

"No. When they see me, they'll expect to go with me. If they don't see me, they won't know you and they won't go with you. And by a week from tomorrow, she may be wed."

"You're sure your father doesn't attend church?"

"Absolutely. He prefers to sleep on Sunday morning."

Lone Wolf nodded, picking up his rifle to clean it.

Sunday morning, Lone Wolf was up before dawn. In a cold fog, he watched Vanessa go to the river and he wanted to follow, to take her into his arms and possess her swiftly. He wasn't certain he would live to see sundown and he knew he would fight to the death anyone who tried to capture her to take her back to her father.

He picked up his things and headed upstream, washing and changing swiftly. He packed his buckskins, then loaded the supplies on the packhorses so Muaahap could travel.

Half an hour later, he heard a rustling and turned toward the river. Vanessa strode toward him, and his heart thudded against his rib cage as he stared at her. She wore a wide-brimmed hat with green-satin ribbons that tied beneath her chin. Her hair was braided and looped around her head, hidden completely beneath the hat that partially hid her face. She wore the green muslin dress without crinolines and hoops, and it clung to her figure as she walked. With her hair pulled back, her green eyes looked larger than ever and she was beautiful in the dress that emphasized her soft curves.

Vanessa strolled up to him and examined him. "My goodness, look at you! How handsome you look. All the ladies in the church will notice you," she said, running her fingers over his black coat. "Maybe you should stay hidden behind the trees and I should go alone. You'll attract so much attention—"

"There is no way I could possibly attract the attention, Vanessa, that you will. And if you think people will notice me, I'm certain they will all notice you, so we shall be as conspicuous as a painted bull roaming into the church."

"We'll sit in the back," she said, pleased by his comments and the look of approval in his eyes.

Sliding his arm around her waist, Lone Wolf pulled her against his chest and bent his head to kiss her. Vanessa's heart thudded because it was the first kiss in a long time. Her hands flew up against his arms, feeling the soft woolen coat sleeves and the strong muscles beneath. He smelled of cotton and wool. She wound her arms around his neck, pressing against him, kissing him back, her tongue playing over his, going deep into his mouth. Desire flowed through her, heating her and giving rise to an ache for more of him.

He raised his head. "I wish we had more time—"

"But we don't," she said, pulling away reluctantly and straightening the hat on her head. "Shall I wake Muaahap now and tell her we go?"

"Yes. You have the derringer?"

"Yes," she said, patting the reticule that dangled from her dainty wrist.

"I would rather you stayed with Muaahap."

Vanessa flashed a smile at him. "But Phoebe would never know you, and you wouldn't know her. We don't look alike. Except you could find her. She will be the most beautiful female there."

"No," he said quietly, shaking his head and touching her cheek. "No, she won't."

Vanessa's lashes fluttered and she drew a deep breath, turning to go to Muaahap and wake her. After Vanessa hugged White Bird, Lone Wolf placed White Bird on a horse while Muaahap mounted up behind her to lead the packhorses. The old woman had a rifle in a scabbard, and she nodded at them as she turned to ride away.

"I hope no one disturbs them."

"Muaahap will take care of White Bird, and no one will bother Muaahap." He turned to help Vanessa into the ancient buckboard he had purchased with her money. It was pulled by a gray and a dun, a team of horses that he had paid little for. Their four best horses followed behind—the black, the bay, a chestnut from the Comanche, and the paint—their reins tied to the back of the buckboard.

Lone Wolf's coat swung open as he climbed up, and Vanessa saw the grip of his revolver in the shoulder holster he wore. He pushed the black hat to the back of his head, and her pulse accelerated because he looked handsome and virile in the black coat and trousers. He still had an air of wildness, and she knew they would be incredibly conspicuous at the church and would have to hang back to avoid public scrutiny.

Her pulse raced at the thought that in a few hours Phoebe and Belva would be safely recovered. She placed her hand on his knee and Lone Wolf's head swung around, his dark eyes blazing with desire as he looked at her.

She leaned close to kiss him. "Thank you."

"If you want to get to church, you should take your hand off my knee," he suggested, his voice husky.

Smiling, she removed her hand and brushed his cheek with her fingers. She smoothed the green muslin skirt over her legs and settled to ride.

The sun's rays slanted above the horizon when they rode down into the draw where he wanted to leave the horses. Sunshine had burned off the fog, and the day promised to be bright and clear with a cloudless blue sky. Bare branches of tall hackberries interlaced overhead, and a rabbit bounded off as they slowed and stopped.

Lone Wolf dismounted to take care of the saddle horses while Vanessa stared at the church. Excitement coursed through her, making it difficult to sit still. They had hours before church time, but Lone Wolf had insisted on arriving early to hide the horses and watch people arrive.

He climbed back into the buckboard and flicked the reins to move to another spot behind a clump of cedars and hidden from the view of the road. There they could see people going into the church.

Vanessa prayed Phoebe came to church, that their father still allowed her to attend, because Vanessa didn't know how she could ride into the fort to get Phoebe and Belva without being discovered.

And if she had to go to Fort McKavett, she did not want Lone Wolf to accompany her, even though she knew she couldn't stop him.

She wiggled on the seat and glanced at him. He sat as still as a stone and she marveled at his patience, reminded again of a predatory cat. If they had to wait until sundown, he would sit just as still and wait.

Wondering for the hundredth time why he was doing this, certain he was riding to his death, Lone Wolf remained quiet. He peered at Vanessa and momentarily forgot their plans and the danger. Sunlight caught the golden strands in her deep red hair, making it look like spun gold. Her lustrous green eyes sparkled with excitement. She was the most beautiful woman he had known, and she could be as forceful as some of the warriors who were his kin. He thought about the upheaval in his life that Vanessa had caused. If they survived the day and were successful, he would have to deal with five females.

The notion staggered him. Vanessa's charm and determination had melted his opposition every time. She had changed his life, and he doubted if it would ever be the same again. And would he want it the same?

As buggies began to arrive, she strained to see, once standing up. "Sit down, Vanessa. You'll see your sisters when they go up the church steps."

She flicked him a smile of acquiescence and sat back down on the seat, wriggling to look at the latest arrivals in the churchyard. He studied her, amused, knowing Vanessa would not make a good fighter because she was too impatient and too excitable.

She was beautiful in the green dress particularly since it dipped low, revealing the curves of her breasts, and cinched her tiny waist. He longed to pull her into his arms and, if they survived this day, he intended to possess her and kiss away any arguments she might give him. Aware they were in great danger and he'd better keep his wits about him, he tried to shift his attention from her.

He glanced again at the church. They had a clear view of the church steps and the area in front where congregates were leaving their wagons and buggies and horses.

As people rode past along the road, Vanessa's palms grew damp. She had seen no sign of the Carters, Phoebe, or Belva.

"We should go now. The churchyard is filling up, and it's almost time for the service to begin. Are you certain they'll come to church?"

"They come with the Carters nearly every Sunday, and Phoebe promised she would continue doing so. As soon as she heard I'd run away from the wagon train, I'm sure she started to look for me."

"Unless your father has kept her away, knowing you might come back for her."

"I haven't seen the Carters yet, and they always attend."

"They're going to be late and so are we. Ready?"

"Yes," she said, gripping the buckboard.

When Lone Wolf flicked the reins, they moved out of the draw and onto the dusty lane. The churchyard was filled with wagons and buggies, and music from a piano carried in the air. They moved slowly along the rutted, narrow road while two buggies approached from the opposite direction.

Vanessa felt a jolt as she stared at a buggy, and she grasped Lone Wolf's arm.

"There're Phoebe and Belva. And the man sitting beside the driver is my father!"

Fifteen

Lone Wolf looked at the approaching buggy, and as his gaze rested on her blue-eyed father, Lone Wolf felt a surge of anger. He remembered Abbot Sutherland, his arrogance and his hatred of Indians.

Sutherland sat in the front of the buggy with another man. He laughed, and Lone Wolf longed to pull him out of the buggy and vent his anger with his hands. He forced his attention to the others, looking at the back of a woman's head, a hat with feathers draping over her brown hair. A young girl with dark brown hair rode beside her. Facing them were two young women, and he knew at once which one was Phoebe.

A golden-haired woman with wide blue eyes and skin so pale it was almost translucent rode facing the woman and girl. The blond's delicate beauty made his breath catch. Her lips were full and rosy and her features perfect. His gaze roamed down her slender throat and full breasts. She was larger than Vanessa, her frame heavier. She looked like the oldest sister, far beyond fifteen, yet he knew she must be Phoebe. And the brown-haired young woman next to her must be her friend Annabelle Carter.

"I recognize your father. Let them get inside. We'll go in afterward."

"If only Phoebe or Belva could see me. Belva has her back to us, and Phoebe is the blond."

"If your father sees you first, we won't be able to get to

them." Lone Wolf had pulled on the reins, and the gray and the dun walked along slowly.

Vanessa gripped the buckboard, praying that Phoebe would look at her. Her sisters sat straight, Phoebe staring ahead, her blue eyes wide. Mr. Carter drove, and Papa was seated beside him. Mrs. Carter and Annabelle were in the back with Phoebe and Belva.

Phoebe's glance swept over them without pause. Vanessa felt a sense of panic because Phoebe hadn't recognized her. Phoebe looked solemn and pale, but as beautiful as ever. While her cheeks had lost their usual pink, her blue eyes were wide, thickly lashed; her golden hair was fastened on each side of her head in long curls. Her mouth was pursed and her gaze swept the area, but she didn't give Vanessa another glance. Belva, her brown hair in braids and a blue hat on her head, had her back to Vanessa.

"Suppose neither one of them looks at me."

"We'll have to see to it that one of them does," he answered. "If Belva sees you, will she cry out?"

"No. She's ten years old and she knows she has to go to boarding school as soon as Phoebe marries. She would rather go to California with us than do that."

"There are the soldiers," Lone Wolf said softly. She followed his gaze and saw four men from the cavalry riding toward the church.

She searched their faces to see if she recognized any of the men. One was Corporal Jed Seibert. She felt cold: Lone Wolf was in terrible danger!

The soldiers rode into the churchyard and two dismounted, filing into church. The other two divided, with Corporal Seibert on the east side of the yard, the private on the west.

"One of them knows me," she said quietly, leaning close to Lone Wolf. "Corporal Jed Seibert. He's standing by the oak."

A buggy with a family approached; and as it entered the

churchyard, Lone Wolf turned in behind it and pulled to the
west side of the yard to park. He helped Vanessa from the
buckboard, and they strolled toward the church. Vanessa
kept her head down, holding her skirt as she took his arm,
praying that the wide hat brim hid her face. They entered
the church behind the family of three children and their
parents.

When the family entered the fourth row from the back,
Lone Wolf steered Vanessa to the pew beside them. She
smiled at the woman, and the woman smiled in return.

Vanessa saw Phoebe sitting between Mrs. Carter and
Papa, Belva out of sight farther along the pew. Would
Phoebe glance around? Vanessa straightened her skirt and
looked over the congregation. One cavalryman stood at the
back to her right; another sat along the aisle on the left.
Vanessa had the sinking feeling that her father expected
her. Could he have wrung their plan from Phoebe?

At the thought that he had, Vanessa went cold. She could
have walked into a trap, leading Lone Wolf into it and to
his death.

She inhaled and was tempted to get up and leave, to try
to think of some other way and time to get Phoebe. She
gripped Lone Wolf's hand, so warm around her cold fingers,
and he turned to look at her. She leaned close to him; he
had to duck his head to get beneath her hat brim. "Papa
might have forced Phoebe to tell him what I planned," she
whispered.

Lone Wolf straightened and gazed at the pulpit, and she
wondered if he had heard her because nothing changed in
his expression.

The minister appeared, his black robe swirling around his
legs when he moved to the pulpit and raised his arms in a
sweeping motion, urging the congregation to their feet. The
music grew louder as people began to sing. Mouthing the
familiar hymn, Vanessa watched Phoebe and remembered
Sundays when she had sat with the Carters and her sisters.

Now that part of her life seemed a long time ago. She glanced up at Lone Wolf as he sang in a full baritone voice and she knew he was the reason her life had changed so drastically.

Lone Wolf was hatless now, his Indian blood as obvious as the sunshine outside. His black hair would not conform to the white man's style. Even with a touch of grease, the black locks sprang in different directions. He was risking his life for her this morning and she felt awed, curious about his depth of feeling for her.

The small church was plain with the smell of freshly cut wood in the air. A Texas flag stood in one corner, and the Stars and Stripes in another. The black-haired piano player listened intently to the preacher as his voice rose and he began his sermon.

During the entire service Phoebe never looked around. Papa did, several times glancing over the congregation. The sermon ended, and the collection plates were passed. New members went to the front to join the church, and the congregation sang another hymn. And then the service was over. The family next to Vanessa stood. When they turned to file out in the opposite direction, Lone Wolf stood up slowly. And then the Carters were coming down the aisle.

Phoebe was in front of Papa! Vanessa didn't dare look at her. She looked down at her lap and prayed Lone Wolf would keep his head down because Papa would cause a scene about an Indian in church.

Suddenly Lone Wolf reached over, his fingers closing around her wrist as he gave her a squeeze. She looked up, gazing beyond him into Phoebe's wide eyes. Papa's head was turned as he talked to someone on the other side of the aisle. Vanessa looked down quickly once she knew that Phoebe had seen her. She hoped that none of the Carters had. Vanessa followed Lone Wolf, and they joined the crowd in the aisle behind the Carters.

At the open door, some people stopped to shake hands

with the pastor. Lone Wolf took Vanessa's hand and eased through the crowd. A large woman with a sunbonnet suddenly materialized in front of them, smiling at Vanessa and studying Lone Wolf.

"You folks are new, aren't you?"

"Yes, ma'am," Lone Wolf said in a drawl that sounded as if he had been born in Louisiana, and Vanessa looked up at him in shock. Where had he learned to talk like that?

"I'm Beauregard Hamilton and this is my wife, Jane Hamilton, ma'am."

"I'm so glad to meet you. I'm Hazel Benjamin, and we're happy to welcome you to Glen Hollow. You live close?"

"We bought some land south of here, ma'am. You'll see a lot of us from now on. It's been right nice to meet you."

"Thank you, it was so nice to meet you."

Lone Wolf hurried Vanessa away from Hazel Benjamin, pushing her back toward the steps of the church.

Another smiling woman who was tall and thin blocked their path. "I'm Priscilla Dartmoor, and I'm so happy you visited our church."

"Thank you, ma'am." Lone Wolf smiled politely. "I'm Beauregard Hamilton, and this is my wife Jane Hamilton. We seem to have left my wife's handkerchief back in the church."

"I'm sure it'll be there. It's nice having you. Come again."

He smiled and pushed Vanessa along.

"Every woman here is looking at you and probably wants to meet you!" she snapped as he nodded right and left, propelling them through the crowd. "What are you doing? The buckboard—"

"Your sisters just went back into the church. Hurry!"

Vanessa's heart raced as they moved against the crowd, climbing the steps. She was blocked by small groups of dawdlers, and Lone Wolf pushed ahead of her, shouldering his way through slowly. "Sorry," he said, smiling.

"Excuse me."

She murmured apologies, and then they were through the throng and easing their way into the church again. Phoebe and Belva stood at the other end of the sanctuary, and no one else was inside. Lone Wolf moved ahead of Vanessa, running down the aisle toward them, his black coat flying open while Vanessa raced after him.

"Vanessa!" Belva cried, turning toward her.

"Let's go," Lone Wolf snapped, cutting her short as she dashed around the pews to them. He reached around her to open a window. "Climb out."

He swung Belva up over the sill, his large hands circling her tiny waist. Her blue hat tumbled off as she gripped his wrists, her eyes huge, and then she dropped to the ground.

He lifted Phoebe out next. She looked pale, her mouth clamped tightly shut. Then his strong hands closed around Vanessa's waist, and he set her outside as well.

He followed, dropping to the ground on both feet, and motioned toward the trees a hundred yards away behind the church. "Run!"

With her heart pounding, Vanessa gripped Phoebe's hand and raced over the ground, her hat sliding behind her head as she held her skirt high. Lone Wolf held Belva's hand as they dashed for the trees. Vanessa ran between cedars and beneath two tall oaks.

"Head for the draw and the horses," Lone Wolf ordered, moving ahead of them toward the west. "We have to get away before you're missed."

They kept to the bushes, and Vanessa realized he had chosen well, because they had cover. In seconds, they reached the four horses. They mounted swiftly, and the whole time Phoebe said nothing. She was white, looking as if she might faint, and Vanessa reached over to squeeze her hand.

"They've missed her," Lone Wolf said grimly, motioning

to the south. Vanessa looked back to see two men run around the church.

"Go!" Lone Wolf snapped. He raced ahead, and Vanessa clung to the horse, praying Phoebe and Belva could keep up with them. They had given Phoebe the bay, and its legs stretched out as they raced along so that it pulled even with Lone Wolf on the paint.

As they pounded over the ground, a shot rang out. Vanessa looked behind to see two soldiers galloping after them.

"Vanessa!" Phoebe's cry was lost on the wind, and Vanessa had a moment of panic. Lone Wolf turned, rifle in hand, and fired behind him. She didn't look back, passing him and riding next to Phoebe. He fired again and the soldiers fired, and then Lone Wolf raced ahead to lead the way.

Vanessa's heart pounded, fear tearing at her, afraid a shot would hit one of them, knowing the soldiers would aim for Lone Wolf. Frightened that they hadn't had enough lead to escape, she leaned over the horse.

They pounded down a draw and around a grove of oaks. Then Lone Wolf reversed their path and rode into the trees, motioning to them to follow. With the horses' sides heaving, they turned. Vanessa rode close to Phoebe, glancing at Belva, who was an experienced rider and more accustomed to horses and the outdoors than Phoebe.

They entered a dense wood and waited. She shivered, gripped with fear, knowing Lone Wolf was in the greatest danger. She heard galloping horses racing toward them and she held her breath as soldiers rushed into view and raced on past them. As soon as they had gone, she glanced at Lone Wolf, expecting him to turn in the opposite direction. Instead he held up his hand indicating that they should wait.

In another few minutes, half-a-dozen men galloped by and she saw her father on one of the horses. He was hatless, his blond hair blowing in the wind, a scowl on his face.

She shivered, knowing that if they were caught the consequences would be terrible. Her gaze went to Lone Wolf, who sat watching the direction the men had ridden, his jaw set, his features impassive. He looked unafraid.

As the sound of the pounding hooves faded, Lone Wolf jerked his head and rode forward, doubling back the way they had come. Uncertain about directions, Vanessa followed him as he wound through the trees along a clear stream. They rode into the shallow, swift-running water, heading upstream and turning west. Lone Wolf kept up a fast pace, and Vanessa became hopelessly lost, wondering how long before they would be able to join up with Muaahap and White Bird.

Finally, along another clear stream with water rushing over smooth rocks, he reined and turned to face them. "We stop a moment."

Vanessa looked at Phoebe, who toppled forward. Lone Wolf vaulted from his horse and caught her before she touched the ground, easing her down. He yanked a handkerchief from his pocket and handed it to Vanessa, and she dashed to the stream to dampen the cloth. Cold water rushed over her hands as she wrung out the linen then went back to sponge Phoebe's face.

While they knelt over Phoebe, Belva dismounted to lead the horses to water. Phoebe's eyes fluttered, and she looked from Lone Wolf to Vanessa.

"Vanessa!" she gasped and reached for her sister. The two hugged as Phoebe sobbed.

"Shh, Phoebe. We're safe now."

"They'll find us, Vanessa. I know they will. Papa is in a rage over your running away. He's made dire threats, and this will make him angrier than ever."

"They won't find us. They haven't found me. Shh. Phoebe, this is Lone Wolf. Lone Wolf, may I present my sister Phoebe Sutherland?"

"How do you do," Phoebe said, gazing at him with curiosity in her eyes.

"We need to ride again. We're not in a safe place."

She nodded and started to get up. He reached down to take her arm and slid his hand around her waist, lifting her to her feet. "All right?"

"Yes, I am."

Her hair had come unpinned in the wild ride. It tumbled in a golden fall around her shoulders, and Lone Wolf studied her. She was a beautiful young woman, but Vanessa was wrong about her sister being the true beauty. There was an earthiness to Vanessa that he found more appealing, and her flaming hair was a special beauty that he would never forget.

And he understood Vanessa's fear for her sister, because Phoebe seemed as frightened and helpless as a small child.

He moved toward the horses, and the younger sister turned to look at him. She was plainer than her older sisters with wide, blue eyes and a wide jaw, yet she seemed stronger and less fearful than Phoebe, more like Vanessa.

"Belva, this is Lone Wolf. This is my sister, Belva Sutherland," Vanessa said.

"Thank you for helping get us away," Belva said quietly. "Papa is so angry already. Now he'll be in a terrible rage."

Lone Wolf smiled at her. "We need to mount and ride again, Belva. We're too close to the church."

She mounted at once, swinging into the saddle with ease. He assisted Phoebe and hoped she wouldn't faint again. He felt a twinge of impatience, knowing she couldn't have cared for him as Vanessa had. He glanced at the youngest and guessed that Belva might be like Vanessa when she was older.

Leading the way, he glanced over his shoulder. Vanessa was the last and he knew it was her doing, but he hated for her to be back where she might catch a bullet.

He had been astounded at the shots which were fired at

them, shocked that Sutherland hadn't ordered the men to refrain from firing so that they wouldn't strike one of his daughters.

Lone Wolf urged his horse to a gallop again, wondering if Phoebe could keep up the pace, suspecting that Vanessa would see to it she did.

They rode across rolling country covered in honey mesquite, cottonwoods, chokecherry, and junipers. They disturbed a herd of mule deer, the black tips of their tails showing as they bounded away. Red squirrels and jackrabbits were abundant, scattering as the horses raced past.

By nightfall, Vanessa caught up with him. "Phoebe is about to faint again. Do you think the soldiers are following us?"

"I don't know. If they have a good tracker, they will. But he'll have to be very good," Lone Wolf said, and she thought about the long way they had traveled up a river until it deepened and they had had to turn out onto the bank.

She reached over to squeeze his hand. "You got them away! We're free!" Joy and excitement coursed through her. "I knew we could get them and escape!"

"Don't rejoice yet, Vanessa," he warned her. "Your father isn't going to just give up. They'll continue searching, and he'll put out word through the military all over the west."

Sobering, she nodded, knowing he was right. She glanced back over her shoulder, aware that soldiers could be on their trail right now.

"We did get them away from the church."

"I won't feel safe until we're far north of Tucumcari."

They were several hundred miles from Tucumcari, so it meant the danger would be great for days. She drew a deep breath, feeling uneasy and glancing behind her again.

"Where are Muaahap and White Bird? Shouldn't we have joined them hours ago?" she asked, turning around to look at him, knowing tonight he would shed the coat and pants and go back to his buckskins. The white shirt made his skin look the color of teak, and she stared at him, thinking him the most handsome man she had ever known.

"We're not there yet," he said, shaking his head. "Muaahap knows where to meet us."

"You didn't tell me they were traveling far."

"I didn't see any reason you should worry about it. We'll be safe if we keep going."

"How did you know where to tell her to meet you?"

He smiled. "You don't remember being here?"

She looked around at the mesquite, rocks, and grass without recognition. "Do you remember being here?"

"Yes, I do. And there they are."

She looked ahead, and her heart leaped with pleasure as Muaahap stood up to greet them and White Bird came toddling toward them. "Mama! Mama!"

"Mama!" Phoebe echoed, looking at Vanessa, who smiled. "She's Lone Wolf's niece. I'll explain later."

They halted and Vanessa dismounted, catching White Bird up in her arms, hugging her as the thin little arms tightened around her neck. White Bird smelled like roses and Vanessa buried her face in the child's hair, thankful they had made it back and she was with White Bird and Muaahap again.

She set White Bird on her feet and glanced up to see Lone Wolf watching her and Phoebe staring at her, a frown furrowing her brow.

Lone Wolf introduced Belva and Phoebe to Muaahap and White Bird. Vanessa was exhausted, and she supposed Phoebe was near to fainting again. They hadn't stopped to eat all day, only chewing on pemmican as they rode.

Since Lone Wolf wouldn't permit a fire, they ate cold chunks of beef, potatoes, and wild plums, and finally Vanessa relaxed.

Belva was enchanted with White Bird, and Vanessa saw that White Bird now would have two doting on her constantly. After supper, Vanessa and Phoebe sat close together on a quilt while Belva held White Bird on her lap and told her stories she couldn't understand. Muaahap stretched out on hides near Belva, listening to her with an interest that rivaled White Bird's. Lone Wolf sat across the camp and cleaned his rifle.

"I couldn't believe it at first when I looked over and saw you. I never expected you to be with a man," Phoebe said, glancing shyly at Lone Wolf as he turned the rifle in his hands. "You left your buggy at the church and your horses."

"We expected to have to leave them. Lone Wolf bought the buckboard and the team with that in mind."

"Vanessa, Papa is livid that you ran away. He fired poor Mrs. Parsons and he's had Sergeant Hollings demoted. He's hired a Pinkerton man to search for you, and put out a military alert."

"I've been careful," Vanessa replied.

Phoebe's gaze drifted to Lone Wolf. "What are you doing with him? Who is he?"

"I found Lone Wolf near our wagon train. He had been wounded in battle and had White Bird with him. He had horses and I saw my chance to escape, so I took it."

"He's Indian!"

"He's Kiowa. He speaks English because he was an army scout for two years."

"Aren't you terrified of him?" Phoebe asked in a whisper.

"He saved you, Phoebe!"

"If Papa catches you with him, he will kill all three of them," she said darkly. "He's already offered a reward for you, and there's no telling what he'll do now."

"Phoebe, we'll take you to a stage to go to California or you can ride with us back to Lone Wolf's people."

"You're going with him?" Phoebe asked, aghast, her blue eyes wide.

"I don't think he'll let me get on the stage with you. Right now, he has agreed to take you to a stage station where you can head west. If you want to go, do so before he changes his mind and takes you back to his people, too."

"You can run away from him!"

"No, I can't. Not if he doesn't want to let me go. Phoebe, he was going to take me back to his people and leave you. He did this for me. I'll cooperate with him now."

"No!" Phoebe cried out and then clamped her hand over her mouth as Lone Wolf glanced at them. "He's a savage, Vanessa!"

"Hardly," Vanessa answered patiently. "Phoebe, Lone Wolf risked his life for you and Belva. Papa has offered a bounty for any dead Indians. *That's* savage, Phoebe. Lone Wolf saved you today—don't ever forget that."

"I won't, but you have to come with Belva and me to California. You can't go with him! It's indecent, and you won't be happy."

Vanessa looked at Belva and White Bird. The tiny girl sat on a hide while Belva sang a song and motioned with her hands.

"I'm not certain that I want to go west any longer," Vanessa said, looking at Lone Wolf. His head swung around, and she met his gaze. She spoke softly because she knew how keen his hearing was.

"You *want* to stay?" Phoebe studied her. "Oh, Vanessa, are you in love with him?" she asked, stricken.

"Yes, but he's not in love with me. He was once married, and men who worked for our father killed his wife."

"Surely not!"

"They did, Phoebe," Vanessa answered calmly, glancing again at him, knowing she loved him more each day. Now that he had rescued Phoebe and Belva, she was overwhelmed with gratitude.

"I'd think he'd hate us."

"No, but he hates Papa."

"I don't want to stay out here with savages and renegades

and soldiers. I don't want to be where Papa and Major Thompkins can find me!"

"Then I suggest we get you on a stage quickly before someone does find you or Lone Wolf decides he wants to take another captive back to his people."

Phoebe shivered and look around. "Who is the woman? His mother?"

"No. She's a Comanche we met along the way who lost her family. She loves White Bird very much and wanted to ride with us."

Phoebe nodded, looking again at Lone Wolf. "He's very handsome, but he terrifies me. You don't fear him?"

"No, I don't fear him," Vanessa said quietly, knowing they should get Phoebe to a stage quickly before Lone Wolf changed his mind or they encountered Comanche or Kiowa who might want Phoebe. Or her father did do something to stir Lone Wolf's rage.

"I'm exhausted."

"Sleep there," Vanessa said, pointing to a quilt and hides.

Phoebe flung her arms around Vanessa and hugged her. "Thank you for coming back to get me. I still can't believe I'm free. Vanessa, I couldn't bear to marry Major Thompkins. I told Papa, but he wouldn't listen and my reluctance made him furious."

"We're not safe yet," Vanessa cautioned, giving Phoebe a squeeze.

"Papa has gotten so much more unreasonable. I'm thankful to be away. And he talks constantly of Ethan and his deeds. Our brother is very special to Papa."

"I don't think Papa ever wanted us."

"Except for his own purposes. He doesn't like to be thwarted." Phoebe hugged Vanessa again. "Thank you for coming back. I'll thank Lone Wolf. I was so afraid you might not return—" Phoebe shivered. "If Papa catches us . . ." her voice trailed away and she moved to the quilt, stretching out and pulling a robe over her. Vanessa crossed the dark campsite to Lone Wolf, who was seated on a rock.

"Phoebe is going to sleep. I'm exhausted, too. Do you think it's safe to sleep?"

"I'll watch for a while, and then Muaahap said she would take a turn."

"Don't disturb Muaahap. She needs her rest. Get me and I'll sit up." She reached out to touch his arm. "Thank you. I couldn't have done this alone."

He studied her and then reached out, his hand going behind her neck, pressing against her nape to draw her closer as he leaned forward to kiss her. His mouth was warm on hers, his lips firm as his tongue entered her mouth. Her pulse jumped, and she kissed him in return, leaning against him as he sat on a rock, his knees touching her thighs. She wanted more of him, so much more. Finally, he pulled away.

"How many days until we reach the stage station?" she asked.

He stared across the campsite. "With five women—who can guess?" His gaze returned to Vanessa. "If we travel fast, we might get there within six or seven days. I don't know whether Phoebe can keep that pace. I think Belva can. We'll head northwest into New Mexico Territory." His dark eyes rested on her. "You're not going on that stage, Vanessa. I'm taking you with me."

She nodded, looking into his dark eyes but unable to guess what ran through his thoughts, longing for more from him than he was willing to give.

"I'm going to sleep now. Call me to take a turn." She walked away, aching to be in his arms. She stepped behind a large juniper for privacy and changed from the muslin dress to buckskin because it was more comfortable.

She heard a footstep and looked around. Lone Wolf stood watching her. He walked toward her. The moonlight spilled

over him, and his dark eyes held a smoldering hunger that
made her heart lurch and race.

"We have something to settle, Vanessa."

Sixteen

She watched him approach and her mouth grew dry, her insides fluttery. After the strain of the long day, she wanted to throw herself into his arms and shower him with kisses as she had the night he told her he would turn back to McKavett. Instead, she stood quietly watching him, her pulse drumming as he walked up to her.

"We rode into danger today that was as great as any I've ever faced," he said in a low voice, drawing her farther away from the campsite. They moved in silence until he turned again to face her, his brown eyes intense, his hands stroking her shoulders.

"I went back to get your sisters and risked my life today; and when I did that, I made myself a promise."

Her heart thudded. She could imagine what he had promised and she stared at him, torn between warring desires. She wanted him to love her and she wanted to avoid any lovemaking with him until he was ready to ask her to be his wife. She did not want to live with him and then be cast aside when he picked an Indian maiden for his mate. With every kiss, each time in his arms, she became even more his woman.

"When dawn came I fully expected this to be the last day of my life. This morning I promised myself that if I lived through this day, you would be in my arms tonight."

"Then you should have asked me this morning, because you made that decision without—"

"Vanessa," he said softly, interrupting her, her name drawn out in a slow drawl that played over her like a lingering caress, a husky tone that held promises of ecstasy. His hands slid to her nape and stroked her and she drew a deep breath, feeling her nipples become taut.

With deliberation, he pulled off his shirt and spread it on the ground, the muscles in his chest rippling as he moved.

"I think that we—" she began again, but he leaned forward, his mouth brushing hers.

He picked up her braid, looking at her as he began to undo it. The faint tugs on her scalp were the same as a caress because his dark eyes held a longing that made her breathless.

He loosened the braids, running his large fingers through her hair, combing free the locks so they fell around her face. He framed her face with his hands, turning her mouth up to his as he bent his head. His mouth slanted over hers, his tongue entering her mouth, sliding in a sensual draw across the inside of her lower lip.

She moaned softly, knowing she could not resist him. She was bound by his caresses and her love. Her hands drifted across his strong shoulders, sliding down his smooth back as his arm went around her waist and he pulled her up tightly against him.

She loved him, wisely or not, and her future was here on this untamed land with a man who was equally wild.

"Vanessa." He whispered her name, trailing kisses along her throat as he removed her buckskin dress. She hadn't put on her underdrawers and she was bare beneath the leather. He inhaled swiftly, stepping forward to cup her breasts and kiss her, his tongue playing over her taut nipple.

With a groan he picked her up and lowered her to his shirt, kneeling beside her. His dark eyes bored through her and Vanessa ached with wanting all of him, his heart as well as his body.

"I love you," she whispered, stroking his chest.

His eyes narrowed a fraction and he stroked her leg, bending his head to trail his tongue along the inside of her thigh, moving higher. She gasped as his tongue flicked over her soft folds, probing, a satiny, heated pressure against her that made her close her eyes and arch her hips and clutch his strong shoulders.

"Please," she whispered and felt him move between her legs and lower himself, his hot shaft entering her, filling her slowly as his arms banded her.

"Vanessa," he whispered and she kissed his throat, her hands playing over him, sliding over his firm buttocks, pulling him up against her as she held him tightly and wrapped her legs around him, wishing she could wrap herself around his heart. For this moment, he was hers; they were one, their hearts beating together.

His control vanished and he thrust hard and fast, taking her as she moved wildly beneath him. Spasms rocked her and she felt his body shudder with his hot release. "Vanessa, love . . ."

Dimly she heard his words and clung to him, wanting all of him for all time.

Gradually they quieted, bodies damp with perspiration while he stroked her. "You're a very brave, strong woman."

She turned her head to kiss his hand, pleased by his words but longing for so much more from him. "If I were really so strong, I would get on the stage with Phoebe and go to California," she whispered. "I can't be satisfied with only part of you."

His dark eyes studied her, and then he moved away, pulling her up into his arms to kiss her again.

"We should go back," he said when he released her. "And we must be up and on our way early. They could ride all night after us and we'd lose any lead we have."

She nodded, realizing she should rethink her future, her

plans to stay, because she would always feel this yearning for him, wanting his love as well as his body.

They walked back quietly, and he left her to return to his chores while Vanessa packed the green dress and lay down for the night.

Stretched out beneath a buffalo robe, Vanessa stared at the hundreds of twinkling stars overhead in the midnight sky. She should take the stage with Phoebe and leave Lone Wolf to his Kiowa way and his memories.

Her gaze shifted to Lone Wolf as he settled with his back against the trunk of a tree, his rifle across his knees, a robe thrown across his shoulders.

The logical thing would be to go to California. She turned to study his arrogant profile, knowing she loved him completely. Could she forget him in time?

Sleeping only a couple hours, she stirred and sat up with the first graying of morning. Lone Wolf was packing the horses and getting ready to ride.

She combed her hair from her face with her fingers and went to wash. When she returned, she went to Lone Wolf, who was seated on a rock eating fruit and jerked beef. White Bird sat close beside him, devouring a plum, her mouth wet with purple juice.

"Get some food. I'll wake the others in a minute."

"You didn't wake me during the night to watch for soldiers. Did you stay up all night?"

"No, I woke Muaahap."

Vanessa stared at him, wondering why, and then she understood. "You didn't want me to take Phoebe and Belva and slip away in the night!"

His dark eyes gazed at her with his unreadable stare. "I didn't want to have to get up this morning and ride across the country to find you."

"I had no intention of running away with Phoebe."

Only the slightest arch of his eyebrow indicated his doubts. "Why would you stay? You told me you don't want to be my woman."

"And you're not going to let me get on the stage," she said, wondering whether he would try to stop her or not.

"No, I'm not." He answered calmly as if she were in full agreement. "I went back for your sister, but you're mine and I'm taking you with me."

Vanessa drew a deep breath, knowing that if she wanted to go to California, she could get away from him in Tucumcari, certain that he would let her go if she really wanted to leave. "Don't get Muaahap up again at night. You can tie my hands to a tree, but she needs her sleep."

A faint glint of amusement lighted his eyes as he studied her. "Very well. Now sit and eat. We can't risk a fire, so this is all you can eat."

"Mama, eat?" White Bird asked, smiling at Vanessa, who knelt down in front of her and smiled in return.

She slanted him a look, aware his knee was only inches away. "If the soldiers do come and are about to take us, we'll divide. I'll go with Phoebe, and you take Muaahap and White Bird and ride away."

Lone Wolf studied her and knew why she was making the request. "You would let them take you so that we could escape?"

"Yes," she said, glancing at White Bird. "She wouldn't be safe and neither would you or Muaahap."

He looked beyond her and felt a surge of anger as he thought about Abbot Sutherland. How badly he would like to meet the man face to face, each free to fight the other. Yet, Sutherland and men like him did not fight their own battles. They hired men to run the risks. He had to be a wealthy man to be a railroader, yet Vanessa gave little indication of coming from wealth.

"Will you do that?"

He looked at Vanessa and curbed the impulse to reach

for her again as he had in the night. Her lips were full and rosy in invitation as she studied him. "Yes, I'll do that because of White Bird."

"Thank you."

"You are brave, Vanessa," he said again.

"Thank you," she said. "That pleases me for you to think so. Now I'll have breakfast. Shall I call Muaahap and my sisters?"

"That will end the quiet, but, yes, you should call them. We need to go as soon as possible."

Within the hour they had eaten and were mounted. They followed Lone Wolf, White Bird with Muaahap. Phoebe followed with Belva, and Vanessa came last. Several times during the day, her back prickled and she looked behind her, praying they weren't being followed and trying to reassure herself that Lone Wolf would know if they were.

As the sun rose in the sky, White Bird became wiggly and Phoebe glanced back at Vanessa more and more often as if looking for an indication that they might stop.

They crossed a wide, clear stream, and the water reminded Vanessa of her hunger.

Muaahap looked around at Phoebe and then pulled out her long stick and jabbed Lone Wolf. He jerked around, looking mildly annoyed, and said something to her in Comanche. He turned back to continue riding.

"Sua yurahpitu," she snapped and jabbed his back again.

He looked around and frowned, his eyes narrowing as she jabbered and motioned and waved the stick at him. Vanessa knew he was losing the battle and reined in her mount. Instantly, Phoebe halted and dismounted.

With a serene smile, Muaahap handed White Bird to Phoebe and then she dismounted and walked away. Frowning, Lone Wolf sat on his horse as Vanessa walked closer and placed her hands on her hips to look up at him. "You might as well get down and rest."

"I've had men under my command in the army. I've had

warriors who obey me without question; and my wife obeyed me, as well as my mother and my sister-in-law. But this—" He broke off and waved his hand. "I think you encourage her."

"I didn't do anything!" Vanessa protested, laughing. He swung his leg over the horse's withers and dropped lightly to the ground.

"It is worth it to see your laughter, but I pray all of you will obey me if I warn you of danger."

"Of course we will, but everyone needed to stop."

"Not everyone, Vanessa. I should like to put Muaahap on that stage to California."

Vanessa smiled, amused at his annoyance and at Muaahap's independence. "I don't think Muaahap would want to go to California."

"No, she wouldn't," he said, leading Vanessa away from the others. They walked through the woods in the cool, crisp afternoon. The land was brown with winter, an occasional juniper dark green against the land. Hawks circled lazily overhead, and she felt safe beside him.

"When we get to the stage station, we will have to be careful. I don't think we should all be seen together. They will have my description from the church in Glen Hollow because of that woman who stood and talked with us. She may remember me and what I look like—"

Vanessa turned to lean against the trunk of a bare-limbed cottonwood with only a few brown leaves turning in the winter breeze. She smiled at him. "Of course. She'll remember exactly what you looked like. She was a female."

He gave her a mocking look and placed one hand on the trunk over her head, leaning closer. She stared at him with curiosity.

"Where did you learn to talk like that, Beauregard Hamilton?"

He shrugged, his dark gaze intent on her. "When I was stationed in Louisiana and when we were in Texas." He traced his finger along her jaw. "Vanessa, I've given some thought to you."

Her heart jumped because he looked solemn as he gazed down at her. He stood close, his arm stretched over her head. His black hair was a tangle, the part she had carefully combed now gone, giving him a shaggy appearance.

"White Bird calls you mama," he said, lowering his hand to her shoulder, a light touch that made her tremble with longing. "I want you for my woman and I intend to keep you and take you back to my camp." He looked at her intently.

"You can't hold me if I don't want to stay," she said stiffly, wondering if she would ever have the resolve and strength to resist him.

"I will marry you, and we will give White Bird a mother and father. If this is what you want, then I will take you as my wife."

Seventeen

Stunned, Vanessa gazed up at him as he waited for her answer. Her heart drummed, and she thought about all he was asking.

Could she marry and know that he still loved and grieved for his wife, that he was doing this for White Bird's sake and to have a woman in his bed at night? She wanted him to ask her to marry him because he loved her.

Vanessa stared into his dark eyes, thinking again of moments in his arms, wanting more than his lovemaking, wanting his heart. Yet if she refused, what would happen? She suspected he would still keep her captive and take her back to his people.

"You ask me to marry, but your heart and your love is ever with Eyes That Smile."

He didn't reply, but he didn't need to because she knew his answer. She ducked beneath his arm and walked away, standing with her back to him, wondering what she should do. If she accepted his proposal and stayed, would she forever regret it?

She could be carrying Lone Wolf's child right now. "When would we marry?"

"When we get back to my people. We will have a Kiowa wedding."

"We should find a local judge as well because in the eyes of my father, a Kiowa wedding would not be binding."

Lone Wolf's fingers closed on her forearm, spinning her

around to face him. "*I* would consider it binding," he snapped, and she realized she had angered him.

"What about Belva?"

"I will take her as my daughter as well as White Bird. According to Kiowa ways, your sisters can become my wives," he said with a sudden twinkle in his eyes, "but I will forego that."

"You'll open your heart to Belva?"

"Yes. You intend to care for her and you love White Bird, so it seems natural that they will be ours."

Ours. She turned her head, watching the few brown leaves flutter in the cottonwood.

"Will Belva want to stay and follow the Indian road?" he asked quietly. "To go from the life she's always known to our life will be a shock for her."

"If she's loved and wanted, she'll be content. You'll see. Phoebe would never adjust. Phoebe doesn't like the outdoors or animals; she belongs in a city, but Belva loves horses and being outdoors."

"I've noticed. She will be a strong woman like you."

As she considered his proposal, Vanessa ran her fingers along the rough gray bark of the tree trunk. Her fingers skimmed the ridges as she pondered her future. With time, would Lone Wolf stop grieving and grow to love her?

He offered marriage when she wanted love. She glanced up at him. He had risked his life for her in riding south to rescue her sisters. Was there a stronger feeling for her than he acknowledged?

Whether there was or not, she was willing to take the risk that love would come. "Yes, I will marry you," she answered solemnly, wondering if she were throwing away her future happiness because his world would be so different from the one she had always known.

He nodded as he studied her. "My grief will end someday, Vanessa."

She gazed up at him, wanting his love, yet excited because she would have a part of him and his feelings for her might grow and change with time. And with children. He smiled, touching Vanessa's cheek with the back of his hand.

"What will we tell Muaahap?" she asked. "She thinks we're already married."

"I'll explain to Muaahap, and she will accept it. She will accept anything you do because she likes you."

"And I'll tell Phoebe then also Belva, so she can think about what lies ahead."

Lone Wolf drew Vanessa to him, his dark eyes boring into her as he bent his head to kiss her, a lingering kiss that was filled with promise. She raised up on tiptoe and laced her arms around his neck. "I want your love and will try to win it," she told him, meeting his gaze.

He kissed her and she wondered if he had no answer and wanted to silence her or merely wanted to kiss her instead of talking.

Half an hour later they were ready to ride again; and as they moved away, she glanced back, reaching out to pick a small cottonwood leaf that was still yellow, knowing she would always remember where he had asked her to become his wife. She carefully placed the leaf in the saddlebag and looked at Lone Wolf riding ahead, his shoulders squared, his short black hair tangled by the wind, as they headed northwest toward New Mexico Territory.

That night when they stopped, she noticed Belva helping Lone Wolf as he unsaddled the horses. Several times Vanessa heard Belva's laughter and glanced at them. After they had eaten a cold dinner of sliced beef, apples, biscuits, and beans, as she cleaned and put away their things, she noticed Belva holding White Bird on her lap while Lone Wolf taught Belva how to tie knots.

"She likes Lone Wolf," Phoebe said, walking up behind Vanessa.

"Yes, she does. And it'll make things easier." She turned

to face Phoebe. "I wanted to talk to you. Lone Wolf has asked me to marry him."

Phoebe's mouth dropped open. "You won't consider his proposal, will you?"

"Yes. I've accepted. I want to marry him."

"You can't!" Phoebe exclaimed, her eyes round. "Vanessa, he's a savage, an Indian! You'll roam the country—"

"I love him," Vanessa said quietly, "and you sound like Papa. There's been nothing savage about him since he helped you escape from Papa. And I won't roam the country as much as I did while growing up."

Phoebe closed her mouth and stared at Lone Wolf. "I suppose I do sound like Papa. Lone Wolf's been kind and marvelous to us, and he's so patient with Belva and White Bird. And Muaahap is kind to Belva, too. She gave Belva a silver bracelet today."

"Muaahap loves her jewelry, so it shows how much she cares to give one of her treasures to Belva."

"What about Belva? Do you want me to take her to California? I can, you know."

Vanessa looked at Phoebe. "I think we should give Belva the choice. Lone Wolf said he will be happy to have her as his daughter."

"That's more than Papa was!" Phoebe said bitterly. "So you'll tell Belva and let her choose?"

"I think she's old enough." Vanessa looked at Belva as she bent over a rope and Lone Wolf watched her tie it.

"I think I know what her choice will be," Phoebe said quietly. "She has always been close to you because you're really a mother to her. Look at her with him now. She'll want him for a father. She already adores White Bird and treats her as if she had a new doll." Phoebe sighed and turned to Vanessa. "Papa smashed Belva's doll collection."

"He *what?*" Vanessa asked, anger shaking her.

"When he heard you had run away, he went into a rage and said he couldn't wait for me to marry Major Thompkins and he would make arrangements for Belva to go to boarding school in Philadelphia the afternoon after my wedding. She could see me wed and then she would be sent away. She started crying and that made him angrier. You know how he hates it if we cry. He pushed her dolls to the floor and stomped on them."

"Oh, Phoebe, he's never been that cruel!"

"He was cruel to you when he gave the dog away that Mama let you have."

"Yes, but it seems worse with Belva. Now I'm doubly glad she's with us."

"Yes." Phoebe turned to Vanessa and hugged her. "And I'm happy for you because Lone Wolf is kind and brave and so handsome, Vanessa!"

"Thank you," Vanessa said quietly, not wanting to tell Phoebe that he still mourned the loss of his first wife.

"Have you told Muaahap?"

"Muaahap already thinks we're married. When the Comanche found us, Lone Wolf was wounded and near death. He told them I was his wife and White Bird his daughter so we would be safe. I've never told her otherwise. Lone Wolf said he would talk to her."

"It won't matter to her. She loves you and White Bird and Belva."

Later, before Belva went to sleep, Vanessa sat down beside her and brushed her hair. The long strands were wavy from being braided, and Vanessa lifted the thick, brown locks to brush them carefully. "Belva, I need to talk to you."

She turned to look up at Vanessa and twisted her arm in front of her. "Look what Muaahap gave me!" Moonlight glinted on the silver bracelet that circled her slender arm.

"It's one of her pretty bracelets. I hope you remembered to say thank you."

"I did, and I gave her the locket that I wore to church. She liked it. I like Muaahap."

"I'm glad. Belva, Lone Wolf has asked me to marry him."

"Land sakes! That's wonderful! You'll be with him always."

"Yes, I will."

"Papa wouldn't ever approve."

"He may never know. I want to ask you—do you want to live with us? We both want you. Or do you want to go to California with Phoebe? She will be glad to take you."

Belva glanced at Phoebe and looked at White Bird, and then her gaze shifted to Lone Wolf.

Vanessa placed her hand on Belva's knee. "You don't have to decide now. You think about it. No decision has to be made until we reach Tucumcari and buy the tickets to California."

"I want to be with all of you as we are now! Can't we talk Phoebe into staying, too?"

"No, we can't. I asked her, and she said she wanted to go to California."

"I don't want us to be separated," Belva said fiercely, and Vanessa stroked her head.

"I don't either, but Phoebe wants to try to get into the opera. She thinks she can, and I have some of Papa's money so she can go to California. She has a friend there who will help her. We have to let her have her chance, Belva."

She saw tears fill Belva's eyes before Belva threw her arms around Vanessa's neck. "I want to be with both of you and with White Bird and Muaahap and Lone Wolf!"

Letting her cry, Vanessa stroked Belva's back and hugged her thin body. She saw Muaahap watching them without a change in her expression.

Belva wiped her eyes, looking at Vanessa as more tears spilled down her cheeks. "Vanessa, Papa smashed my dolls!"

"I'm sorry, Belva. Phoebe told me, and I'm sorry."

Belva pulled open the drawstrings of the dainty beaded

silk reticule she carried. "Look. He missed Delphinia, and I keep her with me all the time," she said, pulling out a china doll with a green organdy dress and black slippers on its tiny china feet.

"Oh, I'm so glad!" Vanessa said, looking at one of her old dolls that their mother had given her and she had passed on to Belva.

"Some time, Vanessa, may I have a dress like the one you're wearing? White Bird has one, and Muaahap has one."

"Yes, you may," Vanessa answered, although she knew that if Belva decided to go to California with Phoebe, she wouldn't be able to wear a buckskin dress.

Belva snuggled down on a hide and pulled a soft buffalo robe up to her chin. "I love you, Vanessa. Thank you for coming back to get us."

"I love you, too," Vanessa said, leaning down to kiss Belva and stroke her brown hair away from her face. "I'm thankful Lone Wolf and I were able to get you and Phoebe, but the danger isn't over yet, so we have to be careful."

"I know. Lone Wolf told me if I see a soldier or hear anything strange to tell him or tell you."

"That's right."

"I don't want to go back."

"None of us do."

Belva closed her eyes and Vanessa stood up, moving to the hide where she would sleep. Lone Wolf sat close, his legs crossed, and he looked as if he had been waiting for her.

"Belva is having difficulty?"

"First she cried because I told her you and I would marry and she would have to choose whether to stay with us or go to California with Phoebe. I told her to think it over."

"And why did she cry later?"

"Because she remembered that Papa had smashed all her dolls except one."

"Why would he do that?" Lone Wolf asked fiercely.

"Because he was furious about my running away."

"She had nothing to do with you." Lone Wolf stared beyond her. "It is best if our paths never cross, Vanessa. It was all I could do to leave your father alone at the churchyard."

"I understand," she said quietly, placing her hand on his. "He's my father, though." Lone Wolf gazed at her and she felt his warm hand beneath her fingers.

"I have told Muaahap that we are not man and wife. I have told her why we said we were and all about your past—as well as Muaahap and I communicate," he added with a chuckle.

"And you told her you will marry me when we get to your camp?"

"Yes, Vanessa," he said, lacing her fingers in his. The touch sent fiery tingles throughout her body. Longing filled her, and she wished she could marry him soon.

She gazed into his eyes, barely able to discern him in the dark night, and wondered how long it would be until they were man and wife. "Do you think your people will be in the same place as they were when you left the battle?"

"No. They'll have moved. There's a canyon about fifty miles south of the battle site—I think that's where they'll be. They had a winter camp by an old fort, Fort Adobe. The Comanche and the Kiowa were camping there when the New Mexico Volunteers attacked. Our tipis were burned, and many of my people were killed. The soldiers had cannons; but by the end of the day, they were driven back. They had started a retreat when I rode after White Bird. We'd never had an attack under cannon fire."

They were silent while she thought about the violence that could come so swiftly on the plains.

"Does that make you want to change your mind about marriage?" he asked finally.

"No," she said. "I was aware of the dangers when I said

yes. It is just as dangerous in many other places. The farm women on the frontier, the women caught in the war-torn states all face danger daily. I'll take my chances," she said quietly, knowing she was taking the biggest chance in risking her heart.

"You're brave and I like that. You're also independent, and I don't know that I like that!"

"I've done what you've asked."

"Vanessa, because of you, I am now traveling with five females. I am a warrior who has traveled alone much of the time, and now we're a band ourselves. Because of you, I had to risk my life and yours to get your sisters. Because of you, I spend my day getting jabbed in the back with a stick by old Muaahap and have to do her bidding." He leaned closer as he talked, his deep voice quiet, almost a whisper, making her pulse drum when his face stopped only inches from hers. "Because of you, I am learning to braid a little girl's hair and lie awake nights worrying about the women in my care. You have ruined my peace, and I'll take my revenge."

She ached with longing, wanting him to move the last bit of distance and kiss her, wanting his arms around her. "You wouldn't respect me as much otherwise. If I were docile and submissive, you would have left me long ago."

"No, I would have kept you with me because of your green eyes and your sunburst of red hair and your body that makes mine as hard as these rocks. No, I would respect you and I would have had more peace. I will teach you, Vanessa, to be submissive."

"I think I *want* you to teach me," she replied softly, her pulse pounding. "And now, I think I'd better move away from you before we do something we shouldn't." She turned and shifted on the hides, lying down and pulling a buffalo robe over her.

*　*　*

The next day they rode hard again until Muaahap jabbed Lone Wolf and they finally stopped. The land had changed as they'd headed northwest, the rolling hills leveling out, the grass thinning. The mesquite was no longer thick, and the oaks had disappeared from the landscape. Occasionally Vanessa saw a lizard scamper across the barren ground, and once she saw wild horses in the distance.

Late in the afternoon, she rode beside Lone Wolf. "Do you think my father will follow us this far?"

"No. No one is following us; and if he had picked up the trail, he would have been behind us long before now. Remember, there are flyers of you posted all over this part of the country, so he can spread the word to watch for us by telegraph and by the military. Even if he hasn't increased the reward, it was large enough that many men will be watching for you. You're a noticeable woman," he said in a lower voice.

She saw the desire burning in his dark eyes. She grew warm as her gaze dropped to his mouth. She missed their moments alone, the intimacy of talking to him at night. Right now, they needed to keep moving as quickly as possible.

He turned his head, flicking the reins to the bay to move ahead. His hair was already a fraction longer and he wore buckskins again. They made him look strong and forbidding, yet she knew how gentle he could be and how kind. She also knew how tough and unyielding he was, and she prayed he did not cross paths with her father.

Soon, she would be Lone Wolf's wife. The thought stirred a fluttery excitement in her every time she contemplated her future with him. And their children would be half-breeds. Her father would never accept them. Nor would some others if she went back to her world. But she didn't expect to return to it, and she would love her children as much as a mother could. Her gaze shifted to White Bird, and she felt another rush of pleasure. Now she wouldn't

have to part with White Bird, and the little girl would grow
up accepting Vanessa as her mother.

For another day, they continued at a fast pace, and then
Lone Wolf slowed. Water was becoming scarcer as the land
sloped gradually upward in a wide plateau. They emerged
onto the staked plains, and later she saw the bluffs of the
llano estacado and the stretches of barren land that shim-
mered in the distance.

They rode into Tucumcari in the evening, entering on a
wide, dirt highway. Adobe buildings lined the thorough-
fares, and soldiers stood in front of doorways or strode
down the street. Vanessa observed the uniforms and her
blood ran cold because the danger was so much greater to
all of them, and especially to Lone Wolf. Three whites and
three Indians. One man with five females. They were conspicuous, and men would remember seeing them.

They drew stares as they rode toward the hotel. She saw
a flyer fluttering on a post and longed to get down and read
and see if it held her picture or if there were now a flyer
out with all three sisters' pictures. Her hair was braided,
looped, and pinned on her head, tucked beneath a sunbonnet. Phoebe wore hers the same way while Belva had one
long braid down her back.

They reined in at the hotel and as she entered the warm
anteroom, she wondered if they would have an argument
from the clerk because of Lone Wolf, Muaahap, and White
Bird. A soldier crossed the lobby, his gaze sweeping boldly
over Vanessa, and a chill ran down her spine as she looked
away from him, hoping the flyers fluttering outside did not
hold her picture. She glanced back to see the soldier was
gone and Lone Wolf stood at the desk talking to the clerk.

Eighteen

While they waited in the lobby, Vanessa watched Lone Wolf argue with the clerk. Finally he finished and returned to her side. "I took three rooms." He touched her collar lightly. "I wish you could be in my room. The clerk told me there's a rooming house where we can eat supper a block away from here."

"The soldiers worry me."

"We'll be safer if only you and I go to dinner and take White Bird. We'll have food sent to the others. Muaahap won't be disappointed, but your sisters—"

"They'll be happy to avoid the risk."

As they followed him down a long, narrow hall, Vanessa remembered the last hotel and the bed she had shared with Lone Wolf and wished she could do so again tonight. The rooms were clean and simple with iron beds and pine wash-stands and chests. She and Phoebe took one room while Muaahap, White Bird, and Belva shared another.

When Phoebe was through bathing and had gone to help Muaahap, Vanessa bathed in a tin tub and changed to the green-muslin dress. As she brushed her hair, Belva entered. One long braid hung down her back and her skin had dark-ened with the days in the sun. She looked more certain of herself.

"I've bathed and now Muaahap is bathing White Bird," she announced. "Vanessa, I've decided what I'll do."

Hearing the solemn note in her voice and knowing the choice was difficult, Vanessa gave Belva her full attention.

"I want to stay with you," she said in a quiet rush.

Pleased, Vanessa reached out to hug her. "I'm glad you want to stay, and I know Phoebe will understand." Vanessa gazed gravely at her younger sister. "One thing you should understand. Until we're with Lone Wolf's people, there's a chance that Papa or someone who works for him or wants the reward he's offering will find us. If so, Lone Wolf won't be able to protect us from many men or soldiers."

"I know. Phoebe told me that, but I want to stay and I've told Phoebe."

Vanessa hugged her again. "Good."

"I told Muaahap last night. She's glad."

"I know White Bird will be happier with you here. Belva, if you ever change your mind, we can contact Phoebe and get you on a stage to California as long as we keep enough money for a ticket."

"I thought of that," Belva said, a smile breaking through her serious expression. "I want to stay here. I like Muaahap and Lone Wolf and White Bird, so I should like his people and wherever we are."

Vanessa gave her another reassuring squeeze.

"I'll go back now and help with White Bird, but I wanted you to know."

"I'm glad, Belva."

"I'm happy both of you wanted me," she said simply, and Vanessa knew she was thinking of their father. "We want you very much," Vanessa said. "I love you, and Lone Wolf said he would be a father to you."

Transformed by a happy glow, Belva paused at the door. "I'll bring White Bird in as soon as I have her dressed."

"Fine," Vanessa replied, knowing there would be more love in Belva's life now.

When Belva returned with White Bird, the child wore

the red gingham dress. Vanessa knelt in front of her. "Don't you look pretty!"

White Bird's large dark eyes gazed at Vanessa and she touched the lace on Vanessa's green dress. "Pretty, 'Nessa."

"She looks so sweet, Belva." Vanessa picked up White Bird, who smelled wonderful from the bath. "I'll bring her to your room after dinner."

Setting White Bird on her feet, Vanessa took her hand and the two of them left to get Lone Wolf. At her knock, he swung open the door to his room. His dark eyes lighted with pleasure when he looked at her. Her hair was hidden beneath a sunbonnet which was far plainer than the wide-brimmed hat and would draw less attention. As she and White Bird entered his room, he shook his head.

"Everyone in town will notice you," he said, removing the sunbonnet, his warm fingers brushing her throat.

"No, they won't. Besides, I won't be with my sisters."

"We'll stop at the hotel dining room and have food sent up to them."

"Phoebe will take the food in our room and pay for it, and she'll be alone when they bring the trays to her."

"We'll go now," he said, taking White Bird's hand and letting her toddle between them.

The evening air was cold; Vanessa looked at White Bird, thankful she had made the gingham with long sleeves. "Tomorrow I want to get a coat for her." Lone Wolf nodded, and she glanced up at him with happiness, feeling like a family.

They found a squat, adobe house with a sign in front advertising rooms and meals. When they entered, tempting smells of cooking meat and corn assailed them. A woman came forward, her eyes narrowing as she looked at Lone Wolf and White Bird. Her gaze returned to Vanessa, who smiled at her.

"Evening, ma'am," the woman said curtly.

"I'm Hepzibah Grant, and this is my husband Robert. We're traveling through and would like to eat supper."

The woman hesitated and then nodded. "This way." She led them into a room brightened by large paintings. Strings of red peppers hung on one wall, and a pot with a tall cactus leaned in one corner. Plain wooden tables with ladder-back chairs stood around the room.

Discreetly seated in a corner, Vanessa and White Bird looked across the table at Lone Wolf. He had removed his hat, and his black hair was combed into a semblance of a part on the right side of his head, but strands had reverted back and hid the part near his wide forehead. Vanessa couldn't decide when he looked the most handsome— dressed in his native attire or in a white shirt and trousers.

He sat relaxed, his hand on the stem of the water goblet as he bent his head to study a menu. She watched him, surprised even though he spoke English fluently that he could also read.

"You learned to read as an army scout?"

He raised his head. "As a matter of fact, yes. I find books interesting, and army life can be long tedious hours of doing nothing. I had a friend who taught me to read."

"Perhaps I shall teach White Bird."

He smiled. "I suspect you will, but you'll be hard pressed to find books."

She shrugged. "I might get a few books tomorrow along with the coat before we leave town and while I still have some money."

After a few minutes he peered at her over the menu, a mirthful glint lighting his eyes. "Wherever we go, you pay my way and White Bird's."

"I have Papa's money, and your way of life requires no money, only horses."

"Actually, Vanessa, as an army scout I earned money. I had little use for most of it, so it's in a bank in Denver

City, Colorado. If we're ever where I can get to it, I can repay you."

"It won't be necessary. Enjoy Abbot Sutherland's gold," she remarked dryly.

With a flash of white teeth, Lone Wolf laughed, and her pulse jumped because he looked so handsome. "As a prospective bridegroom, I should take gifts and horses to your family. But I'm sorry, my love, I wouldn't if I could."

"And Papa would not want your horses." She grinned, refusing to worry about her father.

They ordered tamales and chili for themselves and baked chicken for White Bird. As they ate, Vanessa relaxed, enjoying Lone Wolf's company. Lone Wolf's dark gaze was on her constantly and she sat with her back to the room knowing he could see the door and everyone who entered and left.

"Has Belva given you an answer yet?" he asked.

"Yes, she is staying."

He reached across the table and touched her cheek, drawing his index finger down to her jaw. "You Sutherland women like life in the wild. She is giving up more than you, Vanessa. Her education isn't complete; she's young and impressionable."

"But she also has traveled a great deal. We've been sheltered in many ways, particularly where men are concerned; but in some ways we've had a more varied life than others our age. We lived in many cities and at many forts. We've traveled over a good part of the land. She knows what she wants to do. She's torn between going with Phoebe or staying with us because she and Phoebe are so close."

"If she stays with us and changes her mind, we can always send her to California later. But if she goes now and wants to come back later, she won't be able to find us."

"Is there any way I can get letters from Phoebe?"

He studied her. "Our lives are so different, Vanessa. You'll turn your back on all you have to go with me?"

She gazed into the inky depths of his eyes, feeling drawn to him, knowing the love she felt for him was binding and strong and far more important than where she lived. "Yes. What am I losing?"

"Your whole way of life."

"Which hasn't brought me great happiness. It is my choice to stay."

"I'm sure of that," he said, one corner of his mouth twitching upward. She concentrated on his full sensuous underlip, remembering the feel of it on her mouth.

"Did you like being a scout?"

He shrugged. "I learned what my father wanted me to learn. I did a job. There were men I liked and men I didn't like. But it's the white man's war, and I wanted to return to my people. When this war is over, all our lives will change."

"Did you grow up knowing Eyes That Smile?"

"She was from a different band of Kiowas. We gather together every year when the cottonwood flies for a sun dance, and in her eighteenth year I took her for my wife. Now I'm twenty-four. I was a scout the first two years of the war and in the second year I quit and came back and married Eyes That Smile. She was killed a little over a year ago."

"A little over a year ago we lived in Kansas," Vanessa mused. "The year before that we were in Shreveport, Louisiana. All I can remember is moving."

Their dinners were served, and Vanessa helped White Bird eat. As Vanessa ate, she relished the hot tamales, yet she was far more interested in the man across from her than in the food. He moved as easily in her world as his own, and she wondered about their lives together. Her gaze drifted down across his broad shoulders to his strong hands. She looked up to find him watching her intently and she gazed back at him, feeling a longing that was overpowering.

"When we marry, will we share a tipi with Muaahap and White Bird and Belva?" she asked.

"Eventually, because they're our family, but for the first few weeks, I'll arrange for them to stay elsewhere so we will be completely alone," he said in a deep voice. He reached out to touch her hand as she held her water glass. He rubbed his fingers over her knuckles, a light touch that made her ache for more. Her appetite for her dinner dwindled, and she turned her hand to hold his.

He stopped eating, gazing at her with a fathomless stare that held her enthralled until White Bird wiggled against her.

"Shall we go back to the hotel?" he asked, his voice husky. She stood up and he came around the table to take her arm. He looked down at her as they stood close together. "I want you with me tonight."

Wanting the same thing, Vanessa drew a deep breath. He picked up White Bird and they stepped outside into the cold night air. Darkness had fallen; and during the short walk back to the hotel, Lone Wolf pulled a flyer from a post and tucked it beneath his shirt.

They passed the open doors of the livery stable; a bright lantern glowed on a post in front. When they returned to their rooms, she took White Bird to Muaahap, holding the little girl close for a moment to kiss her good night. Closing the door quietly behind her, she went back to ask Lone Wolf about the flyer.

As she entered his room, he turned. "Are you having second thoughts about staying behind," he asked her quietly.

"No," she said, turning to look at him, her pulse jumping. He was incredibly handsome and she would never have second thoughts. Without having all his love, though, she felt a shyness and hesitation with him that would not have existed otherwise. He removed the flyer and unfolded it.

"He's changed the notice, Vanessa, and all of you are in danger," Lone Wolf said darkly. "The only advantage we

have is that you and your sisters are with the three of us
and people won't be looking for six." He held out the flyer,
and she moved closer to examine it.

Lone Wolf continued looking at the poster over her shoulder and she was aware of his presence and the warmth radiating from his body. These constant brushes against her
and the feather-light touches were like kindling on a fire.
She felt an overwhelming yearning to be in his arms.

"Your father has increased the reward. Bounty hunters
will be watching for you everywhere."

She smoothed out the flyer. "I'll tell—" Shocked, she
stared at the flyer. "He's offering five thousand dollars!"

"Everyone in the west will be on the lookout for three
young women—particularly two as beautiful as Phoebe and
you."

She bit her lip in consternation. "You shouldn't be with
us. This town is filled with soldiers. I saw them everywhere
when we rode in."

"They're from Fort Bascom. Soon I'll take the horses to
the livery stable, which is right behind the hotel. If questions have been asked, I'll probably hear about it."

She placed her hand on his arm, feeling the solid muscle
beneath. "Tomorrow morning, why don't you take Muaahap, Belva, and White Bird and wait outside of town? I'll
meet you after Phoebe leaves on the stage. You would be
safer."

"No," he answered flatly. "If you and I and White Bird
are seen together in town, no one will connect you with that
flyer unless they get a close look at your face. My hair is cut
in the white man's fashion. I wear the white clothing I wore
in Glen Hollow." He glanced at the flyer. "Your father
wouldn't want to acknowledge you were with an Indian."

"No one saw us leave Glen Hollow. They may not have
realized I was with you. And the few people who saw us
together and remembered might not want to tell Papa.
Everyone knows my father's temper and his power."

"I hope you're right."

She turned to look at him. "We'll be safe, although I'd feel better if the three of you would leave town and wait for me."

"No. You're not riding out of here alone with fifty soldiers watching you," he said gruffly. "You're sure you don't want to leave on that stage, Vanessa?"

She gazed into his eyes and knew what she wanted more than anything else was his love. "No, I don't," she whispered, as he reached out to draw her against him and bent down to kiss her.

She slipped her arms around his narrow waist to hold him tightly, kissing him back. His tongue entered her mouth and touched her tongue, playing over hers while he held her tightly.

She held him, deeply in love with him, wanting to be his wife, yet feeling an uncertainty. She pushed away, looking up at him as she touched his jaw and traced her fingers along his throat. "I want to stay. I want to be your wife. I know what I'm doing."

"Vanessa, if I take you as my wife, I consider it binding."

"I'm sure of what I want," she repeated solemnly, longing to hear words of love from him. She stepped back, too aware of their privacy, knowing she should turn and go now before she was in his arms for the night. "I should get back to my room. They'll be waiting."

"In the morning I'll go with Phoebe to buy her ticket to California. I don't think we'll draw as much attention that way, and no man will accost her as long as I accompany her."

"That's fine."

"All of you need to say your goodbyes here at the hotel. If you want to stay behind and have the two of us see her off, we'll do that; but Muaahap, Belva, and White Bird should ride out of town before daylight while no one's stirring."

"I'll tell them," she said, turning to go.

The next morning after breakfast, Lone Wolf left with Phoebe to buy a ticket. He also purchased a coat for White Bird and two black woolen capes for Belva and Vanessa. Upon their return, he followed Phoebe into the hotel room.

Vanessa looked up at him. Once again he was in the white man's clothing he had purchased in Menard. Handsome and tall, he dominated the room.

"The stage leaves at eleven o'clock. Once Phoebe is aboard, we should leave town. We're an oddity and far too noticeable."

"I think you should go now. I can wait at the stage stop."

"Sometimes they're delayed." He shook his head, dismissing her suggestion. "You can't stay here alone. We'll wait together."

Vanessa could not tell from his tone whether or not he felt they were in great danger, but she knew he wanted to go as quickly as possible.

"A man traveling alone with four or five women is not safe," he said flatly. "Many men saw us ride into town. They'll see us leave. I'll get the horses. We'll load up and be ready to go when Phoebe gets the stage."

He left the room and Phoebe turned to her. "I'll miss you. I wonder if we'll ever be together again."

"I hope we will." Vanessa did not tell her sister that she feared they might be saying goodbye for the last time. Phoebe had the portmanteau now and was wearing Vanessa's poplin riding habit. Her anxious blue eyes showed that she understood the seriousness of their situation.

"I'll write to Annabelle Carter, so if you ever need to contact me, you can get in touch with Annabelle or Eleanor Rosati."

They stared at each other and hugged. They had too much to say and no time for more than a few words. "Thank you for coming to get me," Phoebe murmured.

Vanessa nodded. "You go to California. Someday I hope to hear you sing. I'll take good care of Belva."

Phoebe laughed. "You and Lone Wolf and Muaahap will take good care of her! She loves them as much as she does us."

Lone Wolf knocked, then opened the door. "We go now," he said and closed the door again.

Phoebe picked up Vanessa's portmanteau. "Are you sure you want to give all this up?"

"I don't need the dresses. I'll be wearing buckskin after today," she said.

"I mean everything else you're giving up for him. Pretty dresses—"

"I'm certain," Vanessa answered, knowing Phoebe would never understand unless she fell in love.

Lone Wolf appeared. He was dressed in buckskins, the pistol on his hip and a knife in a scabbard fastened to his belt. Looking wild and strong, he wore a deerskin headband.

"The others should be waiting and it's almost time for the stage, so we'll go now."

Impulsively, Phoebe hugged him. "Thank you for coming to our rescue. I'll always be grateful. I'm glad you'll be in our family."

He smiled, returning her hug. Then Phoebe turned to Vanessa to clasp her in a tight, tearful hug. "I'll miss you so much!"

"I hope you find what you want, Phoebe."

They left the hotel and walked the next block to the stage station. The dusty Concord stage waited, its yellow wheels idle, its new team hitched up and ready to go.

Nervous with excitement and anticipation, Phoebe gave Vanessa another quick squeeze. Then, holding up her poplin skirt, she boarded the stage. Her blue eyes sparkled as she settled in the seat. A couple boarded next, and Vanessa was relieved to see their friendly manner as they greeted Phoebe. A tall, balding man in a brown coat and brown trousers joined them, immersing himself in a newspaper as the last passenger, a woman, climbed inside.

A man slammed the door; the drivers climbed up in front, and with a jingle of harness and the creak of springs, the stage pulled away.

The moment the stage began to move, Lone Wolf took her arm. "We go."

They hurried to the livery stable and mounted the horses that Lone Wolf had already saddled. As they rode into the street, they turned in the opposite direction from the stage to ride east out of town.

Vanessa knew Lone Wolf rode slowly to keep from drawing more attention to them. They headed due east instead of angling north because Lone Wolf wanted to stay out of the vicinity of Fort Bascom as much as possible.

As they left the town, they traveled on flat land that was unbroken for miles. Dotted with cactus and sparse grasses, the terrain provided little concealment for riders.

The slight dust stirred by their horses hung in the air, a telltale cloud that was slow to settle. They would be easy to follow, and she suspected Lone Wolf would want to travel through the night.

It was late afternoon before they caught up with Muaahap, White Bird, and Belva. It was mid-day before Lone Wolf began to angle to the northeast.

When night came, they continued. White Bird fell asleep against Belva. Then Belva nodded, and Muaahap dozed. When Lone Wolf halted, they ate cold beef because he wouldn't allow a fire.

He strode to Vanessa as she unfolded her bedding. "We'll rest for about two hours and then we should ride while we have the cover of darkness. In another hour we can turn north again."

"No one has followed us?"

"I can't be certain. No one is close behind, but the soldiers from Bascom could have picked up our trail." He ran his finger along her jaw and she drew in her breath. Each touch was more volatile than the last. She gazed up at him as he moved closer to her. "Still no regrets that you're not on the stage with Phoebe?" he asked huskily.

"No. I haven't regretted it once," she answered, feeling breathless.

"You would be safer."

"Phoebe has a long journey across land that isn't any safer than here. Far from it. And she doesn't have you with her."

He smiled faintly. "No, but once she reaches California, she will never have to worry about battles."

"I don't regret my decision."

"I didn't really think you would. You are as decisive as a man, Vanessa."

"Some things I feel certain about," she said, studying him, wanting to be in his arms and feel his hard chest pressing against her, knowing when she was with him she felt complete and as if her life had a purpose.

"We will reach my people soon and then I will take you as my bride. It will be better for you to have the ceremony and celebration. Then you will feel a part of us."

"I want my own children," she said quietly, blushing at the admission, yet wanting him to know.

He stepped close, his arms sliding around her and pulling her up against him, his face only inches from hers. "I know you do. You told me that once, remember? They will be ours, Vanessa. And we will bring them into a turbulent world, but we will do our best for them. Kiowa children are deeply loved." He smiled at her. "I shall selfishly hope I have a son. I need a man to help me cope with all these women in my life."

"You should have a family. You're unselfish and you're good with the little ones. Belva already adores you."

"If we could just swap Muaahap—"

"She's not that troublesome, and she obeys your wishes when it's important to do so."

"Yes. Only one female disobeys me and cooperates only when it fits her plans, Vanessa," he said, his voice warm, making her tremble. His masculine mouth, the sensual full underlip, was so close. With a lingering look at his mouth, she raised her gaze and stared into his brown eyes, her heart thudding because she loved him desperately.

He leaned forward, his mouth covering hers, his tongue thrusting into her mouth, playing over hers as he held her tightly.

She stood on tiptoe to kiss him back, winding her fingers in his hair. Feeling faint with longing, Vanessa held him tightly while he leaned over her, his arousal pressing against her.

And as she kissed him, her heart sang with joy because she knew this was right. She felt complete with Lone Wolf, certain she belonged with him forever.

When he released her, she stepped back. They both were panting for breath, staring at each other, and it took an effort of her will to keep from going into his arms again.

"I'll keep watch." he said, moving past her to get his rifle. He sat down near a mesquite where it would be more difficult for anyone approaching their camp to see him.

She awoke from sleep to find Lone Wolf shaking her. He jerked his head toward the horses as one of them tossed its head and a bridle jingled.

Frightened, she went to Belva while Lone Wolf shook Muaahap. The old woman came awake at once and hurried to help saddle the horses.

The cold night air added to her chill. Her hands shook as she hastily folded the quilt and yanked it up. She stopped, holding her breath, listening to a faint noise that grew swiftly.

The sound of hoofbeats was unmistakable and then thunderous as horses galloped toward them. Vanessa's fear changed to terror, and she held Belva's hand and rushed toward the horses.

"Go!" Lone Wolf yelled, grabbing his rifle as Muaahap raced with White Bird toward a horse.

Men yelled and the pounding horses burst down the embankment, riding into their campsite and stirring a cloud of dust, spreading out to surround them.

Nineteen

The men rode through their camp, and Belva screamed. Lone Wolf raised his rifle and fired as a soldier bore down on him and clubbed him. Terrified, Vanessa cried out and dashed to kneel beside him.

It was over as swiftly as it had started. A man yelled an order and the others reined in their mounts. Dust rose in a thick cloud that gagged her while the horses milled around and Belva cried. Vanessa leaned over Lone Wolf, rolling him over, aghast at the blood that flowed from his head.

As she knelt beside Lone Wolf, hands closed around her arms and hauled her roughly to her feet. "Let go of me!" she yelled, lunging at a soldier.

"Release her, Edwards," came a deep, commanding voice, and she looked up as a man halted his horse in front of her.

"We'll take them with us. Tie their hands. Lord knows where the rest of them are. One warrior and four women—there should be others nearby. We can exchange them for white captives."

As he talked, he looked down at Vanessa. The night was dark and she couldn't see his face beneath his hat. She wore the deerskin dress and her hair was still in the long braid, and she realized he didn't know they were white.

"Will you release us?" she pleaded. "You can't take us prisoner."

He frowned and dismounted, walking closer to her.

Reaching into his pocket, he pulled out a box. A match flared brightly and he held it out to look first at her and then at Lone Wolf, whose head was turned away, his black hair in disarray.

As the yellow flame flickered, she studied the captain. He had blond hair and handsome features, thickly lashed blue eyes, a full mouth, and a thin nose. His gaze shifted to her and then he looked past her, and she guessed he was looking at the others. "Who are you?"

"I'm Vanessa Sutherland," she said quietly, realizing he hadn't followed her from Tucumcari because of the flyers. "We're traveling back to my family, and this man is accompanying me and my sister. The woman and child are his relatives."

"Redskins," he said contemptuously, and she had a sinking feeling of dread that they were held by a man who hated Indians.

He shook out the match as it burned down and in seconds struck another one. It flared brightly with a hiss and the smell of sulfur. He inched even closer to Vanessa and tilted up her chin.

A chill ran through her. She hated the look in his eyes as he studied her with the same assessing scrutiny he would give a horse he was purchasing. "Get their things and tie their wrists. We'll take them to the fort."

"What about the man, Captain?" a soldier asked.

"The redskin?" he asked. His voice was thick with hatred.

"Please," she said, fearing the officer was about to order his men to shoot Lone Wolf. "If you kill him, you'll stir up the wrath of his people."

"They're already on the warpath," he snapped. "They know we're understaffed because of the war."

"Please let him live," she begged.

The captain held the flickering match and leaned down

to look at Lone Wolf. "I'll be damned," the captain said in an angry tone.

She stared at the blond officer and her blood turned to ice as her terror grew. The captain knew Lone Wolf. He shook out the match.

"Please let him live," she repeated.

The captain walked back to her and tilted up her face again, staring at her in the darkness. "Why do you care?"

"He's important to me."

"He'll live," he said with a grim note in his voice. "He'll live for now. Edwards, tie his ankles."

Lone Wolf moaned and shifted. The captain swung his foot, his boot slamming into Lone Wolf's head.

Vanessa acted without thought, lunging at the captain and shoving him. She caught him by surprise; he stumbled, and she went for his gun. Arms closed around her from behind, yanking her off her feet and squeezing until she cried out. A soldier held her tightly while the captain got to his feet. He kicked Lone Wolf in the side, the blow a dull whack that made Vanessa scream and Belva sob.

"Tie them up!" he snapped, glaring at her. "Take all their things," he ordered as he remounted his horse and cantered away. "Let the two children ride together. It's not necessary to bind them."

Thankful for so small a kindness to Belva and White Bird, Vanessa clamped her jaw shut. She was handled roughly as two soldiers tied her wrists. One ran his hands over her breasts and tweaked her. She turned her head away, his scornful laughter ringing in her ears.

"Two children and an old woman. Too bad they aren't all like this one," one soldier said.

"Get her on a horse," the captain commanded, and the men ceased their banter.

"Tie the redskin's ankles to your saddle horn, Edwards."

"Yes, sir."

"No!" Vanessa cried, turning to the captain. "If you do that, he'll die."

"No, he won't. He's tougher than that."

"Please, put him on a horse. He's already hurt," she pleaded.

The captain studied her speculatively, then repeated his order. "Tie his ankles, Edwards."

Vanessa averted her head, agonized because they would drag Lone Wolf for miles. As they started, she rode stiffly. She focused her eyes straight ahead, hating the captain as much as she would have if he had tied her by her feet and dragged her behind a horse.

More than twenty soldiers closed ranks around them, and she could think of no way to overpower them or break free. She closed her eyes, horribly aware of Lone Wolf being dragged behind them.

After an hour they halted for water at a creek. While the horses drank, she crossed to the captain. A soldier barred her progress, and she glowered at him.

"Get out of my way. I want to talk to the captain!"

The man's eyes narrowed, but he shrugged and stepped aside, allowing Vanessa to pass him. She found the officer beside his horse at the creek bank. He acknowledged her presence with a curt nod.

"Please put him on a horse," she said, fighting to keep her tears from falling. Again she received a cold, speculative inspection.

"Are you his woman?"

"I'm his wife."

He turned and glanced at his men. "Bickers, tie the injun on a horse."

"Yes, sir," a thin soldier answered and moved to Lone Wolf's inert body. Unconscious, he was covered with blood, and Vanessa prayed that the heavy buckskin had protected him.

"Thank you," she said quietly.

"You'll get your chance to thank me fully," he answered, a faint smile on his face. He turned away. "Let's ride!" he called, and the men mounted their horses again.

As they continued on, she twisted around to look back. Lone Wolf was on his belly across a horse, lashed to the animal, his arms dangling and she guessed he remained unconscious. She was terrified for Lone Wolf. She was certain the officer had recognized him and assumed they were old enemies.

Dawn came, and the captain returned to ride beside them. His gaze ran over Muaahap, White Bird, and Belva. He barely glanced at Lone Wolf. His attention shifted to her and he closed the gap between them, giving her another intense appraisal. He studied her thoroughly and she stiffened, raising her chin. "Two whites and three redskins. Tell me how you came to be with them."

"He's escorting us across this country."

"To where?"

"North. I have relatives in Missouri."

"I don't believe you," he replied. "I'll learn the truth. His people probably took you captive, and now you want to stay." He flicked his reins and rode ahead.

By afternoon she was thirsty and exhausted, but her fear overrode all other concerns. She didn't trust the captain and was wary of his intentions toward her. Since, thus far, he had ignored Muaahap and the girls, Vanessa prayed that he wouldn't harm them.

She was amazed that White Bird rode without complaint. She sat in front of Belva, and Vanessa knew she must sense something was wrong because she remained unusually quiet, her thumb in her mouth. Belva looked pale, but not overly frightened, while Muaahap looked her usual stoic self.

"Can't you let the woman and children go free?" Vanessa asked, when the officer returned to her side.

His blue eyes stared at her impassively before he looked

away. "We can exchange them for white captives taken by redskins."

She grew silent, despising the sly touches she received when they stopped for water, the remarks she tried to ignore. Lone Wolf regained consciousness, groaning and then riding limply. Once she looked over her shoulder and he turned his head. His black hair hid his bloody face, so she didn't know whether or not he had seen her.

She hurt for him and was terrified at what lay ahead. Late in the day, in the shimmering distance, she saw the walls of a fort. She guessed they were approaching Fort Bascom.

They halted inside its walls and the captain gave orders briskly, waving his hand. "Take the redskin to the stockade. Take the old woman and children to a room. Bring the woman to my office."

He strode off, and she saw a soldier come toward her. He pulled her off the horse, catching her in his arms, his hands going over her brazenly as he fondled her.

Vanessa clamped her jaw shut, determined to try to ignore as much as she could, watching as three soldiers rode away with Lone Wolf.

As the soldier entered a building, he pulled her along by the arm, turning into a large office. The captain stood on the other side of the room, his back to her while he poured a glass of brandy. Sunlight streamed through the wavering speckled-glass windowpanes. A desk stood along one wall with a cabinet close beside it. Chairs and a leather settee completed the decor.

"Here she is, sir." The soldier left and shut the door, and the captain turned to look at her as he drank his brandy. He had tossed aside his hat and his blond hair was tangled. He had a faint stubble of pale whiskers on his jaw; under other circumstances, she might have considered him a handsome man, but now her dislike for him overwhelmed all else.

"I'm Captain Dupree Milos. You said your name is Vanessa."

"Yes. Please let us go."

"No. I can exchange the others." He crossed the room, and as he approached her, he unbuttoned his blue coat. He set down the glass of brandy and pulled off his coat. From a scabbard on his hip, he removed a knife.

Vanessa drew her breath because she saw he intended to use the weapon. He moved closer, his blue eyes boring into hers as he reached out. Sunlight glinted on the blade as he moved it close to her throat.

She raised her chin and stared at him, wondering if he intended to slit her throat now, here in his office.

"You don't frighten easily, do you, Vanessa?" he asked softly.

She shrugged. "There is little I can do to stop you from whatever you intend, so I'm waiting. I can't overcome you."

"I thought you might fight me."

She wondered if he were toying with her in the manner of a cat with a mouse, trying to torment her and see what kind of fearful reaction he could get. "It seems useless."

"It is," he answered matter-of-factly. His fingers locked in the neck of the buckskin dress and he yanked her toward him as he raised the knife.

Twenty

With strong sweeps of his arm, he slashed the buckskin down the front. It parted and she stood naked before him. He shoved the dress open, looking at her.

Vanessa pulled away from him, holding the torn dress together and backing up.

"You're white, no question about that. Why are you with him? The last I saw of him was a battle we had at the old fort of Adobe Walls. I thought I killed him. Were you one of their captives?"

"No. I met him on the trail. He was searching for his little girl, who had ridden off during the battle. Her mother was killed by your soldiers!" she snapped, angry with him.

"We lost many men in that battle, and they were more important than a few dirty redskins who are no loss to anyone. I'll have a bath drawn for you and I'll find a gingham or calico dress. You're to put it on and clean yourself up for me."

"And if I don't?" she asked, knowing the answer, but needing to hear him say it.

"Then I'll take my anger out on the redskin and you can watch."

"Let them all go, and I'll do what you want."

He drew closer to her and slipped his finger beneath the buckskin and cupped her breast. She drew a breath and stepped back.

His eyes narrowed. "I'll let the women and children go."

"No. Let him go, too. There's a difference between a woman who is willing and one who is all but dead," she argued, feeling the clash with him, desperate to get Lone Wolf and the others to safety because she suspected the captain intended to kill Lone Wolf slowly and painfully.

Captain Milos studied her, tilting up her chin. "Open the dress," he ordered.

Blushing hotly, she did as he asked, looking beyond him, trying to ignore the lust in his eyes as he gazed at her body.

He moved to her to stroke her breasts.

"Your body responds, even if you don't."

She kept her mouth firmly closed, hating his touch and his lecherous gaze. Retreating from his grasp, she covered herself with the slashed buckskin. Her gaze slid back to him as anger filled her. "Let them go, and I'll do as you ask."

"No. If I let him go, then you have to do better than just as I ask. You're to try to please me."

She nodded. "I will if I see them all ride out of here."

"They can't have our horses. Horses are too valuable during wartime. They can go on foot."

"You took our horses and you can give those back."

"No. We need horses and those were good mounts. I won't give them horses. Those redskins are accustomed to walking."

Sensing he wouldn't yield about the horses, she gave up that argument. "I have to see them walk away."

"You don't trust my word?" he questioned sardonically. A smile spread across his handsome face as he leered at her.

"No, I don't. You hate him. I want to see him go and know that he is not being followed by soldiers who will kill him."

"He's not that important to me. If it will put you eagerly into my bed and you'll entertain me, then he can go. I'll arrange for you to watch them leave. In the meantime, I'll get you a dress. I don't want any taint of the redskin on you. You're to bathe and make yourself as pretty as possible for me. This godforsaken frontier is bad enough when I go into town. Out here, it is so dull it could drive a man mad. You should liven up my life. And if you don't," he added menacingly, lifting her chin so she could not avoid his intent, "my men will easily overtake them because the Indians can't go fast on foot. Do you understand? You're to please me fully."

"I understand," she said, feeling as if something were dying inside, but knowing she was trading her body for Lone Wolf's life and the freedom of the others.

"You will come with me to my quarters," he commanded, picking up his glass of brandy and downing it quickly.

She held the buckskin together and followed closely behind him. They left the office and crossed the grounds, then entered a small frame house. The furnishings were spartan, but familiar: a settee and chairs in the narrow front room, field gear hanging on the wall beside a small drop-front desk, a bull's-eye lantern on the desk. Through the open doorway she could see an iron bed and a washstand with a pitcher and washbowl.

"You can have a woman in your quarters?"

"Yes. I run this fort. With a war going on and a shortage of men, no one gives a damn what I do out here as long as I try to keep the redskins under control. I'll have a tub of water fetched for you—and a decent dress and shoes. You won't need underthings. Take down your hair, I want to see it."

She started to turn around.

"No. Don't turn," he ordered. "Take it down."

When she released the buckskin, it gaped open as she reached back to unfasten the long braid and pull the strands of hair free. The air was cool on her bare skin, and she felt humiliated as his eyes roamed over her. His arousal was obvious, and she jerked her gaze up, away from him.

As she stared beyond him out the window at the empty grounds, she heard the scrape of his boots. He crossed the room, his arm banding her waist, his hand sliding over her bare skin as he pushed open the buckskin dress to touch her breast.

He bent his head, and his mouth covered hers in a bruising kiss. He leaned over her while he kissed her for long seconds until he stopped and raised his head to look at her with a frown. "You said you'd cooperate and please me."

"You haven't let them go yet."

"I'm going to, so you start now," he grumbled.

She wound her arms around his neck and closed her eyes, kissing him in return and hating him, loathing his touch, knowing her heart belonged to only one man.

When Dupree released her, he was breathing hard, his eyes glazed with lust. "I want you clean. I want his touch washed off."

"How soon will you release them?"

His eyes narrowed as he looked at her. "You may watch them go this afternoon."

She felt a surge of relief and satisfaction. If she could save every one of them by pleasing him, it would be worth the sacrifice and she would do so for as many days as she thought it would take them to get far from Fort Bascom.

"My sister is returning home. I want to ask her to write to me and send the letter here, so I'll know when they have all arrived safely," she said, wanting him to think she would have some way to check on what he did to them.

"Where's your home?"

"St. Joseph, Missouri," she answered, thinking that would explain their traveling east from Tucumcari.

"And the redskin? Surely *he* isn't going to St. Joseph."

"He was accompanying us there."

He gave her a contemptuous look of disbelief and then he shrugged. "I'll be back to get you and let you watch them go." He left, closing the door behind him. She let out her breath and rushed to the window, her gaze going across the parade ground to the long barracks, the storeroom, and barbershop. She watched Captain Milos cross the parade ground, his long stride purposeful. She would be his tonight and she not only would have to endure him, but she would have to try to please him.

Revulsion filled her while her gaze slid over the buildings. She spotted one with bars over the windows and wondered if that were where Lone Wolf was being held.

Captain Milos headed for that building and Vanessa's pulse jumped. Maybe Milos was going to tell them to release Lone Wolf now. She watched him enter, and she closed her eyes, praying he was going to tell them Lone Wolf was going to go free.

Captain Dupree Milos closed the door behind him and crossed to the cell where Lone Wolf was stretched on the floor.

"Is he alive?"

"Yes, sir," answered Private Nordstrom. "Like some old mule. Just won't die."

"Nordstrom, Rutledge, get him out of there and tie him to the bars."

While the men did as he ordered, the iron bars clanking behind him, Milos selected a rawhide bullwhacker's whip from the corner. He snapped it and listened to the loud pop. "Nordstrom, wait a minute. Revive him. Pour water on him until he knows what's happening. I want to talk to him."

He waited while Rutledge went to the pump. The young soldier returned with a bucket of water which he threw on Lone Wolf, who groaned. The Indian's head rolled as the men held him up, and then he opened his eyes and blinked, straightening up.

"Hold him," Dupree said, moving only yards away from Lone Wolf, standing with his booted feet apart, his fists on his hips. "You dirty redskin. I thought I killed you."

Lone Wolf stared back at him, and Dupree couldn't tell

what was in the redskin's mind. He didn't know if he understood English, but he suspected he did or the woman wouldn't have been so taken with him. "You're going to live. You're going to wish you were dead, but you'll live and you'll walk out of here because your white woman is going to purchase your freedom with her body."

The redskin drew a deep breath, and Dupree felt a surge of satisfaction: The man had understood what he'd said. He moved closer, his voice lowering. "She's a beauty, and she's promised to do everything she can to pleasure me for your safety; so when you're crawling across the stinking desert, think about me between her thighs."

Lone Wolf lunged at him, and Dupree swung his fist. Lone Wolf broke free of Nordstrom's grasp and hit Dupree, who staggered back and crashed over the desk.

"Stop him!" Dupree shouted. Both soldiers grabbed Lone Wolf, but he shook them off. A third soldier came running from the back, and all four of them tackled Lone Wolf, slamming him against the bars. Three soldiers pinned him back, and Dupree pulled away.

"Strip him, turn him around, and lash his hands to the bars," he ordered, rubbing his jaw and shaking with rage. How he'd like to beat the redskin almost to death and then peg him out in the wild, but he wanted the woman's cooperation.

Dupree would have preferred for the Indian to die in a day or two, but his bargain with Vanessa required that the prisoner be able to walk. Still, Dupree could make Lone Wolf's stay as painful as possible. He motioned the enlisted men aside with a crack of the whip. He swung again, concentrating his strength into his arm as he laid the rawhide across the Indian's back.

For the next ten minutes he beat him until his back and the backs of his legs and buttocks were bloody. Dupree stopped, his arm aching, his body trembling from the exertion.

"Get him down and get him dressed. Feed him. Have him on the parade ground, able to stand and walk, in an hour. Give him some brandy. That'll fire him up. Feed him good."

"Yes, sir." Nordstrom answered as they took down Lone Wolf's arms. The Indian sagged to the floor, and they let him fall.

"In an hour bring out the old woman and the children. Don't feed them. Let them fend for themselves when they leave here. I just want them strong enough to walk out of the fort." He looked down at Lone Wolf.

"I'd like to slit the bastard's throat, but I've made a deal for him. Take care of him," he said and walked out. He returned to his office where he ordered a tub to be brought. After bathing and changing, his spirits lifted and his anger dissipated because tonight would be one of the most enjoyable times he had spent in this hellish end of nowhere. The only good thing about it was that it kept him from getting a minié ball through his heart in the War Between the States.

After ordering dinner to be sent to his quarters later, he was ready to go get the woman and let her watch him free the others. He wondered who they were. An odd assortment—one warrior, one old crone, a white child, and a redskin baby. He hadn't known any warriors to travel with only a family of women and no other braves around. He crossed the parade grounds to his house and opened the door.

Vanessa spun around to face Captain Milos Dupree as he entered the room. His uniform was fresh and spotless, his blond hair combed.

Dupree's arousal was swift as he looked at her. She was breathtakingly beautiful with her auburn hair falling freely like a red-gold curtain across her shoulders. The gingham dress was plain and blue, but the neckline was low and revealed her lush curves and pale skin. He wanted to take her right now, but he curbed his impulses, knowing he had to get the prisoners out of the fort. If they died four hours from now, he didn't care. Frankly, he hoped the man would die in a few days. It would give him time to suffer.

"You look beautiful, as I thought you would."

"Thank you," she answered solemnly, and he felt a flash of anger.

"You agreed to please me. I want your smiles. I want you to treat me as if I'm the man you will marry and the man you love with all your heart. Now come kiss me."

Repulsed by him, yet desperate for the sake of the others, she crossed the room, forcing a smile to her lips. She stood on tiptoe to place her mouth over his and kiss him. His body responded instantly, and he slid his arm around her waist to pull her close as his lips hungrily sought more.

He finally paused and raised his head, looking into her wide green eyes. "That's better," he said in a husky voice while he stroked her throat. "For kisses like that, I'll gladly let them go. I've ordered them brought to the parade ground. We'll watch their release and then come back here for an uninterrupted evening."

Vanessa hated the lust in his voice and the way his eyes kept going to her neckline, yet she had made a bargain with him and she would stand by it.

He took her arm and they walked into the sunshine. The wind caught her hair and whipped locks of it across her face. She saw Lone Wolf, Muaahap, Belva, and White Bird standing in a cluster with armed soldiers beside them. They were only yards from the open gates at the entrance of the fort. Two soldiers stood at ready, their rifles pointed at Lone Wolf.

Her gaze went from White Bird to Belva to Lone Wolf, who gave her the same impassive stare she had seen countless times. Even with the blood dried on his temple and cheek, he looked fierce and arrogant. And he was going to turn and walk out of her life. She hurt badly and couldn't stop the spill of tears on her cheeks.

"Can I kiss them goodbye?"

"No," Captain Milos said, tightening his grip on her arm. "My bargain was to release them unharmed and to allow you to see them go." He nodded, and one of the soldiers motioned to them.

Belva waved and wiped her eyes, taking White Bird's hand. Lone Wolf gazed at Vanessa and then turned, walking slowly, and she wondered if he were suffering from being dragged behind the horse. Her tears streamed freely now, and she didn't care. At least they would live, because Muaahap and Lone Wolf were at home on this land.

Suddenly White Bird yanked away from Belva and ran back to Vanessa, holding her arms out, crying, "Mama! Mama!"

Vanessa knelt to scoop her up, holding her close, feeling the tiny body, White Bird's thin arms around her neck. She didn't want to let go of White Bird, but she knew she had to or Captain Milos would part them by force.

"I love you," she whispered, kissing White Bird's cheek, handing her to Belva, who had come back to take her. A soldier stood in front of her, but Vanessa ignored him and placed White Bird in Belva's arms.

Tears ran down Belva's cheeks as well, and Vanessa hugged them both. "Take care of them and yourself. I'll be all right," she whispered. She stepped away and Belva turned when the soldier took her arm.

Now four soldiers stood with rifles drawn on Lone Wolf, whose angry countenance was fierce. Vanessa stared at him, feeling as if something inside were crumbling.

"She called you *mama*," Captain Milos said coldly.

"I taught her to call me that."

He glanced at them again. "If he tries anything, he's dead."

She watched as Belva caught up with them while White Bird cried and held out her arms to Vanessa. Muaahap and Lone Wolf turned to walk with them, and they moved slowly toward the gate.

"I wish you would let them have horses."

"That wasn't in our bargain and they don't need horses. The redskins will find their own people and they know how to survive out here like the snakes and the cactus."

He took her arm and she jerked away. "No! You said I could see them go. I want to go to the gates and stand where I can see them safely away from here. My seeing them go was part of our bargain," she snapped.

He studied her and then nodded. "Very well." He reached out to touch her cheek, his expression filled with contempt. "You cry for a redskin. You're a squaw, his woman."

She looked directly into his blue eyes. "Yes, I am. I love him."

His nostrils flared and for a moment Vanessa thought he might strike her. "Bitch," he said coldly. "Come along. You can watch them go, and then we'll return to my quarters and you'll keep your part of the bargain." He held her arm and they walked through the gates. She could see the small party moving slowly, White Bird walking now with one hand in Belva's and the other held by Muaahap.

With every step they took away from her, Vanessa felt as if they were walking out of her life and she would never see them again. She had never dreamed it would hurt so badly to part with them. Tears poured down her cheeks as she cried silently, aching, feeling as if her heart were being torn out. Would she ever see any of them again?

Captain Dupree wouldn't keep her a long time, because he would tire of her, but by then Lone Wolf might be so far away with his constantly moving tribe that she wouldn't ever find him.

And what if Dupree sent her somewhere when he tired of her? After a few weeks, Captain Milos might not care whether she stayed or ran away.

Her tears finally stopped as she watched the figures diminish and grow smaller in the distance.

"How did all of you get together?"

"I encountered them after the battle. He was wounded and needed help and his niece was with him."

"That's not his own child then. Who's the crone?"

"She's a Comanche who wanted to travel with us."

"And the girl is your sister?"

"Yes."

"You would rather she go with them than stay here with us and be returned to your family?"

"Yes. She's fine with them."

Now she couldn't see any of them. She felt reassured that they had gotten away from the fort and that no men were riding out loaded and armed. Milos took her arm. "We can go back now."

"No. I want to wait a little longer. I want to feel satisfied that you haven't sent any soldiers after them," she argued, knowing she was prolonging what was inevitable. He had kept his part of the bargain, and now she would have to keep hers.

He paced impatiently behind her. "You can watch the gate from my quarters; but I promise you, I am not sending anyone after them. I don't want them. They're not important to me."

"He is," she said flatly. "I saw the anger in your expression when you realized who he was."

"He wounded me at Adobe Walls. They make those war arrows with barbs so they'll do the most damage and tear the flesh if you try to pull them out. Yes, I remember him—and he remembers me because I killed his woman."

"She was his sister-in-law," Vanessa said flatly. "You killed the little girl's mother."

"She was an Indian. They would have killed me if they could have."

Vanessa felt a wave of revulsion toward him, wanting to leap at him and claw him and tell him that he had taken a child's mother from her. "She was unarmed and not fighting. She was only trying to protect her little girl," Vanessa said, remembering what Lone Wolf had told her about White Bird's mother.

He shrugged. "She would have been as savage as any of them if I had been her captive."

The sun was on the horizon, splashing the sky with pink, as Vanessa watched the empty land. Then dusk came and the first stars twinkled. "You've waited long enough. I kept my part, now you keep yours. We go."

Reluctantly, Vanessa turned to walk beside him back to his quarters. When she stepped inside, she watched as he lit a lamp and shed his coat. He pulled off his shirt and tossed it aside, standing bare-chested and studying her. She saw the large jagged scar on his right shoulder.

"That's where you were shot by Lone Wolf?"

"Yes." He crossed the room to her, putting his arms around her to kiss her.

Vanessa slid her arms around his neck. She felt cold inside, as if she had fallen into a pond of icy water. All her thoughts were on Lone Wolf, seeing his dark eyes, his impassive gaze, knowing he could do nothing now to help her. She prayed that he could get the others to safety and that Milos had kept his word and not sent any men after them.

Milos's hands roamed over her and her flesh felt prickly, but she tried to cooperate, fighting tears and a burning in her throat. If she cried, he would be enraged, yet she hated his touch, hated what he wanted from her.

His fingers worked at her buttons and the dress fell, billowing around her ankles. He stepped back to look at her as he pulled off his belt. "You're damned poor at your part of the bargain."

"I'm trying," she said, hating his eyes on her. "I'm not accustomed to men."

"Just to a dirty redskin," he sneered. Dupree looked at her, bursting with his desire, yet wanting to take his time to try to stir her to passion. He suspected she was capable of great depths of passion. The cascade of riotous red curls couldn't belong to a cold woman, and her body was enough to set him aflame. He cupped her breasts, bending his head to take one in his mouth.

He paused to look at her while he shed the rest of his clothing and his boots. He pulled her warm, soft body against his, his arousal pressing into her flesh as his hand slid between her thighs.

His mouth covered hers and he kissed her, trailing kisses to her throat as her hands slid over his back, but her efforts were half-hearted. He no longer cared; he was lost to passion, ready to possess her.

"Taps," she murmured, and he dimly heard the bugle, his attention on her soft body. And then he paused, raising his head to look at her. He tilted her face up, his fingers pinching her jaw, and her eyes widened.

"How the hell do you know that's taps? If I've got me a damned soiled dove or camp follower—" he snarled.

"No. My father was in the military," Vanessa admitted, suddenly not caring what happened. She felt as if she were dying, knowing she would recover from Dupree's lust and passion, but hating it, consumed with revulsion, aching for Lone Wolf and White Bird, Belva and Muaahap.

The captain's fingers shifted to her shoulders and he gave her a shake, his hands holding her tightly. "He's not in the military now?"

"No."

"Where's he live?"

For the first time she heard the earnest note in his voice. "What difference does it make? You and I have our bargain."

"It makes a hell of a difference if he can ruin my career! Where's he living?" he snapped, winding his fingers in her hair and jerking her face up to stare into her eyes.

"He's at Fort McKavett."

"Then he's a military man! What rank is he? Who is he? Dammit, whose daughter are you?"

She debated whether or not to lie, but it no longer mattered, because she might not ever see Lone Wolf again.

"Who is he?" Dupree shouted, pulling her hair until she cried out.

"He's Abbot Sutherland. He's working for the President, building railroads."

Dupree Milos's eyes narrowed, and he released her. His body burned for satisfaction, but he knew Abbot Sutherland and the man was powerful. Dupree crossed the room, trying to control his urges before he lost himself in passion and made a blunder that might cost him his career. "Get dressed!" he snapped.

For an instant, Vanessa stared at his bare back in shock and then she scooped up the dress, needing no further urging. Her hands shook and she felt faint with relief because it was obvious that the mention of her father had stopped Dupree. He was having second thoughts about bedding her.

He paced restlessly, seemingly unaware he was still nude, and she turned her back, dressing and buttoning as swiftly as she could.

Dupree turned to look at her. Vanessa's back was to him as she struggled to button her dress. He wanted to charge across the room, shove her to the floor, and possess her. His body ached for release, for she was a breathtaking beauty, but Abbot Sutherland's daughter gave him pause. Something nagged at him about the name. Where had he heard Sutherland mentioned recently?

Why was she out here on the plains with her sister and three redskins? Her father hated and despised Indians, and everyone had heard how Sutherland had offered ten dollars for any dead Indian when he was trying to get his railroad built in Kansas.

Why would she be here with such a strange assortment of people? Why was the sister with her? McKavett wasn't impossibly far away. He had seen them in Tucumcari, and he had observed her at the stage station seeing someone off. Had it been Sutherland? No. Abbot Sutherland would never have left her with the redskin.

Dupree's eyes narrowed as he studied her. Had the girls run away from home? The nagging thought returned, and he remembered stopping in Tucumcari to read a flyer nailed to a post.

"Great God!" he exclaimed. Dupree yanked on his pants and buttoned them. "You and your sisters have run away from your father!"

She turned around, and he had a suspicion she was weighing what to say to him. "My father wanted to marry my sister to an older man, and Phoebe didn't want to wed him. I helped her to escape."

"And you put her on a stage in Tucumcari."

She flushed and nodded her head. "Phoebe is gone now. I would rather you didn't notify my father."

Suddenly Dupree realized he'd let the youngest sister go. "I'll be right back," he snapped, charging across the room and out the door.

He remembered a large reward; but if he returned Vanessa to her father, Sutherland might be grateful enough to reward Dupree in a way that would further his career.

Vanessa hurried to the window and watched him stride across the parade ground. She wondered if he intended to send a telegram to her father now.

She looked at the open door and hurried outside. At a nearby building a saddled horse was tethered at a hitching rail. There had been no guards at the gates earlier, and she couldn't see well enough to tell whether or not there were any there now, but she was going to take the risk. She hurried to take the reins and she mounted, wheeling the horse around and kicking her heels. The black horse plunged forward.

"Stop her!"

She recognized Dupree's voice as she leaned over the horse and galloped toward the open gates. She heard him yell again behind her, the noise torn away by the wind rushing against her and the sound of the horse's pounding hooves.

The black galloped through the gates, racing in the direction she had watched Lone Wolf go so many hours earlier. Only he was on foot and she was on horseback.

She glanced back, her eyes adjusting to the night, and she saw one rider racing after her. She urged the horse faster, feeling a desperate need to get to Lone Wolf.

The rider drew alongside her. Panicky, Vanessa urged the horse faster, seeing her hope of escape dwindling. Dupree Milos galloped beside her and gradually pulled ahead, crowding her horse. Suddenly he grabbed her reins and tugged, pulling back to stop both horses.

Desperate to escape him and get to Lone Wolf, she flung herself out of the saddle the moment the horse halted. She knew it was useless to run, but she had to keep trying to get away from Milos until there was no chance at all. He continued at her heels and yanked her up before him, crushing her against him, his arm banding her tightly.

She beat against his chest, struggling to break free, until he grabbed her hair and yanked her face up. "Stop fighting me! It'll do you no good. I'm taking you back."

Eight soldiers rode past them, and he returned a salute. She watched them and went cold suddenly. "Where are they going?"

"After your sister. If you're Abbot Sutherland's daughter, he's going to want both of you back."

"What about the others? You made a bargain, and I tried to keep my part."

"I told them I only want the sister."

"You'll hurt the others," she exclaimed in fright. "Please, I'll do whatever you want. Please, stop those men."

"I told them I just want the white girl."

"Please go after your men and call them back. Leave

Belva where she is. Leave the others alone." The strain of the day was finally too much, and Vanessa broke into sobs.

Ignoring her, Dupree rode back in silence. At his quarters he swung down off the horse, and Vanessa dismounted swiftly.

Inside, he kicked the door shut and crossed the room to pour two brandies.

A knock on the door interrupted him, and he opened the door to motion two men to come inside. Two privates brought in trays of food and set them on the table.

They hurried out and closed the door.

"We'll eat shortly," he said, picking up the glasses with brandy and bringing one to her. "Drink this. It'll help," he said in a kinder voice.

She drank the fiery liquid and coughed. He drank some of his and motioned to her. "Go ahead. Drink more. You'll feel better."

Vanessa took another long drink. She watched him as he faced her. He stood only a few feet away, his blue eyes full of speculation as he studied her. "Why are you out here?"

"I was being sent to a convent—"

"A convent!" he exclaimed, interrupting her. He reached out to touch her hair. "You should never be in a convent. Your father was sending you?"

"Yes. I was with a wagon train headed to Denver where I was to enter the convent."

"Why wouldn't your father marry you to someone?"

"The men he approved of didn't want to marry me."

"The devil you say! I find that impossible to believe, Vanessa. You're a beautiful woman."

"Thank you," she answered, his words leaving her cold. Her thoughts were on the soldiers riding after Belva to bring her back to Fort Bascom.

He studied her, and Vanessa's heart beat quickly because he knew now she had run away. He could do what he wanted with her and her father would never know. Her reprieve from his bed was only temporary.

"I can't believe that there wasn't anyone who wanted to marry you," he said, regarding her.

She shrugged. "No one my father could accept wanted to marry me. He wanted a successful man with a promising future, not someone eighteen who had just joined the army. Unfortunately, I was more interested in a young man nearer my age than the colonels and majors and generals I met."

Dupree stroked her shoulder, letting his fingers trail down over her breast. He saw the flicker in her eyes and knew she didn't like his touch. He debated with himself. She admitted to running away, so he could do whatever he wanted with her and she would have no protector. There would be no one he would have to answer to if he got rid of her after he was through with her.

On the other hand, Abbot Sutherland was a powerful man with friends in the military and in Washington. Dupree studied her. If he could control his lust and think straight, this might be an opportunity for him. "Sit down, Vanessa."

She noted the change in his tone. She sat in a wing chair, and he took down the decanter of brandy. He refilled his glass and sat facing her, setting the decanter on a table beside him. "You were on your way to Denver to a convent when you ran away and encountered the Indian and the child."

"That's right, and later Comanche warriors found us and took us to their camp. When we left them, Muaahap, the older woman, went with us because she had grown to love the child."

"Three females traveling with the warrior?"

"Yes. I wanted to go back for my sisters, and finally Lone Wolf agreed to go with me. We got both of them, and I put Phoebe on a stage in Tucumcari."

"You're in love with him."

"Yes, I am. He's asked me to marry him."

"You know how your father will feel about that," Dupree said. "Most soldiers who've served in the West know Colonel Sutherland's hatred for Indians and his bounty for dead ones. He wouldn't consider the marriage binding, and he'd kill the warrior."

She turned her head to look at the crackling fire. "It doesn't matter now because Lone Wolf is gone and I don't know where or how to find him."

Mulling over possibilities, Dupree continued to study her. She was a beauty, intelligent, from a good family, and her father could help him greatly with his army career. On the other hand, Dupree could take her right now, keep her as his mistress for as long as it pleased him, and no one would know or care.

At the thought of the last, he weakened, thinking about her lush body, his gaze going over her. She was staring at the fire, her lustrous eyes brimming with tears again while she probably thought about the redskin. She sipped the brandy with which he suspected she was unfamiliar and which had already mellowed her slightly. Which did he want, to take her now, possess her body and have immediate satisfaction, or to wait, try to win her and her father, hoping Sutherland would help his career?

Dupree sipped the brandy, feeling the heat warm his insides. "You were taking your youngest sister to live with the Indians?"

"Yes. We gave her the choice of going with my sister or staying with me. She chose to stay with me."

"Tell me their names."

He listened as she talked, her voice growing listless, and he suspected she was feeling the influence of the brandy. He needed to come to a decision because they would soon return with the sister.

All three girls had run away from home—that meant that all three were unhappy, so it had to be they wanted to get away from the father. Vanessa was being sent to a convent and she didn't want to go. Phoebe was being married to a man she despised, and they hadn't wanted to leave Belva behind.

He made his decision and stood up, crossing to Vanessa to take the snifter of brandy from her hand and set it down. He picked her up and sat down with her on his lap.

As she started to get up, his arm tightened around her waist and he held her. "Be still. I want to talk to you."

She settled, sitting stiffly on his knees. She smelled of roses and he longed to peel away the dress, knowing what she looked like beneath it. Trying to get his mind back to the problem at hand, he fingered her collar.

"You know your father would never allow you to stay with a tribe or be married to a redskin."

"He wouldn't find us."

"He has the U.S. Army at his disposal in his work for the President."

"He doesn't know about Lone Wolf. All he knows is that I ran away from the wagon train and came back to Fort McKavett."

"He'd find out. You've traveled and people have seen you together. Now I know."

She looked at him sharply, and he felt a twinge of cynical amusement, knowing the brandy had fuzzed her sharp thinking. And he was thankful it had. "He'd find you and kill the Indian."

She stared at him, mulling over what he had said. He let his hand rest against her soft breast as he smoothed the lace on her dress with his fingers. "Vanessa, I can take you now and make you my mistress. You promised to please me, and I can do whatever I want."

She nodded, her eyes round and solemn.

"I want more than that. You don't want to live in a convent, do you?"

"No, I don't."

"I saw you with the little Indian girl. You were meant to

have your own little girls. You'll make a good mother. You'll forget the warrior; and you should, because your father would kill him and take you back and put you in the convent."

"No," she whispered, but there was no force in her voice.

"You know he would," Dupree declared emphatically. "I think I can give you things that would make you happy, and you can give me things that would make me happy. If your father wanted to, he could help my career because he has influence in high places."

She nodded solemnly, and he wondered if she were so fogged by brandy, she didn't know what he was saying. He saw opportunity sitting on his lap with a lush body and big green eyes. This was his chance for a big promotion, for powerful contacts in Washington.

"Vanessa, will you marry me?"

Twenty-one

Vanessa stared at Dupree Milos as his words swirled in her head. She felt hot and dizzy and wanted to get away from him. Uncertain she had heard him correctly, she stared into his blue eyes. "Why would you want to marry me?"

"I told you, I can give you things you want. I think you can give me things I want. Or your father can. Even if we don't wed—your father is offering a big reward for you. He'll be grateful to me for returning you and your sister to him. As enticing as your body is, I'd be foolish if I let the reward go by." He smiled at her. "But I'd rather marry you, Vanessa."

Vanessa scooted off his lap, moving away from him to stand in front of the fire and hold out her hands, the warmth of the flames doing little for her chill. She debated how to answer, aware he could so easily go after Lone Wolf and kill him. Finally, she turned around. "I'll have to give your proposal thought; but if Belva tells me your men murdered Lone Wolf, then the answer is no."

"I don't think that will happen. I told them I just wanted the white girl. I told them to tell your sister that you sent for her. I think she'll come willingly. He can't fight. He doesn't have a weapon and he's injured."

Vanessa nodded. Her head was spinning, and she knew it was from the brandy because she was unaccustomed to spirits. He stood up and crossed the room to her, placing his hands on her shoulders.

"We could have a good marriage, Vanessa. It would be better than being locked away in a convent. I saw how you love the little girl. Think how it will be with your own children."

She gazed up at him, thinking that at one time she would have accepted his proposal. He was handsome, young enough to suit her, probably of high enough rank in the military to suit Papa. But all she could see now was Lone Wolf's dark eyes.

"I'm thirty-one. I have savings and I can provide for you quite well. My family lives in Illinois and my father has his own saddlery shop, a successful business."

She didn't love Dupree Milos and didn't want to marry him, but she was afraid to tell him until enough time had passed that Lone Wolf would be safely beyond his reach.

He slid his arms around her, pulling her to him. This time his kiss was less passionate, far more gentle. She was afraid to annoy him, so she stood quietly in his arms while he kissed her.

When she stepped out of his embrace, Dupree gestured toward the table. "We'll eat now."

He took the covers off the plates to reveal thick slices of roast beef, potatoes with brown gravy, green beans, biscuits.

He pulled out a chair for her and sat down facing her. "If you're Abbot Sutherland's daughter, you're accustomed to living on a post."

"Yes. That's where I've spent a lot of my life. We've moved constantly." As he started to pour brandy into her glass, she waved her hand. "No, thank you. I've had enough."

He smiled and poured the brandy. "You might change your mind, Vanessa."

She realized he was trying to charm her and she tried to reciprocate, wishing she hadn't had the brandy to drink, knowing she should try to keep her mind clear. He would find other quarters for her and she would be alone, but she suspected he would post a guard so she couldn't try to leave again. Now, even if she had a chance to escape, she couldn't leave when the soldiers might be returning with Belva. And when a few days had passed and she told the captain she wouldn't marry him, would he try to force himself on her? Then he would have Belva to use as a threat.

She smiled at him, only half-hearing what he was saying as she studied him in the golden glow of the lantern. Once Belva was with her, they would have to get away from Fort Bascom.

"I'd like to go into Tucumcari and get some material to make a dress. I don't have anything to wear besides this, and it doesn't fit me."

"It looks pretty on you, but you should have something else. I'll return your gold—your father's gold, actually, to you and take you to Tucumcari tomorrow."

"May Belva go along? She won't have anything to wear either."

"Of course. Whatever you want," he answered cheerfully.

She ate slowly, wanting the evening to be over, knowing he would kiss her again and wishing she could eat and go to her quarters without touching him. She wondered how far away from the fort the others had gotten?

"What if your men can't find Belva?"

"They'll find her. There's nowhere they can hide."

"How soon do you expect them back?"

He shrugged. "My men may have to wait until daylight to look for them. I'd guess they would be back midday or the middle of tomorrow afternoon. The Indians are on foot, so they can't have gotten far."

She looked at the curling flames and thought about Lone Wolf and the others walking away from the fort. How bad were Lone Wolf's injuries? She remembered that last moment when she had looked into Lone Wolf's dark eyes, and pain stabbed through her.

"After being dragged behind your horse for miles, Lone Wolf may not be able to walk far."

"He'll survive. You saw him leave. Tomorrow he'll be stronger and better." He glanced at her plate. "You should eat."

She shook her head. "I'm not hungry."

"You pine over the Indian," he said with contempt in his voice.

"I was where I wanted to be when you brought me back here. When my father learns where I am, he'll take me to Denver."

"You have another choice and a damned good one."

She looked again at the flames, her thoughts constantly turning to Lone Wolf. Would he try to fight the soldiers to keep Belva?

"Have you thought about a home or children?"

"Not often," she answered, studying him. "What do you want in the future?" she asked, curious what he hoped to get from her father. "An Army career?"

"Yes. I want to make general. I want a good command. I want out of this godforsaken territory and back where there are more amenities. But right now, I'm missing a war and I don't mind that. I'd rather face the redskins than Rebel cannons."

She stood up, pulling on her cape. "I'm exhausted. It's been a long day and I'd like my own room." She wondered whether he would let her go. To her relief he stood.

"Certainly. I'll show you to your quarters. Right now, there are no families here as there have been in times past, so we have some small houses available."

Stepping into the cold night, he escorted her a short distance to a small frame house. He opened the door and went ahead to light a lamp.

She entered a furnished one-room house that was slightly dusty and held only a table, bed, desk, washstand, and chairs.

"There's a privy in back and I'll post a guard. You won have another chance to escape."

The lamp gave a golden glow that bathed him in its ligh catching glints in his thick yellow hair. They stared at eac other, and his gaze went over her in a quick assessment.

"Think about my offer." He moved close to her and tilte up her chin. "I let him live so I could have you in my be tonight. I still want you, but I want more from you. You' never get back to that Indian, so face what lies ahead. You' see I've made you a generous offer."

She nodded, determined she would try to get back Lone Wolf.

"Think about marriage, Vanessa. I can make you happy. Dupree said, as he placed his arms around her and pulle her to him to kiss her long and passionately. She slid h arms around his neck and stood still, aching for Lone Wol wanting to push Dupree away, yet wanting to cooperate unt she saw a chance for escape.

Finally, Dupree released her. "We'll breakfast in th morning before I have to start the day. I'll come wake you

She nodded, following him to the door and closing Putting out the lamp, she moved silently across the roo to the front window. A lantern burned on a post outsid and she saw the guard standing with his back to her.

The guard could see the gates and anyone who tried go through them. Discouraged, knowing she couldn't leav without Belva, she stood at the window, staring in the d rection in which Lone Wolf had walked away. She glance at the stars, thinking that Lone Wolf was under the sam stars. How badly had he been hurt? She reminded herse how tough he was and of the terrible wounds he had su vived before. He should survive this.

The next morning she washed, combed, and braided h hair, and then waited for Captain Milos.

Within the quarter-hour, he knocked on the door. Sl swung it open, realizing again that he was a handsome ma

His blue eyes swept over her, and he smiled with a flash of white teeth. "Good morning!" he said cheerfully, coming into the room. "I thought perhaps I would have the chance to wake you."

"I've been up a long time."

"So have I. So we're both early risers. Something we'll have in common. I thought we might eat breakfast together, and then I have work to do. This afternoon, I'll accompany you to Tucumcari, and you may get some material for a dress."

"I'd like that. I need clothing," she said, her spirits soaring because in Tucumcari she would have a chance to get away from him. "I want Belva to go with us."

"Of course she may if she's here."

"I'd rather wait for her. If she doesn't come until late, we can go tomorrow."

"Fine, Vanessa. Whatever pleases you. I have another surprise for you."

She felt cold, looking into his blue eyes. Surely he wouldn't harm Lone Wolf and then tell her with a smile. "What surprise?" she asked, afraid to hear.

"Just before I came here, I sent a telegram. And I've received an answer."

She stared at him, her blood like ice.

"I sent a telegram to your father that you're here and you're just fine and Belva is with you. I've received one back from him. He's on his way to Fort Bascom now."

"No!" she exclaimed. "He'll take me to Denver to the convent."

"No, he won't. I'll ask for your hand in marriage, and if you cooperate, you won't ever have to think about a convent." Dupree draped his arm around her shoulders. "Let me handle your father. You'll see. I think I can get him to accept me as a son-in-law." Dupree turned her to face him and placed his hands on her shoulders. "The real question, Vanessa, is—will you accept me as a husband?"

"I told you I wanted to give it thought. You did little yesterday to endear yourself to me," she stated bluntly. Anger flared in his blue eyes and then was gone.

"Think about the advantages of what I'm offering. Now let's go to my quarters and have breakfast."

All through a steaming breakfast of pink ham and hot biscuits, scrambled eggs, and hot coffee, he tried to charm her and she tried to respond politely.

As she drank coffee, she gazed out the window. "I think our wagon train passed close to Bascom, although the area was grassier than this. We were along the Canadian River."

"The Canadian River runs hundreds of miles across western lands."

"It's just north of here, isn't it?"

He raised his head, his blue eyes focusing on her with amusement as he lowered his coffee cup. "Yes, we're beside the river, but it won't do you any good to know that. I know you didn't have a chance to make any arrangements with the Indian and they won't stay around here."

"So where we camped was farther west along the river," she said, knowing it was east, but hoping he would continue talking about locations.

"No, it was east of here. You were probably fifteen or twenty miles west of where we fought. They won't be camping in the same place now, so it wouldn't do you any good to look there for him if you did get away. Which you won't."

"Actually, I was worrying about Belva. I don't suppose she has returned?"

"No. You'll know immediately," he said. As soon as they finished eating, he escorted her back to her quarters and left to take care of military duties. She didn't see him again that day. When late afternoon came and then early evening and there was no sign of Belva, Vanessa's curiosity rose. That night when Dupree came to escort her to his quarters for dinner, his good spirits were gone and he seemed solemn.

"Where is Belva, Captain?"

"They're aren't back yet, but that doesn't mean anything. There are hundreds of reasons why they could have been delayed. They'll be here with her tomorrow."

"Tomorrow you'll take us to Tucumcari?"

"Yes. I told you I would."

"You're young to be a captain. You shouldn't really need my father's intervention."

"He can speed things and he can help. A man can be forgotten out here. I would like to get back to Washington. I like the East."

She nodded and hoped he thought she was listening as she wondered about Belva and why the soldiers hadn't returned.

Finally that night, after a few goodnight kisses and caresses that she endured, she was alone in her quarters again. Standing in her darkened room, she gazed toward the gates. They were on the Canadian River. Tomorrow, in Tucumcari, she wanted to look at the town; and if any chance came to escape, she would take it. If he hadn't found Belva now, she didn't think he would. Vanessa stared into the darkness and wondered about Belva and Lone Wolf, Muaahap and White Bird. Where were they? Why hadn't the soldiers returned with her sister?

Lone Wolf staggered and fell, sprawling on his face as dizziness overwhelmed him. Muaahap knelt beside him and motioned to Belva to sit down.

Muaahap saw the blood on his neck and frowned. She raised his shirt and drew in her breath as she looked at the lashes across his bloody back. She heard Belva cry out and turned to see her staring at his back. Muaahap motioned to her to take White Bird away.

Guipago could not go on in this condition. Muaahap stared at him, touching a leather pouch on her belt that held medicine. She needed water to clean him. She stood up, her gaze scanning the horizon.

Holding White Bird's hand, Belva walked back to take Muaahap's arm and point behind them.

Raising her hand to shade her eyes and squinting, Muaahap frowned. Knowing her eyesight was not as sharp as the girl's, she saw nothing and she couldn't understand Belva's words or motions. Turning again, less than a quarter of a mile ahead, she saw a wash with a few junipers scattered down it.

Muaahap knelt beside Lone Wolf, patting his face. "Guipago! Guipago! *Kai'wa! Aho,*" she said loudly in his ear.

His lashes fluttered and he raised his head, focusing on her. She pointed toward the trees. She held her right hand out, motioning to go.

He struggled to get up and she reached beneath his arm to help him, calling to Belva, who came quickly with White Bird. Belva got on his other side, and the two helped him to his feet, staggering toward the trees. Muaahap caught White Bird's hand, and the four of them slowly covered the distance.

Before they reached the trees, he sprawled again. Belva clutched Muaahap's arm.

"Muaahap, look! Riders!" she exclaimed, pointing.

Muaahap peered behind them, now seeing the dust rise in the air, at last certain that someone was following them. She guessed the soldier had sent his men out to kill them. She looked at Belva, who, though still a child, was a female nonetheless, and Muaahap knew the girl would not be safe with soldiers.

She motioned to Belva to take Lone Wolf's ankle. She picked up the other one and began to tug on it. Belva protested in words Muaahap could not understand, but it was obvious Belva didn't think they should drag him.

Muaahap nodded vigorously and pointed toward the dust on the horizon and then toward the trees that were only yards away now. Belva clamped her mouth closed and took his ankle, tears falling as she helped pull him across the rough ground.

Muaahap knelt to motion to White Bird and talk to her in Comanche and, finally, White Bird nodded solemnly. Muaahap glanced at the dust again, judging the distance and the time it would take, and knew they would have to hurry to hide. She pulled a knife from her moccasin and hacked away a stout juniper branch, cutting two of them and giving one to Belva. She took the other and began to dig, scraping away the soft sand in the wash beneath the junipers, motioning to Belva to do the same.

With a perplexed look, Belva also began to dig beneath the branches, struggling as the bushes scraped her and pushed against her. Muaahap nodded and went back to the spot where Lone Wolf had fallen. With the juniper branch she brushed away their tracks, walking backward, sweeping the ground and then turning to dig.

They scraped out shallow indentations, and Muaahap rolled Lone Wolf into the large one, covering him quickly with the sand and dirt until only a round circle of his face was exposed and branches of a juniper hung directly over him. She stepped back to study the effect. If the soldiers looked closely, they would spot Lone Wolf; otherwise, he wasn't noticeable because of the thick branches.

Belva dug quickly beneath another juniper, and Muaahap helped her enlarge the space near the trunk of the tree. Muaahap climbed the rise to peer over the bank. Eight soldiers rode toward them.

She brushed away her tracks and slid back down to help Belva. Finally, she motioned to Belva, who stretched out in the shallow space, and Muaahap hastily scooped the dirt over her until only her face was exposed and, like Lone Wolf, she was partially concealed by juniper branches.

Muaahap took White Bird's hand and went to the space she had dug beneath the other side of the tree. She scooted and crawled beneath branches, patting the ground beside her, talking again to White Bird, who nodded. Muaahap scooped dirt over her feet and legs and lap, turning to motion to White Bird, who nodded again and crawled under the branches. Muaahap spread sand and dirt over both of them and, as she worked, she heard the jingle of harness and the horses' hooves, as well as the deep voices of several men.

She continued to cover herself as best she could, knowing she and White Bird were barely hidden except for the thick juniper. She held White Bird's hand tightly.

"They have to be here somewhere," came a deep voice. "The tracks stopped in the middle of nowhere."

"They can't be far. The tracks are fresh. He's covered them, but they had to have come this way. Otherwise, we could see them."

Scarcely daring to breathe, Muaahap lay unmoving, holding White Bird's hand tightly, rolling her eyes as she heard horses within yards.

"I think they went the other way."

"If they went any other way, we could see them unless they were hours ahead of us. But they can't be far ahead. He said the redskin was almost beat to death."

"We'd better get the girl. You heard the captain."

"They had to have come this way. Head on up this wash. Toby, you and Will go on north for another hour and then turn east. The rest of us will head east. They won't turn west because it would be back toward Bascom."

Muaahap listened to them ride past. She lay still and felt White Bird start to move. Muaahap squeezed White Bird's hand tightly, and White Bird became still.

Hoofbeats faded, and then Muaahap heard the jingle of a bridle. One of the soldiers had stayed behind; the horse walked slowly past and turned. Hoofbeats faded, but she continued to wait. Finally, she crawled out from under the juniper and helped White Bird to crawl out. Their faces were scratched by the juniper, sand and twigs twisted in their hair. Muaahap surveyed the horizon, then she hurried to Belva and helped her up. Together, they uncovered Lone Wolf, dragging him out from beneath the tree.

Muaahap took a small medicine pouch from her belt. With Belva's help, they worked Lone Wolf's shirt up. He stirred, looking at her, and she motioned to him. He removed the shirt, and Muaahap knelt behind him to tend to his back.

While Muaahap worked on Lone Wolf, Belva took White Bird, and they walked away.

That night they sat huddled near Lone Wolf, who slept. White Bird was curled in Belva's lap, asleep. Muaahap motioned to Belva to stay where she was.

Muaahap moved east down the wash, following its winding course and the tracks of the soldiers' horses. Satisfied that horses had passed this way earlier, she walked carefully without making noise.

Two hours later, she climbed a bank and scanned the area. A quarter-moon shed enough light to see the mounds on the ground and the horses nearby. Less than half a mile away was the soldiers' camp and their picketed mounts.

She moved quietly and slowly, remembering times long past when she had ridden with her husband and stolen horses. The soldiers were spread in a circle, their feet toward a burned-out fire. From the condition of the camp, she knew they hadn't worried about anyone's attacking them. Utensils were still scattered, and if they had to leave in a hurry, they would have to go without their possessions.

She moved closer, tiptoeing and pausing between steps. Their saddles lay on the ground, and she wished she had the strength to carry one. A gunbelt lay close to a soldier's head, the revolver in the holster.

Creeping closer, Muaahap knelt only yards away from his head. When she reached for the belt, her fingers closing on the hard leather, he shifted and she froze, staring at him.

If any of the men woke and saw her, she wouldn't be able to escape.

Waiting, listening to one of the men snore, she finally picked up the belt in one swift move. Holding it tightly, she crept away.

She fastened the belt over her shoulder and then picked up an iron skillet and a canteen. As she moved toward the horses, she picked up a blanket.

The soldiers slept without a man on watch. She moved silently to the horses, taking out the knife to cut the ropes to the long metal picket pins. She placed the blanket on one horse and then stuck the pan down the back of her dress, her belt keeping it from falling to the ground. She hung the canteen on her belt. Slowly, she led the two horses away.

Two hundred yards from camp, she looked back at the sleeping soldiers, tempted to return for more horses, but deciding against it.

With a deep breath, she threw herself up on the back of one of the horses and straightened up, holding the rope and moving ahead, leading the other horse.

When she reached Lone Wolf, all of them were asleep, Belva curled around White Bird.

Muaahap shook Lone Wolf, patting his cheek until finally he raised his head.

She motioned to go and doubled her fists with thumbs down to indicate soldiers. Groaning, Lone Wolf sat up, pain stabbing him, his legs and back feeling on fire.

He studied Muaahap as she continued to make the sign of soldiers. He heard a soft whicker and turned to stare at two horses. Astounded, he looked at Muaahap. She had taken the horses from the soldiers! The Comanche could get horses better than anyone. They had taken horses out from under the noses of soldiers before, but it had been agile warriors in their prime, not a little old woman who jingled when she walked. She gave him a sly grin and stood up.

He stared in amazement as she unbuckled a gunbelt. Feeling a surge of hope and strength, he returned her grin, holding his fists in front of him and raking his right fist down in the sign for bravery. Almost laughing out loud, she pulled an iron skillet from the back of her dress.

Ignoring the pain for a moment, he stood up with an effort, groaning because it felt as if flames licked at his flesh. He reached out to hug her. This time, she did laugh— and gave him the gunbelt.

He took the belt from her and then realized he couldn't wear it until his back healed. He put down the gunbelt and motioned to her, signing a question. Where were the soldiers?

She pointed east, and he guessed they had ridden down the draw. Looking at Belva and White Bird, he wondered how they had escaped the soldiers' notice, suspecting Muaahap had fashioned them a hiding place in the junipers. He gestured to the north and waited while Muaahap bent to waken Belva. In minutes he was mounted on one horse with a sleeping White Bird in front of him while Belva and Muaahap rode pillion on the other.

As they headed north, he kept looking toward the east for any sign of the soldiers, judging they had about two more hours until sunup and needed to get as far north as possible. The sun would be behind the soldiers, an advantage to him. He tried to close his mind to thoughts about Vanessa, knowing he couldn't ride back for her without help, bitterness gnawing at him with the knowledge that the captain had already possessed her.

Lone Wolf's fists clenched and he turned to look over his shoulder to the west, wanting to ride back to get her. He wasn't physically able now and he had to get White Bird and Belva to safety. He remembered standing on the parade ground, facing Vanessa. She had lifted her chin, and her green eyes had widened, filled with pain. The thought of parting from her had torn through him as badly as the loss of Eyes That Smile.

When White Bird had broken free to run to Vanessa, he had wanted to charge across the parade ground and smash his fist into the captain's face. He had held back because he had known it would have gotten him killed and White Bird and Belva and Muaahap needed him.

Now, he glanced at Muaahap, realizing she didn't need him as much as he had thought. He wondered about her age. She was pleased with herself and she had a right to be. And when he had a chance, he would give her a horse and get a bracelet and earrings fashioned for her because now with horses and a gun they had a chance to escape and survive.

Dawn came in pink streaks, and he continued to watch the east, knowing they needed to turn soon and ride in that direction if he wanted to get back to the Kiowas.

His thoughts shifted back to the captain, who had made a bargain with Vanessa but had then sent out soldiers, breaking his promise. Lone Wolf guessed that they were sent to kill and that the captain's word had proved worthless. Captain Milos. He had heard the men say his name. And laugh about the captain and Vanessa. Anger surged in Lone Wolf. He intended to meet the captain again.

Frustrated, he ached for Vanessa, hurting over leaving her and surprised at the depth of the hurt. How had she won her way into his heart?

He thought of the nights with her in his room, the hours of talk and kisses and lovemaking. And her determination to rescue Phoebe. When had Vanessa become a vital part of his life? A future without her seemed empty, and he ached more than he would have ever guessed.

He thought about his marriage proposal and her solemn acceptance. Now he wished he could do it over and tell her that he wanted her for his wife because he wanted her at his side, because he loved and needed her.

He looked back over his shoulder. He would recover from his wounds and the beating. Then he would take a war party and they would ride back to get her, and he would kill the captain for Tainso and for Vanessa.

By midday, he was exhausted and in constant pain. They found a river and Muaahap insisted on tending his back. They moved away from the others, and he stripped to let her apply her medicine, finally getting relief.

They mounted again and rode east another three days into grassy country. By the third night, as the moon rose high overhead, Lone Wolf rode in the lead. Scanning the horizon, he spotted the slash in the earth and rode toward it. As they neared, he could see a wide chasm.

In another half-mile, Lone Wolf rode to the rim to look down into a deep canyon. Moonlight splashed on the landscape as he gazed below with satisfaction.

Smoke curled skyward from the large circles of tipis. He motioned to the others and began the careful descent, glancing back over his shoulder once more, feeling as if he had left his heart behind with Vanessa, knowing his grief for Eyes That Smile had ended, that now Vanessa Sutherland held his heart.

He turned on the horse, the north wind whipping against him, the pale moon above, and he thought about Vanessa beneath the same moon. "I'll come for you," he said quietly. "Wait, my heart, because I will be back."

Twenty-two

Five days later, Vanessa sat across from Dupree as they finished breakfast. Through the window she saw a soldier striding toward the captain's quarters.

"Someone's coming," she said, and a sharp knock followed her words.

"Come in," Dupree called, pushing back his chair to turn toward the door.

A sergeant entered and saluted, and Dupree returned the salute. Then the sergeant's gaze shifted to Vanessa, and he stared.

"Karns?" the captain asked, his voice rising in curiosity.

"Sorry, sir," the man said as his gaze returned to Dupree.

"What do you mean, sorry?" With a scrape of his chair, Dupree stood. "Step outside. Excuse me, Vanessa, military business." He spoke curtly and closed the door behind himself and his officer. She contemplated the look the sergeant had given her, and a chill ran down her spine. She slid out of her chair and rushed to the door to listen because she was sure whatever he had to tell Dupree concerned Belva.

"What the devil? Why couldn't you find them? He was half-dead!"

As she eavesdropped, Vanessa frowned. Lone Wolf hadn't appeared half-dead when he had walked out of the fort. His head had been bloody, but he had walked away. What had Dupree done to him?

"What!"

At the outburst from Captain Milos, her attention shifted back to the men. She leaned even closer to the door.

"How in hell could someone get into a camp of eight soldiers and steal two horses?"

"I don't know, sir. I just know they were gone. We're in Comanche territory, and you know how they take horses right under . . ."

His words trailed away, and Vanessa returned to the breakfast table. The soldiers hadn't found Belva and the others. Where were they? Had they gotten away safely?

She heard Dupree raise his voice again, but she was unable to distinguish what he said. However, there was no mistaking his anger and she took a perverse pleasure in it and the fact that the soldiers had not found Belva.

When the door re-opened, Milos stormed inside. "I'm going to my office. You can walk back to your place, Vanessa. Sorry, but I have business to attend to."

"Where's Belva?"

His eyes blazed with anger. "I don't know. My men couldn't find them. I'll send out another detachment to search for her. I want her here when your father arrives." He took his hat from a peg and left, slamming the door behind him.

She watched him from the window, her thoughts on Belva and Lone Wolf. Where were they? Had they gotten safely away and the soldiers couldn't pick up the trail?

On Tuesday, Dupree had taken her to Tucumcari to get material. He had also returned to her what little remained of her gold and greenbacks. Most of the money she had spent or sent with Phoebe. But she had had enough to purchase yards of blue velvet and purple gingham and order a pair of shoes. And as they rode around Tucumcari, she had tried to get a feeling for the town. In the dry goods store, she had asked the direction to the Canadian River.

Now, while she wondered about Belva and the others,

she returned to her small room to go back to her sewing, bending over the velvet and thinking about Lone Wolf.

That night Vanessa paced her room, her white nightgown billowing around her. She had to get away from Bascom before her father arrived. He would either make her marry Dupree Milos right here at the fort or he would get an army escort and go with her to the convent in Denver.

If only she knew where Belva was. Vanessa rubbed her head, feeling certain Belva was still with Lone Wolf and that they had reached his people.

He had said that in the winter they camped and didn't move around as they did in the summer. If she could escape, could she find him? He had drawn a map in the dirt of where they were going from Tucumcari, where he thought his people would now be camping.

She could remember Lone Wolf's deep voice as he had told her, ". . . There's a canyon about fifty miles south of where you were, I think that's where they'll be . . ."

She rubbed her head again, knowing the first problem was to get away from Bascom or Tucumcari.

All during the next day she pondered ways to escape and what she would need to take with her. She sewed the velvet dress. She had chosen the fabric because it would be warm on the cold winter nights, and she had lined the skirt with several deep pockets in which she could hide things to take with her. She spent hours sewing when Dupree was away during the day. That night at dinner, she asked him to take her to Tucumcari again because she needed more material to complete her dress.

He obliged, coming to get her Saturday morning. As she opened the door, his gaze raked over her and desire flared in his eyes. He stepped inside to look at her again, his gaze going over the velvet dress.

"You look beautiful, Vanessa!" he said.

"This is a fancy dress for a ride to town, but I'll be warmer," she said, pulling the woolen cape around her, aware that the pockets on the underside of the velvet skirt held her gold. She had carefully wrapped the coins so they wouldn't jingle, lightly stitching them into the pockets along with the greenbacks. Only if he picked her up would Dupree notice anything awry.

"I won't argue with you. You look wonderful in that dress," he said, helping her with the cape, his hands roaming over her shoulders. He pulled her into his arms to kiss her.

She stood quietly, longing to shove him away and hating his kiss, but knowing she had to cooperate or she wouldn't get to Tucumcari.

He raised his head, his blue eyes blazing with desire. "I want you to marry me, Vanessa."

"You should wait and marry a woman you love," she answered, stepping away from him. He followed her toward the door.

"Love is foolish." Pausing to look at himself in the oval mirror, he smoothed his hair. "Shall we go?"

When she nodded, he took her arm to lead her outside in the sunshine to a waiting buggy. Four soldiers rode behind them, and she glanced at them as they left the fort.

"Is it dangerous to go from here to town?"

"Anywhere on the frontier is dangerous. We fight the Apache, Comanche, Ute. I don't want to encounter a war party while I'm alone with a pretty woman. And every man on the post is happy to go into town."

As soon as they reached Tucumcari, he climbed down and came around to help her out of the buggy, his hands closing around her waist as he swung her to the ground.

"I want to go to the dry goods store. I need to get material and some feathers and ribbon for a bonnet," she said. "Mr. Slocum has such pretty things," she added, remembering that on the first trip Dupree hadn't left her side, but his boredom with her shopping had been plain.

Dupree looked beyond her as if his attention was elsewhere. "How long will it take?"

"I like to take my time and look at everything."

"Vanessa, you like to shop too much for you to have ever been happy with that redskin. I'll give you half an hour."

"You may join me, but I'd like an hour to look. This is the only chance I get to shop and talk to people."

He glanced across the street at a cantina. "One hour. I'll come to the dry goods store and meet you."

"Thank you."

"I'll take care of the bill, Vanessa."

"Thank you," she said, giving him a broad smile. "But Papa will do that when he arrives."

"No, I insist."

She smiled at him again and turned away, glancing back in seconds to see Dupree striding across the street to the cantina. Turning around, she rushed into the general store. She purchased a canteen and a large supply of jerked beef. While she paid for the purchase, her pulse drummed because if Dupree discovered what she was doing, he would know she intended to run.

As soon as she had paid, she hurried to the dry goods store, relieved when the door swung shut behind her. She glanced through the oval glass, looking down the street at the cantina. The sun shone brightly and men milled around on the street, but there was no sign of Dupree.

"Morning, Miss Sutherland," Thad Slocum said, smiling at her, revealing a wide gap between his front teeth.

"Good morning, Mr. Slocum," she said warmly. "I came to look at material again while Captain Milos runs some errands. You have such pretty things."

"Look all you want."

Several men sat around a pot-bellied stove, and a few women shopped. Vanessa drifted down one aisle and moved slowly to another. She inched her way toward the back of the store and paused to watch Thad Slocum and his customers.

Slocum stood talking to the men, while the women were busy looking at goods. Vanessa quickly moved through the back room and out a back door. She turned, remembering her way to the livery stable, and hurried along the block, her back tingling because if Dupree caught her now or a soldier spotted her, she would go back to Bascom and not be allowed to come to town again.

In the next block she could see the livery stable. The weathered structure had its double doors thrown open; a horse was tethered in front at a hitching rail. The smell of horses and straw was strong.

She passed the livery stable and then turned in at the back, hurrying to the side to look around the stable. Leaning against the rough boards, she waited, and in a minute heard two men talking.

She looked again as they walked outside, a horse between them. They turned toward the sorrel tethered to the rail. Vanessa rushed behind them toward the open door and slipped into the stable.

To her relief the place was empty. Without hesitation she ran to a ladder to climb into the loft. She heard the men returning and lay down in the hay, praying they wouldn't come up.

After a time they walked outside again. With a rustling of straw, she moved to the front of the loft near a window where she could see the street and glimpse the main street. She piled straw high in front of her and settled to wait.

Over an hour later, she heard shouts outside, the sound carrying through the open window. She raised up cautiously to listen, afraid to look out.

"Have you seen a woman wearing a blue dress? She's pretty and young. This is a picture of her."

"Wish I had. Nope, not around here. You think those women are here?"

"One of them is, and we have to find her." The voice

trailed away. She settled back on the straw and closed her eyes, knowing she should sleep and rest now if she could.

When she stirred, it was dark. Her eyes adjusted to the faint moonlight coming through the open window in the loft. She sat quietly listening for anyone else in the stable. In time, she moved cautiously down the ladder and gazed around. Five horses were in stalls.

She went to the front door and pushed. It was locked as she had expected. She turned and saw the doors to the corral that were barred from the inside. Hurrying, Vanessa lifted the bar. She placed two gold coins beside a stall and led a black gelding out to saddle it. In ten minutes, she opened the corral gate and led the horse through, her pulse pounding because now she would be in terrible danger.

She closed the gate, mounted, and rode quietly out of town, looking at the stars and darkened houses, knowing she would draw less attention if she went slowly. Her nerves were taut, her ears straining for any sound. Once she turned to glance at the empty street behind her. Far down the street where light spilled from a cantina, she saw a man move into the street.

She left town, heading north for the river and breaking into a gallop. Her nerves were raw, and panic gripped her until she saw the silver ribbon glistening in the moonlight. She had reached the river, and she turned east.

During the next day Vanessa followed the Canadian River, aware she would ride too far north and have to drop back south, but afraid she would get lost otherwise.

Riding through the night and all day, stopping to give her horse rests, she hoped to widen the distance because she had no doubt that Dupree would come after her. With her father on the way to Tucumcari, Dupree would want her back desperately.

The following night she kept riding, dozing and almost falling from the saddle only to jerk upright and wake. A cold north wind blew, and she pulled the cape tightly across her shoulders.

During the next day, she had to stop to sleep, terrified that she would wake as Dupree's prisoner, but unable to go on.

When she mounted again to ride, she continued following the river. She realized how much she had learned about traveling across country from Lone Wolf. Losing count of days and nights, she continued along the meandering Canadian until she began to worry because she should have reached the place where the wagon train had camped or where the battle had been fought. She might miss the wagon train site, but she expected the battleground to be easy to recognize. Adding to her fears, the supply of jerked beef dwindled.

Late in the afternoon of the next day, she saw the first saber on the ground. She rode past it and, in a few minutes, saw a scrap of a uniform. She halted, studying the land and the river, then she dismounted to rest and let her horse drink. She refilled the canteens, knowing the worst part of the journey lay ahead because now she was uncertain about where to find Lone Wolf. He had said some fifty miles south of the battle site, and she prayed she could locate him because she wouldn't have the food or water to return.

She turned south, looking back once at the scrap of blue on the ground. She rode for several hours and then stopped to sleep. During the night a cold north wind whipped her until she was numb, forcing her to stop again and wait for daylight and sunshine. The next day she began to run low on water.

After another three days, she tried to curb her panic. She didn't want to admit that she was wandering on the plains, hopelessly lost. She lifted her chin and paused, deciding to turn west before she rode too far south.

Time began to blur; she lost track of the days and wondered if she would wander on the empty land until she died of starvation or thirst.

Had she wandered in circles? Was there anyone within miles of her? She hadn't seen a town since she'd left Tucumcari and the few times she had seen riders in a distance, she had hidden near mesquites until they passed.

She ate the last of the jerked beef and knew there was little water left. She knew Muaahap and Lone Wolf would have eaten berries they found and cactus, but she was uncertain about the cactus and she hadn't found any berries. It was late afternoon and she rode hunched on the horse, the wind whipping at her. Ahead was a break in the land. Maybe there was a creek with water. She rode closer, seeing that the gap was a wide chasm.

Weak with hunger and exhaustion, she continued, riding to the edge of the ridge, where the gelding stopped. She stared a moment, dazed, thinking she was imagining the canyon. The deep sides were layers of colors, reds and yellows, brush growing along canyon sides; and at the bottom, the canyon was filled with more tipis than she had ever seen in her life.

When another gust of wind buffeted her, she blinked and straightened up. Smoke spiraled into the air from the tipis, and people moved about. She glanced around, seeking the easiest way down the embankment, afraid that when she reached the bottom, the village would vanish, that it was merely a sight that her desperate imagination conjured up. She turned the horse and found a place that wasn't as steep, urging the gelding down the slope, winding her way to the bottom.

She heard a drumbeat and then men calling, saw them running back and forth. Her head spun and she felt dizzy, faint with weakness, as she rode forward. People came out of tipis toward her, standing to stare at her as she rode into their camp.

She tried to remember the words Lone Wolf had taught

her, but her thoughts spun away and she felt a light-
headedness. As she rode closer, the gelding walked past
a cluster of men. A warrior with black streaks on his
face and feathers in his hair strode toward her. She
gazed into his dark eyes and he stopped, frowning and
staring at her.

She rode past more warriors who watched her intently, and then she saw Lone Wolf walking toward her,
his black hair flying out behind his head. Looking
strong and powerful, he was dressed in buckskins, a
red band encircling his head. In long strides he approached her, his dark eyes fixed on her as Vanessa
felt blackness enveloping her.

Twenty-three

Lone Wolf had been talking with two warriors when he heard Claw of Eagle yell that a white woman was riding into camp.

A shock jolted Lone Wolf and he stood up abruptly. He saw people moving toward the southwest and he strode forward. Muaahap emerged from a tipi and glanced at him, her eyes round with curiosity.

As a cold gust of wind struck him, he lengthened his stride. He heard the words *red hair*. He stretched out his long legs, his pulse jumping, his curiosity rampant as he moved beyond the last ring of tipis. People stood staring and he looked up, shock stabbing him.

Riding toward him on a gaunt black horse was Vanessa, her green eyes enormous, her hair a tangle, a black cape wrapped tightly around her. She was thin and pale and swayed as she rode.

Stunned with disbelief, he raced toward her, his heart pounding violently. Her eyes closed, and she went limp.

As she fell, he caught her, pulling her from the horse and turning to stride with her in his arms back to the tipi that Muaahap and Belva had carefully made for him. Vanessa was incredibly light in his arms, fragile and no heavier than a child, and fear for her gripped him. Muaahap turned around to rush ahead of him, and his people began to murmur, their questions floating in the air, but he couldn't stop to answer any of them. His panic ran deep. Vanessa might not have eaten or had water for days. And beneath all his fear a surging joy coursed in him that he held her in his arms again.

How had she ridden from Tucumcari and found him? He rushed into the tipi where Belva was already building the fire up and Muaahap was getting out her collection of medicines and a container of water.

He laid Vanessa on a bed made of hides placed on rawhide lashed to poles so it stood off the ground a few feet. He knelt beside her to hold her head and raise the water to her lips as Muaahap went around to Vanessa's other side to wipe her face with a damp rag. When Muaahap placed a thick buffalo robe over her, Lone Wolf wanted to pull her into his arms to try to get her warm.

Instead, he held her head and watched her lashes flutter as he tried to pour a little water between her chapped lips. When she opened her eyes and looked up at him, Lone Wolf felt as if the breath had been swept out of him and everything inside him pulled into a tight knot. With a shaking hand, he set down the water and drew Vanessa into his arms gently to hold her, burying his face in her hair and feeling hot tears stinging his eyes.

While she wrapped her arms around him, he tried to keep from holding her too tightly, but he wanted her against his heart.

"Vanessa, my love," he whispered. "My love."

Leaning back, he picked up the water to hold it to her lips. All the while she drank, she kept her large green eyes fixed on him. He couldn't look away from her or talk for the knot that burned in his throat. He stroked her head and looked around at Muaahap, who had something cooking over the firepit, causing a delicious smell of stewing meat to fill the tipi.

"You're here and you're safe," he whispered, kissing Vanessa's forehead and her cheek while she patted his shoulder and gazed at him as if she were too weak to talk.

"Guipago!"

He turned. Muaahap held two leather pouches and a gourd in her hand and motioned to him to move away. Reluctantly, he stood to let Muaahap tend Vanessa. He left the tipi to explain to the others who she was and how she came to ride into camp.

When he returned to the tipi she was asleep, and Muaahap sat close beside her, combing her hair while Belva stirred the bubbling stew. He ate and sat nearby, waiting patiently for Vanessa to waken. He had unsaddled her horse, which was in need of water and food, and again he wondered how she had come all the way from Fort Bascom. How long had she been alone?

When she stirred, he moved to her side. He had never seen the blue velvet dress before. Muaahap had unbuttoned it, and Vanessa's soft curves were revealed. The velvet was muddy along the skirt, covered with twigs and dust, wrinkled, as if she had worn it since starting her journey. She'd had an empty canteen, and he hadn't found any food in the saddlebags.

She hadn't been riding an army saddle, so she had left from somewhere besides Fort Bascom. Questions swirled in his mind as he stood over her.

Muaahap indicated she had fed Vanessa earlier, and he sat beside Vanessa to lift her into his arms. After a time, when he glanced around, he saw that Muaahap and Belva were gone.

He cradled Vanessa in his arms until her eyes opened. She gazed up at him, her green eyes enormous. Slowly, she raised her arm to place it around his neck.

"I was afraid I'd never find you," she whispered.

His heart thudded and he bent his head to kiss her gently, his lips touching hers lightly, trying to curb the devouring hunger he felt for her until she was stronger. He held her against his heart, stroking her head, rocking her in his arms, murmuring softly to her in Kiowa words.

Vanessa held him tightly, her fingers sliding across his shoulder and arms, reassuring herself he wasn't a dream. "I was so afraid I wouldn't find you," she repeated, and he pressed her head against his chest.

"You did, love. I couldn't believe my eyes." He shifted to look down at her. "You rode here from Fort Bascom?"

"Yes," she answered. "You showed me the way, remember?"

"Only a vague description," he said, looking at her. "Who came with you?"

"I came alone," she said, watching him close his eyes as if he had received a blow.

"Alone? Vanessa—" He bit off his words and pulled her closer to hug her, burying his face in her thick hair.

"I got away from Dupree in Tucumcari."

"Vanessa, you could have missed us so easily."

"I thought I had. I followed the river until I reached the site of the battle where you had camped before. Then I turned south as you'd said to. I ran out of food and water. I don't do too well at traveling without you," she murmured, feeling exhausted now that she was safe with him.

He held her again, rocking her, his arms tightly around her. Finally, he leaned back to look into her eyes. "Did he hurt you?"

"No," she answered, knowing he was referring to Dupree.

"Then we will forget he ever existed. I'll make you forget him."

"He didn't take me to his bed."

Lone Wolf frowned, staring at her with disbelief. "You escaped?"

"No. He learned who my father is and he thought Papa could help his career. Dupree wanted me to marry him."

Lone Wolf's breath went out in a hiss. Without waiting for his comment, she continued. "He sent for Papa and Papa was on his way from Fort McKavett when I ran away."

"I can't believe you came alone. Vanessa, you could have been lost or picked up by others."

"There are not many others out here," she answered, closing her eyes. "I'm exhausted."

"You'll feel better tomorrow, love. Go to sleep. I want to hold you in my arms and never let you go."

With a faint smile, she placed her head against his chest. He stroked her head, his hand sliding over her shoulder and back until he realized she was asleep. He hovered over her while Muaahap tended her, and that night he slept on a bed close to hers.

The next morning he left while Muaahap fed and bathed Vanessa. Mid-morning he returned to the tipi with White Bird at his side because he had promised her she could see Vanessa. The moment he stepped inside, his pulse jumped.

Vanessa stood across the tipi and she turned to look at him, her wide, lustrous eyes focusing on him with a look that made his blood heat. He held White Bird's hand, and she gave a cry of delight, holding out her arms to run to Vanessa, who picked her up and held her tightly.

" 'Nessa. I love you," White Bird said, squeezing Vanessa's neck.

"And I love you, precious," Vanessa said, hugging White Bird who smelled clean and sweet. She gazed past her at Lone Wolf, who stood watching them.

"She's missed you. She knew you were here last night and wanted to come see you, but we told her she had to wait."

"I'm back now and I won't leave you again," Vanessa said to White Bird while White Bird turned a lock of Vanessa's hair in her tiny fingers.

"I'll return and get her shortly," Lone Wolf said, leaving Vanessa with White Bird. She sat down to hold the little girl on her lap, hugging her again, so thankful to be back with all of them because they seemed like her family now.

Half an hour later, Belva came to the tipi, and when she

left, she took White Bird with her. Vanessa stood up, moving around, feeling her strength returning after Muaahap's feeding and care. She brushed her hair and heard a rustle.

Lone Wolf entered and closed the flap to the tipi. Wearing buckskins, looking handsome and strong, he crossed to her, his dark gaze intense.

Vanessa's heart pounded wildly as he came toward her and took her in his arms. His mouth touched hers and hers opened; his tongue met hers swiftly. She held him, her heart pounding as she returned his kiss, still amazed to be with him. Joy coursed through her along with an overwhelming longing for him. He felt solid and powerful, and finally she was in his arms. Breathless from his kisses, she leaned away to look up at him, her gaze going over his dark hair.

"I had to find you," she said quietly. "Papa was coming to Tucumcari. I knew he would make me marry the captain or he would escort me to the convent himself."

"If I had known you were riding out here alone—" Lone Wolf stroked her hair. "What will I do with you? Headstrong, self-willed, beautiful. Vanessa," he said solemnly, "we agreed to wed. I want to do so as soon as you're strong enough."

With joy she kissed him, leaning back, finally, to look at him. "I'm strong enough."

Amusement glinted in his dark eyes and then it was gone, replaced by desire. "I would like to have the wedding this next hour, but within the next few days we will wed."

She held him tightly, her heart pounding with happiness while his hand continued to stroke her head and back.

"Vanessa," he said in a husky voice, and she looked up at him again. His dark eyes were intense. He framed her face with his large hands, holding her gently as he gazed down into her eyes. "I love you," he said quietly. The words took away her breath as she looked up at him. "You've healed my grief. I loved Eyes That Smile, but now my heart fills with love for you."

Her joy soared, and she tightened her arms around his neck, standing on tiptoe to kiss him long and passionately, her heart pounding with happiness. She had never expected to hear those words from him before they wed. His arms tightened as he kissed her, his tongue going deep, his arousal pressing against her.

He raised his head. "I forget. You are all bones now, and I don't want to hold you so tightly that I hurt you."

"You'll never hurt me," she assured him. "I didn't think I'd hear those words from you for a long while—if ever. I hoped that you would grow to love me with time—"

"Back at Bascom when I saw you across the parade ground, I knew what I was losing, Vanessa. I've loved you for a long time now, but I was so blind to it."

"You love me now. That's what's important," she whispered joyously.

"When I left you with the captain, I knew how strong my love for you is. If it hadn't been for White Bird and Belva, I would have tried to fight him—"

"Thank heavens you didn't! They had rifles on you and would have shot you at the first move. And that would have been unbearable."

"Life with me may not be easy for—"

She placed her hand on his mouth, then stood on tiptoe to pull his head down to her, and his arms tightened around her as he kissed her.

Two days later Vanessa sat cross-legged in a small tipi while Muaahap combed and braided her hair, fastening it with silver wire. Silver hoops dangled from her ears and on one arm she wore one of Muaahap's silver bracelets and on the other a silver bracelet Lone Wolf had fashioned for her. Women sat in the circle surrounding her.

Vanessa looked down again at her dress, touching it lightly, feeling the soft doeskin. A muted yellow, the dress was beaded and painted with geometric patterns that were made and designed by Lone Wolf's family. Anticipation and excitement filled her and she wriggled with impatience as Muaahap continued braiding her hair.

Finally, she emerged from the small tipi that faced another across the center of the camp. The sun was shining brightly, and there was a crisp coolness in the winter air. As she moved forward, Lone Wolf emerged from his tipi and her breath caught. He wore eagle feathers in his hair and a buckskin shirt and buckskin pants. His face was streaked with ocher paint, emphasizing his large dark eyes and his prominent cheekbones. He looked wild and handsome, and her pulse raced. She met his dark gaze and forgot all else as they stepped in front of the medicine man who would marry them.

She didn't understand the words of the short ceremony as the medicine man chanted prayers and fanned smoke over them that rose skyward. Afterward, Lone Wolf took her arm and led her away while the camp began their celebration.

They entered his tipi and he secured the flap, giving them privacy. He turned to look down at her, reaching into a leather pouch on his belt to withdraw a small piece of folded deerskin.

"Vanessa," he said, taking her hand, his voice husky. "I have taken you as my wife before my people, which is as binding to us as the white man's way is to his people. I know the white man gives a wedding ring that binds the woman to him and my people do not do this. But our women wear silver and shell bracelets and rings and necklaces. So I want you to have this ring as a sign of our marriage. I want you to take my way of life; but in this, I take your way because I want all to know you're my wife. We may never again walk the white man's road, but you have strong ties with your sisters. I want a ring on your finger proclaiming you're my woman."

Her heart drummed with joy at his words, and she watched as he unfolded the leather. A small ring of gleaming silver lay on the brown deerskin. Lone Wolf picked up the ring and took her pale, slender hand in his large dark fingers.

"What are the words, Vanessa?"

"With this ring, I thee wed," she said in a quiet voice. She looked into his dark eyes. "To have and to hold from this day forward."

"With this ring," he repeated solemnly, gazing into her eyes, "I thee wed. To have and to hold from this day forward." He slid the ring on her finger, and she moved into his arms, winding her arms around his neck to hold him tightly and kiss him, her heart beating wildly with joy.

"We have the next seven days when we will be left alone as much as possible and Muaahap, Belva, and White Bird will stay elsewhere. Then life returns to normal except that you will be in my arms every night."

She thrilled at his words, kissing his throat, her hands going across his chest. He stepped back to pull off his shirt, the muscles rippling in his broad chest. He picked up the end of her braid. "I want your hair unbound," he said in a husky voice, unfastening the silver wire and beginning to pull free the plaits of hair, tugging lightly on her scalp. She watched him, her hands tracing the contours of his chest as she marveled that they were finally man and wife. Her love for him welled up, and she wanted to touch and kiss him and learn what pleased him. As he unwound the braid, her scalp tingled and she felt as if she were drowning in his dark eyes.

He combed his fingers through the braid and her hair spilled over her shoulder. Continuing to watch her, the tension building between them, he shifted to unravel the other braid while she reached up to remove the hoops from her ears.

"Let me undress you, Vanessa," he said solemnly, taking

the hoop from her ear, his fingers lightly stroking her cheek, the faint touches tickling her erotically.

"Sometimes when I stopped to rest on the way here, I dreamed I saw you. And sometimes I didn't think I would ever find you."

"I don't know how you did."

"I turned east, finally, because I was afraid I had passed you, and then I was going to ride back north except I wouldn't have lasted that long. I thought if I went east, I might find a town and food . . ."

"Vanessa, you are still that storm wind in my life." He pulled up the doeskin dress, and she raised her arms as he eased it over her head. He inhaled, his chest expanding while he cupped her breasts with his dark hands.

"I don't want to lose you ever again," he whispered, leaning down to kiss her and flick his tongue across her nipple.

She wound her fingers in his hair, her heart pounding as he kissed and stroked her. She pushed away his buckskins and touched him, wanting to drive him to the frenzy that he created in her.

She still felt stunned that she was finally with him. And she was still amazed by his deep declaration of love that filled her with joy. She slid her hands over his virile body, feeling the solid muscles, his hard thighs, his manhood.

She stepped closer to kiss him, trailing kisses on his smooth flesh, moaning softly when he caressed her, his hands stroking her breasts.

Relishing the heat and strength of his body, she pressed against him. As her hands slid over his back, she looked up at him. Instead of smooth taut flesh over strong muscles, she felt tiny ridges. She caught his upper arms, her fingers closing on his biceps. He paused and looked down at her.

"Your back?"

He straightened up and his expression changed, a flash of anger surfacing in his eyes. "I have much to settle with

Captain Milos. But he'll not interfere with my marriage night."

She gave a small cry, turning him, looking at Lone Wolf's broad, bronzed back, now lined by scars that streaked his skin. "He did this to you?" she asked, aghast, remembering watching Dupree stride across the parade ground. She had thought he was going to tell them to release Lone Wolf; instead, he had done this. "He promised me he wouldn't harm you!"

Lone Wolf turned to look down at her, holding her shoulders. "Vanessa, I don't want to hear another word about Dupree Milos tonight." He frowned, wiping her tears away with his thumb. "Don't cry. I survived and I'm mending and the scars will fade."

"I love you," she whispered, "and I hope I can learn to live with the dangerous life you have."

"I'm not so certain," he said, leaning down to kiss her throat, trailing light kisses to her mouth and ear, stroking her back, his hands sliding down over her buttocks with feathery touches that made her pulse pound. "I'm not so certain," he repeated, "that I have any more risks than you do."

"Of course you do, riding in raids and battles—" she murmured, kissing his chest, her hands trailing over his narrow hips, down to his strong thighs.

"Riding across country alone," he added, "rescuing sisters, offering yourself to save me. No, my life isn't more dangerous."

He turned her face up to look into her eyes. "I love you, Vanessa," he whispered, bending to kiss her passionately, his tongue touching and stroking hers.

Later, when he lowered himself between her thighs, entering her slowly, she pulled him against her.

"This is the way I want you," he said harshly in her ear. "All mine. I want your body and heart, Vanessa."

"And I want yours," she said, her eyes opening wide to

look up at him. When she saw the hungry look in his gaze, her heart beat wildly with need and joy.

"You have mine," he said in a gruff, husky voice. All thought spun away as she held his powerful body and moved beneath him. "I want to drive you wild, Vanessa, to feel your fire," he whispered, withdrawing partially, easing back into her, stirring an exquisite torment.

She climaxed, dimly hearing him cry her name, holding him tightly. "I love you," she whispered. "I love you so much."

They slowed, their bodies damp, and he held her tightly against him, turning on his side, his legs tangled with hers. She stroked his strong body, joyous that he loved her, knowing she loved him with all her heart.

"Now, I have you to myself for days with no interruptions," he said, gazing at her.

She ran her fingers through his hair, smiling at him. "I keep having to touch you because I feared I would never get back to you. I constantly saw your face in the clouds and thought I saw you on your horse in the shimmering distance."

"I would have come to Bascom to get you, but I had to get well and we had to wait for a war party to prepare for the right time."

Surprised, she gazed at him solemnly. "I wouldn't have wanted you to fight them for me."

He shrugged his shoulder. "We intended to. I wasn't going to leave you."

"You could not have fought all those soldiers without losing a lot of men."

"We wouldn't have made a direct attack in broad daylight."

"How did you get back here? Did you walk all this way?"

He looked amused as he stroked her throat and wound his fingers through her hair. "Old Muaahap surprised me and saved us all. So before you say it, yes, I'm glad I allowed her to come with us—although I don't think I ever really had a choice."

"What did she do?"

"She hid us from the soldiers that rode after us, and that night she slipped into their camp and stole two of their horses while they slept."

Startled, Vanessa sat up. "I heard Dupree and a soldier talking about some horses being taken, but I didn't dream it might have been Muaahap!"

"As much as I hate to admit it, I owe my life to her as well as to you. I had a silver necklace and bracelet made for her, and she wears them constantly. And now that we're safely in camp, she clinks with every step she takes," he said, his gaze drifting over Vanessa and his voice growing husky.

"No wonder Dupree was so angry. When the soldier returned from riding after Belva, I couldn't hear everything they were saying, but I knew he was furious." Feeling that panic that had come so often when she was traveling, she hugged him. "Lone Wolf . . ."

She trailed her kisses lower over his chest, and he inhaled deeply, winding his fingers in her hair. His hand drifted across her breasts, and she moaned softly. As his gaze met hers, he drew her down against him to kiss her and she was lost to his loving again.

Mid-day the next afternoon, she lay in his arms, her fingers trailing along his chest down to his flat stomach while she talked. His touch was languorous, and she felt exhausted from their lovemaking. "You have changed my life—"

"*I changed yours!* You've uprooted mine and it will never be the same. Yours was changing when we met."

She rolled on her side to gaze at him solemnly. "Now I have love all around me. I have a family filled with love—

something I never had before. And sometime soon we'll have children."

"I am sure of that," he said complacently, his fingers trailing on her cheek.

Someone yelled, and a horse raced past. Lone Wolf turned his head, listening and frowning.

He stood up abruptly. "Danger comes." He yanked on the buckskins and moccasins, pulling on his shirt and reaching for the gunbelt to fasten it around his hips.

Fear for him shot through her like a knife stabbing into her, and she wondered if she would ever be able to accept or cope with this part of his life.

"What should I do?" she asked as she pulled on her plain buckskin dress.

"Muaahap will come. If we have to move camp, she'll show you what to do and Belva will watch White Bird." He caught Vanessa up tightly to kiss her hard and then he was gone. She stepped outside to see mounted warriors, men running and yelling. Lone Wolf jumped on a horse and rode forward.

Muaahap came with White Bird in her arms. She motioned to Vanessa, who hurried to meet her. Everyone was moving toward the west and she wondered what was happening. She stopped walking, standing immobile as she looked at the rim of the canyon and saw what had disturbed the camp.

Silhouetted against the sky were soldiers strung out along the ridge with two riders approaching down the sloping canyon wall. One of the two mounted men was carrying a large white flag.

A warrior with feathers in his hair moved forward. Lone Wolf urged his horse ahead and the two rode to meet the soldiers.

Stunned, she felt as if ice poured into her veins as she looked at them because she could guess why they were there.

She looked around and saw Belva standing yards behind her. Wide-eyed, Belva held White Bird in her arms.

Clamping her jaw closed tightly so she wouldn't cry, Vanessa went to them to take White Bird and hug her tightly. She handed White Bird to Muaahap and kissed them both on the cheek.

"Belva, we have to go." Taking Belva's hand, she moved forward.

"I don't want to leave here."

"We have to go, Belva. They've come for us, and if we go willingly, maybe they won't attack."

With tears spilling down Belva's cheeks, she ran back to hug Muaahap and White Bird. She turned to walk beside Vanessa, a scowl wrinkling her brow.

They moved past people who watched them silently until only Lone Wolf and Chief Wind on Cloud were ahead.

Lone Wolf turned to look at her and rode back to her, dismounting and blocking her way. His brown eyes were filled with fire, and his jaw was set in a stubborn line.

"I won't let you go."

Twenty-four

"You have to let me go now. This is not the way to fight them," she whispered, struggling against tears and staring at him as if memorizing him because she felt she was losing him forever. "I won't have others killed now because of me. You can come for me later and you'll have an advantage when you fight them."

"No!"

"I won't stay. I won't let your people be killed because of me! You can't hold me here and fight at the same time. If a battle begins, I'll run into the thick of it."

She saw the rage in his expression, yet she would not let a battle take place like this when the soldiers had the advantage.

"You can come later. It'll only be days," she whispered.

"No, I'll tie you—"

"And Muaahap or someone else will untie me because they won't want this either. The army has the advantage now."

She moved closer until she stood in front of him "Do this for me. Let me go now, and come for me later. It's a long journey to Denver. There won't be as many of them, and your people won't be in as great a danger as they are now."

He stepped forward, his eyes blazing as his arm banded her waist and he pulled her to him to kiss her hard and long. Clinging to his wide shoulders, she returned his kiss, terrified it was a final goodbye.

He released her and lifted her to his horse and Belva up behind her. He stood with his hand on Vanessa's thigh. "I will come for you. I only do this because I know so many would be hurt and you'd do something foolish to try to stop the battle."

She nodded, fighting desperately to hold back tears and turning away quickly. The soldiers turned to ride beside her, and they headed toward the side of the canyon.

As the wind whipped her, she felt as if her heart were being torn out and left behind. She kept her eyes ahead, unable to turn around and look back at him. Blinded by tears, she followed a soldier, the other one coming behind as they climbed to the rim. A gust of wind blew her hair across her face, and she pushed long strands away. Glancing below, she saw Lone Wolf seated on a horse, still watching her, his people standing quietly.

The wind caught Lone Wolf's black hair, blowing the ends slightly. He sat like a statue, gazing up at her. Pain tore at her as she looked at him. She turned away and only a few feet from her was her father, riding toward her on a fine chestnut.

Abbot Sutherland's blue eyes burned with rage. Dupree rode beside him, his face pale and his jaw set grimly. Her father reined in alongside her, and his face was florid with anger.

He reached out to strike her, his palm hitting her cheek with a sharp crack. She flinched from the stinging blow and raised her chin. "You should not take me back."

"I'd like to destroy every one of the damned redskins; but I want you and Belva, and this way I know for certain I'll get you back. We'll talk at Bascom."

He turned to ride ahead and Dupree moved alongside her. "I don't know how you escaped. Was he in Tucumcari?"

She raised her chin not wanting to talk to him, tears still streaming down her cheeks.

"Answer me, Vanessa. It'll go harder on you with your father if you don't cooperate with me," Dupree said in a tight voice. She turned to look at him.

"I rode out here alone."

His eyes narrowed, and she saw the fury blaze in his expression. "It's useless to lie. And there's no way you could have ridden here alone. You would never have found them. I've had scouts searching the area for days now. Your father will wring the truth from you."

He rode away and she cried quietly, feeling Belva's slim hand reaching over to squeeze her hand.

"Lone Wolf will come for us," Vanessa said. "Just be ready, Belva, because we may be separated."

"Papa will be more careful now. He won't let us out of his sight."

Vanessa's cheek still stung from her father's slap, but nothing hurt like the parting with Lone Wolf, because she was afraid for him to come for her, afraid for him to fight soldiers at Bascom. She wondered if they would even return there or just head north now to a convent. If they did, Lone Wolf would never catch them.

As they rode two days later, she realized they were returning to Bascom. She remembered her long, lone ride out and the hope burning within her. Now she knew it would be better for Lone Wolf and his people if she never had returned because then he would be safe.

When they rode into Bascom, she was shown the same quarters and, within minutes of their arrival, Dupree entered to face her.

"You can make the future easy, Vanessa, or difficult. Your father is livid. I think he would like to beat you for running away, but I've prevailed on him and told him I would like to marry you. If you cooperate, we can have a good future."

She raised her chin. "I'm married now." She held out her hand with the silver ring.

Dupree's lip curled in contempt as he shook his head.

"No one recognizes a marriage to a redskin by a white woman. Least of all your father. He would never accept such a marriage. Think about it before you throw away your chance at happiness. In time you will forget the Indian, and I can give you so much."

"We have no love for each other. You would be as miserable as I would be."

"Your father can help me advance and get where I want to go. That's what is important. And I'm willing to take you as a wife even after this incident. You should consider yourself fortunate, because not many men would."

She raised her chin in defiance. "I'm married. I pledged vows that I intend to keep as long as I live."

Dupree's eyes narrowed, "You'll regret your stand."

"You didn't keep your word to me to not harm him."

Dupree's blond brows arched. "So you know about the beating. I did keep my promise. I said I'd release him and I did. He lived because of your offer. Right now our manpower is low. If we hadn't been outnumbered as badly as we were at the battle at Adobe Walls, we would have attacked the winter camp when we came to get you. And if I ever get another chance at him, I'll finish the job. But the beating was a pleasure and should have caused him pain for days, particularly trying to travel across country."

She drew a deep breath, hating Dupree. "We'll never marry."

"You'll regret your decision," he snapped angrily. "A few years from now, remember what you could have had."

"I suppose my father paid you the reward for Belva and me."

"Your father is a very generous man. He paid me the reward for finding all three of you. And he understands my ambitions. He has high hopes that we'll marry, but you don't give much thought to pleasing your father."

She turned away from him, wanting him to go, remembering the scars across Lone Wolf's back.

"Your father brought your things. There are three trunks and I suggest you get out of the buckskin that angers him so much. He'll be in to see you soon. Look at me, Vanessa."

She turned around and he held her by her shoulders, his fingers biting into her flesh. "Think about marriage. You'll never get back to the Indian. Just remember that life as an officer's wife will be infinitely more interesting than being locked away in a convent."

He turned and left, and she put her hands over her face to cry, missing Lone Wolf dreadfully, feeling in her heart that disaster lay ahead and not wanting Lone Wolf to go into battle for her.

She wiped her eyes and nose, glancing at the silver band on her finger and touching it lightly, knowing her father wouldn't accept her marriage either.

She bathed and changed, dressing in a pink silk, combing her hair. She had no appetite and left dinner untouched.

A small lamp burned against the dark when she heard footsteps outside. The door opened and her father entered. He had changed and wore a black coat and trousers; his thick blond hair was combed neatly. His blue eyes blazed with anger as he closed the door and faced her.

She could feel his rage as he glared at her and she steadied herself as he struck her again, the palm of his hand snapping her head around, stinging her cheek. He moved away. "You're trouble, Vanessa. Nothing but trouble."

After a moment, he turned around. "Sit down. We need to talk," he ordered in a cold voice. "I want to know where Phoebe is. Captain Milos said you put her on a stage for California. You know where she's staying and you're to tell me."

"Papa, let her have this chance," Vanessa said. "She wants to sing in the opera."

"Great God! Phoebe doesn't need to go on stage like a saloon singer! She had a chance for an excellent marriage, and you've ruined all that! It is only by the interjection of

Captain Milos that I don't beat you, Vanessa. You deserve it for all the havoc you've wreaked."

Still facing him, she gazed at him calmly, feeling removed from him. He moved impatiently and stared at her.

"Where is she?"

"I'll tell you, but I wish you would reconsider. She has a marvelous voice and singing in the opera is not like singing in a saloon."

"I'll consider it, Vanessa, but it isn't likely I'll find it acceptable for my daughter. Where is she?"

"She's with friends in San Francisco. Please think about it before you do something."

"Now about you, Vanessa. I should have taken you to Denver myself; but I thought with an army escort, you would be delivered safely to the convent. This time I'll personally take you there."

She stared at him, wondering if he had forgotten Dupree.

"But there is a chance you won't have to go to the convent. Captain Milos is taken with you and he has asked for your hand in marriage. You have a choice, Vanessa. I would prefer you marry the captain; but you can be troublesome and if you don't want to marry him, I don't intend to force you into it. I'll simply place you in a convent and you will have hours upon end to realize your mistakes."

She drew herself up. She held up her hand, and his eyes narrowed as he looked at the silver band on her finger.

"I'm married, Papa."

"To whom?" he asked, his voice cold and abrupt. She expected him to strike her again when she answered him.

"To Guipago, Lone Wolf, a full-blood Kiowa."

Abbot Sutherland drew in his breath, rage making him clench his fists as his face flushed. "Dammit, Vanessa, I should beat you senseless. The marriage doesn't exist. It is meaningless except that now the captain won't want you. So it's settled. You go to the convent."

"Dupree knows and he still wants to marry me," she said.

Her father's blond brows arched as he stared at her. "Dupree still wants you?"

"Papa, there is no love between us. He wants me as his wife because he thinks you can further his career."

"I probably can. And I'd be willing to do so if you marry him." He tilted his head to study her. "You're like your mother, headstrong, wild, uncontrollable—yes, I'll help Milos if you wed. I admire ambition. A man with a cool head who is not ruled by his heart will go far."

She walked to a window to stare outside as dark settled. Out there to the east was Lone Wolf. "I'll never marry Dupree," she said quietly. "I'm already married."

"I think after you spend a few days shut away in these small quarters alone, you may see what lies ahead for you in Denver and change your mind. Either way, I shall be glad to see you placed where you can no longer cause me trouble. And you've been trouble, Vanessa, since the day you were born," he snapped.

She turned to look at him, knowing at one time she would have been crushed by his words, but now she didn't hurt because she had another family that was filled with love and someday she hoped she could return to them.

She stared at her father, feeling his anger as he gazed back at her. He turned abruptly and left, slamming the door behind him. She moved listlessly across the room to stare at the parade ground. As long as she was at Bascom, she didn't think Lone Wolf would attack. It would be when they started to Denver that the battle would come.

And what would happen when her father and Lone Wolf confronted each other? She drew a deep breath, knowing that as cruel as her father sometimes was, she loved him. He was her father and she had grown up loving him and wanting his love, and she prayed that Lone Wolf and her father never again crossed paths.

She turned restlessly, looking around. Three trunks were in the room and she realized her father had packed all her belongings. Had he intended to get her out of his life forever? Again, she realized that Lone Wolf's love cushioned her against hurt by her father. She could view the trunks calmly without being devastated by them because she didn't want to return home. She turned the silver ring on her finger, hearing Lone Wolf's deep voice, *". . . with this ring, I thee wed . . ."*

She closed her eyes, pulling memories around her like a cloak that warmed her and protected her from the coldness of her father. She remembered Lone Wolf's dark eyes on her, his lovemaking, his long body stretched next to hers as he held her tightly against him. She thought of White Bird's thin arms hugging her and Muaahap's doting care.

Vanessa touched a trunk, her fingers slipping over the brass lock. She didn't want to go to Denver, but she didn't want Lone Wolf or his kin killed in battle and she didn't want her father slain.

The following morning, she heard a knock. When she opened the door, she expected to find Dupree. Instead, it was a private with a tray of food. He handed it to her and hurried away without looking back. She glanced across the parade ground. Her father stood in the doorway of a building and he turned away.

She took the tray inside, having little interest in eating, but knowing she had to keep her strength up because she was certain Lone Wolf would come to get her.

Twenty-five

Lone Wolf squinted down the rifle barrel and lowered it as he cleaned the weapon. He was readying for war, knowing others would follow him when he rode after Vanessa. He paused, looking at the flames in the firepit. What would happen when he encountered Abbot Sutherland? She had said she loved her father—and it would be natural that she did—but Sutherland had been cruel to her. Lone Wolf's jaw tightened as he remembered that moment when she had reached the top of the canyon, halting on the rim, wind blowing her long red hair. He had seen her father ride up to her and strike her.

Without thought he had raised the rifle to fire. Chief Wind on Cloud had grabbed the gun and lowered it, reminding him of the others.

Lone Wolf stared at the flames dancing in the firepit as Muaahap sat on a robe and combed White Bird's long hair. His thoughts were on Vanessa, fear tormenting him that her father would force her into a marriage with Dupree Milos. Neither her father nor Milos would recognize the Kiowa marriage.

Lone Wolf knotted his fist, knowing Vanessa would fight a marriage, yet she might not be able to stop it if two determined men intended that she become Dupree's wife.

Warriors could not ride into Fort Bascom and get her; they wouldn't fare well in a direct confrontation at the fort, so he had to wait until someone took Vanessa out. He glanced down at the folded yellow-doeskin dress, running his fingers on it, remembering Vanessa in the dress, in his arms.

Anger burned in him as he thought about her father and Captain Milos. As soon as the medicine man deemed it the right time, Lone Wolf would lead the war party to get Vanessa back. His heart raced every time he thought of her.

He left to join in smoking the pipe to get ready for the long ceremony.

Four days later, it was time to go. With his face streaked with ocher paint, Lone Wolf wore eagle feathers in his hair. He mounted the bay that had red stripes painted for the number of times he had counted coup, and touched an enemy in battle. A handprint on his horse indicated success in combat. Moving ahead, raising his hand with his rifle, he gave a high, rapid call. He glanced back to see the warriors coming behind him.

Muaahap stood watching him go. As he rode out of camp, Lone Wolf glanced back once at the tipi where he had spent one night with Vanessa. Longing shook him, and he prayed she was all right and that she was not married to Dupree Milos.

They rode steadily during the day and camped at night, and each day he felt more determined to get her. He was also facing the fact that soon he would clash with Abbot Sutherland and he was not going to be able to hold back his anger toward the man who had struck Vanessa and caused her so much heartbreak, who had paid a bounty to Eyes That Smile's killers.

As they approached Bascom, he could feel Vanessa's presence; he dreamed they were together. He stood while the moon was bright and high in the sky and gazed across the empty land to the west. Soon he would ride to get her, fighting Sutherland, the soldiers, and settling with Captain Milos. They were still at least two days away from Bascom. They would camp while a few of the party rode closer, watching to see if a small group left the fort to take her to Denver. Lone Wolf felt a bond with her, knowing she was his woman no matter what was happening.

"Vanessa," he said softly, praying she was all right.

By the end of the week, Vanessa had made three rag dolls for White Bird. She hadn't seen or talked to anyone. She had been deliberately isolated because her father thought this would make her want to accept Dupree's proposal.

She turned a doll in her hand, looking at its smiling yarn mouth and button eyes and wondering if she would ever get to take the doll to White Bird. Vanessa placed her hand against her stomach, wishing she carried Lone Wolf's baby now, even though it would enrage her father beyond measure.

During the middle of the afternoon the next day, she heard footsteps. She looked up from her sewing as the door swung open and Dupree entered.

"Sewing?" he asked, looking at the material bunched in her lap. "I wondered what you would do with your time." He crossed the room. He looked strong and full of vigor. He picked up one of the dolls she had made and turned it in his hands. "Making rag dolls. For the future?"

"Yes," she answered.

"You should give some time to pleasing your father."

"I gave up long ago trying in every way possible to please my father. Only my brother Ethan can do that. I'm already married. Papa refuses to acknowledge it, but that doesn't make it any less so. It's as binding as any marriage."

"No, it's not. You're joining me for dinner tonight. I still want you for a wife because I know what your father can do. A large home in Washington and a good appointment would be excellent. You won't inherit from your father because everything is going to your brother; but if we had a

Washington home and contacts, think of the chances Belva would have when it came time to marry."

"That's years away! And if my brother Ethan doesn't like you, you'll be out of Papa's favor instantly."

"I won't interfere with your brother Ethan. Far from it." Dupree crossed the room to her and pulled her up. "I can give you a lot, Vanessa."

"And you hope my father can give you a lot."

"You have a sharp tongue." His arm slipped around her waist and she stiffened, pushing away.

Frowning, he stared at her. "I'll come to get you for dinner about seven o'clock."

"I'd rather not," she said flatly.

He shook his head. "You'll have to—"

She heard footsteps running outside, and Dupree turned his head as the door flung open.

"Vanessa! Vanessa!" Belva ran inside, her brown hair swirling across her shoulders. Her cheeks were tearstained and her face was pale. "Come quick. Papa—" She broke off and began to cry.

Dimly aware of Dupree beside her, Vanessa rushed across the parade ground with Belva. They entered an office and Vanessa paused in the doorway. Her father stood by the window with his back to them, a paper in his hand.

"Papa?" she asked, startled because he appeared fine. "Belva, what is it?" Vanessa asked.

Abbot Sutherland turned around, and she received another shock. His face was ashen and tears streamed down it. He held out the paper in his hand and shook it. "My Ethan, my son—"

She felt a leaden weight, knowing what must be in the letter. She took it from him, seeing the splotches and tearstains on it, hurting for her father, remembering her blond-haired older brother who had had little time for his sisters and had always been so sure of himself and his endeavors.

She raised the paper, scanning it as she heard Belva's high voice, "Papa, I'm sorry—"

"Leave me alone, Belva!" he said sharply.

The letters seemed to leap out at Vanessa. ". . . regret to inform you that your son, Major Ethan Sutherland, was killed while fighting valiantly in the line of duty . . ."

She lowered the letter and looked into her father's teary eyes. "I'm sorry, Papa," she said quietly.

"Why Ethan?" he exclaimed, shaking his fists. "All my life has been devoted to him. He was the perfect son! Why him? He should have come home to me. I have so many plans for him. And Ethan never complained. He never fought me. He accepted everything I wanted him to do."

Vanessa glanced around and saw Belva step outside. She turned back, knowing it was useless to try to comfort Papa or to go to him, because he didn't want her sympathy or her company. Even so, she felt he needed someone because she had never seen her father sad, hurt, or filled with regret.

His gaze rested on her, and she felt for a moment that he longed for it to be her the letter was about and Ethan standing in the room with him.

"All I have left are three girls who are headstrong and troublesome. All my plans for him have died along with him."

Vanessa could not think of anything to say to him; she had no words with which to console him. She motioned with the letter. "His body is in Virginia."

"I'll get his body and bring it home. I'll buy a home in Denver and place his body in the cemetery nearby. I'll not have my Ethan resting in a burial ground on some distant battlefield."

Abbot stared at her, his expression hardening. "So I'm left with the three of you. I've already decided to wash my hands of Phoebe, and I plan to send Belva to boarding school."

"If you had ever given us the chance, we all wanted your love and we all tried to love you," Vanessa said quietly.

His blue eyes were cold as he stared at her. "You're not even my child, Vanessa."

Twenty-six

Stunned, Vanessa stared at her father in open-mouthed wonder, thinking she had heard him wrong. *Abbot Sutherland was not her father!*

With a grim set to his mouth, he gazed at her. "Your mother . . ." He paused and Vanessa waited, immobile with shock, curious, yet dreading to hear more. She loved her mother and she didn't want that love to be destroyed by something her father might say.

He looked out the window. "Your mother ran away with a man. He was black-haired, one-quarter Chickasaw."

Shocked again, she thought of all the years she had wanted her father's love and he had been so cold and harsh. Ethan was golden-haired, the image of their handsome father, but Vanessa had given little thought to her looks being different.

"That's why you hate Indians," she whispered, suddenly knowing that it wasn't prejudice alone, but a hatred born of anger and revenge and perhaps envy that made her father so vindictive toward Indians. "Did she love him?"

"I made her come back so no scandal would hurt Ethan, but she was carrying a child from the union. I told her I would be father to her child because otherwise my son would have grown up with a black cloud surrounding him. We moved so often that no friends knew. It was easy to move to the next fort, live a military life, and have everyone accept the birth of the second child as mine. Thank God, you don't look like him! But you're not my blood," he said in a harsh voice. "I raised you as my child. I've given you fancy dresses, lessons, all the things you should have had, and it was to no avail. You have a wild streak in you that is part your mother and probably part your father."

"Phoebe and Belva? Are they—"

"They're my daughters. I wanted sons and I had daughters," he said bitterly. "And after Ethan, I never loved your mother."

"She kept trying to give you another son," Vanessa said, thinking how he had dominated all their lives and caused so much misery. "We all loved you and wanted your love," she said more to herself than to him. She gazed beyond him, still shocked by his revelations, thinking over the years. "I'm part Chickasaw."

"Yes," he answered flatly, and she wondered if he hated her when he thought about her heritage.

He gazed out the window and wiped his eyes. "All the money I have saved for Ethan—"

She felt a strange mixture of pity for him and sadness that he had never wanted the love of any of the rest of them. "Papa—and you will always be Papa to me until you tell me not to call you that—let me go. You don't love me. Give me my happiness and let me go back to Lone Wolf. I'm bound to him; I'm his wife. I don't want to live in a convent."

He looked at her, tears filling his eyes. "Leave me alone, Vanessa."

She nodded and turned to step outside where Dupree stood talking quietly to Belva.

"Should I go talk to him?" Belva asked.

Vanessa shook her head. "No, I think he wants to be alone right now, Belva. Let's wait."

"I'm sorry, Vanessa," Dupree said. "You were the closest in age to your brother."

"Ethan was five years older, always busy with his own

things, so none of us knew him well, but I loved Ethan because he was my brother. Papa adored him."

"That damned war—so many dying. That's the only advantage to this frontier. It isn't safe here, but it's not as bad as the war has gotten to be." He placed his arm around her. "I'm sorry about your loss."

She moved away. "Thank you, Dupree. Belva, why don't you come with me and we'll go back to my quarters. Excuse us, Dupree."

Belva joined her; and as they crossed the open ground, Vanessa debated whether or not to tell Belva about her parentage.

When they were inside, Vanessa closed the door. Belva picked up two of the rag dolls. "Did you make these?"

"Yes, and you may have one. I have one for White Bird and there's one more for either of you."

"It's wonderful, Vanessa!" she said, hugging the largest one. "Thank you. Will you teach me how to make one?"

"Yes. Belva, Papa told me some things just now. He's distraught and he was franker with me than ever before. And he said things—" she paused "—I didn't know."

"Like what?"

"I'm not really his daughter." Belva looked up, her eyes round.

"You're not Papa's child? Whose daughter are you?"

"Our mother ran away one time—"

"Mama did?" Belva asked, surprise in her voice. "I guess none of us could get along with Papa. Where'd Mama go?"

"I don't know. He just told me she ran away because she was in love with another man. Papa brought her back, but that man was my father, and he was one-quarter Chickasaw. So I'm part Chickasaw."

"Land sakes!" Belva exclaimed, staring at her with an open mouth. "You're not my sister?"

"Yes, I'm your half-sister. We have the same mother, Belva."

"That's right. You don't look like you're Chickasaw. Maybe that was why Papa was always so angry with you."

"Maybe it was."

"I think he was the cruelest to you," Belva said quietly. "Am I his daughter?"

"Yes. Mama returned to Papa, and you and Phoebe are both his daughters."

"He still didn't love us."

Vanessa drew a deep breath, knowing there wasn't any good answer to give Belva about their father's love. "Belva, he wants to send you to boarding school. I don't know whether I can talk him out of it. I've asked him to let me go back to Lone Wolf."

"I want to go with you."

"Listen to me for a few minutes. You're eleven. If you go to school, you can get an education. In a few years, you may want to do something else besides live out here. Think what you're giving up."

"I don't mind giving any of it up. If I go to boarding school, I would still be with Papa in summers, and he doesn't want me. You said you and Lone Wolf do want me, and I love Muaahap and White Bird."

With a rush of love for Belva, Vanessa hugged her tightly. "We do want you. I love you, but I'm trying to think what's best for you."

"I want to stay with you."

Vanessa nodded. "We may not have a choice, Belva."

Belva touched the doll. "Can I stay with you tonight? I don't like it here, and I never see anyone except soldiers."

"Yes, of course, you can stay. They always bring dinner, so we'll eat soon."

After supper they sewed and talked until Belva went to bed. Later, wearing a cotton nightgown, Vanessa stood in the darkness at the window as she had done every night since her arrival. Where was Lone Wolf tonight? In his tipi at the canyon? Would he ride with a war party to the fort?

Questions played in Vanessa's mind and she knew there would never be an answer to some of them. What had happened to her blood father?

She turned to stare into the darkness. Would Papa relent and let her go? She felt he would never let Belva go now because she was the only child he was not furious with; yet she didn't think Belva had any more of his love than Phoebe or she.

She finally climbed into bed, stroking Belva's brown hair away from her face. With all the days in the sun, Belva's skin had darkened and her brown hair was already dark, so that she looked more like she had Chickasaw blood than Vanessa. Vanessa turned away to sleep.

The next morning they ate breakfast and then dressed, Vanessa wearing a green moire trimmed in black ribbon and intending to talk to Papa again.

"Belva," Vanessa said solemnly, feeling a cold prickle of fear every time she thought about leaving the fort. "Lone Wolf said he would come for me."

Belva's eyes brightened and she sat up. She was bent over the table, working on a doll. "Vanessa, that would be wonderful!"

"No, it wouldn't because it would mean a battle. Papa won't leave here without an escort of soldiers. It would mean a fight between Papa and Lone Wolf."

Belva's eyes grew round. "That would be terrible," she said quietly. "Surely they wouldn't—"

"Yes, they would, Belva. They hate each other. But I don't want him fighting Papa, because one of them wouldn't survive the fight."

Belva blinked and leaned back in the chair, biting her lip. "Is there any way to stop it?"

"If Papa would let me go back to Lone Wolf, there wouldn't be a battle."

"You have to talk him into letting you go back. Will Lone Wolf leave him alone if he goes back to Fort McKavett?"

Sara Orwig

Vanessa looked out the window and saw the soldier standing guard. He leaned against a post, a tall, lanky man with a pistol at his side. Her gaze swung back to Belva. "If Papa goes without me, I think he'll be left alone."

"I'm going to the room where I've been staying to get my things and move them here. Papa brought a trunk of my clothes."

"He brought all of my things from home."

"Why did he do that?"

"Because he doesn't expect me to ever go back," Vanessa answered quietly.

Belva frowned. "I'll go get my things."

She left, slipping across the parade ground, and Vanessa watched her, aware that Belva was growing up quickly and making some major decisions now about her life. She saw her father striding toward Belva. They stopped to talk a moment. He nodded and glanced toward Vanessa's quarters, and then he headed in her direction.

She smoothed the green moire dress and waited, wondering if he had made up his mind about going to Denver, feeling a tight knot inside because he seldom backed down from a decision.

She glanced at the small oval mirror, staring at her reflection, wondering about her Chickasaw heritage. Who was her father? How did her mother meet him? Questions swirled in thought, questions that might not ever be answered because the answer was locked away with her parents, perhaps some answers known only to her mother, who was gone now.

Footsteps were loud outside. "Morning, Colonel," came the greeting from the guard.

"Good morning." Papa entered without knocking, stepping into the room and closing the door behind him. His eyes were red, his face haggard. Startled by the change in his robust good looks, Vanessa stared at him. He looked as if he had lost pounds and nights of sleep when it hadn't been twenty-four hours yet since he had received the letter about Ethan.

"I want to talk to you." He moved about impatiently. "I've had a long night to think about my life, my loss of Ethan." He paced the floor and pulled out a handkerchief to wipe his eyes. "I don't understand why this happened. Now I'm alone. None of you love me—"

"We tried, Papa."

He looked at her, his expression harsh. "Perhaps you did and I was too busy, too involved with Ethan. I know that all three of you want to be away from me."

"You want us away from you!"

"If I wanted you at home, all of you would still like to leave."

She realized he was right. Phoebe wanted the opera; she wanted Lone Wolf, and Belva wanted to stay with her. "A few years ago that wouldn't have been so, but Phoebe and I are grown and Belva is maturing. We want other things now."

"After all these years, I'm alone. I have no one. I have a fortune, but Ethan is gone, and it will be meaningless to you if you're in a convent. I can't see settling it on Phoebe when she ran away from home. I feel as if I barely know Belva."

"That's your fault, Papa," Vanessa stated bluntly. "We're your daughters and we always loved you and wanted your love. But since you never returned it, finally, we gave up."

Haggard, his fists clenched, he stared at her. "I failed you, didn't I?"

"Not your son—only your daughters," she answered truthfully.

He ran his fingers across his eyes and turned his back to her.

"Who was my father? And where did they meet?"

There was such a long silence she wondered whether he

had heard her or not. But then he inhaled deeply, his shoulders heaving.

"I was stationed at Fort Washita in the Indian Nation when Ethan was a baby. In those days, the soldiers were there to protect the Chickasaws and Choctaws from the plains Indians. The fort was a stopping place for migrants and the overland mail. I was a young officer with my wife and child at the fort. We went to parties and dances in the homes of the Chickasaws and Choctaws, and they came to the fort to dances."

Abbot's voice sounded strained, and he paused. She waited patiently, curious, understanding that what he was saying was difficult for him.

"There was one Indian in particular who wasn't married, and your mother went with him to Arkansas. I went after her and I shot and killed him."

Vanessa drew a deep breath, staring at her father as he turned to face her. "I killed him in Arkansas and brought her back with me because I wasn't going to allow her to ruin Ethan's life. No one knew what happened to him. I asked for a transfer, and we were sent to Virginia, where you were born."

Vanessa looked down at her fingers, wondering how much her mother had suffered over what had happened. "Let me go, Papa."

He studied her. "Belva told me you rode from here to that encampment all by yourself."

"Yes, I did."

"Dupree said that's impossible."

She shrugged. "I desperately wanted to go to Lone Wolf."

"How'd you find it?"

"Lone Wolf told me it was south of the battle site when soldiers attacked their winter camp near an old fort called Adobe Walls."

"I know where that is."

"It's on the Canadian River. I asked in Tucumcari how far the river was from Tucumcari and how to find it. Once I found the river, I followed it until I found where they had camped and fought. Then I turned south." She waved her hand slightly as if in apology. "I suppose you know that when I left the wagon train, I took your gold."

He looked mildly amused. "I knew you did. The Parsons woman was hysterical when she talked to me and told me the money was gone."

"I gave some of the money to Phoebe."

Abbot studied Vanessa with speculation in his eyes. "You're a brave woman, Vanessa."

"I did what I had to do," she answered quietly, knowing at one time she would have been thrilled to receive such a compliment from him, but now it no longer mattered.

"And I never would have guessed Phoebe had the courage to go alone to California." Abbot ran his hand over his face again, wiping away tears. "I've not only lost Ethan, I've lost all of you. Except Belva. Maybe it isn't too late with her."

Shocked, Vanessa stared at her father, wondering if Ethan's loss had jolted him so much he was changing. "She wants to go with me because she knows we love her. Lone Wolf is a father to her."

"The father I haven't been!" Abbot exclaimed bitterly. "I suppose, Vanessa, I've made dreadful mistakes. I don't have Ethan and I rejected love from the three of you and now I'm alone."

"Papa, if you let Phoebe go with your blessings and support her in what she does, she's still young," Vanessa said, her hopes rising as she stared at him, wondering if he could possibly change.

He turned to look at her. "You're a brave woman and I should be proud to have you for my daughter," he said quietly. "If you married Dupree, you would have so much, Vanessa—"

"Papa, I'm already married. I wouldn't have love with Dupree and I know how important that is. With Lone Wolf and White Bird I have a family filled with love. Will you let me go back to my husband?" she asked, holding her breath.

His blue eyes focused on her and he crossed the room to her.

"Let me go, Papa," she urged.

"You had your own mind when you were a tiny child," he said, touching her red hair. She couldn't recall the last time he had touched her gently. "I know I lost you long ago due to my own selfishness. Yes, go back to him. I'll get an army escort to go with you to the Kiowa winter camp. I don't want you traveling alone again, and Dupree can take enough men to see you there safely."

Vanessa barely heard the last as she closed her eyes, swaying, relief washing over her like a surging ocean wave. She grasped his hand. "Papa, thank you! Thank you! That gives me so much joy!"

He stared at her, unable to respond. She hugged him impulsively, and he patted her shoulder. "Thank you!" she exclaimed again.

"I don't know how you can give up the life you've always known, the life Dupree offers, to trail after a warrior. I think you'll regret your choice, Vanessa," Abbot told her solemnly.

She shook her head. "No, I'll never regret it."

Her father moved away, looking out the window again. "Vanessa, I didn't sleep last night. I was planning my future, and I've decided to divide my estate. A share will go to each of you."

"You don't need to include me."

"I'm going to include you. Life is changing on the frontier, and when the war is over, it will change more. I'm a railroader and I talk to railroad men. I know what the trains can do and what a difference they'll make in our lives. I'll have my attorney draw up the papers and I'll place your share in a bank. If you ever want it, you may contact Phoebe, Belva, or the attorney. He's Paul Devlin and he lives in San Antonio. I'll leave a stipulation that if you never touch it, in fifty years it will revert to Phoebe and Belva or their heirs."

"Thank you, but it's not necessary."

"It's there. Always remember that. I'll talk to Dupree today about an escort for you to the camp. If they ride with a white flag of truce, there shouldn't be any fighting."

"Papa, thank you! This gives me much happiness!"

"Perhaps it will make up for the past. I'm going to talk to Belva. I'll give her a choice, but I'm going to try to convince her to stay with me and go to school."

Vanessa nodded, wondering how much her father would change, realizing how totally devastated he was by Ethan's loss.

He gave Vanessa an appraising glance. "Maybe I underestimated all of you."

"You hurt Belva badly when you destroyed her dolls."

"The dolls seemed so foolish and silly."

"If they had been wooden soldiers of Ethan's, would you have smashed them?"

He flinched. "No, I wouldn't have," he answered forthrightly, and Vanessa realized Ethan's loss was causing a giant upheaval in her father's life. At the door, he glanced back at her once more. "You went all alone from here to that camp?"

"Yes."

"Dupree can't figure how you got away from him in Tucumcari either. He thinks you had help."

"No, I was alone."

"That's remarkable, Vanessa, really remarkable."

"I just wanted to get back to him," she answered quietly.

"Perhaps we should have spent more time together," he

said with a note of regret. "But time for that is past." He glanced at the window. "I'll talk to Belva."

He left and she went to the open door as a cold wind whipped inside. Her father strode across the open ground and he looked as strong and determined as ever, yet Ethan's loss had shaken him, perhaps changing him for all time. She looked up at a winter sky, gray with clouds, and she wondered if snow were falling farther north. Then any thought about weather was gone. *She was going home to Lone Wolf!*

She wanted to run outside and shout with joy and jump in the air. And she wanted to get on a horse right now and go. With a broad smile, she turned to run inside and pack what she wanted to take with her.

She looked at the trunks, knowing Muaahap and some of the other women would love the bright-colored silks and satins. Deciding to take most of her things, she began to fold the dresses. She could pack the belongings on horses and leave the trunks for Papa to take home.

An hour later she had bathed and washed her hair and dressed in a blue gingham. As she brushed her hair dry, she heard voices and footsteps and a knock at the door.

She opened it to face her father. He stepped inside, cold air rushing in with him as he turned to face her, and she shut the door.

"I've talked to Belva. She's going with me back to McKavett."

Astonished, Vanessa stared at him. "How did you talk her into going?"

"We had a long discussion and I made some promises to her. And I think part of the reason she changed is because I'm letting you go back to your Indian."

"Papa, call him Lone Wolf or my husband, please," she said.

He shrugged. "I find all the changes in my life difficult,

Vanessa. That one seems impossible, but with time perhaps—"

"Belva will go to boarding school?"

"No, that's one of my promises to her. She won't this year and maybe not at all. She'll continue with a tutor and we will also travel to California to visit Phoebe."

"Oh, Papa, that's wonderful!" Vanessa exclaimed, engulfed by a mixture of emotions. "I'm happy because I think Belva was too young to decide to go with me; yet at the same time, I love Belva and I'll miss her as well as Phoebe."

"I've promised her many things to get her to stay. I told Belva we will go to Denver and build a house. We'll have a home, and she can stay in Denver when business demands that I travel. That way you and Phoebe will know where to find us. And she can make friends and not move away from them."

"I think that's grand!" Vanessa said. She was happy for Belva and felt in her heart that staying with Papa in Denver might be best for her sister, but also had a pang of loss. "Papa, it's not too late with Belva. I hope you see that. It's not too late with any of us in some ways because we all love you."

"As you said, children love freely. I look back, Vanessa, and I see how I shut the three of you out. I shut your mother out," he said quietly, "because I was so angry with her."

Vanessa was silent, having no answer to what had happened between her parents.

"Dupree is making arrangements for Belva and me to leave tomorrow morning for McKavett. I have to make arrangements about things there and then we'll go to Denver. In the afternoon tomorrow, Dupree said he will take a detail and they'll escort you back to your husband."

"Oh, Papa, that's the most wonderful thing you've ever done!" she exclaimed, hugging him again.

"I'm glad we can part on a good note, Vanessa, because I feel I'll never see you again."

"Papa, Lone Wolf speaks English fluently and was an army scout. He knows our way of life. I think he'll take me to Denver sometime so you can see your grandchildren."

Abbot frowned, glancing down at her. "Are you with child?"

"No," she said, shaking her head, "but I want a family."

He nodded. "Will you talk to Belva?"

"Yes, right now," she agreed, throwing her woolen cape across her shoulders.

They stepped outside, and the wind whipped against her. She noticed the guard was gone and she guessed he wouldn't return. Joyous, she hurried across the compound.

"I'll leave you so you'll be alone with her. She stays in that building," he said, pointing to a long, frame structure. "She's in the first room to your right."

Vanessa knocked on a closed door. When it opened, she entered to find clothing strewn around the narrow, sparsely furnished room that held only a bed and desk and washstand.

"Papa told you," Belva said, pushing long strands of brown hair away from her face. "I'm going with him."

"Yes, and I think that's fine."

Belva ran across the room to hug Vanessa. "I'll miss you! I'll miss White Bird and Lone Wolf and Muaahap."

Vanessa squeezed Belva's shoulders and stepped back, wiping tears from her eyes. "I'll miss you, too, Belva, but you're probably doing what's best."

"Papa said if I'm not happy by next winter, we could come back and try to find the Kiowa winter camp so that I could go with you."

"That's a wonderful offer." Vanessa looked at the sparkle in Belva's blue eyes and smiled.

Belva became solemn. "I'll still miss you."

"I know you will, and I'll miss you." Vanessa glanced around. "I'll help you get ready to go."

As they filled Belva's trunks, Vanessa's thoughts kept going to Lone Wolf, hoping that he was still in the camp and that a war party had not yet started toward the fort.

A few light flurries of snow swirled through the air and caught on the ground around posts. The cold north wind whipped against Vanessa and she pulled the cloak more tightly around her as she stood beside a wagon. Papa, Belva, and twelve soldiers were ready to ride for Fort McKavett. The soldiers had accompanied Papa to Bascom and would return with him. Belva stood gazing at the wagon while Dupree waited beside Vanessa.

Papa came across the grounds, leading two horses, and Vanessa looked at him with curiosity. "Vanessa," he called to her as he stopped at a hitching rail.

Holding the cloak tightly closed under her chin, she hurried to him.

"I went to Tucumcari yesterday and bought these horses. I know how important horses are to Indians, so these go to you and your husband as a wedding gift."

"Thank you!" she exclaimed, shocked more by his thoughtfulness and relenting than by his generosity, astounded he would give something to Lone Wolf. "Thank you, Papa," she said, giving him a hug which he returned stiffly with one arm. He stepped back and held up his other hand, holding out a rifle. "This is a gift to your husband."

She looked into her father's blue eyes, amazed that he would give Lone Wolf a special gift. "I'll take it to him."

"I don't like what you're doing, but I like even less losing all of my children—and I almost did. If you'll come back, Vanessa, I'll let you do what you want."

She shook her head. "No, Papa. This is my place now. I'll take the rifle and horses. Thank you."

He glanced at the cluster of soldiers milling around the wagon, Dupree talking to Belva. "Dupree said he will pack and start out within the hour to take you to Lone Wolf."

She nodded. "Be good to Belva."

"I will be." Abbot looked down at her. "Everyone is waiting. Shall we go?"

They walked to the wagon, and he turned to extend his hand to Dupree. "Thank you, Dupree. Thank you for returning my daughters to me and for taking Vanessa back to her husband."

"Thank you, sir, for your generosity. I'm sorry about your son. Don't worry about Vanessa. We'll get her there safely."

Abbot nodded and turned to Vanessa. "Goodbye, Vanessa," he said.

She stepped up to kiss his cheek and hug him, and then she turned to Belva, who had tears spilling onto her cheeks. They hugged each other tightly.

"Come on, Belva," Papa said and helped her into the wagon.

He climbed up to drive, and they turned out of the fort while the soldiers rode with them. As the wind whistled across the open ground and blew the cloak tightly around her, Vanessa watched them go. When they turned, Belva waved and Vanessa returned the wave.

"Will you be ready to leave soon?"

She looked at Dupree and nodded. "Within the hour."

"I'll send someone for your things."

She nodded, gazing to the east, knowing within days she would be with Lone Wolf.

She bathed and changed, dressing in a heavy woolen riding habit and putting the thick woolen cloak around her shoulders. Her hair was in a long braid. When the soldiers arrived for her things, she motioned to the bundles she had tied up. They lashed her bundles on packhorses and, at last, Dupree appeared. He was mounted on a black horse and he halted, the horse prancing nervously in front of her quarters.

"Ready to go?"

Closing the door, she nodded and mounted the gray horse that was saddled and waiting for her. They rode out of the fort as gusts of wind buffeted her. She rode beside Dupree, and twenty soldiers followed. Four more rode in front of them.

Her gaze swept the horizon, looking at the flat land, hoping there would be no war party and she could arrive at the winter camp without incident.

"Your sister made a wise choice," Dupree said dryly, glancing at her. There was a cold tone in his voice, and she realized he was angry with her.

"With Ethan's loss, Papa changed. I think this will be good for Belva and for Papa."

"It'll be damned good for Belva," Dupree remarked with cynicism.

They fell silent, and she continued to look over the countryside. "If there is a war party, you'll raise the white flag at once, won't you?"

His head swung around, and he looked at her with a faint smile.

Fear stabbed her as she studied him. "You'll fight?"

"We will if we're attacked."

"You told Papa you'd take me back in peace."

"We're doing that. Your father will hear we rode out to take you to the Kiowa winter camp. Along the way, if we're attacked, we'll fight. That's different."

"No, it's not! It may be Lone Wolf coming for me. He said he would."

Dupree shrugged. "If he attacks us with two or three hundred, then yes, I'll raise the white flag and hand you over. If he comes with twenty or thirty or forty, then we'll fight."

"You won't be attacked if you raise the white flag," she

snapped, anger replacing her fear. "You know Papa thought you were escorting me to my husband, not going out to fight him."

Dupree shrugged, and she felt a leaden weight and a rush of anger. "He won't attack us if he wants you back."

"With the soldiers in front of us, no one can see that I'm with you until they're close to us."

"If he comes in peace, he may have you. If he attacks, he'll get a fight."

"You'd better not turn your back on me, captain," she snapped.

He looked mildly amused. "And what would you shoot me with? The rifle your father bought that has no ammunition. You don't have a revolver, Vanessa, and you won't get your hands on one during this ride."

"Dupree, my father will hear about this, and you won't be in his favor then."

"I don't think he'll hear about anything."

She closed her mouth, looking at him again and then shifting her gaze to the horizon.

As the afternoon wore on, the cold seemed to seep through her cape and bite at her skin. By the time the sun was setting and Dupree called a halt, she was huddled on her horse, chilled, tired, and ready to stop traveling.

She watched while Dupree gave orders and men put up tents. As soon as Dupree motioned to one, she hurried toward it. "This is yours, Vanessa. Right next to mine so I can hear if you want anything."

"Thank you."

She hurried inside and found a bedroll, a lantern, blankets, and utensils. As soon as she stepped out of the wind, she felt warmer. Shedding the cape, she listened to the canvas tent flap as the wind struck it. She could hear men moving around outside, and Dupree giving orders.

The tent had a canvas floor and cut off the wind completely. She unrolled the bedding.

Within the hour she could smell something cooking and stepped outside. Lighting the night, a bonfire roared, shedding a large circle of light, and the men milled around it. Dupree appeared at her side, taking her arm.

"Let's eat. We brought along beef and there's some stew. But come to my tent for a minute. I have something to warm you up."

Dry grass swished against her skirt as she walked beside him. They entered a tent like hers; both were roomy enough to stand and move around, and his held a small field desk. Hanging on a post, a lantern glowed brightly. He opened a flask and poured two tin cups with brandy, turning to hand one to her. "Drink it. It'll warm you."

She took the brandy and sipped it, feeling the fiery liquid go down and heating her as he had said it would.

"I hope Papa and Belva travel out of this cold."

"They should; they ride south," he said, stepping to the flap and tying it shut. She frowned at him, her gaze going from the flap to him.

"What are you doing?"

He straightened up, a faint smile on his face, his eyes heavy lidded and filled with lust as he let his gaze lower over her.

"I'm going to enjoy the night with you, Vanessa," he said quietly and started toward her.

Twenty-seven

Her pulse pounded with anger as she stared at him while he removed his coat. "Get out of here, Dupree. If you harm me, my father will ruin you."

"Your father will never know what I do with you," Dupree answered slyly. "Are you going to write to him? Go back to see him?" he asked in a cynical voice. "Hell, no. He left you with a band of soldiers to go to the middle of nowhere. No one knows where you are except me and my men, and the men with me were carefully chosen. I can trust them."

She felt cold, suddenly realizing how vulnerable she was, how much she had trusted Dupree when she should have known better. His pleasant cooperation the last days with Papa present had lulled her into forgetting the first hours with Dupree and his deceit about Lone Wolf.

The lantern glowed with a yellow light, highlighting Dupree's pointed chin and his broad cheekbones, leaving his cheeks in shadows. He unbuckled his belt and moved toward her.

"Lone Wolf will kill you if you harm me."

"I hope he comes after me. Then I'll get to finish the job. I hoped he would die after the beating I gave him. And it will give me pleasure to do as I please to his squaw," Dupree said with contempt.

"Someone will get word to my father. You'll never do this and get away with it," she said, moving from him, thinking about the rifle she had let him pack on one of the horses. "He'll learn about it, and it'll be the end of your army career."

She shifted to one side, backing away as he unfastened his shirt and pulled it off.

"I held back that first night with you, but not tonight. Your father will never know. When I get back, I'll send a telegram that I delivered you safely to the redskin camp. I have two dozen men out there who will back me up and be witnesses that you were safely taken to the camp. They'll be happy to lie because I've told them they each get a chance with you."

"I should have known what you would be like once Papa was gone."

Dupree shook his head. "You won't go back to tell him."

"I'll scream."

As Dupree smiled, her blood ran cold. "I hope you do. I told you I trust these men. I've promised you to them when I'm finished with you, Vanessa."

She inhaled swiftly, frightened now, her mind racing. She glanced at the lantern, but he stood closer to it than she did. It hung against the center pole several feet behind him and above his head.

"One of the men will talk or I'll get back. And Lone Wolf will come after you."

"He won't ever know," Dupree said softly. "You disappear out here on this godforsaken land and who will know? Lone Wolf will think you're with your father and he won't know where to look. Your father will think you're with Lone Wolf, so he won't expect to hear from you again."

"You're a monster! I trusted you," she said, edging away, knowing in a minute she would be backed against the canvas.

"You'll regret turning down my offer. You could have had a life of ease and wealth. Between your father and me, you would have been pampered and cared for. Instead, Vanessa, I'm going to spend a couple of days enjoying you and then let my men have you and then we'll leave you. Only this time you won't have a horse and you won't have food and you won't have anyone to help you. I doubt if you'll even feel like walking when twenty men have pleasured themselves with you."

"Someone will find out, Dupree," she said, trying to control her fear, to choke back the scream that threatened. She was terrified of him because she saw no way to stop him this time.

She lunged for the flap, her fingers yanking at the ties.

He caught her, pulling her back against him. He was strong and her struggles against him were useless. He caught both her wrists, lashing them together with his belt. He turned her to face him, his fingers going to her throat to unbutton her dress.

"Don't do this, Dupree. You'll regret it," she said, standing so close to him, knowing she wouldn't gain anything by running outside because one of the men would bring her right back to him. She looked around the tent for a weapon to use against him and found that there was nothing.

His hands moved over her breasts as he unfastened buttons and opened her bodice to stroke her, pushing away the chemise and cupping her breasts. He drew in his breath. "You're a beautiful woman. I want your hair down."

He reached around her, unfastening the braid swiftly, combing out her hair with his fingers. "Now," he said, pushing open her bodice.

The air was cold on her skin, and she gazed beyond him, trying to ignore his hands as he stroked her breasts. His fingers returned to the buttons and he pushed the dress open and ran his hands over her. His touch was loathsome and her skin prickled while a cold fear gripped her. He unfastened her wrists, tossing down the belt. She looked at the heavy buckle, wondering if she could use it as a weapon, but realized it was not enough.

Dupree pulled her closer, yanking down the dress, shoving it off her arms, and letting it fall around her ankles. He ripped away her underclothing until she stood with only her stockings and shoes.

Desperate, Vanessa saw nothing in the tent that she could use as a weapon except the lantern, and he still stood between her and the center post where the lantern hung. His hands drifted over her, sliding between her legs, and she stiffened.

Panting, he wound his fingers in her hair and held her, kissing her hard, and then he released her as he began to unbutton his trousers. As he stepped out of one leg, balanced on one foot, she lunged at him, throwing herself against him and slamming him into the center post, grabbing for the lantern.

Her fingers closed on the metal base and she tried to pull it off the nail where it hung.

Dupree seized her and they went down together. She clawed at him and kicked him, biting his arm.

He pinned her down swiftly as she struggled beneath him. His eyes glittered with lust.

On the keening wind another high shrill sound rose, tearing her attention from Dupree and sending a thrill surging through her. Dupree stilled suddenly.

His head jerked up, his nostrils flaring as he froze over her. "Dammit! Damned redskins!"

The piercing cries continued, a series of yips that sent a chill down Vanessa's spine while at the same time she wanted to scream for joy.

Outside, men yelled. The pounding hooves of galloping horses thundered in the night.

"Damned Indians!" Dupree repeated. A shot was fired as Dupree yanked on his clothes and ran from the tent.

Lone Wolf! Vanessa's heart leaped, her fear shifting and changing like water in a swirling stream. With shaking hands, she yanked on her dress.

The cries and pounding horses were unmistakable now. It was a war party tearing through the camp. Guns blasted the night, and men yelled, the constant cries of the raiding Indians a wild challenge carried on the wind.

Something struck the canvas, and the tent burst into flames.

Her hands shook as she fastened buttons and grabbed up her cape to rush outside.

Arms locked around her and Dupree grabbed her, sweeping her up on a horse in front of him and turning to wheel into the darkness and gallop away with her.

Lone Wolf tore across the camp, firing the rifle, searching for Vanessa. He had crept through the darkness close enough to see her near Dupree at one point. Both of them were here. But where was she now? And where was Belva? He hadn't seen Belva all night. Had Abbot Sutherland taken Belva back to McKavett? And why was Vanessa heading *east?*

Tents were flaming and suddenly Lone Wolf was cold with fear. Had Dupree tied Vanessa and left her in one of the burning tents. He galloped to a tent, swinging down over the side of his horse to look inside, straightening up to ride furiously to the next tent as a battle raged behind him.

Ignoring the guns of the soldiers, his fright for her safety grew when he couldn't find her. And he couldn't find Dupree. In minutes, the smoke would be too thick to find anyone.

A warrior rode past and motioned to Lone Wolf as he fired his rifle, waving his hand in a wide sweep toward the west.

Lone Wolf urged his bay forward, the horse racing into the darkness away from the burning tents and flames.

It took a while for Lone Wolf's eyes to adjust, and he wondered if he were galloping away from Vanessa and leaving her to burn in a tent or die at the hands of a soldier. And then he saw a shadow ahead of him.

He leaned low over the bay, kicking its sides, feeling the surge of its powerful muscles as the horse stretched out and pounded across the land. Wind tore at Lone Wolf, and he strained to see, gradually narrowing the gap until he glimpsed a man leaning low over a galloping horse. Was it Dupree? And did he have Vanessa or was she back at the camp?

Lone Wolf wanted Vanessa more than he wanted to take revenge on Dupree. Torn between going after Dupree and going back, Lone Wolf galloped behind the other horse, hoping Vanessa was only yards ahead of him.

In spite of the cold, his palms were damp with sweat because he was terrified he was leaving her when she needed him. He glanced back to see the raging flames dancing high in the dark night.

He remembered Cloud in Sky motioning to him. Cloud in Sky wouldn't send him out after Dupree. Most of the warriors didn't know Dupree. Determined to catch up with whoever was ahead of him, Lone Wolf kicked the bay.

The horses raced, the bay slowly closing the lead. Suddenly, the other horse was drawn up short and wheeled around.

"Stop where you are! I'll kill her!" Dupree shouted.

Lone Wolf reined his horse, recognizing Dupree Milos's voice. He could see Milos as he held Vanessa against him and kept the prancing horse in check.

"Get down off the horse and put your hands in the air," Dupree shouted. "I've got a knife against her throat and I'll cut her if you don't do as I say."

"Ride away from him! He has a rif—" Vanessa cried and gasped.

"Don't hurt her!" Lone Wolf snapped, yanking the knife from the scabbard and raising his hands. In the dark, he didn't think Dupree could see well enough to spot the knife.

Lone Wolf held the knife flat against his wrist as he raised his hands.

"You didn't gain anything by attacking. I'll take her and when I'm through with her, my men can have her. This time you won't live to know about it," Milos yelled.

Vanessa cried softly, as the knife cut into her throat. She knew that if she moved or struck Dupree, he would stab her, yet he couldn't get the rifle out of the scabbard and hold her at knife point at the same time. "Please go!" she sobbed, knowing he would kill Lone Wolf the first chance he got, and Lone Wolf wouldn't attack him as long as he ran a chance of hurting her.

She could make out the dark bulk of Lone Wolf's wide shoulders, his black hair blowing in the wind as he held his hands high over his head.

Suddenly, Dupree flung her away from him. She tumbled, falling through the air off the horse's back and sprawling on the ground as Dupree yanked up his rifle.

Vanessa screamed a warning.

Twenty-eight

Vanessa slammed against the earth, the jolt dazing her and knocking the breath from her lungs, her hands and face scraping on the rough ground. She twisted as the rifle fired, the blast loud in the night.

With a cry she rolled over and came to her knees. A knife glinted, protruding from Dupree's chest. He toppled off the horse, and she turned while Lone Wolf ran to her.

His strong arms closed around her and she flung her arms around him, clinging to him, relishing the strength in his shoulders and arms, knowing she was safe now. She sobbed with relief to be in his arms while he tilted her head up. "Are you hurt?"

"No! He fired his rifle—"

"He missed. The moment he released you, I threw the knife. Vanessa," Lone Wolf said her name in a husky voice filled with longing. The warmth and love in the one word made her shake with relief and joy.

"I trusted him when he told Papa he would take me back to you. I shouldn't have—"

Lone Wolf framed her face with his hands. "You're sure he didn't hurt you?"

"No, he didn't. I'm all right."

"Why was he bringing you back to me?" Lone Wolf asked, frowning at her.

"Because Papa had a change of heart. I will tell you

more later, but Papa agreed I could return to you. He sent horses as a wedding gift and he sent a rifle for you."

"Your father? Abbot Sutherland sent me a wedding gift?" Lone Wolf asked, his brows arching, disbelief in his voice.

"Yes." She reached up, placing her hand behind Lone Wolf's head to pull him down. His mouth covered hers and he kissed her hungrily and hard, all his pent-up longing pouring out, making her tremble with eagerness. He pulled her up against him, his tongue going deep into her mouth, touching her tongue, desire and reassurance both evident in his kiss while his hand caressed her throat.

With a hiss he pulled away and looked down. "That bastard—"

She looked at Lone Wolf's hand, which was dark with blood. He leaned closer, peering at her throat. "He cut you!"

"I felt something, but I didn't think it was a bad cut."

Lone Wolf pulled out a soft thin strip of leather from a pouch on his belt and placed it against her throat.

He glanced over his shoulder. "I'll get the knife Muaahap gave me and see if he is still alive."

Lone Wolf set her down gently and moved away. Vanessa watched him lean over Dupree's body and finally return to her.

"He's dead." Lone Wolf placed his knife in his scabbard. He picked Vanessa up and placed her on his horse. Then he went back one more time, and leaned over Dupree. She saw the knife glint in the moonlight.

Lone Wolf fastened a bit of Dupree's hair and scalp to his lance. Clamping his jaw closed tightly, he held the lance toward the gray sky while he remembered the moment when White Bird's mother had died in his arms. He gave a high, keening wail. "Tainso, he is gone," Lone Wolf added quietly.

He turned and walked back to the horse, seeing Vanessa watching him, her eyes large as she looked at the lance.

She shivered and turned away. With ease, he mounted behind her, his arms winding around her.

The moment his arm slid around her, Vanessa turned, throwing herself against him to kiss him wildly. Startled for a moment, his arm tightened around her while he kissed her in return. Leaning over her, he tried to remember not to hold her too tightly. He had been so fearful that he wasn't going to find her in the camp, and the moments when Dupree had held the knife at her throat had been agony. Now here she was in his arms, kissing him joyously.

He wondered if he would ever become accustomed to that exuberance and fire that could burst forth so swiftly from her when she was excited or pleased. He held her tightly against his pounding heart, his shaft hard with wanting her. He kissed her, feeling her hands flutter over him.

She raised her head to stroke his cheek.

"I would take you now, but we have to join the others or someone will come searching for us," Lone Wolf said, his voice raspy with the need for her.

She turned to look ahead at the flames that still curled skyward, a pall of smoke hanging over the camp.

"If they're still fighting—"

"They're not. There's no gunfire, Vanessa. I'll leave you in the darkness outside the ring of light while I let someone know we're here and that we're all right."

"You don't have to leave me. I don't want you to."

"It's a battlefield now and it won't be a pretty sight."

"I can close my eyes. You have two horses from Papa if they're still alive. All my things are on the packhorses."

"We'll find your belongings. The horses should be fine."

He urged his horse to a canter and then slowed again as they neared the camp.

She turned her head, placing her forehead against his chest, feeling his strong arm across her shoulders while she closed her eyes. She could feel his warmth and she wanted to be in his arms, alone in his tipi, instead of facing a long, grueling ride back to camp.

As he talked, she leaned against him and felt the slight vibrations in his chest. Around them, flames still crackled, and the smell of burning canvas, gunpowder, and woodsmoke hung in the air. Men's voices were loud; a horse whinnied. Finally, a man gave a cry and she felt Lone Wolf urge his horse forward and the bay broke into a run.

Horses galloped and she started to raise her head. Lone Wolf's hand cupped the back of her head, pressing her against his chest so she couldn't see the campground or the dead.

She held him as the dark night enveloped them again. She raised her head, and this time he didn't stop her. When they slowed to a walk, she turned to him.

"Did you get the horses?"

"Yes. We have all the horses."

She shivered. "Dupree said he would spend a couple of days with me and then give me to the men who were with him."

"That's over," Lone Wolf said flatly. "And I have avenged Tainso's death and his cruelty to you."

She turned to look ahead. Warriors fanned out in a broad line and rode silently. Lone Wolf followed slowly behind them, letting the distance widen. Her gaze ran over the warriors who were streaked with paint and had feathers in their hair. Their ponies were painted with stripes on their legs, circles around one horse's eye, a palm print on the another's withers.

As the wind whipped against them, Lone Wolf sheltered her, his body giving her warmth. He looked down at her. "When you returned to the fort," Lone Wolf said quietly, "what happened?"

"Papa wanted me to marry Dupree. I told him you and I were wed, and at first he didn't want to accept our marriage. I was shut in quarters where I didn't have anyone to talk to and I didn't see anyone for days."

Lone Wolf's arm tightened around her. "What made your father change so much?"

"He received a letter." She twisted to look up at him. "My brother Ethan was killed in Virginia."

"Ah, Vanessa," Lone Wolf said, regret in his voice. "I'm sorry you lost a brother."

"It tore Papa up. I've never seen him upset like that. Then he seemed to realize he had shut all of us out of his life. By the next morning when he came to talk to me, he said he would let me return to you. He talked Belva into going with him. He changed—I think he felt completely alone and lost. He intends to build a home in Denver and stay there so Belva will live in one place long enough to have some lasting friendships. He'll buy her a horse, and she doesn't have to go away to school."

"He meant all this?"

"Yes, he did. You can't imagine how his life revolved around Ethan." She paused and looked up at Lone Wolf again. "And I think I know one reason for his hatred toward Indians."

"Other than building railroads, what?"

"Papa was distraught over Ethan's death, and he talked more openly with me than ever before. He told me that my mother ran away with a man who was one-quarter Chickasaw. Papa found them and killed him and brought her back. I'm not his daughter. My blood father was the Chickasaw."

Lone Wolf gazed over her head into space beyond her. "So all that time he was offering bounties for Indians, he was trying to get back at your father," he observed.

"I imagine that's right. He took Mother home and killed my father. He said no one knew what happened because they had run away to Arkansas. Papa requested and received a transfer to Virginia, where I was born. Phoebe and Belva are his own daughters."

Lone Wolf ran his hand over her hair. "Maybe that explains some of the clashes you had with him and his withholding love from you."

Suddenly she threw her arms around Lone Wolf. "Thank heavens you came!"

His arms tightened around her, and he leaned down to kiss her.

Three days later, as they rode down into the canyon, snow swirled and blew against them. Pressed against Lone Wolf, Vanessa was warm. Everyone came out to greet them, and they circled the camp with the horses brought from the raid. Vanessa saw Muaahap and White Bird waving.

"There—" she started to point to them.

Lone Wolf swung her to the ground, and White Bird ran to her with her arms held out. Vanessa caught her up, holding her closely to hug and kiss her cheek while White Bird hugged Vanessa's neck.

"Mama! Mama!"

Lone Wolf dropped to the ground and walked over to her, snow white in his dark hair, flakes on his long lashes. "I think it's time she calls you *kkaw-kkoy'*. I will tell her about Tainso, but you will be mother to her," he said, his arm encircling them both.

"Kkaw-kkoy'," White Bird repeated, her dark eyes gazing at Vanessa. Vanessa held her tightly, love filling her heart for White Bird. Muaahap came up, grinning at Vanessa, who turned to hug her. She said something to Lone Wolf, and he nodded.

Vanessa looked at him curiously. "What did she say?"

"She reminded me that she knew I would get you back without harm and that I would get my revenge. She had a dream about it. She had told me not to ride too hard and push you because she wouldn't be along to tell me when to halt."

Vanessa smiled, touching his cheek.

"I want to be alone with you now, but it's our tradition to celebrate a victorious raid so we'll have to wait until tonight when the festivities are under way. Muaahap has gone to our tipi to wait for you so White Bird can be with you. We will be alone tonight," he said quietly. "We didn't get our time together, so Muaahap and White Bird will sleep elsewhere for the next two weeks."

Vanessa stood on tiptoe to kiss him, a lingering, heated kiss that escalated as his arm tightened around her waist and he held her against him.

She walked away to find White Bird and Muaahap. Snowflakes pelted her, but she barely felt the cold as she looked back at Lone Wolf, who looked back at her.

That night she left the dancers early, stepping out of the circle away from the roaring blaze. She hurried to their tipi and entered. She wore the yellow doeskin dress she had worn for their wedding, and her pulse raced in eager anticipation of being alone with him.

As she knelt to build up the embers in the firepit, she felt a rush of cold air behind her. Lone Wolf entered and tied shut the flap, closing out the cold and the wind.

As her gaze ran over her strong, handsome husband, her heart drummed. Eagle feathers were in his hair, and his face was streaked with paint.

When he looked at her, she felt pulled into the dark depths of eyes that smoldered with desire and love. He stepped toward her to slide his arm around her waist and pull her up against him, looking down into her eyes.

"My woman. I haven't known peace since you came into my life. You are still the wild wind storming through my days."

"And you're the love I've never known, filling my life," she said softly, running her fingertips over his cheek. He lowered his head to kiss her long and hard and then he released her. He caught the ends of his buckskin shirt and pulled it off.

Orange flames from the fire cast dancing light on his bronzed skin, and Vanessa ran her hands over his powerful muscles, stepping close to kiss him.

His hands closed on the hem of the doeskin dress, and he eased it up over her head to remove it. Fires of love danced in his dark eyes as he gazed at her. "My woman, you're a beauty and a storm. I love you, Vanessa."

She wound her slender arms around his neck, pressing against him and raising her mouth for his kiss. "I love you," she murmured as his mouth brushed hers. She stood on tiptoe, kissing him passionately, her heart racing with joy, knowing she was where she belonged—in the arms of the powerful man she loved with all her heart.

About the Author

Married and the mother of three, SARA ORWIG is a Midwesterner, having lived in Oklahoma, Kansas, and South Dakota. With an abiding fondness for the Old West, its history and legends, she is an avid collector of western history books and enjoys research trips to old forts and historical sites. Her previous Zebra historical romance was *Texas Passion,* and she is currently completing her next, *Comanche Temptation.* Sara loves to hear from readers. If you would like a *Warrior Moon* bookmark, please send a self-addressed, stamped envelope to Sara Orwig, P.O. Box 780258, Oklahoma City, Oklahoma 73178.

JANE KIDDER'S EXCITING
WELLESLEY BROTHERS SERIES

MAIL ORDER TEMPTRESS   (3863, $4.25)
Kirsten Lundgren traveled all the way to Minnesota to
be a mail order bride, but when Eric Wellesley wrapped
her in his virile embrace, her hopes for security soon
turned to dreams of passion!

PASSION'S SONG   (4174, $4.25)
When beautiful opera singer Elizabeth Ashford agreed
to care for widower Adam Wellesley's four children, she
never dreamed she'd fall in love with the little devils—
and with their handsome father as well!

PASSION'S CAPTIVE   (4341, $4.50)
To prevent her from hanging, Union captain Stuart
Wellesley offered to marry feisty Confederate spy Claire
Boudreau. Little did he realize he was in for a different
kind of war after the wedding!

PASSION'S BARGAIN   (4539, $4.50)
When she was sold into an unwanted marriage by her
father, Megan Taylor took matters into her own hands
and blackmailed Geoffrey Wellesley into becoming her
husband instead. But Meg soon found that marriage to
the handsome, wealthy timber baron was far more than
she had bargained for!

DISCOVER DEANA JAMES!

Taylor—made Romance From Zebra Books

WHISPERED KISSES (3830, $4.99/5.99)

Beautiful Texas heiress Laura Leigh Webster never imagined that her biggest worry on her African safari would be the handsome Jace Elliot, her tour guide. Laura's guardian, Lord Chadwick Hamilton, warns her of Jace's dangerous past; she simply cannot resist the lure of his strong arms and the passion of his *Whispered Kisses*.

KISS OF THE NIGHT WIND (3831, $4.99/$5.99)

Carrie Sue Strover thought she was leaving trouble behind her when she deserted her brother's outlaw gang to live her life as schoolmarm Carolyn Starns. On her journey, her stagecoach was attacked and she was rescued by handsome T.J. Rogue. T.J. plots to have Carrie lead him to her brother's cohorts who murdered his family. T.J., however, soon succumbs to the beautiful runaway's charms and loving caresses.

FORTUNE'S FLAMES (3825, $4.99/$5.99)

Impatient to begin her journey back home to New Orleans, beautiful Maren James was furious when Captain Hawk delayed the voyage by searching for stowaways. Impatience gave way to uncontrollable desire once the handsome captain searched *her* cabin. He was looking for illegal passengers; what he found was wild passion with a woman he knew was unlike all those he had known before!

PASSIONS WILD AND FREE (3828, $4.99/$5.99)

After seeing her family and home destroyed by the cruel and hateful Epson gang, Randee Hollis swore revenge. She knew she found the perfect man to help her—gunslinger Marsh Logan. Not only strong and brave, Marsh had the ebony hair and light blue eyes to make Randee forget her hate and seek the love and passion that only he could give her.